SHACKLES OF GOLD

Shackles of Gold

ISABELLE M GUERNICA

Guernica
Publishing

THE GEMS AND GLORY SERIES
BOOK TWO
Shackles of Gold
By Isabelle M. Guernica

Guernica Publishing LLC.

Cover Art by Barbara J. Kennerly
Edited by Jaime Ryter at The Ryter's Proof

This is a work of fiction. Any similarities between real people, places, or situations is completely coincidental. This book is recommended for readers eighteen and older due to language, depictions of blood, gore, and sexually explicit scenes.

WARNING

This book contains plenty of violent and sexually explicit
scenes. Not to mention, it is a why-choose. Which means the
FMC will enter a completely consensual relationship with multiple male love interests.
There is no cheating. This book does end on a cliffhanger.

Proceed if you dare, but know that if you do, you'll be swept
away into an incredible world full of monsters, murder, hot alpha
males, and some beautiful, badass females.

Welcome back to the kingdom of Hell, fellow nightmares.

THE GEMS AND GLORY SERIES
BOOK TWO

Shackles of Gold

Isabelle M. Guernica

For the ones that came back.
Thank you.

Atticus,

    You don't know me as anything other than the creature of your contempt. The being that harbors your hatred. The Child who stole everything from you, and then was stolen from you.

Well, rest assured. I am alive and well and ripe for the taking. Though, I must warn you that such an act would not go over well with your eldest brother. He has since taken a liking to me, and I to him. Should you choose to take me without his knowledge nor my consent, there will be hell to pay.

Nonetheless, this power I have belongs to you as much as it does him and Atlas. Therefore, I have faith I will hear from you soon, and when that time comes, we may bargain. Until then, I'll bid you a swift farewell, Deity of Chaos and Control.

Best regards, Rhesamyre.

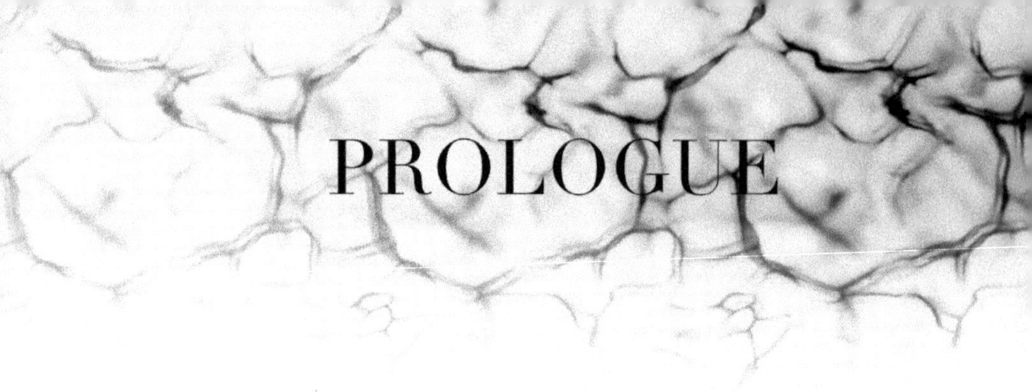

I press my muzzle further into the fresh kill, ripping apart muscles and tearing through flesh, devouring the life I have taken while lapping at the caribou's blood that stains the snowy, forest floor and my dark fur. A few dire wolves prowl on my perimeter, and I growl at them all when they get too close to *my* feast. The pack of five whines and growls, tearing into other slain caribou and snapping at one another as they fight amongst themselves to claim the first few bites.

I feel eyes on me, then lift my head as I lick my chops to gaze into the eyes of a curious hellhound, who no doubt heard the carnage and came to investigate. My hackles rise as my fur bristles, and I snarl at the hellish beast. He may be larger than me, but the power that pulses in my blood has me snapping my jaws in his direction and releasing a low snarl in warning. The hellhound whines and paces back and forth for a moment, and the rest of my pack locks their gazes on the beast ahead.

I bark to reprimand him once more, and he finally scampers off into the forest. Feeling satisfied, I turn my attention back to my meal and greedily take my fill, and soon, my pack and I are on the move again. We travel through the snow, the wind ripping through my fur as we lope along through the forest in search of cover from the coming storm.

Howls echo through the woodwork ahead, reaching our supernatural ears, and we halt as the frosted wind reveals multiple scents swiftly closing in on us. I sniff the air, my hackles rising as a low rumble sounds ahead of us. Hellhounds yip and bark as a much larger beast prowls forward, his breath visible in the frigid air, which comes from three heads at differing times as six red eyes zero in on my smaller form. The three-headed hellhound, flanked by another hellhound just a touch smaller with two heads, roars and howls at me, preparing to charge.

I snap my jaws and snarl in return, baring my teeth in challenge. He takes me up on the offer and launches forward as his younger brother and their pack leap at my soldiers of five. Blood and gore follow suit as jaws snap around necks and appendages, and the three-headed beast swipes at me in a daring attempt to swallow me whole. Then, when he rears one of his great heads backward to open his mouth, preparing to breathe fire, I beat him to it. Feeling power and heat radiate from deep within me, my body ignites and burns the alpha hellhound.

My teeth latch around his jugular and threaten to rip him apart as my flames of orange and silver devour and snuff out his own. Whines and low growls of submission rumble from the beast's throat, which remains in my mouth, and he shifts, lowering himself onto the snow as I keep ahold of him. Around me, I vaguely acknowledge the other hellhounds, as well as the two-headed beast, bowing and baring their necks or rolling over to show their bellies in submission. My own pack of wolves promptly sit on their haunches and howl, then sink into the snow out of respect.

I remove my teeth from the three-headed hound and take a step back, and every hellhound in the area remains lowered with their weaknesses bared. I peel my lips back as though to grin, then tip my head back and howl in both triumph and forewarning to the other monsters of this strange, snowy land. I dare claim it is a stranger to us, too, as something about the crisp air here does not remind me of home.

Home . . .

Now where might that be again? I can't quite recall. Not since I awoke a few moons ago in this feral body. The other five wolves were with me, too, and they have since refused to leave my side.

However, as I stand before these hellhounds, something about their spiced scents does remind me of a place far from here. Perhaps somewhere warmer and a bit darker in nature, but I find that to be only fitting. We are all darker in nature, too. And I . . . *I want to go there.*

I want to go home.

"You have forgotten your name," growls one of the three heads.

I cock my head, ears pricking at the hellhound as I sit back on my haunches. *"My name?"*

The third head moves forward and noses me gently, and I bare my teeth at him, but he is not deterred as he rubs his big head along my side.

"You do not belong here. Not in this land. And you have not claimed such an appearance in centuries," he says, though his jaws do not move. I can simply just . . . *hear* him.

"I do not understand."

"In time. In time . . . in time, the spell will be broken. The rumored vow that claims our silence forgotten."

These words make no sense to me. *"Will you take me away from here?"*

"If that is what you so wish."

The air shifts around us as the soil quakes, and I could swear the stars twinkle brighter in the sky as a tunnel appears before us, hellhounds and dire wolves alike. The largest, multiheaded hounds of the pack rise to their paws again and seem to glance at me before looking to the glimmering tunnel that smells of them once more. I prowl forward into that tunnel, following the scent of subtle smoke and the pine of the woodwork that greets us on the other side. There is no snow beneath our paws here, only a welcoming, warm ground that glows beneath me in subtle recognition and respect of my presence. I don't understand why, but I do not question it.

I at least know better than to question the properties here.

The mountainside we stand upon glitters with black stone, and further down, beyond a proud set of iron gates, lies a place alight with gentle fires and candles. I can just barely make out other beings walking between the structures and interacting with one another, but it is easy enough to tell that this cluster of creatures is different from the others my wolves and I had come across in that strange land. I cock my head at the sight but then turn around to nip at the ears of the two-headed hound that nudges against me, whining gently.

His red eyes are gentle and kind, and he pushes me away from the mountainside, away from the strange, bewitching, and beautiful sight before me. I comply with a low growl, then follow him and the other hounds deeper into the woods of the dark mountain.

CHAPTER ONE
ALASTAIR

The demons of hell shout and bang their fists against the tables before them as I enter the great hall, moving straight toward the head table situated at the front of the room where the seven assassins and four generals lounge. Their lieutenants stand behind them, leaning against the back wall with daggers in their eyes and crossed arms; Pollux is amongst them, too.

"What'd I miss?" I mutter, sauntering up to the archangel clad in hellion battle leathers.

He shrugs. "Nothing new. The demons are still outraged, demanding answers. Turns out, they all get pretty unruly without a king . . . or queen." He sighs, and the sound of utter exhaustion clashes with his professional scowl. "A few have even stepped up, claiming *they* should be named king."

I raise my brow, slightly tickled by the ridiculous notion. "I take it that didn't go over very well."

Pollux smirks. "Pride was quick to rip out the first demon's heart, and the rest have promptly shut up as far as *that* is concerned." He loses his smile now, glancing at me with a fair bit of irritation in his eyes. "And what is your dear brother up to this morning?"

I roll my eyes, growling. "Sulking about like a damned fool." I shake my head in defeat, a rare phenomenon outside of where Rhesa is concerned. "He doesn't know where Rhesa could have run off to, either, despite them apparently exchanging *letters*."

He chuckles again. "Sly little princess . . . *queen*." He sighs again. "Quite impressive that she managed to keep that from both of us for as long as she did. That and her claim of the forbidden power once more, as well as Tally. And you're no closer to finding her?"

I lower my head. "Unfortunately not. Her trail went cold quickly, and I'm still unable to reach her through our shared branding. She's quite adept at hiding from me, even with that well of power simmering inside her."

Pollux places a hand on my shoulder in comfort, then jerks his chin toward the table of eleven high-bred demons and *others* that predate even my existence of these spheres. "They'll bargain with beings worse than the Pythoness if it means finding and securing her safety once more, and so would I."

I nod, patting his hand on my shoulder in gratitude. "I know, and I thank you for that. And, despite his pissy attitude and resentment toward me, I know Atticus will help, too. He'll do it for her."

"And what of Atlas?"

"No word yet. Atticus claims he hasn't heard from our middle brother in quite some time."

"Yet that ex-genie of Rhesa's claims she had contact with him, too, no?"

"So Tallullah claims."

Pollux hums. "Then I suppose it's also only a matter of time before he comes prowling about, looking for Rhesa."

I nod again, then turn my gaze to the raging hall of demons. Finally, War bangs his fists on the table, nearly cracking it, as he rises to his feet, pulsing his power across the room and causing tremors to shake the fixtures and rattle the tables. Plenty of demons fall on their asses or to their knees, and I can physically *see* the way their bones quake beneath their varying shades of skin. Whereas some wretch over the side of their tables as that power slithers inside their bodies, staking a dangerous claim that promises death.

"Silence," orders War in Babel, his voice dangerously low. Lower than I've ever heard it. *"Until the return of our queen, we shall remain in power. All concerns of leadership shall be taken up with us, and I can assure you, your concerns shall be heard, but I cannot promise heads and hearts will not roll afterward."*

The demons remain quiet, and after War dismisses them, they shuffle out swiftly and silently. When the doors click closed, the remaining demons of the court collectively sigh and slump further into their chairs. Some hold their heads in their hands and rub their temples or pinch the bridges of their noses. Seems as though the loss of their king is affecting them more than they're leading on, and the stress of losing Rhesa is eating at them, too.

Can't say I'm faring much better at the moment, either. I haven't slept in days, and most of my time is spent either training, hunting Rhesa, or avoiding my brother.

"Please," mutters Greed, turning to face me. "Tell me you found her trail?"

I clench my jaw, and my silent scowl seems to be answer enough. The demons nod, remaining quiet, but I know they're far from satisfied.

"I'm curious . . ." drawls a low, accented voice.

I don't bother to hide my irritation as I face my brother.

Atticus leans against the far wall, twirling an obsidian blade as he stands in a styled suit of silver and obsidian leathers. Tattoos similar to my own peak out around his cufflinks and collar, revealing sigils and scriptures in Old Latin that weave between inked chains and thorns that cover his hands and neck. Emerald eyes glow eerily as he surveys the demons before him with a scowl similar to my own, and half his black hair is braided and tied over his left shoulder, while the right half is shaved off, revealing the mandala patterns that slither up his neck and curl around the word *entropy* that is inked above his right ear.

Looking at him is not like peering into a mirror, though no one can doubt we are related as we share similar noses and sharp jaws. And once upon a time, our eyes had been the same color, too. But since claiming our titles and powers, each of us has shifted into something *other*.

"Were any of you ever going to tell her she is the Child so many sought after for years?" he inquires, pushing off the wall to stride toward us. He chuckles, sparing me a feral grin.

Atticus has always been anything but tame.

"Seems as though she had to go behind *all* your backs to figure it out herself. Bargaining with all sorts of beasts and monsters in the process. How amusing . . . and how *dangerous*," he seethes. "For if *I* had gotten ahold of her, I would've—"

"*You* would've *what*?" snarls Envy, slowly rising from his seat. "Ripped her apart, limb from limb? Drained her of her blood? Devoured her whole?" Envy is head-to-head with my brother now, the two about the same height, though Atticus is a bit *bigger*. The assassin gins, cocking his head. "I'm curious what *you* would've done. *So please*, enlighten us."

Atticus smirks again, and the look is nothing but pure arrogance. Then he glances at me as he claims smugly, "I would've made her *mine*. Though, it seems Alastair already beat me to it. A few times, I might add."

"You would do well not to speak of our *queen* in that light behind her back, Atticus," growls Lust. "Few good things tend to come of it."

Atticus's grin widens again, and he puts his hands up in mock surrender as he backs away from Envy. The glow in his green eyes mixes with radiant mirth and something akin to the promise of murder. Often times, when Atticus finds something amusing, heads start to roll, and hearts end up on the floor.

"I wouldn't dream of it," drawls my brother, looking more somber now. "In the short time I was able to both speak with and gaze upon our dear queen of hell, I have to say, she is quite the formidable female."

"And when have you *gazed upon her*, Chaos?" inquires Pride, and honestly, I find myself wondering the same.

"*Those eyes*," mutters Malcolm, stepping forward as he cocks his head with a curious, calculating gaze. "You wore the lord of Temptation's skin for a while, did you not?"

Atticus smiles once again. "Out of all the beings here, I didn't think *you* would get it so swiftly. Though, it does make the most sense, seeing as it was you and that other lieutenant with her when you visited the pillars. Good catch, Mini-Conquest."

I snarl. "Figures *that's* where you've been all this time. What has befallen the real Siren?"

He waves me off. "He's fine. He was too busy whoring himself out to his own underlings to notice I had taken up residence in his home for a little bit. Claiming his own title of sin and *skin* for as long as it suited me."

"You can shapeshift?" Silas inquires, looking between my brother and me.

"We can," I answer the lieutenant of War. "But often times, it's more like a glamour. It's how we hid for as long as we did after the Great Betrayal. We can change our forms and mask our scents from time to time." I spare my brother another irritated glance. "Figures my brother here chooses one that is constantly surrounded by whores and demons that reek of sex and lust."

"*Watch it*," snarls Lust, sounding offended.

"You're just jealous you didn't do it first, brother," coos Atticus, ignoring Lust. "I found it to be a rather pleasant way to pass the time."

"Thus leaving Alastair to find the Child all on his own, right?" inquires Pollux with a grin.

Atticus nods, though I can spot a tightness in his smile that wasn't there before. "It worked, didn't it? He found her, but I guess I shouldn't have trusted him to *keep* her."

"If you think Rhesa is capable of being *kept*," drawls Death quietly, "you're in for quite the surprise."

"I recall your initial question was whether or not we had ever planned to tell her of her origins?" inquires Famine, seeming tired of the banter.

Atticus finally loses that smug smile of his and nods for the horseman to continue.

"To be honest," drawls Wrath, "we are unsure. Sam loved her. Claimed her as his daughter, and we swore to protect her and cherish her as a part of this family. No questions asked. However . . . I only ever recall her asking about her mother *once*. When she did, Sam brushed her off and said she was a low-bred demon whom he loved, but who died in a complicated childbirth. Rhesa always believed herself to get the short end of the stick when it came to magic, since Mamba took the forbidden power before she was old enough to recall ever having it in the first place. Though I don't believe Sam ever made any moves to explain that to her."

"He wanted to protect her from it," claims Sloth. "Protect her from herself, too." He looks at me, then at my brother. "You deities were too busy trying to track her down, as were a few other creatures that wanted to use her against you. But on top of that, the power was beginning to eat her alive from the inside out. *Burning* her alive. Removing it was our only option to both hide and save her."

"Yet none of you ever sought to use the power yourselves," I find myself noting. "Why?"

Pride chuckles a little. "Long before even the first king of hell, the Cruel One, claimed the Obsidian Throne, Hell was an unruly wasteland where sinful creatures roamed. All of us existed, but in similar fashions to how creatures like those in the Forbidden Cities exist nowadays: separated and usually isolated, and operating under the same belief that silent neighbors are the best neighbors, though common demons fought often, and the land was no stranger to bloodshed."

Pride lifts his shoulders, and even that action is calculated and pristine. "Things got a little better under Abaddon, but not by much. Many even argue it was *worse*, but when Sam became king, he banded all of us together *properly*. Samael gave us a real *home*, one that was worth fighting for. He defined our roles in the spheres in a manner that was just and fair and gave us ways to better focus on ourselves and control our desires, needs, and magic. More productive methods to let off some steam and regulate our powers that had previously been eating us alive . . . and then he gave us this little girl to look after. To chase and protect and love."

"We understood that the forbidden power would do more harm than good," continues Greed for his brother, clapping him on the shoulder. "It would serve to tear hell apart and invite our enemies inside if they ever learned we had such a well of magic at our disposal. That we had *Rhesa*, and nothing was getting any-where *near* that baby girl. *Nothing*. She was . . . pure. A light that just drew you in. It was a choice to grow fond of her and call her ours, but it wasn't our choice to protect her. Not if we're honest with ourselves . . . it was just . . . instinctual."

I glance at Atticus to find all humor has disappeared from his features, and only an unreadable scowl remains. Slowly, he nods and then looks at me.

"And you don't know where she is?" inquires my brother with a strange quietness.

I shake my head. "Not yet."

He inclines his head, but our attention soon diverts to the sound of knocking on the doors at the other end of the hall. Conquest waves a lazy hand to unlock the doors, and I raise a brow at the sight of the soulless mortal as he strolls forward. Most of the demons around me consider him to be Rhesa's latest *pet*.

"Apologies for interrupting," begins Dexter, bowing. "But I believe I have news you'll want to hear."

"Out with it," orders Gluttony.

"There are reports of hellhounds leaving their posts and not returning. In addition, it seems as though the Alpha Brothers have gone missing, as well."

"*The Alpha Brothers*?" I furrow my brows at the title. "Regarding hellhounds, that would have to be Cerberus and Orthrus, correct?"

"You'd be correct," says Death. "Though, those two are strict rule followers. They never stray far from their posts unless something or *someone* provokes them."

"Someone powerful, then," notes Pollux. "Perhaps even someone that could change up the very rules they worship. What is Rhesa's relationship with them?"

War raises his brow. "Same as her father. They respect her, as they respect all of us. You think she has something to do with this?"

"*I* certainly believe it is worth looking into," quips Atticus, raising his hand like an imbecile.

I roll my eyes. "Admittedly, I find myself agreeing. Let's see if it is indeed our queen."

Conquest nods. "Very well. We leave in ten."

I dip my chin and take my leave to stroll back to Rhesa's room, then get busy strapping the rest of my weapons to my sides. A knock sounds at the door a few moments later, and Pollux strides in. I glance up at him as I finish fastening my grey battle leathers, finding him surveying the room with his nostrils flaring lightly as he takes in Rhesa's scent, which has now mixed with mine since I've been staying in her room these past several days. Though unable to sleep, at least her shelves of smutty books have been keeping me company, as well as her journals of diary entries and short stories, all of which are well-written and quite entertaining.

Rhesa loved playing pranks on the court when she was younger.

Pollux regards me with a skeptical scowl. "War and Conquest will accompany us to the den . . . as will your brother. Apparently, the hellhounds' ranks have grown with the addition of the dire wolves that roam these Obsidian Mountains."

I raise my brow. "Rhesa has been busy."

He watches me carefully. "Assuming it is her."

"It has to be." My thoughts move faster than my mouth can. "She's gathering an army. She's looking to avenge her father."

Pollux remains casual, careful. He doesn't want to hope. It's a brave endeavor, and sometimes foolish. "I don't think an army of hellhounds and wolves is going to accomplish what she wants.

Certainly not against celestials. Her teeth may be sharp, but I dare say their swords are sharper."

I shrug halfheartedly. "Maybe it isn't for the celestials . . . not yet, at least."

"Then for who?"

"I don't know yet."

He hums. "Very well. Are you ready to go?"

I nod, and the two of us head toward the palace courtyard to meet up with War and Conquest, as well as my obnoxious little brother. Atticus pays me no mind, and while that pisses me off, I know meeting his eyes would only serve to piss me off even more. The Horsemen ignore us, and then we're walking through a conveyance deep into the dark pines of the Obsidian Mountains. All remains quiet as the sun casts shadows through the forest of spice and smoke, and distant animals shuffle amongst the branches while the feathered wings of birds flutter. Ravens watch us with beady eyes, and the black buck of this land are ballsy as they remain still, bowing up as though to charge.

Prey or not, everything here is dangerous when provoked.

"What can we expect from the wolves and hellhounds?" inquires Pollux.

"They patrol these woods and warded perimeters of Hell," answers Conquest. "And their den is a warded cave set in the mountains. And naturally, beasts of their calibers tend to be overtly territorial."

"Will we even be able to get close to them if that's the case?" asks Atticus. Even his voice grates on every one of my nerves.

I grind my teeth.

"The hellhounds may have found themselves a new alpha," drawls War, "but they'll still listen and respect us. At least"—he shrugs—"they will long enough for us to get in and confirm if Rhesa is there. I believe, anyway."

Pollux nods. "Very well. And what if she does not desire to go back with us?"

"Naturally, we won't force her into anything," I reply. "However, I *will be* demanding answers."

"As will we," agrees War. "We shall come to understand her mindset and hopefully convince her to return and claim her throne before an internal civil war breaks out."

"Is that something you see happening in the near future?" inquires Atticus.

Conquest grins, glancing back at us as he replies, "Oh, *yes*. Especially since the demons already know how Sam was slain in the first place. We'll be faced with a civil war for the throne on top of a war against the celestials, and while I may hope for the latter, I would like Rhesa to be leading the charge before that happens."

I hum. "Then I suppose we'll have to explain as much to Rhesa."

War and Conquest seem to silently agree, and we soon near the warded den of dire wolves and hellhounds. The cave is nestled into the base of the mountains, and surrounding the entrance are *dozens* of wolves and hounds. All of which raise their heads and sniff the air, then begin to emit low growls in warning as their hackles rise.

War steps forward from the woodwork and growls in return, successfully shutting a few up as they take in this new predator. Hellhounds are quicker to recognize him and lower their heads, but the dire wolves take a bit more convincing. I step forward and snarl lightly, causing the wolves to lower their heads and bare their necks to me. Behind me, Pollux scoffs, muttering *showoff.*

The five of us continue into the den, the walls and ceiling beginning to glow orange with glowworms, while faint runes of wolves and old languages shimmer upon the walls. Plenty of hellhounds and dire wolves prowl and rest along the rock formations of the narrow hall, regarding us skeptically and emitting low rumbles in warning. However, none of them dare take a step toward us, seeming to think better of it as they size up the two hellion generals in their midst. Never mind the two deities amongst them, too. One a hunter of hunters, and wolf in my own right.

Plus Pollux, too, I suppose.

"I've never seen this many gathered in one place," mutters War, eyeing the canines skeptically.

"I know," agrees Conquest. "A few of these dire wolves don't even belong to this sphere. Some are too mortal or celestial kissed to call Hell their home."

I listen to their commentary as I keep an eye on the wolves surrounding us, but my attention is soon directed toward the large cavern that opens ahead. Hundreds more wolves and hellhounds rest amongst each other, and at the front of the cavern, the largest of the beasts snooze: Cerberus and Orthrus, the Alpha Brothers of Hell.

I waste no time, inhaling deeply to search for her, and I can vaguely pick it out from the hundreds of canine smells contaminating it. But her unique, luxurious smoke and spice scent remains unmistakable.

Hell, I've been holding up in her damn room, surrounded by it for the past few days and nights. Torturing myself with the intoxicating scent of her that drives me wild.

"She's here," I mutter. "Though, her scent is highly diluted with *dog*."

"I don't see her yet," says Pollux, eyeing the largest of the hellhounds with a trained eye that intends to ascertain threats and weaknesses.

The three-headed hound, Cerberus, and the two-headed hound, Orthrus, finally snap their eyes open and give us their undivided attention. Well, I suppose their attention is divided between their numerous heads. They knew we arrived, but until now, they didn't bother to show they *cared*.

"*Cerberus,*" calls War quietly in Babel, and the hellhound whines a little.

Huh. So he's just a massive puppy dog. *Noted.*

"Have I ever mentioned how much I really don't like canines?" mutters Pollux. "Like, *this is fucking terrifying.*"

I can't help but bark a sudden, quiet laugh at that, my chuckle abrupt and resounding throughout the cavern.

Cerberus and Orthrus shuffle, and from between them, another dark form rises. The sleek, black dire wolf is far smaller than the rest; however, the rest of the wolves and hounds seem to shuffle around and lower themselves in acknowledgment of the newcomer. Then, obsidian eyes with flecks of amber, which nearly glow from the light of the worms above, snap toward me.

"*Fuck,*" I mutter. "That's Rhesa."

"*What?*" snarls Atticus.

"Rhesa . . . she's . . ." I shake my head. "It is *technically* possible for her to shapeshift, too. And here she is . . . the alpha she-wolf herself."

"Do you think she's actually aware of herself?" inquires Pollux, watching her with a gaze I've never seen on the archangel before. He almost looks . . . *scared.* "Does she know who *we* are? Who *she* really is?"

I clench my jaw. "Only one way to find out."

I step forward, deeper into the wolves' den, and Rhesa watches my every footfall. Her familiar hellfire eyes flick back and forth from me to my traveling companions, her very own family and friends. *Hell below*, I hope she recognizes me. I hope she turns back into the female form I have come to adore and lust after. The one I wish to cherish and worship, devote everything I am to.

"Rhesa," I call softly, stopping just before the larger, multi-headed hellhounds that shuffle and snarl lowly in my direction.

The beautiful, sleek black wolf who smells of her and shares her eyes, peels back her lips and snarls at me, baring her teeth as she rises to her full height as her fur bristles. Around me, other hounds and wolves rise to their feet and stiffen as growls rumble from their own chests as their new alpha sizes me up as a *threat*.

One which she appears unafraid to neutralize.

"Rhesa," I call again, my voice a plea. *A fucking prayer.* "Come on, my love . . . you know me."

I take another step toward her, my hand extended outward despite her obvious warnings. Fangs flash, and she pins her ears back while her eyes nearly glow in the shadowed lights.

"Alastair, I don't think—"

"*Quiet*, Pollux. She *knows* me." *She has to know me. Has to remember me.* "You know me, my love."

My hand gets closer to her head, and her growls only grow louder as she opens her mouth to reveal the rest of her teeth. Her face contorts into a menacing, vicious snarl as her eyes shimmer. Then, just as I am about to lay a hand on her, she snaps her jaws at me. I swiftly pull my hand back, narrowly avoiding her gnashing teeth as she lunges for me. Around us, wolves and hounds bark and lunge for War, Conquest, Atticus, and Pollux behind me.

I throw Rhesa off me as gently as I can, and she rolls and skitters backward but doesn't stay back for long as she lunges for me again. Her eyes set on my throat with her mouth open wide and nearly unhinged.

"I think we've overstayed our welcome!" calls War, throwing a few wolves backward without killing them.

"I couldn't agree more!" replies Pollux.

I know they're right, but I want to grab her before we retreat through a conveyance. However, as Cerberus and Orthrus enter the fray and step between Rhesa and me, they successfully sabotage that plan.

"Alastair, *she's fine*!" calls Conquest. "*We won't be* if we remain here! I have no desire to harm our hounds, nor risk hurting Rhesa in the crossfire!"

With one last longing glance toward Rhesa's snarling wolf form, I turn away and enter a conveyance with the others. We're successfully deposited back into the throne room, where the others lounge stiffly with drinks in their hands as they await our news. I see Pollux shutter out of the corner of my eye, repeating to himself quietly how he *hates canines, and it sucks because his queen is now one of the damn dogs.*

"Well?" prompts Pride, rising to his feet. "Where is she?"

War chuckles, but the sound is devoid of proper humor. "*Oh, she's with the dogs, all right. I believe she's got every single hound and wolf within the spheres tucked away in that damned den upon the mountain.*"

Lust quirks a brow, drawling, "Well, is she okay?"

"She's a fucking dire wolf," growls Atticus.

Death raises his brows, defaulting to me for answers. "She's a *what*?"

"I . . ." I begin, though I'm still quite stunned myself. "I suppose when I erupted, I shifted into Grief. It seems as though Rhesa went a different route, becoming the wolf that nearly bit my hand off and later, went for my head."

Envy chuckles. *"She did what?"*

"She didn't . . . she doesn't . . ." Famine tries to find the right words, looking between us. "She didn't *recognize* you? *Any of you?* Does she even know who *she* is?"

"Doesn't appear that way," replies Pollux quietly.

I nod. "Unfortunately, I'm inclined to agree. I believe, at the moment, the Rhesa we know and love is gone. Replaced by this wolf who has built herself an army of canines. Including Cerberus and Orthrus."

"Well then," starts Damian. "How do we get her back?"

"When we shift," drawls Atticus, "most of the time, we can do it willingly and keep ahold of our power, mentality, and memories . . . save for that time after the Great Betrayal. I've never seen anything else like this."

I incline my head in agreement. "Rhesa's hopefully *temporary* amnesia stems from *why* she erupted in the first place. All of this is due to Samael's murder."

Pride nods, working a muscle in his jaw. "Very well. Then how do we at least get her here safely, preferably without losing any limbs in the process?"

"I would imagine waltzing right into her den isn't going to work a second time," says War. "We could before, thanks to our status, but Rhesa seems to outrank even us now."

"So . . . maybe we can draw her out?" suggests Silas. "Get her alone, isolated from the pack, *the army*, she has accumulated. Then, we just snatch her up and toss her through a conveyance.

Perhaps once she is here, somewhere familiar, surrounded by her family and friends, something will jostle a memory?"

"That's certainly a start," I say. "She can't stay out there, that much is certain. While she is heavily guarded and protected, once word gets out that the queen of Hell and the Child herself is in such a vulnerable state, hunters will come looking. It doesn't matter if we're in the Hellion Sphere. We need to act fast."

"Well," drawls Pollux, grinning. "You and I are pretty good at provoking monsters and *poking proverbial bears*. I'm sure we can poke at your lovely wolf, too."

CHAPTER TWO
RHESAMYRE

My ever-growing pack patrols the warded boundaries upon and below the mountains near the gates. I can't recall where the gates lead; the other side is still foreign to me as I continue through the forest with my snout to the ground as I trot along. The five wolves that accompanied me when I awoke never leave my side, and trail behind me obediently and silently as I patrol the lands that reek of scents I struggle to name.

The scents that plagued my den a few hours ago were different from the ones of this forest, in addition to the ones that surround the clusters of shelters at the edge of the woods where different beings roam and gather. *They* reek of *prey*, but the ones who invaded my den smelled of grander predators. Specifically, the one who dared to come near me; the sound of the strange noise he made had rattled my core, and his *scent* . . .

I don't know the words, but he smelled of the hardwood forest, yet he had a sweeter air about him that was tinged by fire, revealing how dangerous he may yet be.

It made me angry. And I wanted nothing more than to sink my teeth into his throat and drain him of his blood that surely must taste as delectable as he smells.

The wolves by my side whine lowly, and I halt my tracking to survey the land around us. Then, in the distance, I hear fire snapping and crackling, and curiosity gets the better of me as a low snarl rumbles from my throat at the possible threat. I lope toward the sound and varying smells of prey, my pack on my heels, and we halt before a few beings that walk upon their hindquarters and stand upright.

They surround the fire, their forms tense as they seem to sense my arrival. However, the whines I hear next have me snapping my head toward another being who slumps against the base of a tree. A female, with her form bound and flat muzzle covered by something that inhibits her ability to bark.

"Just fucking wolves," mutters one of the three males, going for a weapon.

Foolish.

Another male chuckles, but his fear does not go unheard nor unscented. "Must have smelled her blood and heard her pretty little whimpers. They'll devour her whole. None would be the wiser of us fooling around with her."

The female whimpers, and I cock my head at the smell of her fear. She is fearful of me, but her fear was already potent enough with just these males present. As I continue to survey them as they watch my pack and me carefully from where we lurk in the woodwork, I find her scent to be all over them. And in turn, their scents intertwine with hers, too. Blood coats their hands, and something about the way they bare their teeth and chuckle at the female's distress has me baring *my* teeth and releasing another low snarl.

The men give me their full attention once more, and one by one, they reveal their weapons. However, my pack and I don't give them much time to rethink their rash decision to put up a fight, and we launch ourselves at the men. It doesn't take long before they're cowering away and screaming. My teeth latch onto limbs and *tear,* ripping skin and muscles from bones and tendons as blood splatters my coat. The males' cries are pitiful and, in my opinion, end all too swiftly as they die from trauma and blood loss.

The bound female is all but sobbing now, and I release the male I was latched on to, relishing in the way he *thumps* into the wet mush of red soil. I stalk toward her, and her cries only grow louder as I sniff her throat and face, then down to where her limbs are tied. I snarl at the bindings and latch my teeth around the odd texture, snapping it off her instantly. The female quiets down, and I only take a moment to peer into her green eyes before growling to my pack that *we're finished here.*

However, before I can turn to lope off, I feel my fur being tugged on gently. I whirl around again to snap at the female's hand, and she cowers and cocks her head at me as tears fall from her eyes.

Then she grins at me, and it sets me on edge. "My, my. I didn't want to believe it at first, *las*," she coos. "Yet the rumors spread like wildfire, and here you are."

I growl and jump backward, but strange bindings have already appeared and slithered around my limbs. Black, thorny vines pierce my skin and draw blood, causing me to whine and snarl. The sound attracts the rest of my pack, but when the female glances their way, those same bindings halt their movements, too.

"I will admit, the trip out here was a bumpy one. Though, it seems it'll be well worth it. And using your own instincts to be *merciful* against you." She cackles. "Certainly well worth it."

I growl as she rises to her feet, and before my very eyes, her form shifts from that of a young woman into a frailer, greyer one.

"Wicked spellwork it was to do that, even for a short amount of time," she complains, now binding my jaws closed so I can't snap her head off.

"Used to be easy before the betrayals," she mutters to herself. "A great deal used to be *much easier* back when they called me *queen*." She sighs. "No matter. One plan may have failed, but I am under the impression another will soon replace the last. Those mortal, soulless slaves certainly had no qualms taking me up on my offer to catch the lone wolf that has been roaming about these hellish woods. Certainly not, if I could guarantee their freedom . . . though, I suppose I forgot to mention the only freedom they would receive would be through death. *Oh, well.*"

She shrugs, then grins and kneels to better meet my eyes. "You're mine now, las. And we have a rendezvous to make, so we best be on our way to meet him."

Tugging me by my hind legs, the female that now reeks of swamps and rot drags me through the woods up to another creature of four legs that is much bigger than me, but still smells of prey. Its paws are oddly shaped and much harder in nature, and the animal snorts and stomps at the ground restlessly. The female ungracefully hoists me onto a strange, uplifted cot that is settled behind the animal—*the horse*—and then ties me down so tight I can barely twitch.

Once she is mounted upon the horse's back, she takes off, trotting away from the rest of my pack members. All of whom whine and howl in agony as I am dragged away from them, and they are left there, bound amongst the males we butchered. I howl for them to the best of my ability despite the restraints over my muzzle, but as the horse lopes onward, I eventually tire myself out.

It isn't until much later, when we are further away from the mountains, that we go through another one of those strange tunnels, and the rotten scents of this new land nearly make me gag.

"That was quick," calls a new male, this one smelling of feathers and an odd sense of self-righteousness and entitlement that baffles me. It makes me want to gag again.

I do so, hacking through my restraints, and the sound seems to catch his attention. The shiny, golden male adorned with broad wings moves around the horse to survey my form, and he grins at the sight of me.

"Hello, princess," he coos. "Though, I suppose your rightful title is *queen* now, is it not?"

"Her title is whatever you choose, my beloved," says the female, coming to stand beside him, glowering at me smugly.

I growl at her.

He chuckles, then kisses her temple. "I agree. You've got her bound rather tightly. No wonder she's having trouble breathing. It wouldn't be in our favor to kill her so soon."

"Don't let her fool you. She's quite resilient."

"*Oh*, I'm well aware of that. It took me a few days to completely recover from that blast of power she sent my way. She's got the forbidden power now."

"At least you recovered. The same cannot be said of Adriel, though, correct?"

"Correct. She managed to slay him quite impressively."

The female hums. "Well, no matter. As promised, here she is. They didn't sense nor scent me in that form, though I'm sure it won't take them long to figure out she's gone."

"I'm counting on it."

"I still wish you had included me in this contingency plan of yours."

The male chuckles in a sweeter manner, and the sound nearly makes me sick again. He grabs the female's cheeks to embrace her, kissing her forehead. "Had I done that, then others would have learned of it too soon. We need to trust each other, so trust me when I say it was the best course of action to pursue."

"Which means that you always knew my plan for the Reformation Spell would fail," she accuses.

"I had hoped it wouldn't, but just in case, I had a plan for that. This is merely phase one."

"Very well. I trust you."

"I know you do, and soon enough, you'll have the power to permanently retrieve your youthful form once more. We'll be together again, and Andrew will finally be with us."

"I'm looking forward to it."

"As am I, but for now, I best get going. Taking my new *pet* with me."

"Now *that* is a far better title for her than *queen*." The female cackles, then leans down to pat my head mockingly. "Be a good, *bitch*, las. I'll see you again soon enough."

The winged male doesn't waste any more time and hauls me upward so we may step through another one of those tunnels into a different land of unsavory smells.

He places me down on the cold ground roughly, then snarls to the others around us, *"Keep those bindings tight, especially around that fang-riddled snout of hers."*

I feel pressure on my paws and legs, tying them together again with new materials, and even though I try to bite at the hands that touch me, a knee resting on my airways plus more hands holding me down has me struggling to do so. My jaws are tied shut in a more convoluted manner, keeping me from biting, and I am roughly hoisted upward and thrown over the shoulder of one of the males clad in white and gold. I struggle and wiggle in my bindings, but it's no use, and I only succeed in tiring myself out again.

We follow the golden male through double doors that lead into a nearly blindingly bright chamber riddled with more celestials and winged creatures. Various scents infiltrate my nose, making me want to sneeze as my head spins when I try to decipher them all. Most, including the one that took me from that rotten female, smell familiar, for some reason.

However, as I am roughly placed down on the floor and held by the scruff of my neck before a bunch of dark beings, I neglect the idea of trying to remember where I have smelled these brutes before. Instead, I busy myself with growling and snarling, attempting to break my bonds, but the rough hand still nestled in my scruff shakes me violently in warning.

"Easy, Apollo," calls one of the faceless beings seated before me. *"Don't harm the little wolf yet."*

"I didn't want to believe it at first when we heard the rumors," says another. *"Yet here she is. The esteemed princess of Hell and daughter of the devil . . . reduced to appear as a sniveling, snarling, smelly beast."*

"I don't see much of a difference," chuckles a third.

"Of course, we're still curious as to exactly how *this happened,"* drawls the last.

"Nonetheless, this doesn't change anything," claims the original. *"In fact, it might just make things easier for us. Now, make her presentable. I fancy something gold."*

Rhesamyre,

You're quite arrogant.

But fret not, I like that in a woman. And you have the potential to be quite spicy, yet I've already heard plenty of rumors that the Princess of Hell is quite sweet when she wants to be. I'm curious to know which side my brother has seen, and in turn, which side he prefers.

Does he love fucking the demon of kindness, or the killer? I'm now curious to know which one I would prefer over the two, as well.

But that can be a conversation for another time, for you now claim to be the child we once had stolen from us. Very well, I'll play your game. What are the rules?

Sincerely,
The best of my brothers, and the best lover you have yet to taste,

Atticus

CHAPTER THREE
ALASTAIR

"We have a problem," claims Damian as he enters the study we occupy.

"Don't we always?" mutters Lust, glancing up from the documents he reads, a drink in hand as he works.

The court of demons have been busying themselves by dealing with internal matters. While Pollux, Atticus, and I ponder and plot the best way to get Rhesa back. Though still a challenge, capturing her will be the easy part; it's changing her back and ensuring she remembers us, *remembers me*, that I'm more concerned with.

Death sighs, glancing at his reaper. "What's the matter, Damian?"

"A bounty has been placed on Rhesa's cute little wolfy head by the current governing mortals of Goldfinch," says Damian. "Rumor has already spread to the neighboring spheres of Rhesa's current . . . um . . . *state of mind*."

"No big deal," claims Atticus. "A bounty was bound to appear after all that shit that went down over the mirror, right?"

"Correct," agrees Gage, appearing beside Damian. "However, that's probably the least of our concerns." He holds up a letter between his fingers, one sealed with the celestial crest—the north star adorned with angel wings. "We just received this from a messenger on our way here."

Death reaches his hand out to retrieve the letter, but Atticus, *in all his impatient wisdom*, snatches the letter before the Horseman can. Death scowls, but Atticus ignores him as he slices the wax seal with a dagger, then turns away from us to read it without the worry of us reading his facial expressions. However, the action doesn't seem necessary, since only a second passes before I hear him crinkling the parchment and growling in rage. All while his *wings* rip outward from his back straight through his jacket and leathers. The feathers are darker than my shade of silver, but still metallic in nature as faint symbols and scriptures delicately trace the veins of his remiges.

"Brother," I call, and he tenses at the title before ruffling his feathers out of view again and turning to face us. His scowl is back in place as he hands the letter back to Death.

Death bristles, cursing angel names under his breath. "Seven devils . . . *we have your wolf. Hand over the Obsidian Throne and all those affiliated, and you can have her back in one piece. Fail to do so within the next twenty-four hours, and you can rest assured she will not be undamaged by the time you manage to get her back. In the meantime, here is another gift for you. Be sure Pollux reclaims what he seems to have misplaced. Sincerely yours, the Zodiacs.*"

"*Give me that,*" snarls Pollux, snatching the letter. I see his eyes reread the text too many times for it not to be true, and his nostrils flare as his wings twitch. He meets the eyes of the lieutenants, and Malcolm steps forward with a burlap bag that is stained red at the bottom. Pollux claims the *gift* and peers inside it with a snarl.

"What is it, Pollux?" I inquire.

Pollux dumps the contents onto the floor, and five different heads belonging to both males and females roll out.

"*My informants*," he snarls. "No doubt Apollo sniffed them out. That *bastard*."

Plenty of us scowl at the sight of the severed heads, and Pollux continues to nearly vibrate with rage.

"How the fuck did this happen?" inquires Wrath quietly, though his aggression and fury are barely reined in as he crushes his glass in his palm, shards digging into his skin messily. "She was still in Hell last time I checked! Mere *hours* ago!"

"*Lilith*," hisses Pollux again, his Enochian accent thickening even though he speaks Babel with ease.

"*What*?" growl a few of the Seven, cursing amongst themselves again.

"It had to have been Lilith," the archangel reiterates. "She's the only one capable of getting into hell as something *other* undetected. If she opened a conveyance far enough from the wards, near the gates out in the wilds, most likely glamoured with a plethora of black magic, none would be the wiser. Not while the hellhounds are busy hiding out in Rhesa's den. No archangel could accomplish that, as their aura is too strong. And neither could a mortal on their own. The crone is still alive . . . and she and Apollo were once a thing. *Are a thing.* She snuck in and retrieved Rhesa for *him*."

"Wolf or not," drawls Atticus, "she should know better than to trust the *fucking Pythoness* of all beings! Did none of you ever teach her the meaning of *stranger danger*?"

"*We did our best*," snaps War. "Obviously, there is more to this than we know. She must have been ambushed or tricked or something of the sort!"

"Or perhaps," drawls Sloth, the assassin looking more exhausted as the days without Rhesa pass, "she is more wolf than we realize. She may not understand even the simplest desires other than defense and offense. *Instinct*, if you will. And, knowing Rhesa's stubborn nature anyway, it's possible she saw whatever form Lilith took to get near her as more of a challenge than a threat. Rhesa's never been one to back down from a fight."

"That much is clear," quips Greed.

"So, how do we get her back now?" inquires Envy.

"*I'll fucking demand her back*," I growl lowly. "I'm done playing nice. I'm done tip-toeing around the pathetic rules and wards of these spheres." I look to my brother, and he nods at me.

"Seems as though these spheres need a reminder of who we are and what we're capable of," he claims.

"Dangerous words, you two," chuckles Death, looking between us. "But I know all of us are starting to agree with such methods."

Pollux shakes his head. "No, no. Something is still amiss here. We need to know *exactly* how she was taken."

"Why does that matter?" asks Famine.

"Because we've been *wrong* about her! I—*we've*—been wrong about *everything*! We thought she was amassing an army to attack the celestials, *but she wasn't*. And dare I say, she wasn't even the one calling the wolves and hounds to her side . . . they went of their own volition. To protect *her*. Not Hell. Not the gates. And certainly not any of the surrounding subjects. More so, I don't believe Rhesa is out for blood right now. She isn't going out of her way looking for trouble. In my opinion, something had to have been *very wrong* for her to even approach the Pythoness. Rhesa may be stubborn, but she's no fool. Something happened out there, and we need to know what."

"Again," demands Atticus, "we ask *why*?"

Pollux snarls. "Because it'll give us a better idea of her mindset and, from there, how long we have before they *break* her. Or how long we have until this wolfish attitude remains *permanent*."

Gluttony scoffs a little, though he doesn't seem all that confident in his words as he claims, "That won't happen. We'll save her before then, and she won't break easy."

"I agree, she won't," Pollux declares. "But my brothers." He shakes his head. "*Apollo* and the *Zodiacs* can get quite creative with their methods of torture when they get a bunch of overzealous, religious mortals to do their bidding. And the current leaders of the mortal kingdom already want Rhesa dead. So don't think they won't draw it out for as long as they can."

"And here I thought the best tormentors resided right here in hell," quips Atticus.

Conquest scowls. "How do you think we came to possess such creatures skilled in the arts of torture? When humans want to be cruel, they're quite skilled at hurting one another. Far better at it than any demon or monster could ever dream of being. Even in our worst nightmares, we haven't been able to come up with even half the shit they do to each other."

"So many want to blame the devil for their misfortune and misdeeds," muses Sloth. "Yet all they need do is glance in the mirror."

"We oughtta usurp that throne next," quips Atticus, rolling his eyes. "Or eradicate them all. Whichever is easiest. I guarantee the species will not be missed."

Wrath scowls at my brother. "We already have one throne to fill. The last thing we need is another kingdom to feed. And the longer we stand here bickering about what to do next, the longer they have to start *breaking* her."

"Agreed," I growl. "Pollux, let's go learn of what really happened in the woods. Then from there, we're going to the Celestial Cities."

"I'm going with you," states Atticus, and I nod.

"What about the rest of us?" inquires Damian.

"Most of us are still needed here, lieutenant," says Death. "In order to ensure a hell still remains for Rhesa when she does return. I wouldn't put it past the celestials to attempt a siege if most of us are away. The deities and archangel should suffice, much to our dismay."

Damian looks torn but obeys his general's order all the same. The rest seem compliant enough, and once again, Atticus, Pollux, and I set off through another conveyance into the woods of the Obsidian Mountains.

We follow Rhesa's scent further away from the gates and den where she had surely been patrolling before Lilith snatched her up and soon come to find a bloodbath of soulless slaves and black magic. Five other wolves remain bound upon the blood-soaked soil near the fallen bodies of the men, and they growl and snarl viciously as we near them, revealing teeth that appear more like steel than bone.

I curse angel names under my breath. "*Bloody hell*, these are the Soldiers of Sorrow."

"*What?*" growls Atticus. "They shifted with her?"

"Certainly appears that way." I bend down to better observe one of the dark dire wolves, pressing a knee against his head to survey his steeled teeth, and I run my finger down a fang to feel the sharpened edge that mimics their infamous swords. "And their teeth have since become their half-light weaponry."

"That's disturbing," quips Pollux. "Intriguing, but still horrifying."

I roll my eyes, then press my hands against the wolf's head and flush my power through it. Closing my eyes, I allow his memories to flood through me, revealing what happened here only a few hours ago. Then with a low growl, I remove my hands again.

"Unfortunately, you were right, Pollux," I drawl. "Rhesa was tricked into believing Lilith was a young girl being tortured and raped by a few escaped slaves. The witch took Rhesa away upon a celestial-bred stallion. Apollo is definitely involved."

"Dammit! Then let's go get her," snarls Atticus.

Pollux nods, then jerks his chin at the wolves. "What about them?"

"I'll send word for the court to retrieve them," I say. "Rhesa can decide what she wants to do with them once she gets back."

Seeming satisfied with that, Pollux moves to open a conveyance into Ursa Major. However, after a few seconds of waiting, and him cursing under his breath quite frequently, I am forced to regrettably ask, "*What*?"

"I can't open it," he snarls. "They must have removed my runes worked into the wards. And odds are, neither of you will be able to, either."

"So now *what*?" snaps Atticus, scoffing. "We actually have to send a formal reply to those winged fucks?"

"Seems that way," the archangel growls. He sighs. "And since they butchered all of my underlings in Ursa Major, I'll have to reach out to the few others I have scattered about the rest of the spheres. They'll hide and gather information until receiving further orders from me."

"You don't think they'll be bought off?"

Pollux scowls, but still manages to look smug all the same. It's a talent, really. "Contracted genies are usually a little bit more loyal and cunning than common spies and servants."

I raise my brow. "Excuse me?"

Atticus almost smirks as he shakes his head and chuckles lowly. "I know better than to inquire about you running out of wishes. So what brilliance did you come up with instead, angel boy?"

Pollux snarls at the old nickname that mirrors an insult. "I wished for their unyielding loyalty and then for them to serve me until I am through using them to gather information on my behalf. They have the ability to shift their forms and access unlimited wells of information, and I haven't been using individual wishes to seek what I desire. Instead, I wished for them to *always give me* information when I inquire it. Simple as that. However, I have to be mindful of how often I ask them to dive into those endless pits that lie within the cracks of our spheres, as many that go under sometimes do not resurface again, leaving me to dispose of their bodies since their souls and minds remain trapped in the depths of wherever they travel to find what I am after. The magic takes its toll, even on me. Patience is key, as is a steady pace when inquiring what most are too afraid to ask."

Hence why most genies are only limited to three wishes per *master.* The depths of information and raw magic they dive headfirst into are vast and more like voids than pools, and things lurk there under the surface, in the dark. It would make sense that Pollux has to be careful about how often he instructs those spies of his to go swimming, lest they want to drown.

I narrow my eyes, thinking aloud. "That genie Rhesa fished from the leviathan's den . . . how'd her lamp get there in the first place, Pollux?"

The shit eating grin he spares can only be described as *devilish*, and he chuckles darkly. "I threw it into the river to keep you and your brothers from potentially snatching it up. The rest of the genies back then were already serving me, and I wasn't able to contract another one at the time. It would have stretched my power too thin, and I wouldn't have been able to keep them hidden and protected from you bastards. Apollo had met a few in Ursa Major in the past and unfortunately remembered their mannerisms, catching them even with my shielding."

I shake my head. "It always comes back to you somehow, doesn't it?"

He shrugs at me, though he doesn't deny it. "We'd best get back to the palace if I am to send word to my remaining genies in the other spheres, *Your Majesty*."

Atticus and I glance at one another, then nod and reach for the soldiers-turned-wolves so we may haul them back to the heart of Hell.

CHAPTER FOUR
RHESAMYRE

"This isn't right, Apollo."

I slowly wake inside my narrow cage, and although my legs are unbound, the collar they placed around my neck just about crushes my airways every time I try to inhale. Not to mention, there is another piece of odd equipment clamping my jaws shut, too. My entire body aches, and I'm *starving*.

Plenty of wounds litter my skin and cause my fur to mat together with dried blood, and my paws often pulse with pain from where my captors forced me to walk upon sharp edges on the hard flooring of this strange chamber as they poked me forward with hot irons. However, I remain unable to lick my wounds thanks to the bindings, and my paws have since begun to itch as my pads attempt to heal around the invasive shards.

"Nonsense," replies the one called *Apollo* to a few of his fellow winged celestials in that strange wording. *"She's been rather biddable thus far. The mortals certainly know how to cook up impressive means of torture. We'll guarantee her loyalty soon enough."*

One of them snarls, *"You have* nothing. *Nothing but a wounded pup who can hardly lick her wounds."*

"Agreed," says another, sounding just as enraged. *"You should stop while you're ahead. Before you've done too much damage."*

Apollo scoffs. *"And since when do you lot stick up for hellion natives so passionately?"*

"Unlike you, we don't wish for war, brother. There is a difference between a broken will and a broken heart, and what you see when you look at her is the latter."

"As soon as she recalls how vicious and powerful she truly is," says yet another winged male, *"she'll tear you limb from limb. Just as she nearly did before, and just as she did Adriel."*

"And do you, my dear brothers, not seek vengeance in Adriel's name?" inquires Apollo.

"Adriel made his fucking bed. You and Adriel slaughtered *Samael, and conspired with that witch to do it. This isn't right, brother. And there will be hell to pay."*

"You're already guilty by association, so you might as well see it through till the end."

"You're sick in the head, Apollo. We want no part in this, so leave our names out of it. And you'd best start praying to the Great Star and Fern above that when the deities *do get ahold of you, they'll end you swiftly."*

Apollo scoffs, and they finally seem to end this pathetic conversation as I hear them stomp off out of the chamber. *Good riddance.*

However, it isn't long after I close my eyes that my cage is suddenly rattled, and I'm jostled about and startled awake again. I growl and whine and snarl, making all sorts of noises in protest, and the one who literally kicked me awake comes to kneel before me.

It's the same young female from the woods, the one who shifted into an old hag and hung upon Apollo's arm like some bitch in heat as she handed me over to him. She cocks her head at me, looking smug as she holds a bowl of some rotten meat in her hands.

Though, she must assume the bloodlust in my eyes is for that meat rather than for her, and she says, "*Oh*. Hungry, are we, las?"

Feeling a sudden spark of defiance and strategy fill my bones, I whine at her pathetically.

Very well. Let's play games, *witch*.

She makes a pouty face at me. "*Aw*, such an odd sound coming from the likes of you. Very well. Sit tight. Of course, it's not like you have much of a choice."

Bitch.

Slowly, she places the bowl of rotten meat aside, then moves to unlock my cage with a series of hand gestures. She backs up a few strides to allow me to exit, and I hobble and stumble out upon my wounded paws that howl in pain. I whimper and whine again, putting on a show while struggling to reach the bowl that I have no intention of eating from. For on top of the rotten smell comes something else wickedly vile and *evil*, and I know better than to believe this meat isn't laced with some cruel poison designed to torture me from the inside out.

I sniff at the contents, then look at the young witch again.

"*Oh*, well, silly me," she coos, sniggering. "Of course you'll need some assistance getting that thing off your face. Sit still, las. Or your punishment shall be quite severe."

Doing as she instructs, I sit back on my haunches and raise my head, but close my eyes as she feels around the straps of the muzzle. It goes against every instinct inside me to let her *pet me* like I'm some prized *dog*, but she seems to take the action as genuine submission as she remains close by. I lower my nose to the bowl, sniffing at its contents as her hand continues to stroke the matted fur upon my back, and when I lick the meat, she relaxes just a touch more.

"Good las," she coos, then cackles quietly again. "The Obsidian Princess dripped in gold. What an unholy sight to behold."

As I suspected, there is something severely wrong with this meat, but I suppose she thinks I'm hungry enough not to care or notice.

Fool.

Faster than she can react, I have my jaws wrapped around her wrist, successfully crushing her bones and tendons and snapping her hand from her arm. She screams bloody murder as her form shifts into the old hag once more, but I am already upon her. Tearing into her jugular and ripping her head from her shoulders. But I don't stop there. I bathe in her blood, lapping it up as I disassemble her piece by piece. I want nothing left. I want all of her gone.

Thoroughly disemboweled, her organs litter the floor, staining the white stone red with blood and gore. Her bones splinter, and her eyes pop between my teeth, and I'm too busy enjoying the kill and succumbing to the bloodlust to bother noticing the other forms that have since entered the chamber with us.

Another blood curdling roar reaches my ears, and a second later, I'm flying through the air and landing against a wall with a heavy thud and *crunch*. My own lungs feel as if they're underwater now, and I can barely breathe as my organs feel as though they've caught fire within me. Apollo stands above me, screaming in rage, ready to plunge his sword into me. However, his brothers are there to hold him back and drag him away from me while he still curses my name and entire existence as a whole. I can hardly appreciate the sound of his anguish, though, since my own pain worsens with every breath I fail to take.

"For fuck's sake, Rhesa," curses one of the winged males as he kneels next to me. "You couldn't have waited till later to do that? *Seven Devils . . .*"

My ears fail me, and my vision begins to fade in and out as he presses his hands against my wounds.

"She's fading . . ."

"We need to get her to Pollux. Now . . ."

"I don't think . . . no time . . ."

"We don't have a choice but to try! . . . I will not be responsible for . . ."

No. Wherever they wish to take me, I won't have any part in it. I've had quite enough of winged males hauling me around like cheap luggage.

Something within me whirls and growls to life at the declaration, and I feel the air shift around me as the ground falls away. Shouts of protest come from the males nearby, but I pay them no mind as I allow another odd tunnel to consume me. It deposits me upon another dusty land I vaguely recognize from some far-off memory, but I don't have the strength to place it right now. Not as I whine and huff pathetically as my lungs still refuse to work correctly, and my limbs twitch in the hot sand as the sun beats down on me from a cloudless sky above.

I don't scent anything other than hot air and sand, nor do I see anything but a vast desert beyond the never-ending horizon.

What a desolate place to gaze upon before I die.

I can't help but whine again at the thought, and though I want to stand up and snarl at whatever may come to steal my soul away, my legs refuse to move. Not as more blood pools beneath me on the sand, and I am forced to close my eyes again.

. . . .

"Easy does it, little wolf."

I open my heavy-lidded eyes, feeling myself lift into strong arms as he carries me through yet another strange tunnel. This one deposits us into a quieter, open-aired hut surrounded by the shade of mighty trees upon the small land of an oasis. I whine and growl at the stranger pathetically, and he chuckles gently in response.

"I know, Rhesa," he says softly. "Just hang on a bit longer for me. I'll make you better."

He places me down on a hard, but lightly cushioned surface above the ground. Then, much to my dismay, he binds my legs and mouth again, and I snarl and snap at him, finally getting a good look at him.

To put it simply, he's quite dull; however, there is still an air about him that causes me to rethink that initial statement.

This . . . this isn't his true form.

He raises a brow at me, his pinkish eyes looking kind and . . . *sad* as he watches me struggle. The sight makes me pause, and he smiles gently at me while rubbing my ears softly.

"I can't very well have you biting off my hands when I pull these glass shards out, nor do I trust you to stay still while I do it. I know it hurts, and you have no reason to trust me, but I need you to try. Okay, my little wolf?"

Okay, I want to reply, but it comes out as a pathetic whine once more.

He smirks a little, then presses his forehead against my own for a moment before he leans back to concentrate on fixing my paws and other wounds.

It's excruciating.

He has to reopen and stretch a few of the cuts upon my paws to get the shards out completely. Poking and prodding and picking at my bloody, angry, and inflamed wounds over and over again. Then on top of that, he has to go in and clean out and sew up a few other burns and wounds upon the rest of my body that refuse to heal, thanks to whatever poison those males forced down my throat within the hours of claiming me as their *pet*. It was rotten and vile and slid down my throat in thick globs, and it left me feeling powerless and weak afterward, thus causing my wounds to heal slowly and, in turn, fester with the poison in my blood.

Finally, his painful work comes to an end, and he finishes by removing the bonds as well as the golden collar. It peels off my skin and fur in a sticky manner, thanks to the thorns and studs embedded into it, and the male above me curses at my state.

Gently, he hoists me up into his arms once more, then strides across his hut toward a plush-looking oversized seat, layered with more blankets and pillows. And despite the heat of the air and my fur, I shiver in his arms. He sets me down upon the soft cushions, pulling a few blankets over me as he kneels in front of me to rub my ears gently, and I let him, releasing a low whine in the process.

"Hush now, my fierce, little wolf," he says softly. "You're safe here. Your wounds will heal soon enough, and the fever will pass, too. I'll be able to give you something for the pain once that poison makes its way out of your system, and most of it has, now that you've nearly bled to death." He spares me a gentle smile. "I'm quite impressed you were able to open a conveyance in your state, too. You're quite remarkable."

He presses his forehead against my own again, kissing my eyes and nose gently before sighing and standing once more. However, before he can completely remove his hand from my muzzle, I lick his palm.

What is your name, I want to ask.

He seems to sense or see the question in my eyes. "My name is Atlas. Rest easy, Rhesamyre."

The names *almost* spark a memory, but I'm still too tired to chase after it and make an attempt to decipher it. So instead, I do as he instructs, and I sleep.

Atlas,

Rumor has it that while your youngest brother has been off fraternizing with whores and lustful wildlings, you've been residing in silence elsewhere. Alastair has since found the Child once stolen from you, and while he remains with me, I write to both you and Atticus in hopes the you'll aid me in a little problem of mine.

Our enemies are once again conspiring to condemn and betray those closest to and against them. And yes, I say OUR ENEMIES. Perhaps they never quit conspiring, to begin with. Not since you and your brothers erupted so violently, but my initial point still stands.

One by one, they are coming out of the woodwork.

So what of you, Deity of Sacrifice and Devotion? Will you remain a quiet, complacent, and forgotten king? Or will you finally bare your fangs and show just how cruel you can be? The old texts claim you were forged from bloodstained gems and bred for bloodshed, yet I don't believe it to be true. Maybe once upon a time, but certainly not now.

I beckon you to come prove me wrong.

Best regards,
Rhesamyre

CHAPTER FIVE
ATLAS

Struggling to hold her furry, slick form in my arms, Rhesamyre manages to escape my embrace once more as she jumps from the tub and scurries away, slipping and sliding on the wooden floors as she goes since her paws are wet.

I sigh from where I kneel beside the bathtub, my hands and arms covered in soap suds that smell of desert flowers and herbs.

Three times.

I've tried three times now to bathe her properly, intending to finally be rid of the last bits of dried blood, dirt, grime, and wicked celestial and other rotten scents that still cling to her matted coat. However, she's having none of it.

I suppose I should just be thankful she hasn't bitten my hand off, though she's certainly threatened to a few times, nipping a few of my fingers in the process, too.

Message received. No baths. *Got it.*

Rising to my feet again, I grab the towel to dry my face from the water she sprayed when she shook earlier, then proceed through my hut to find where she scampered off. In the past few days, she's found a few different hiding places throughout my desert abode that she prefers. I've found her underneath the bed, within the walls and shelves of the pantry, and even in the bathtub, when it isn't full of water.

But despite my numerous offers, she has *yet* to clamber up onto the bed or sofa with me in the evenings after we've finished the farm chores. Well, after *I've* finished the farm chores. Watering the goats, gathering eggs from the coop, restocking the grain feeders for the wild birds that prefer the palms and shrubbery of my oasis, and harvesting a few of the herbs, fruits, and veggies that can thrive in this heated climate.

This far into the wide-ranging desert of the West, there isn't much else to do. I travel here and there and into town plenty of times throughout the month, but now that Rhesa has arrived, I don't believe I'll be going anywhere for a while. Not until she is more comfortable around me, at least.

Besides, I don't trust her not to *eat* anyone. The desert is no stranger to coyotes and wild dogs, but a dire wolf of her caliber is certainly going to raise some suspicions.

Rounding the corner of the den, toward the open porch that overlooks the pond, I frown at the sight before me. There she goes again, chewing on that injured front leg of hers. No wonder it has yet to heal; the damn wolf keeps nagging at it and irritating the injury that nearly cost her the entire leg as a whole.

Snapping my fingers to get her attention, I scold her, "*Hey*! You're gonna rip your stitches again! Knock it off!"

She growls at me, her leg still in her mouth as she watches me with wild, amber eyes. However, after a moment of me refusing to yield, she finally succumbs to my command and releases her leg, then lies on her side upon the porch with a heavy *humph*.

I sigh to myself, as well, running a hand through my cropped hair that, even after all these years, still feels foreign to the touch. I can't recall the last time I took my proper form. I suppose it was sometime after the eruption when my brothers and I parted ways for the last time.

Seven Devils, that was a long damn time ago.

And now here she is. The Child that arguably started it all . . . snoozing on my porch as a wolf with sopping wet fur.

Fucking hell . . . how did this happen?

Of course, even the rumors of what happened in hell and the mortal regions reached the ears of us Western vagabonds, but plenty of other rumors have circulated before this one, too. None of them ever came to fruition, though, so what made this one so different?

How were the royals of both hell and the magicless slain so carelessly? And how the hell did she turn into *this* and end up *here,* of all spheres?

I shake my head at my inner inquiries, then step back into the hut once more and make my way toward the kitchen. She's at least gotten her appetite back, though it did take a while. I had to eat in front of her and reassure her that what I made was in fact *edible* and therefore not poisoned. And even then, she was very measured and tentative when she nibbled on the dishes of meat, veggies, and fruit, often glancing up at me from the floor to ensure I hadn't moved from my place at the table.

Though I tried to sit on the floor to eat with her, or perhaps even feed her, she once again didn't find that idea to be all that pleasant. She has preferred to keep her distance from me, yet every time I glance over my shoulder, she's often there. Lurking and prowling about in curiosity, but not daring to get much closer, despite my invitations. Getting her into the bath was no easy feat, and I was only successful due to my using dried fruits dusted with sugar as bribes. Though, I'm sure if I tried again, she'd definitely bite my ear off this time.

Feeling eyes on me, I glance back over my shoulder to find she has returned to sit in the middle of the carpeted den to observe my culinary skills from a distance she deems safe.

"Curious about what's for dinner tonight, my little wolf?" I inquire, though I don't expect an answer.

Not including our first evening together, she hasn't given me any indication that she's truly still *Rhesamyre* in there. I've seen her side glances and the way her ears or nose twitch in recognition of my voice, but another silent inquiry has yet to hang between us again. For that first night, I swear I *heard* her.

And it was a beautiful voice indeed. Certainly something more befitting a high-bred, demonic female of hell than that of the beastly wolf that has since taken up residence in my home.

Rhesamyre's little snout twitches at me, and I nod as I turn my attention back to the cutting board and chopped veggies.

"Well," I drawl as I work. "You've been gobbling up everything I give you, but I know you'll grow tired of lamb and goat soon enough. We have eggs for breakfast every morning. So how about something thicker for dinner tonight? I've still got a good chunk of steak left in my ice box, and I might as well let you have a taste of it since you're here. Of course, I can't promise it'll be as tasty as the steaks you've had in hell, but it'll satisfy the craving well enough, I suppose."

I glance back at her again, raising my brow. "Good enough, yes?"

She blinks at me, then lies down.

I nod. "I agree."

As I move about the kitchen to cook and light lanterns and candles since the sun has begun to set, I peer at her out of the corner of my eye every so often, watching in amusement as she ever-so-slightly tries to sneak her way closer into the kitchen. She crawls across the floor gently on her tummy while stretching her legs until she's finally sitting below the edge of the counter near me.

I peer over the side at her, just about done with plating dinner as I inquire, "May I help you, little wolf?"

Her nose twitches again as she stretches her neck to better scent the meal I have prepared, and she licks her chops and just about starts drooling.

I smirk, placing her dinner down before her as I note, "Begging and drooling isn't very queenly of you, Rhesa girl."

She ignores me, obviously unphased by the insult as she sniffs at her steak and chows down. I remain standing at the counter above her, cutting into my own dish slowly as I survey her form. She's not healing as quickly as she should be, especially given the fact that I know she has *all* of the forbidden power coursing through her veins now.

Granted, those dammed Zodiacs poisoned her a great deal before wounding her, thus stunting her ability to heal; however, I had figured most of it would've passed through her system by now. Certainly, since she had almost bled to death by the time I got to her—once I realized my furthest wards had been tampered with, that is.

A conveyance could be opened within those runes, but I would still be made aware of the infiltration immediately. However, here within this oasis, a conveyance cannot be opened unless the traveler has my invitation to do so. But it's not like anyone knows I'm here, anyway.

I don't have many visitors.

"Slow down, Rhesa," I say, not liking the way she's begun to scarf her meal down so recklessly.

She growls at me through a mouthful of food, and I roll my eyes. I've had plenty of time to perfect my culinary skills over the years, but I've never had anyone to cook *for*. So despite the circumstances, it does bring a small smile to my face to see that she at least enjoys my dishes. Wolf or not, I'm sure she's quite picky when it comes to her meals.

Licking her plate clean, Rhesa rolls her tongue over her teeth as she sits back on her haunches to observe me. Well, more specifically, the forkful of meat I currently hold.

I raise my brow at her. "Little glutton . . . though I suppose that is fitting, given how you were raised."

I lower my fork toward her. "The beloved final bite. Would you like it, little wolf?"

Rhesa sniffs the bite of food, then nibbles on it gently before ripping the meat from the metal. While she's busy chewing, I bend down to grab her plate, then proceed back to the sink to clean the dishes. However, what I don't expect is to hear her little pitter-patter of paws after me, but I do my best not to make a big deal of the action as I ignore her. She sniffs about the kitchen behind me, and then much to my surprise, jumps and places her front paws on the counter next to me to survey my hands in the sink.

I glance down at her. "Can I help you with something, little wolf?"

Her ears twitch, and with my soapy hand, I tap her on the nose gently.

"Boop."

She snarls a little at the sight of the bubbles upon her nose, clearly insulted, then jumps away from the counter in annoyance. I chuckle to myself, then finally finish cleaning up from dinner with every intention of retiring for the evening momentarily. However, the sound of rumbling thunder in the distance has me taking pause, and I soon find myself smirking at the sound of Rhesa's answering growl.

She's positioned near the open patio again, her sights set on the glittering stars and darkness that lie just before the thunderous clouds that rumble and flash with lightning.

"Looks like a good-sized storm," I note, coming to stand beside her. "My doorways are all warded with weatherproofed runes, so we won't have to worry about rain or sand flying in uninvited."

The sky lights up again, and Rhesa flinches at the sound of the thunder before snarling and growling once more. I chuckle, then bend down to meet her eyes and stroke her ears.

"I know they have storms in hell, little wolf. So don't tell me you're afraid of *thunder* of all things?"

She snarls lightly, and the message is clear enough.

I fear nothing.

Thunder shakes the soil below and the sky right above us as lightning crackles, and Rhesa all but whirls around and jumps into me as she growls again. Though she snarls and puts on a brave face, her limbs all but quake against my chest.

I wrap my arms around her, squeezing gently as I coax her to relax in my embrace. However, as per usual, she wiggles around and refuses my company, then stalks off to the other side of the den where she can better watch the sky, despite flinching every time it rumbles.

I sigh, then rise back onto my feet again and make my way toward my bedroom and bathing chamber.

....

Her whines and soft cries wake me up in the middle of the night; the dry lightning storm is nothing more than a faint echo of thunder in the distance now. I groan as I roll onto my back, listening and deciding that the whines are coming from directly under my bed again. She often sneaks under there at night to sleep, but similarly to other nights, she'll wake early due to nightmares around midnight. I often fall back to sleep after ensuring she's all right, but I'm unsure if *she* actually goes back to sleep again, as she is usually up before I am, come dawn.

Her whines sound louder than usual, thus making me fear she may have hurt herself again. I pull back my sheets and step out of bed, then get down on my hands and knees to locate her under the bed. She's in the very center, lying on her side, her paws and face often twitching as if she's running and snarling in her dreams.

Or her nightmares, I suppose.

"Rhesa."

She growls in her sleep, her tail thudding against the wood as her fur bristles.

I reach for her, though stop short of stroking her paw. I've nearly lost my hand once already, and I'd hate to scare her again.

"Rhesa girl, come back to me. Wake up for me, little wolf."

She snarls and whines again, sounding hurt and distressed, and I feel the power inside her surge briefly before settling down again.

Knowing this can only end poorly, I sigh to myself and prepare to get bitten as I swiftly grab her and haul her out from beneath the bed. She startles awake and snarls and whines and growls, the human equivalent of cursing up a storm as I pull her toward me to hold her close. I tuck her against my chest with my legs encircling her, laying her head over my shoulder while cooing gently in the hopes that my presence will calm her rather than stress her out more.

And then, much to my surprise, she settles against me and allows me to bury my face in her fur. Running my hands up and down her back and over her head and ears, I listen as her heartbeat settles and her whines finally quiet down. I'm not sure how long we remain there on the floor together, but once I deem it safe to pull away, I do so in order to meet her gaze. And her eyes seem . . . *sad*. Her ears are lowered and her body is heavy as her amber eyes, which usually glow with a predator's gaze, now appear dull and depressed again.

I rub her ears and stroke her face. "You're okay, my little wolf. No monsters can get you here. You're safe."

She presses her forehead into my chest once more, leaning all her body weight against me in the process. Slowly, I scoop her up into my arms to return to bed, placing her on the other side and crawling in behind her to keep her back tucked against my chest. She lets me position her to where it's more comfortable for me, and once we're properly settled, she sighs and closes her eyes. I stroke her fuzzy belly as I drift off, the rhythmic sound of her snores soon lulling me to sleep once more.

CHAPTER SIX
ATLAS

Waking up to find Rhesa positioned above me with all four paws spread out on either side of me is, needless to say, an *alarming start* to the morning.

I blink up at her, and she just stares down at me with that wolfish, predator's gaze of hers. The one that could turn feral with little to no warning in less than the blink of an eye, and yet, she doesn't.

"Good morning," I breathe, not daring to move yet.

Rhesa sniffs at my face, then *licks* me.

Alarmed, I sit up slowly and bring my hands up to cradle her; however, she jumps off my bed and thus out of my embrace before I can. She lands on the floor and spins around to face me, her tail swishing from side to side every so often as she watches me go about my morning routine.

"You seem . . . *chipper* this morning, little wolf," I note, now heading into the kitchen to fix her some breakfast.

Rhesa sniffs about quietly for a moment, then disappears outside to go about her own private business for a bit. While she paces the perimeter of the oasis and wards, I brew some morning tea and fix food for us to share. I don't need to call her back when it's ready, since she's already near the patio chairs, waiting for me. I take a seat as I lower her plate down next to me, and she nibbles at the scrambled eggs and bacon while I sip from my herbal tea.

"I was thinking," I begin, and one ear flicks toward me while she licks her plate clean. "Perhaps if you're feeling up to it, and I can trust you not to *eat* anyone, we could head into town?"

She licks her chops and stares at me, her gaze flicking between my leftovers and my face.

"You'll have to stay by my side the whole time," I continue, now beginning to feed her my last strips of bacon. "So no wandering off, and no threatening the townsfolk, either. If there's a threat, let me handle it, yes?"

After licking my fingers clean, she sits back on her haunches again and cocks her head. I purse my lips at the sight, not quite liking how . . . *docile* she is all of a sudden.

"Rhesa."

Her nose twitches, and then she sneezes.

I chuckle, then massage her ears and scrunch up the skin of her furry face to place a kiss on the tip of her nose.

"Very well. This will be a test of trust, okay? Perhaps it may be too soon, but I am still needed elsewhere if I am to keep up my façade. It would be best if you came with me so I can better keep an eye on you."

She whines at me, then escapes my hands and proceeds toward the edge of the patio to lie down. I sigh, nodding to myself and muttering a small *okay* as I clean our dishes and prepare my gear and cloak. When I return to the patio a few moments later, Rhesa is still there, staring off into the distance. She's deathly still as she gazes at nothing, her body barely giving me any indication that she's even breathing properly.

"Rhesa."

She gives me no indication that she even hears me, either.

Allowing my footfalls to be louder than necessary in hopes that it will get a reaction out of her without scaring her; I step forward and try again. "Rhesa."

Her ears twitch, and then she looks at me with colder eyes again. Not the predator's gaze that promises pain, but instead the dull gaze that sometimes befalls her features when her mind wanders somewhere I cannot follow. I am familiar with it, that dark place that whispers cruel, sweet nothings full of hollow promises that surround broken vows and betrayals. It's a cold, lonely, and seemingly never-ending road that slopes upward to encourage your legs to give out first. And then your eyes betray you next, for the light at the end is forever misleading and unforgiving in its trickery of distance and purpose.

Perhaps it is death. Perhaps it is the Yonder Star itself. Or perhaps it is something far more sinister.

Softening my gaze as I watch her, I call her once more. "Come on, my little wolf. You've been cooped up in here with me for too long. Getting out to breathe different air will be good for you."

Seeming to believe my words, Rhesa rises again and saunters up to me. I rub her ears gently, then pull my hood over my head and open a conveyance. It drops us onto the dusty road that leads into the small sand village of Jules, and when I walk on, Rhesa seems content enough to follow and stay close as we near the cracked runes upon the low sandstone walls.

The sand people of this village are poor but kind souls who often retreat here when their homes are claimed by the desert storms and raiding parties that patrol these dusty wastelands. The Hussars do their best to keep order, but the West is vast and foreboding, with a cruel habit of ripping all one is and has away from them. The coarse sand often makes it easy, and few thrive out here.

Rhesa's head is on a swivel as we proceed through the sleepy town toward the pharmacy and clinic. The streets are quiet but not necessarily empty as a few tend to their livestock or count their spices in hopes of trading in either this town or the next. I know they're curious about the dire wolf at my side, but when they gaze at me, they know better than to gossip. They all have their own issues to deal with, and an uncommon creature of her caliber is the least of their concerns at the moment, for too many of them are injured or starving as is, struggling to move their families to safer places.

"Easy does it, little wolf," I mutter down to her, and her ears flick up at me while she watches everyone around us with a stern gaze. "These people are no threat to you or me. I trust them, and you trust me, yes?"

She looks at me now but gives me no real hope that she truly understands or believes me. I sigh, then turn into the clinic I service and often support financially. Rhesa follows me through the door, then stops short at the sight of the few folks who sit against the walls and cough into their torn cloaks. Mothers clutch their babes while fathers clench their other small children and wives, and while plenty flinch at the sight of my wolf, none of them comment on her appearance. Instead, they focus their tired, sick gazes on me as I assess their situations.

"Thank the bloody stars," exclaims the head physician in a version of butchered Babel as she returns from the back. Her skin is as dark as the night sky, thanks to her desert heritage, but her eyes are alight with a golden glow as bright as the sun. Her black hair sits braided in tight cornrows that don't venture far from her scalp, and white patterns and facial markings paint her chin and cheekbones while piercings line her ears. Many of them signify her craft and religion, which often fall under the subject of witch-

craft. *"I knew it was about time for you to show up here again, but I was beginning to get worried as the days dragged on."*

I smile gently at the mortal woman in her late forties, placing my bag down on the nearby counter while pulling down my hood.

"I was a little preoccupied," I reply, glancing down at Rhesa, who sits next to me in a stiff manner.

Imani raises her brows at the sight of the dire wolf but doesn't question me as she just nods and sighs. *"I see . . . . No matter. You're here now, and that's enough."*

I dip my chin. *"Seems busier in here today."*

"The raiders are getting ballsier, and the Hussars can hardly keep up, even with those quick horses of theirs."

I raise my brow, alarmed as I inquire, *"The raiding party doubled again?"*

"Tripled."

I curse angel names under my breath, and Rhesa looks up at me while cocking her head. *"That's troublesome."*

"Agreed. You can start with them," says Imani, pointing toward a family with three kids between the ages of six months and three years. However, she hesitates before she returns to work as she glances at Rhesa once more. *"Do I need to be aware of anything?"*

I shake my head. *"Pay her no mind."*

Imani nods, then wastes no more time with me and gestures for the next patients to follow her into the back room.

Opting to leave Rhesa where she is, I proceed toward the family that appears battered and bruised in a number of ways.

"Can you stand?" I ask the couple, my eyes darting across all their shared wounds.

The man shakily nods and rises to his feet, extending his hand to shake my own.

"My name is Ali. We traveled with many of our neighbors here from Seaglass."

I hum. *"Seaglass is very much south of here. A three-week ride at the least."*

"We know . . . but it is as Doctor Imani stated. The Hussars can only do so much across this dusty sphere to police the people . . . and now that hell is in a frenzy . . ." He shakes his head, seeming to rid his mind of his thoughts before he inquires, *"Are you a doctor?"*

"Something like that. Will you let me help you and your family?"

He nods. *"Please."*

"Then you can head back into that other room across from Imani's, and I'll be there shortly."

He nods, then helps his wife to her feet while clutching his children close. I watch them stagger back into my clinic space, then turn my eyes to Rhesa once more. She hasn't strayed far from where I left her and keeps her eyes trained on me as I survey her form.

"Come along, little wolf," I say, jerking my head in the direction of my office.

Rhesa huffs once quietly, then follows me back into the room. Being mindful of her tail as I shut the door, I turn my attention to the family before me once more as Rhesa settles below the window to keep her eyes trained on the outside as well as my actions.

I get to work healing these people one by one, treating injuries the old-fashioned way the majority of the time, but effortlessly providing my Alchemic services to heal bigger wounds and aid in relieving fevers when need be. Then I prescribe herbal infusions, powders, and salves for the rest.

"I haven't seen them that bright in a while."

I bring my attention up from healing and wrapping the latest mother's wrist. A raider man had broken it something fierce a few weeks ago when beating the shit out of her, and the only reason he wasn't able to rape her was thanks to her husband interfering, though it cost him his life, thus leaving her alone with their four kids to trek across the desert alongside the rest of these people.

Following her gaze, I glance outside the window to find her children, as well as a few other kids, laughing and running amuck, with Rhesa snapping at their heels playfully. She grew bored of lying in here after a few hours and has since taken to babysitting. Surprisingly enough, she's quite skilled at it and has coaxed smiles out of the older children who originally could hardly breathe and hadn't eaten or slept properly in weeks.

"It gives me hope, seeing them smile again," continues the mother in front of me, her eyes wet with unshed tears. *"After everything happened . . ."* She hiccups a little, her good hand rising to cover her mouth as she sobs quietly. *"I didn't think I'd ever see them smile that bright again. Or jump and play so carelessly . . . Oh, to be a child again. Capable of forgetting as they grow older."*

I nod as I watch Rhesa play with the children. The massive dire wolf looks incredibly out of place, yet at peace all the same. Her little nips are gentle as she herds and chases the screaming kids who laugh and snuggle with her. And she licks their faces and growls and barks at them, her tail nearly *wagging.*

"Mister Sawbones?"

I snap my attention back to the woman, then clear my throat and finish assessing her injuries before clearing her and allowing the next patient in. After the last of the families are through, Imani finally knocks on my open door with her boot, as her hands are otherwise occupied, holding two glasses of desert alcohol.

I smile at the sight, chuckling as I thank her and reach for the much-needed whiskey after the long day we've had.

She clinks her glass against my own, glancing outside the window at Rhesa and a few slumbering kids as she says, *"I can't thank you enough, Sawbones. As always, you come when I need you without me ever reaching out first."*

I nod. *"I knew things were bad, but I wasn't aware just* how bad.*"*

The witch doctor shrugs. *"No one ever does. I worry for our world, Saw . . . I'm sure you've at least heard of the most recent talk concerning Hell and the midlands?"*

I sip from my glass, watching as Rhesa settles down to relax alone since the last of the children finally leave. *"I have."*

Imani places her hand on my shoulder, successfully dragging my eyes away from the wolf to properly meet hers once more.

"My practice with the Dark Arts and Old Commands may be limited, friend, but I am no fool . . . that wolf out there—"

"If you enjoy having your vocal cords intact and tongue properly located in your mouth, you won't *finish that sentence."*

She removes her hand as she surveys my steeled gaze, and she swallows thickly before nodding once.

"I meant nothing by it," she claims, her eyes sliding to look at my wolf again. *"She kept the children busy and made them smile, which in turn relieved some of the parents' stress . . . I only wish to repay the debt one day, if at all possible."*

I hum, then down the rest of my drink in one swallow. *"I don't think it's* impossible *. . . though I wouldn't deem it all that necessary, either. That little wolf out there . . . I dare say it is simply in her nature to help those in need."*

Imani hums. *"Perhaps . . . perhaps not. Even so, should you need my help with her, I am here for you, my friend."*

"And I thank you for that, as well as your discretion on the matter, faithful witch."

. . . .

Toweling my hair dry after a good soak in the bath, I glance outside my bathing chamber to find Rhesa snoozing atop my bed. Smiling gently at the sight, I grab a book from the shelf and proceed to lie with her. She shuffles and growls in her sleep as I move her around so I can fit beside her, and then she huffs quietly and starts snoring once again. I chuckle, then open my book and proceed to resume reading.

Feeling eyes on me a few pages in, I glance over to make eye contact with Rhesa. Her head is buried between her paws, but her ears are pricked toward me as she studies me.

I lift the book a little to show her the title upon the spine that reads *Folklore at its Finest*. A romantic fantasy decades old, but a timeless piece all the same. One of my oldest favorites, if I may be honest.

"I bet you didn't take me for a hopeless romantic, huh?" I inquire.

She blinks at me.

"Yeah. It surprises most folks. I'd be curious to know what your preferred genres and favorite titles are, little wolf."

She stretches and shuffles toward me, scooting closer. I raise my brow at her but dare not move as she comes to rest her head on my arm and stares at the pages for a moment before her eyes shift back up to me again.

Clearing my throat, I begin reading again. Aloud this time.

"For a single moment, all was well. Perfect, even. Assuming such a thing even exists, that is. Happiness no longer eluded me as I watched our children dance and play with one another. Our enemies were defeated, and the war was won . . . but that was years ago. And now I find myself unsheathing my sword once more, dusting off my armor, and praying to gods I don't believe in. Stars I have lost faith in.

"Yet here I stand, all the same, ready to defend and protect the one I love from a burning world that seeks to devour us and our memories whole. I see no greater life ahead, but I know looking behind me isn't an option, either. So here I'll stand. Sword in hand, flares in the smoky sky, and only the beating heart of my lover beside me to keep me grounded. To keep me sane in the horrors of what now brings. And despite the fucking terror of what stands before us, I grab her hand, kiss her bloodied knuckles, and declare my love for her just as I did years ago on our wedding night. Before that, even.

"'You are mine,' I claim as arrows rain down on our men, painting the battlefield red. 'Now until the end. And when we lose, I will find you again.'

"'Perhaps we can choose somewhere sunnier this time,' she prompts, grinning despite the bloodshed and screams around us. 'Until then, we are warriors. We are comfortable in bloodshed, and we're willing to give violence its proper debut.'

"I can only nod and think to myself how much I love this woman. This unruly, reckless, wild woman."

I glance down at Rhesa again, finding her eyes have closed as she continues to rest her head on my arm. Quietly, I shut my book, place it on my nightstand, and then snuggle against my wolf to sleep.

CHAPTER SEVEN
ATLAS

Closing up the chicken coop after retrieving the morning's eggs, I count them absentmindedly while I glance around my property for Rhesa's little wolf form. The chickens believe her to be a menace to our quiet society here, and have since deemed it safer to hide within the coop, literally *cooped up all day,* in order to evade her.

Meanwhile, Rhesa has since marked them as pathetic prey not even worth stalking, and much prefers swimming about the shallow waters of the pond after the few waterbugs, tadpoles, and pupfish. Seeing her snap her jaws into the water after the schools of critters have often left me unable to finish the chores since I'm too enamored with watching her.

And once again, a smile forces its way onto my lips as I watch her splash about without much care in the world.

Good.

Turning away to head into the barn to feed the goats and complete the rest of the chores, I'm not drawn out of my work again until I feel my remote wards shutter from a recently opened conveyance. I pause from deseeding the most recent batch of sour fruit from the garden as I feel the foreign newcomer agitate my wards, and then next thing I know, I'm sprinting outside to find Rhesa after hearing her release a menacing, territorial growl.

I skid to a stop in the sand just behind Rhesa, who's lowered herself to the ground, snarling with raised hackles at the winged male before us.

Releasing my own quiet snarl, I demand from the Archangel of Perception, "Does anyone else know you're here?"

Pollux scoffs a little. His icy, calculating gaze darts between the wolf and me as he replies, "*That's* your first question? *Really*?"

"It's the only one that matters in my book. So. *Does anyone else know you're here*?"

He snarls, and Rhesa growls and snaps her jaws at him, clearly warning him to watch his tone and attitude, and I'd be lying to myself if I claimed my chest didn't swell a little at that.

Pollux cocks his head at the wolf, something in his eyes softening at the sight of her. However, his gaze hardens with his next blink as he looks at me once more. His wings ruffle and twitch behind him as he finally draws them into his back after flying here, the hellion battle leathers he sports glittering in the sunshine like Rhesa's midnight fur.

"No," replies Pollux at last, glancing around the oasis. "I'm here alone, and no one knows of my whereabouts."

"And you'll be keeping it that way."

He quirks his brow at me. "You want me to *lie* to your brothers about your location? About *her* location?'

I shrug. "It's never stopped you before . . . I know better than to bother asking how you found us. So instead, I'll simply ask why you've come alone in the first place."

"I figured it would be easier like this. One thing at a time . . . for her sake." He glances down at the wolf between us once more, and Rhesa has yet to relax. "How is she?"

"Nearly feral, but we've come to *somewhat* of an understanding. I feed her, and she doesn't eat my face in my sleep."

Against himself, Pollux's scowl cracks as he allows himself to smirk and chuckle. "Yeah, that sounds about right."

"How did this happen, Pollux? I've heard the rumors and stories from the desert townsfolk, but I'd hardly call them reliable sources of intel."

Pollux nods to himself, seeming to mentally search for the right words on how to proceed, but then makes the mistake of taking a step forward.

Rhesa comes unhinged.

She's a flash of glittering, graceful black fur when she launches herself at the intrusive archangel, and neither Pollux nor I are quick enough to stop her from attempting to sink her teeth into his arms when he goes to defend himself. He hisses at the impact and does his best to grab her and keep her gnashing teeth away from his throat and nose. He holds her paws together with one hand while keeping her muzzle closed with the other, and she wiggles, growls, and whines in his arms.

"You're gonna hurt her," I snap, stalking toward him.

"*I'm doing my best here, Atlas,*" he snarls. Then quieter, he coos to Rhesa, "I need you to calm down, darling. Then once I trust that you won't bite my head off, I'll let you go."

Rhesa snarls through clenched teeth around his hand, her eyes darting over to me, and I'd once again be lying to myself if I claimed not to feel a little relieved at the sight of her hostility. It means that she's *feeling something*, and although it may be mostly wrath and indignation, at least it's better than the dull look of distress and trepidation she's often had in the past days, as exhibited the other evening when she finally allowed me to embrace her throughout the night.

I reach out to stroke her ears, muttering for her to *calm down* while claiming that Pollux won't hurt her, and I believe that.

She seems to believe me, too. And slowly, she quiets down and quits squirming.

Pollux surveys the interaction with narrowed eyes, then carefully, hands Rhesa to me. I take her with little difficulty, and she presses her wet nose into my neck to inhale my scent.

"You two," drawls Pollux carefully, cocking his head. "You seem *close*."

I shrug, then place my little wolf down so she may stand by me on her own four paws. She's still impressively wary of Pollux as she growls lowly from behind my legs, but seems content enough to allow us adults to speak for the meantime.

"How has she been?"

"She was a bloody mess when I found her, I believe this will be a lengthy discussion, yes?" I hesitate, but then inquire, "Would you like to come inside?"

He glances down at Rhesa again, then nods. "That seems appropriate."

Nodding in agreement, I head back into the hut with Pollux. However, Rhesa remains standing where she is, just watching us from a distance.

"Is she okay?" inquires Pollux *again*, taking a seat on the patio.

I slip into the hut to pour myself and Pollux a heavy drink. "She doesn't trust you."

Pollux makes a humorous sound of disagreement. "I've known her for a bit longer than you have, *Your Majesty*."

I return to the patio, handing him his drink while sipping from mine, taking a seat to overlook my property.

"Unfortunately," I drawl, "I don't think your previous relationship matters much at the moment. She isn't quite *herself*."

Pollux scoffs. "Yeah, *no shit*."

"I mean, besides the obvious." I sigh, meeting his steeled gaze with my own. "Pollux, the first day I had her, she was beaten, bloodied, and I'm certain that if she isn't what she is, she would've died out there in the desert. Honestly, I'm still surprised she *is* alive now. And she was *alone* . . . so what the *fuck* happened?"

Pollux takes a slow sip from his glass, his eyes darting over to Rhesa again. She's at least laid down, but her gaze is still transfixed on Pollux and me. Then when Pollux removes the glass from his lips, he tells me all that has transpired in the past months.

When he's finished with his story, he tosses the last of his drink back, then leans forward to run his hands through his hair. His half-bun comes undone in the process, but he doesn't seem to mind nor notice as he glances up with wet eyes to watch Rhesa again. She's inched only a little bit closer, but it's clear she's not a fan of his at the moment.

"My brothers tried to get her out," explains Pollux quietly. "They didn't agree with Apollo nor the Zodiacs' methods, and certainly not Lilith's. So when the wicked witch pushed Rhesa too far, Rhesa slaughtered her in cold blood, and Apollo came undone. He truly would've killed Rhesa if not for my brothers interfering, but before they could get her back to me, back to Hell, she managed to open a conveyance and flee. As to how or why she ended up within your territory, as wounded as she was, I'm not entirely sure. Even my remaining informants couldn't give me a straight answer there. Though right now, that isn't as important. She's safe and alive . . . yet she's not herself, is she? That's not Rhesamyre in that wolf body."

I follow the archangel's previous example and down the rest of my drink in one go, relishing the burn as I shake my head.

"No," I agree. "That's not Rhesamyre. At least, I don't think she's in there at the moment. The first day, though . . . I could've sworn I *heard* her." I shrug, confused. "She didn't speak. She didn't make any real attempt to communicate, and yet *I heard her.*"

Pollux leans back in his chair, his wings readjusting with the motion as he leans on them. "You had already fixed her up when you heard her?"

I nod. "Did my best to heal her the old-fashioned way. They did a number on her, but yes. I had just placed her on the couch to rest when I heard her inquire about my name."

"And you gave it to her?"

"I did."

"And then?"

I shrug. "Then nothing. She woke up the next day and was steadier on her feet but would barely eat. She didn't trust me, but she didn't try to run off, either. I dare say by that point, she was more wolf than woman, but she still suffers from nightmares and night terrors after dark. It was only the other day I managed to get her to sleep with me on a proper bed."

Pollux hums. "Assuming I recall the phenomenon correctly . . . I think you two *imprinted*, Atlas."

I raise my brows. "*Imprinting* . . . no, no. That can't be."

Pollux's gaze is still that of steeled calculation, but he remains patient as he explains, "It isn't something we have any control over, Atlas. It's an Old Command that happens instinctually by way of predestined constellations mapped out by the Evergreen Fern and Yonder Star. Divine intervention and fate, if you will. The bond can mean many things, and can be formed between family members, friends . . . or even lovers, eventually."

I shake my head, rising to my feet to pace. Rhesa's ears perk up at the action, but she doesn't rise with me.

"I . . . I don't think—"

"You're a protector, Atlas. You always have been. And you were there to protect Rhesa when she was truly in need of it and vulnerable. And she's . . . she's usually *not vulnerable*. Not at all. But when Sam was killed, a part of her died with him, and she *broke*." He chuckles a little. "Hence why we currently have a wolf stalking us."

Pollux and I glance over at Rhesa again, and she halts her crawling and pricks her ears once more. I laugh a little, smiling in her direction, but she snarls at me in return.

I nod, sitting down again to better meet Pollux's inquisitive gaze.

"I've come to care about her. I *do* care about her," I admit. However, I still shake my head at the thought. "But *imprinting*? What makes you so sure?"

Pollux shrugs. "Truly, it's just an educated guess. Putting together what you described, as well as the fact that she still trusts you despite seeming a bit feral." He chuckles again. "What else would you call it?"

I match the timbre of his low laugh, nodding again. "Imprinting . . . I suppose it does have a nice ring to it."

"It does." Pollux sobers up again. "The initial issue still stands, though. She needs to come home."

"She does . . . and she will. I'll bring her home."

He raises his brow at me, seeming unconvinced. "You're going to Hell? To where your brothers are?"

"I believe I am. Seems only fitting after all this time. She is the thing that tore us apart, even if it wasn't her fault, to begin with. Now she's the one who'll bring us back together."

Pollux smirks. "Poetic."

I chuckle. "Pathetically so, yes . . . though, I'm not sure how we get her to shift back into a woman."

Pollux stands up and claps me on my shoulder. "Perhaps you should show her the first step in doing so by shifting back into your old form, Your Majesty."

. . . .

"C'mere, my little wolf," I coo, though Rhesa doesn't seem to be having any of it. She snarls at me when I reach for her again, gnashing her teeth dangerously.

"Maybe you should've waited until we had her in Hell," quips Pollux while standing next to me with crossed arms and tense wings.

I roll my eyes, growling at him. "*Hindsight*, yes. And maybe instead of just standing there like a useless angel, you could help me out here."

He throws his hands up dramatically, making Rhesa brace and growl again. He seems apologetic as he glances at her and frowns, but then he still manages to snarl at me, "You said she doesn't trust me. What good could I possibly do?"

"*I don't know.* Something!"

"*Look.*" He sighs, rubbing his temples. "How do you usually get her to come to you? Do you shake a bag of treats at her or something?"

I gape at him. *Un*-fucking-*believable.*

"Yes, yes. I'm aware of how bad that sounds . . . but maybe it's worth a try?"

At a loss for words, I just shake my head and mutter, "How the hell are *you* deemed one of the intelligent archangels?"

"Have you *met* my brothers? It's not much of a competition."

"*Obviously*," I snarl, then sigh again and think aloud, stating the obvious, "This isn't going to work."

Despite being a few steps ahead of her, I crouch to better meet her eyes on her level. She snarls at the movement, her nose twitching as she filters through my unmasked scent. Shedding the form of *Sawbones* was easy enough, and I now stand as tall as Pollux and only a touch leaner. I was always a bit smaller than Alastair and Atticus growing up, but not by much, and we just about evened out after being promoted to deities.

Now with a different face and longer, darker hair. Rhesa seems to have pegged me as a complete stranger again. Tattoos that are all but foreign to me litter nearly all of my tanned skin again, painting me in sigils, old scriptures, wicked mandalas, and intricate layers of weaponry. I'm sure in her eyes, I look far more menacing than I did prior to the shift, and I don't blame her for being wary. Her instincts are top-notch, and she knows I am not *common*.

"Rhesa," I call, and she cocks her head at me and whines.

"She's scared," Pollux breathes, admitting what must be hard to accept after knowing what she's capable of. "It's not just mistrust . . . she's *scared* of us."

"I know you don't want to be," I call to her. "And you don't need to be, little wolf. I'm still *me*, Rhesa. I'm . . ." I release a careful breath. "I'm still yours."

She whines again, lying down now and pressing her face against her paws. Her fur still bristles while her ears twitch, and it's clear she's at odds with herself. Instinct is telling her one thing, but the imprint is telling her another. I can't imagine how confusing it must be, especially when she isn't quite in her right mind anyway.

I take another careful step toward her, and her ears prick forward again, though she doesn't raise her head.

"Rhesa."

Atlas?

I halt. My head tilts to the side as her *voice* echoes inside my
head. Unbelieving, yet curious to know if it'll happen again, if it
even *can* happen again, I call her name once more.

Silence answers me, and I write it off again as my own false
hopes taking a form of their own. When I finally reach her, she
rises onto her haunches again and growls but doesn't bare her
teeth at me. I smile as gently as I can, kneeling once more in front
of her while extending my hand.

"Listen to me, my little wolf. We want to take you home. *You
need to go home* . . . your friends and family miss you, and if I were
a better male, then I would have taken you to them the minute I
found you. But I didn't. Because I'm selfish and I wanted you all
to myself."

I lean forward just a little bit more, and she lets me stroke
her ears, but she's still tense beneath my tatted hands. "But you
deserve more than this desert life. You're bred for more and are
worth more. So let us give it back to you. Let us help you reclaim
it all. Let me take you home."

A beat of silence, then I hear her whisper again, *Home?*

I nod, pulling her close to hug her to my chest. "Yes, my fierce,
little wolf. Home."

Hello, Rhesamyre,

It seems you're a busy girl, so I'll keep this short.
I am content with where I am. I am somewhere
that I can be of use to folks without harming
them. Our enemies are everywhere, as they
always have been. They're always scheming, and
even after we're gone from these spheres, they'll
still be scheming against our legacies, too.
To put it simply, I'm tired of fighting.

Atlas.

CHAPTER EIGHT
ALASTAIR

The throne room is tense.

Understatement of the *fucking* decade.

The Four Generals and Seven lounge, but no one relaxes. Plenty sit upon the steps of the dais or lean against walls, and even the oversized serpent hasn't slithered about in some time as he slumbers around the Obsidian Throne. The lieutenants keep to themselves, and not even my brother has made some crude, inept remark in some time, either.

Pollux disappeared in the early hours of the morning, off to only stars knew where, and I didn't quite care at the time. However, when we received word that he had found not only our queen, but my brother . . .

Well. Needless to say, my interest in his whereabouts was suddenly piqued, and it took all my willpower to not only hold myself back, but Atticus, too, from hunting the archangel down to find Rhesa and Atlas.

The recently added runes that allow my brother, Pollux, and myself free range to open conveyances within the wards of Hell ripple in warning, and then a moment later, a glittering conveyance opens to reveal the long-awaited trio.

Atlas strides forward in his proper form, dressed in desert cloaks, but still looking as regal and menacing as ever. The delicate and dainty Old Latin inscription that translates to *strength* rests in the corner under his right eye, and power similar to my own wafts off him in waves as he assesses the demons and Hellion Court before him. His hand absentmindedly rubs the fur atop Rhesa's head.

He makes eye contact with me first, and then Atticus next. My gaze darts to where he casually pets Rhesa's ears, and something vile surges through me at the sight.

Jealousy.

This jaundiced emotion nearly rips a growl out of me, but I stifle it so as not to spook or provoke Rhesa again, as the wolf has proven herself to have a quick temper and even quicker response time.

Feeling eyes on me, I tear my gaze away from Rhesa's canine form to meet the dark eyes of Envy. The assassin cocks his head at me, daring me to act on the emotions that are his namesake.

Begrudgingly, I turn my gaze away from him to study the trio once more, but Pollux has already stepped forward to claim his own space away from Atlas and Rhesa.

I take a calculated breath, opting to speak first with an incredible sense of self-restraint in order to keep the growl out of my voice. "Atlas. I would be lying if I said it wasn't good to see you again. You're well I presume, brother?"

Menacing pink eyes glow eerily in the enchanted lights of the room, and he scans me with a scrutinizing gaze as he sizes me up.

The wolf under his hand does the same, and she growls first.

Atlas goes to a knee next to her, rubbing her ears and the scruff of her neck, and I feel my *trouvaille* tattoo start to itch at the sight.

"I'm well enough," he claims, rising to his feet once more as soon as he deems it safe to do so. "Better than you lot, it seems."

Atticus, *ever the temperamental fool*, growls. "*Watch it*, Atlas."

Rhesa snarls menacingly, and the sound and power within her nearly rattle the entire room. Atticus has yet to take his eyes off her, and she doesn't retreat, either. In fact, she takes a step forward, her hellfire eyes set on my youngest brother, promising pain.

"I see you're still an imbecile, little brother," calls Atlas, unfazed by Rhesa's reaction as he crosses his arms, looking smug.

Too smug.

It's inevitable that I'm going to hurt him. It's merely a question of *when*.

Atticus, seeming to at least have *some sense* still left in his dumbass, empty head, slowly raises his hands to show Rhesa he means no harm. Though, I doubt the pledge extends to our brother, and I second the notion.

"*Rhesamyre*," calls Atticus gently, and she pauses her prowling.

My youngest brother by a mere few minutes looks at war with what to do next, and honestly, as am I. This version of Rhesa is one I've had little experience with, and so far, it hasn't been all that pleasant.

"Hello, sweet spice," coos Atticus, and his next move surprises all of us.

He lowers himself to his knees.

Rhesa cocks her head, her ears twitching, and then she looks back at Atlas as if unsure of what to do next. Atlas smiles gently at her, then extends his hand and gestures for her to go meet Atticus. However, she simply whines, then lies down and remains where she is. Her fur bristles and her eyes are wary, and it's obvious she doesn't trust anyone. She seems to barely trust Atlas as it is.

I slide my eyes over to Pollux, and sensing my gaze, he turns to face me.

"Care to share?" I quip.

Pollux's jaw tenses as he works a muscle there. "I was able to contact the rest of my informants after we received word from my brothers about what went down in Ursa Major . . . though even they don't exactly know the *why* behind it. But my genies informed me of where she was dropped."

"It seems as though it is as we feared," states Death, and Rhesa raises her head to study the bearer of the new voice. He attempts to smile at her, but she simply grumbles and lowers her head again. Sighing, Death nods. "That's not Rhesa."

"Well," drawls Pollux, his eyes on Atlas again, "not quite."

"What did you do?" inquires Atticus, and this time, he thankfully keeps the growl out of his voice for her sake. However, the implication is still there as he accuses Atlas of whatever he can, and Rhesa knows it as she growls again.

Atlas hesitates, then continues slowly, softly. "It wasn't something I had any control over."

Understanding washes over all of us in waves, and it is Pride who snarls next, "*You fucking imprinted.*"

Rhesa snarls from her place in the center again, and Pride spares her a little glance in apology before setting his sights back on Atlas.

"Before you rip him a new one," interjects Pollux, "I suggest you let him finish. It will be imperative if we hope to get Rhesa back as a *woman.*"

"On with it, then," orders Conquest.

"After I found her and nursed her back to health," explains Atlas, "I heard her voice. It went away for a bit, but then I heard it again earlier today after I shifted and had to regain her trust."

"What do you mean?" inquires Greed.

"I mean it quite literally. I *heard her voice* echoing in my own head, but she didn't speak like you and I are now."

"You're delusional," claims Atticus. "That doesn't mean anything."

"It does, though," drawls Pollux. "It means a great deal, because I hate to break it to you, but Atlas remains the only one of us successful in even getting anywhere *near* her. Let alone being able to console and hold her without fear of losing a finger. In addition, if this imprint does exist, it means that *Rhesa* still exists somewhere in that wolfy head. If we can find a way to strengthen their bond, then perhaps we can communicate with Rhesa and coerce her into shifting back into a woman again. Remind her of who she is."

"As I said, though," begins Atlas again. "I heard her the first day, and then I heard her this morning. Outside of those two times, nothing."

"It's better than nothing," says Sloth. "It's a start. It's better than where we were a mere hour ago, that much is certain."

"So then, *what*?" scoffs Atticus. "We just wait her out? Let those two get all *lovey-dovey* until she's ready to come out of hiding?" He levels his gaze onto Rhesa, smirking. "I'm quite surprised and disappointed in you, sweet spice. I didn't take you for a *coward*."

I close my eyes and tip my head back, muttering a few curses and prayers to whatever may be willing to listen out there.

Rhesa's answering growl echoes through the throne room again, rattling the chandeliers above us, and I direct my attention to her as she rises onto her paws once more. Her body is tense and ready for action, her mouth open and nearly unhinged as she sizes up my youngest brother.

"Rhesa," calls Atlas, but while an ear flicks back to hear him, she doesn't listen.

Instead, she launches herself full speed at Atticus. My youngest brother chuckles darkly and welcomes the challenge, but I don't miss the *oh shit* look he allows to slip through his scowl as she tackles him to the stone floor. I would spare a moment to laugh at his expense if I wasn't so worried about her hurting herself in her assault. All of us brace and take a few steps forward to better intervene as we watch them roll and brawl.

Rhesa was relentless and tended to be reckless before becoming a wolf, no doubt about it. However, this beast, with her eyes, has every intention of *killing* my brother, and while a small part of me wouldn't mind seeing him get roughed up a bit, the majority of me knows this will not end well for any of us.

Rhesa's gnashing teeth go for his throat and nose while her claws scratch his torso and arms. And while he is mostly covered in proper leathers, her weight and underlying power still factor into her assault. They may be paws instead of fists, but they still pack a punch.

Atticus, doing his damn best not to hurt her, is already bleeding from his nose where she head-butted him. He holds her back by her torso and under her front legs, and she wiggles and snarls and howls at him in anger.

Atlas dives in to wrap his hands around her middle to pull her off our brother, and I come to his aid when she struggles in his grip and turns her gnashing teeth onto him instead. Limbs and teeth tangle, and Atticus grunts when her fangs sink into his arm when he goes to prevent her from biting Atlas, but that doesn't stop her from nearly clawing Atlas's eyes out. Blood drips from my middle brother's face, and I narrowly avoid her teeth next as she struggles in my grasp.

"*Fucking hell!*" I snarl. "*Rhesa my re!*"

She stills momentarily and then starts whining and yowling as if I injured her. Fearing the worst, I drop her, and she scurries away before whirling around to keep her front to us. The Hellion Court remains upright and tense around us, ready to intervene if she goes for the kill again, though they do *hesitate*, a rare phenomenon. However, Rhesa just backs herself onto the dais against the throne, snarling and whining often with trembling limbs as she nearly trips over herself ungracefully on the stairs.

"Easy, *easy*, my little wolf," coos Atlas, attempting to step toward her with a bleeding face. "You're okay. I promise you're okay."

Rhesa *barks* at him, snarling viciously. However, the sound of slithering scales and faint hissing has her hackles rising higher, and Mamba peers around the edge of the throne to make eye contact with her. She snarls in his face, snapping at him, but the serpent just seems more confused than threatened by the sight of her.

Her growls are low and getting quieter as the seconds tick by, and much to all of our surprise, they soon cease completely as she *boops* her nose against the menacing snake's. He slithers around the throne again, nudging Rhesa onto the empty seat as he slides around her protectively. She curls up on the throne, resting her head over the armrest while side-eying us warily, and Mamba takes point.

The entire room seems to collectively release a careful breath, and Atticus curses quietly to himself as he surveys the puncture wounds in his forearm. Atlas glowers at him, then slaps our brother upside the head with an impressive *whack*.

"*The fu—*"

"*Happy now*?" sneers Atlas in our brother's face, and Atticus merely scowls.

Atticus lifts his shoulders, an attempt at nonchalance. "At least we know she's got some fight left in her. I'm sure we can all agree that rage is better than submission. Better than dismissal and better than dissociation. Now we know what we're working with, so you're *bloody damn welcome*."

Stomping off, he doesn't even spare Rhesa a final glance as he leaves the throne room, slamming the doors hard enough behind him to make her *flinch*.

Sighing, I turn to face the rest of the court.

"Unfortunately," drawls War, "I believe he does have a point. Between the supposed imprinting and her reaction to being threatened and challenged . . . maybe Rhesa isn't that far gone, after all."

A few nod in agreement, though they don't seem settled or satisfied with the news.

"So then," prompts Gage slowly, the fellow wolf unable to communicate with her despite his best efforts. "What now?"

Seemingly at a loss, no one replies. An agreement is eventually made to ensure she is never alone, but even so, no one approaches the slumbering wolf again.

....

"C'mon, baby girl," calls Pride, *kneeling* on the floor a few paces away from the throne where Rhesa lies, watching us skeptically. "You need to eat."

Neither she nor Mamba have moved much in the past few days, and while the snake still takes his offerings greedily, Rhesa has yet to eat anything we attempt to give her. All of us have tried, including the lieutenants, and I've even seen Mamba attempt to share with her, too. However, she remains unconvinced and stiffly remains on that dark, stone throne where she can remain alert to any threats.

I also know she only leaves when Mamba does, the two of them often disappearing for a bit to relieve themselves before returning to the throne, taking no shortcuts or field trips on the way to and from this room, but I know she must eat or drink at *some point*. It's just never when we're around.

Pride clicks his tongue in disapproval, the plate of steak and mixed fruit and veggies growing cold in his hands since Rhesa has refused to move.

"Still no appetite?" inquires Famine as he enters the throne room with his wolfish lieutenant, Gage.

I shake my head, sighing. "No."

"Not for Gluttony's cooking, anyway. Nor Atlas's," explains Pride, finally just setting the plate down on the first step and backing away.

Famine nods his head, his eyes downcast as he sighs and runs a hand through his pale hair.

"Maybe the *mutt* can try again," calls Atticus from where he leans against the wall near the doors.

Gage bares his teeth but refrains from snarling at my brother for Rhesa's sake.

"I may have the blood of a wolf," claims Gage, irritation evident on his hybrid face. "But that doesn't guarantee she'll trust me. In fact, as we've already learned, it seems to agitate her more."

True enough. She *did* try to bite his tail off when he dared to approach her the second day.

Atticus grins, and I can only pray he doesn't say something utterly *stupid* that causes another fight to break out. Either between all of us, or Rhesa again.

"That's true," he replies. "I suppose you do reek of *dog* in such an unsavory manner that she just can't stand to be any closer to you."

"I don't see her curling up in your lap, either, *Chaos*," growls Gage.

Rhesa huffs, and Gage spares her an apologetic glance.

"Before you opened your fucking mouth to spew useless nonsense," drawls Famine, "we did have a point in coming here."

"Did they find something?" inquires Pride, referring to Death, Sloth, and Atlas, who have been slaving away in the libraries, attempting to figure out a possible way to shift her back using magic.

"Not yet, but the lieutenants have an idea."

We all look to Gage expectantly, and the lieutenant inclines his head. "The girls have been asking about her . . . Tallulah, Althea, and Feronia. And we think that maybe it's time for a woman's touch."

I survey Rhesa's form as I contemplate it, and at this point, I'm willing to try anything.

"Is it wise to risk their safety, though?" asks Pride. "She may still take exception to females after the ordeal with Lilith. And I know that *when* she becomes a woman again, she'll be distraught to know she harmed her girls in this state."

Gage shrugs. "I agree, but we won't know until we try. The girls want to . . . they're worried."

I find myself nodding in agreement, but it is Atticus who speaks up next. Thankfully in a tone more befitting the grand commander rather than my idiotic brother. "We should be open to anything at this point, because it's clear that, despite our best efforts, nothing is working. In addition, even with that imprint between her and our brother, odds are, the longer she remains in this state, cut off from us, cut off from her humanity as a whole, the more challenging it will be to turn her back. So, I concur. We should let the girls try."

I meet my brother's gaze, then nod in approval. He doesn't react to me, though, and instead takes his leave without uttering another word.

Rhesa's hellfire eyes watch him go, her ears twitching when he quietly clicks the doors shut behind him.

CHAPTER NINE
ATLAS

"You need to come see this," calls Greed, tapping his knuckles on the doorframe of the library to catch our attention.

Death, Sloth, and I all exchange quick glances, then follow the assassin wordlessly as he leads us to one of the grand balconies that overlook the courtyard and garden. Scattered across the lengthy railing are my brothers and the rest of the Hellion Court, and I take my place near Atticus and Alastair to peer over the side to survey the scene beyond.

I'm speechless. For in the center of the garden, sprawled out upon blankets near baskets and trays of snacks, is my little wolf and her three girlfriends.

The three females giggle often, indulging in various conversations while petting and brushing Rhesa gently. The wolf seems more than content as she lies between them, getting fed cookies and sandwiches often by the girls as they play card games or read underneath the shade of the center tree in the warm air and sunshine.

"It was the lieutenants' idea," explains Alastair quietly. "The girls even managed to bathe her and have since taken up residence in the garden."

My eldest brother shakes his head in disbelief, but I can tell even through his scowl, he's relieved. And so am I. So is everyone.

"She's eating," I remark.

"She is," replies War. "She never gave any indication that she wanted to hurt them, either. Still a little wary at first, but somehow, the girls managed to coax her away from Mamba to follow them."

"It was almost laughable, to be honest," chuckles Wrath, albeit darkly. "Here we've been, attempting all sorts of tricks to get her out of that damn throne room. And yet the *minute* the girls show up, she's nearly *wagging her tail*."

I release a breathy laugh—something crossed between a sigh and a chuckle, I'm not entirely sure. All I know is that I'm *relieved*. Very relieved to see her eyes alight with laughter and happiness as she relaxes with the girls. Even allowing them to use her as a *pillow* while she takes snacks from their hands gently.

Death claps his lieutenant on the shoulder, sounding proud as he says, "Job well done, Damian."

The reaper releases a quiet huff, smiling and nodding as he surveys the females in the garden.

....

Lounging a few feet away from her, leaning against one of the garden trees, my brothers and I watch over the group that surrounds my little wolf. The lieutenants now sit with the girls and Rhesa since the wolf has yet to chase them off, and though she still seems wary of the males, she seems satisfied enough with a full belly to remain snoozing on Althea's lap while unshifted wendigo, Feronia, uses her fuzzy tummy as a pillow.

"So all of you have essentially grown up with Rhesa here in the palace, right?" inquires the ex-genie, Tallulah.

"Just about," replies Silas. "Rhesa is undoubtedly credited with getting us in here and off the streets. That much is certain."

"Oh? In what ways?"

Gage chuckles at whatever memories surface, allowing the mortal woman, Althea, to lean back against his chest, thus giving him access to Rhesa's ears, which he rubs with one hand leisurely without the worry of her snapping at him, thanks to Althea's presence acting as a buffer between them. I can't help but notice the lieutenant's other hand wraps around the female's plump navel, his fingers caressing the soft flesh there underneath her hellion summer dress.

Something akin to jealousy rears its wicked, vile head within me at the sight of his hand placed so causally on my wolf's head, but I tamp it down so as not to spook Rhesa and ruin this moment.

"A few decades back," drawls Silas, and I can't help but be a little curious, too, "I was making a living running an illegal gambling ring under Gluttony's and Greed's noses. Rhesa was sent to infiltrate my ranks and shut me down, and boy, did she ever. However, curious as always and forever scheming, Rhesa challenged me to a game of chess. The game lasted close to twenty hours with over two hundred moves between us, and even then, it still ended in a draw in order to preserve both our sanities. However, instead of throwing me on my ass in some cell or slaver's pit, she gave me a choice instead.

"'*Your potential and power are limitless,*' she claimed. '*And of no use to me down here. Perhaps you would like to do what you're best at and get rewarded for it?*'" He smiles at the memory, glancing down at the slumbering wolf. "From there, she vouched for me on many occasions, and soon enough, General War took an interest in me."

Gage nods along, and Tallulah cocks her head at him, prompting the demon-wolf to continue. He does.

"As you're aware, I'm a low-bred hybrid who was fortunate enough to inherit my father's blood of the wolf, but he had no higher claims. Consequently, I grew up on the lower streets of Heart. Often thieving and scheming to feed myself and find work, hustling where it counted, and often killing others when they would steal from the kids weaker than them. Rhesa was sent to neutralize the mutt bred in the streets, but upon finding me, she decided on another path. '*There are finer things you could be stealing, and worse people you could be killing. Your skills are wasted on the streets.*' It was as simple as that, and with her guidance, I eventually found myself serving the devil as Famine's second in command."

"You left out an important piece of that story, Gage," chuckles Damian.

Gage grins, nodding. "I suppose I did . . . . I forgot to mention that when Rhesa found me, she beat the ever-loving *shit* out of me. I think I frustrated her, but piqued her curiosity all the same. Every time she knocked me down, she would order me to get back up. And I did. *Repeatedly.*"

"Why?" inquires Tally. "Why not order you to stay down and be done with it?"

Gage shrugs. "Couldn't tell you. She just saw something in me that no one else did. It wasn't pity, I know that much. Rhesa doesn't believe in pity, but she does believe in *opportunity*. As exemplified by all of us being here now. Rhesa saw an opportunity to strengthen her court, and she didn't hesitate to risk taking a chance on even a simple nobody like me."

"She gambled her reputation when she saved me from myself, too," adds Damian, his fingers tracing patterns on Feronia's calves that rest over his lap. "Having recently lost my family at the time, I was out for blood. I wanted to butcher the mortal men who had broken into my home and lain waste to my siblings and parents, and I eventually did. However, by the end of my journey, I was ready to end it all there. I was satisfied that they were gone and had gotten what I deemed they deserved. Rhesa caught me before I could reunite with my family in the next sphere far from here. '*You may take your own life if you so choose; I will not stop you. However, I will dissuade you, for I believe your life is still worth something. If not to you, then to me. If you are to have faith in anything, have faith in me. Death is always certain, but I am far better at bargaining, and the Great Star is not satisfied with your soul yet.*'"

Nodding along, Malcolm adds soon enough, "'*You're capable of more than this,*' she once told me. '*You crave more than what you have been given but have only taken what you needed. Never what you wanted. It is time you started living for yourself whilst fighting for something greater.*' I wasn't alone for a long time, but when my folks and sisters grew sick, and we couldn't afford the necessary medicine, I resorted to thievery, then later, murder. I was able to stay out of Rhesa's peripheral for three months with a kill streak of fifteen mortal men, and then she finally caught me." Malcolm grins. "I suppose I impressed her with my ability to *hide* from her, as very few have succeeded in doing so for as long as I did. Still to this day, no one has beaten my record."

"Cocky bastard," teases Damian, grinning.

"Jealous?" quips Malcolm.

The reaper shrugs. "Not anymore."

"But once upon a time?"

"Maybe a long time ago, when I used to brood in dark corners," admits the reaper.

Gage laughs abruptly at that. "*Used* to?'

"Hush it. You'll wake the wolf."

"Sounds like a puny excuse to me," quips Silas.

Damian scowls. "Go ahead and keep talking shit then if you're so brave."

"I'm good, thanks. I quite like my balls where they are."

The girls snicker softly to themselves as the males bicker quietly, often rubbing Rhesa's fur soothingly when she snarls absentmindedly in her sleep, thanks to whatever dreams or nightmares interrupt her slumber.

I can't help but think back to a few days ago when *I* was the one consoling her, cuddling her. And *of course,* I want her to feel safe and happy, and this is exactly what she needed. But even so, a part of me had hoped I would be the one she would seek out. And maybe one day, I will be again. She just needs space from us overbearing males who, truthfully, have ulterior motives that are confusing enough for *us* to decipher, let alone her in this primal state. She needs time, and I know the rest of the court will give her that time, but I worry for my brothers. Certainly Atticus more than Alastair, the hot-tempered fool who often seems to forget he's been bred and built for command.

Alastair may be the eldest of us and our acting leader, but it is Atticus who is often held responsible for many of our triumphs in the old days during the Wild Hunt. The Four Horsemen are all but strangers to us now, but there was a time when he, War, and Conquest worked closely together to ensure victory. Staying up for days at a time, poring all their attention and time into discussing battle plans and contingencies. However, as I survey Atticus's form now, one wouldn't think that at all. For even I have trouble distinguishing between his brilliance and his brash, *shit for brains* façade.

Sensing my gaze, Atticus meets my eyes, envy swirling in his own emerald eyes as his mind surely wanders to draw similar conclusions as my own.

"You know what she looks like, right?" he inquires softly.

"That lone wolf that used to stalk us when we were boys," replies Alastair, his eyes focused on Rhesa.

Atticus nods. "Uncanny, I'd say." He works a muscle in his jaw, grinding his teeth. "I'm not a patient male by any means," he vows lowly.

I nod, and out of my peripheral, I see Alastair turn to watch us out of the corner of his eye.

"With that said," continues Atticus quietly, his more obvious emotions sealed off behind a steeled scowl. But I can always read him and Alastair with ease, and right now, Atticus is *livid*. "I am willing to give her another day. Perhaps two, if she keeps up this good behavior. But after that, we need to take more proactive steps to ensure we don't lose her." He looks between Alastair and me. "I don't feel like repeating history."

I nod again. "I know, and neither do we."

....

Atlas . . .

My mind is hazy with sleep, but her voice echoes in my ears in an odd but soothing manner. It's enough to make me wake and blink the sleep from my eyes; anxiety washes over me at first, but then I hear her whisper my name again on some foreign, Alchemic wind, thanks to this damn imprint.

I close my eyes again, and when I do, *she's* there. A beautiful woman with midnight hair and obsidian horns. She stands with her bare feet buried in the desert sand of my oasis in the West, her body covered in transparent silks. However, they don't leave much to the imagination, thus revealing her few tattoos and the curves of her mouthwatering body.

She is every bit the incarnate of unholy desire and sensuality.

However, as she turns to glance back at me, sizing me up, I still at the sight of the white eyes that take the place of her amber ones. What does Alastair call them again? Hellfire, was it?

There are no hellfire eyes here. Only white, luminescent voids that shine with raw magic that, dare I say, don't quite belong to any of our known spheres.

She cocks her head at me, studying me as I steel myself to close the gap between us, reaching her in a few strides. She doesn't yield and instead turns to face me with a scowl, though something akin to mirth dances in her white eyes.

"Atlas."

I tilt my head slightly at the sound of her voice, as it sounds . . . *different* from the other times she has called my name. It is still Rhesa's voice, yet not, as if her accent and tone are wrong. It is the slightest shift in her timbre that makes all the difference, and this . . .

This is not Rhesamyre.

As if she can read my thoughts or see the question and revelation in my gaze, her lips pull into a smirk as she claims in Old Latin, *"The girl is still slumbering—well, wallowing in her grief is more like it. Though, I suppose that is because I am keeping her there."*

"For how long?" I inquire softly, not entirely sure how to handle speaking to this one who wears Rhesa's face and uses her body but claims to be someone or *something* else entirely.

It's fucking startling, to say the least, but I keep hold of my scowl and steady my breathing so as not to raise suspicion and potentially spook this one into possibly harming Rhesa in any way.

"For however long she needs to come out of this stronger than before, and she will," claims white eyes. *"She's already fighting me quite impressively, even if she doesn't truly realize it. Nonetheless, Rhe-*

samyre will return . . . when you and your brothers prove yourselves worthy of having her, that is."

"And how might I go about proving myself?"

She grins. *"You already are, and you all but already have . . . . It will come down to Atticus again, just as it once did centuries ago when you received your magic and titles."*

I stiffen. *"How do you know of such matters?"*

"I know a great deal of all matters, boy. And it is as I told your eldest brother. You share powers with Rhesamyre, and your souls seek to be whole again. Only then will I be satisfied. Only then will our girl be safe."

Slowly, I reach toward her to place my hands on her cheeks. This one doesn't stop me, and I study her eyes before I lower my gaze to study the rest of Rhesamyre's form. Noting the *trouvaille* tattoo that brands her inner right forearm in a similar manner to Alastair's ink. And through the sheer silks, I can see the fern tattoo on her right thigh, as well as the patterns that mark her breasts. They're beautiful, and I'd also be lying to myself again if I said I didn't appreciate our height difference.

"Can I speak with her now?" I inquire, meeting its eyes again.

This one shakes her head. *"No . . . but she will hear you. I will ensure she knows of your intentions, Devotion. Speak your truth."*

I take another calculated, steeling breath. *"I know our letters weren't all that productive, but recently, I've had an . . .* epiphany *of sorts, I suppose. And being with you, even though you were a simple wolf . . ."*

I chuckle a little, leaning forward to press my lips to her forehead despite the warning brewing in her gaze at my closer proximity. *"I know what I said before . . . but things are different now. We're* different now. *And I'd be lying to myself if I said I didn't care for you, Rhesa. The emotions are still raw, and the relationship has yet to be properly defined. But even so, I cannot deny there is something here, and for the first time in a long, long time, I find myself* want-ing *to fight for it. Fight for you. Us. Whatever we may be . . . I don't quite know yet, but I know I want* something. *I want to be someone to you."*

For a moment, hellfire eyes flash; black consumes the white as it recedes enough to allow me to see her proper irises and pupils, and they *smolder* as she scowls at me. Her own ability to close off her emotions and focus on nothing more than the multiple ways to skin me alive takes hold. I find myself grinning at the sight; that familiar, but long-forgotten feeling and desire for bloodshed beginning to settle deep within my core once more. She brings it out of me, and I find myself ready to welcome it.

For now, I gaze upon the unhinged predator who enjoys sipping the blood of her enemies from obsidian chalices. The blood-stained monster that *is* Rhesamyre. The one who harbors her hatred, her lust, and her unquenchable thirst and desire for death and decay and destruction in copious forms.

What a beautiful sight it is. *What a beautiful sight* she *is.*

Her eyes flash again, and the white voids return

"She senses you nearby. She knows she can trust you."

Not a question, but still, I nod.

"You're hers."

Nodding again, I lean forward to press my lips to her forehead once more. *"In whatever way she'll have me. In whatever way you and her want or need, I'm yours, my little wolf."*

A heartbeat of silence passes between us, and then this one mutters, *"Little wolf, little wolf. Unable to be caged. Unable to be kept, but she will choose to remain by your sides. She belongs to all three of you. Cherish her, Atlas. My trust does not come easily, but you earned it once before. A long, long time ago. All four of you did."*

Power somewhere far away from here flares and rattles the spheres with the declaration, but I don't pay much attention to it as I continue to watch her.

CHAPTER TEN
ATTICUS

She's exquisite.

The princess of Hell is a beauty. And I'm sure that even though the few cultures of the Spheres have different definitions of beauty, Rhesamyre still qualifies as gorgeous and alluring in all of them.

She's quick to take notice of me as she exits Draven's castle, even quicker than her bodyguards, or whatever *the hell they're playing at by coming here with her. However, despite the intelligence shining in her unique, demonic gaze, she's still not immune to the influence that Siren's abilities have over most beings.*

The baku continue to growl quietly as I stride toward her, and my hands nearly twitch as I reach for her. Covering her eyes, her body language changes immediately, and I smirk to myself as I feel her inner beast bristle at the challenge I lay down between us.

"I do apologize for it," I begin with a voice that isn't quite my own, as Siren's vocal cords are quieter in nature than mine. Sultry and husky at all times so he may better bed males and females alike on a whim.

I rotate around her while keeping my hand gently laid over her eyes. The two males on either side of her stay stock still as they watch me, and while I know defiance brews in their eyes, their bodies betray them. I can't help but smirk a little at the sight, and as I bring my gaze back to Rhesamyre, her scent encourages me to breathe her in deeper. So I do. I trace my nose along the side of her neck, and it takes all my strength not to dart my tongue out to taste her in the middle of Draven's fucking courtyard.

"I am the embodiment of temptation, after all. And even princesses of Hell are often unable to resist my charms."

"That has to get old after a while."

"It does. For it can often get in the way of simpler conversations."

"Are you one for simpler conversations?"

"Sometimes."

Though with you, I think I would like to save the conversations for the morning after.

Because for you, *there* would be *a morning after. Many,* many *mornings after nights full of sinful work. Where I take my time learning your quirks and where your most sensitive spots of pleasure are.*

"Though I doubt your succubus and incubus feel the same, Lord of Temptation."

"Call me Siren, Princess."

"Siren."

"Better." No. *That is not what you will call me. That is not my name.*

"But not perfect?"

"Not yet."

"What do you want, Siren?"

Right now? You. *I want you. I want to . . .* know you, *Rhesamyre. In every possible way. I want to know what you taste like, what you sound like, and what your deepest, darkest desires are. What are your fantasies? What would you like to eat for breakfast the morning after? And is there any chance I can eat* you *for breakfast?*

Though from the subtle, smoked scent of my brother that stakes a claim on her own sweet spice, I would imagine that last question would be answered with a no.

Unless . . .

"A common question, yet the answer always eludes me," I finally reply, and with startling cognizance, I find it to be the stars' honest truth.

With great difficulty, I remove my hands and disappear. Her scent lingers in my nose, messing with my mind even hours after she's gone from the pillars.

. . . .

Keeping my eyes trained on Rhesamyre's wolf form, I absent-mindedly move one of my chess pieces to advance on one of my opponent's forces. Conquest and War curse under their breath, and I smirk to myself as I best the Horsemen *again*. Two boards sit between us on one of the stone tables settled in the garden, and I play against these two simultaneously while Rhesa snoozes in the sunshine as her girlfriends read to her.

Those books are practically porn, but I'm not complaining, and apparently, neither is the wolf.

"This'll be the third time he's gonna win, *dammit*," curses Pollux from the shade. "I've got money bet on you two, so you'd better fucking shape up."

Conquest growls quietly so as not to disturb Rhesa. "If you're so bloody confident, then why don't you get in here and take a crack at it? Because despite the absolute *dumbass* Atticus is, he's alarmingly skilled in the art of winning and thus pissing off his enemies."

I grin. "It's truly a gift."

Literally.

War rolls his eyes, moving one of his chess pieces while muttering, "Where's Rhesa when we need her? She'll knock him down a few pegs."

"And I think he'd let her," quips Sloth, peering at us over his book as he reads in the shade, lounging upon one of the couches.

"I'm not going to dignify that with a response," I reply, moving a new pawn and successfully drawing yet another aggravated sigh from War.

"So that means you would," notes Pollux, and I scowl at him.

The archangel grins and puts his hands up in mock surrender, then glances back over his shoulder as he notices Atlas returning to stand near Alastair, the latter busy playing card games with Greed and Gluttony.

I survey Atlas's form, noting the red ring he fiddles with upon his left hand as he stares out at Rhesa.

Choosing to ignore the appearance of that ring for now, I inquire, "How's the West? Still a wasteland?"

He chuckles quietly. "That's putting it mildly. The raiders are relentless."

"But that's not exactly anything new," quips Pollux.

Atlas shrugs. "The West has always had its fair share of problems, but I feel as though things have gotten worse since Samael died. The Hussars are made up of plenty of beings, but a few of their faster ranks contained demons and hell-horses. With our king gone, they don't have enough to replenish their ranks after raiders plow through them. So, needless to say, the outlying villages and people are being ripped to shreds, and the Hussars, *ironically enough*, can't keep up."

Conquest nods. "That will certainly prove to be troublesome as time goes on. Hell's always prided itself on being able to protect and aid our allies. If we can't stop a few raiders from laying waste to whatever may remain of the West, then who's to say a few more groups won't get ballsy and start inching toward Hell as a whole?"

"The demons here are sated for now," adds War. "But I wouldn't bet our lives on that lasting much longer."

"At least that much we can agree on," says Alastair. "But there's only one ruler who can fix that, and she's currently still a canine."

Nodding, I find myself glancing at Atlas again when I notice his jaw working as if he wants to say something else. It's a subtle shift in his scowl, but enough to have me narrowing my eyes at my brother.

"Spit it out, Atlas," I demand.

Atlas meets my eyes, glances at Rhesa, and then casually mentions, "I spoke with her last night."

"*Excuse me*?" snarls Alastair.

Rhesa's ears twitch toward us, but she doesn't sit up.

"In whatever mindscape we share, thanks to this damn imprint," my middle brother explains softly while keeping a close eye on the wolf. "She was a woman, and we were able to have a civilized conversation. However, it wasn't exactly *Rhesamyre*."

"What do you mean?" I demand.

Alastair curses quietly, inquiring, even though he seems to already know the answer, "You met the white-eyed bitch, didn't you?"

Atlas quirks a brow at that, but nods all the same. "That isn't exactly the terminology I would use . . . but *yes*. We spoke."

"*Well . . .*" I drawl. "In the midst of your reunion, did you happen to mention the shit we're dealing with out here while she's busy playing cowardly *dog*?"

Atlas scowls. "Rhesa is not to blame. Whatever the hell inhabits her body . . . it's more powerful than Rhesa and is claiming to be the one keeping Rhesa locked away in her wolf form at the moment. However, it did reveal that Rhesa is fighting it. She's trying to break free of it, but I fear she isn't strong enough."

Greed nods along, and I look at the assassin. "We have found that to be the case in the past, too. It always released Rhesa in a timely manner, but that's just it. *It* would release *her*. I don't believe Rhesa truly knows she shares her body with another ancient being of suspiciously powerful origins, and we've been no closer to figuring out what *it* is or what it wants, either."

"It wants Rhesa safe," says Atlas matter-of-factly.

"That was my impression, as well," agrees Alastair, nodding.

"It always speaks in Old Latin," adds Gluttony. "And it always mutters about power and prayers and keeping Rhesamyre safe. About her being worthy, and us needing to constantly prove ourselves if we wish to be anywhere near her."

"Never mind any of that," drawls Alastair. "What are we to do if this time it doesn't . . ."

He needn't finish that sentence, as it's obvious what he's thinking, and it puts everyone on edge. Even me, though I haven't met the *white-eyed bitch* yet. However, the implications of what it is capable of are obvious enough to me, and the fact that it may or may not have a monopoly over Rhesa's mind and body irks me more than I care to admit.

Atlas shakes his head. "It claimed that Rhesa has to fight her way out." He looks between Alastair and me now. "And that we must prove ourselves worthy of claiming her as ours."

I scoff at that, but Alastair remains still and silent.

"Well, then . . . maybe we've been going about it all wrong," I voice, and I continue no matter how wrong I may be. "From what I understand of Rhesamyre, she doesn't like to be *coddled*. She's passionate in all her emotions, and that includes love, anger, you name it . . . but she doesn't get *sad*. She gets angry, and then she gets even. It was grief that drove her into this state, yes. But it wasn't grief alone. It was uncaged, unhinged, bloody, and unfiltered *rage* . . . so maybe that's how we turn her back."

Atlas looks as if he wants to disagree, but as he ponders my words, he inquires, "So . . . you want to . . ."

"I want to make her bloody *fucking* angry," I clarify.

"*That* . . ." drawls Wrath, but then he barks a humorless laugh. "That might just work."

"It's alarming and unsettling when you remind us of how intelligent you can actually be at times, Atticus," quips Pollux. "I, for one, prefer the dumbass."

I scowl at the archangel. "From one imbecile to another, I can concur with confidence that I prefer it when you're a moron, too."

"*Oh*, just you wait," quips Alastair, a rare grin upon his features in place of a scowl. "When Rhesa's back, she'll make all of us look like fools."

I vaguely register Sloth nodding his head in agreement out of the corner of my eye, but I would imagine all of the Hellion Court is in agreement.

I believe I agree, anyway. And although between the three of us, Atlas, and especially Alastair, have had far more time with Rhesa than I have, I've already seen a kernel of that infamous, wicked, and competitive intelligence. It flickered in her eyes the day I met her as *Siren* and then again the second time when she sensed me from across Wicker's courtyard.

The day she called me by my real name in that dead language my brothers and I once called our native tongue.

"Though, while I concur," drawls Conquest, pulling me out of my thoughts, "how would you pursue *pissing her off*? Because if we're honest with ourselves, she's had plenty of chances to be angry and shift back, yet she hasn't."

I sigh. "Right . . . perhaps threatening *her* isn't the best way to draw her out."

"So, *what*?" scoffs Atlas. "You want to threaten her friends or something? Brother, with all due respect—"

"Which is very little at the moment," mutters Pollux.

Atlas ignores him, and for Rhesa's sake, so do I as my brother continues, "If we threaten her friends and family in any way, when she returns, it's highly likely she won't forgive you for putting them in harm's way."

"I don't think I really give a *shit* if she likes me or not," I claim. "So long as she's a *woman* when she hates me, she can hate me forever, for all I care."

Pollux cocks his head at me, sparing me a sly grin. "Liar."

Maybe I am, I realize. However, my declaration still stands. If risking my potential relationship with Rhesamyre is the way to ensure she returns, then so be it.

But *damn*, that would fucking suck.

"While I share similar sentiments, and am willing to do just about anything for Rhesa," begins Alastair, "I have to agree with Atlas on this one. Yes, threatening her friends may do the trick, but Rhesa's not quick to forgive such actions. She's good at holding quiet grudges and striking back when you least expect it."

"It sounds as though you're speaking from experience," I quip.

Alastair sighs. "One of my many mistakes in life is assuming I know someone when in actuality, *I don't*. And even though Rhesa and I had grown closer, she still kept plenty of secrets from me, and I doubt that will end any time soon. But if we do it this way, then Rhesa's walls will remain up, and I—*we* will never be able to get close to her again. It will take a long time to rebuild that trust, and I fret that time isn't exactly a friend of ours at the moment."

"Well, as it stands, *none of us* have a steady relationship with her. And you're right, time isn't an ally. For the longer she remains a wolf, the more likely we are to lose her as a whole, *dammit!*"

"When she pursued answers concerning her dreams about you, Alastair, where did she go?" inquires Pollux, though I have a sneaky suspicion the shifty archangel already knows. He's just trying to be dramatic and prove a point, that asshole.

Typical.

"She went to speak with Draven," I answer for my brother. "That's when I saw her the first time."

Pollux nods. "And then she later convened with Wicker, yes?"

"When we were searching for information about Feronia," supplies Conquest. "Wrath and Pride were with her when the Lord of Fear had her walk off a *fucking balcony.*"

"Right. I bet that was stressful. Immortal or not, that would've hurt."

"Is there a plan forming or not, Pollux?" inquires Alastair, getting more peeved by the minute. "Because I believe I know what you're thinking, but I'm not sure if I like it or not."

Pollux shrugs. "From what it sounds like, it'll be the lesser of two evils. So take your pick . . . either you fools threaten her friends, or we enlist the help of Draven and Wicker to entice Rhesa to get angry and vengeful in her dreams. Maybe if she fights hard enough to survive in her nightmares, then her resolve and power will spur a shift here on the outside."

Conquest chuckles darkly. "I've certainly heard worse plans."

"*You've* come up with *worse* plans," War deadpans. Then, he looks to Pollux and us deities as he nods. "I'm game. For better or worse, I think it's worth a shot."

I glance around to survey the other few members of the Hellion Court, and no one objects.

"Okay," drawls Alastair. "Then I suppose we should go pay the lords a visit."

. . . .

"We want Rhesa back, too . . . but *this* . . . " drawls Feronia, shaking her head as she stands near the lieutenants and the other females, our wolf seated between them. "This feels *wrong*."

"We won't disagree with you there," agrees Atlas softly. "But what other choice do we have?"

"If you've got a better idea," I quip, "we're all fucking ears."

The little wendigo looks taken aback by my comment, and I vaguely feel Alastair elbow me in the ribs in warning. I ignore him, then lower my gaze to the obsidian wolf that is beginning to look too *tame* for my liking.

Feronia finally rolls her eyes as she crouches next to Rhesa, and the wolf licks the wendigo's cheek gently.

She giggles softly. "We'll see you again soon, Rhesa. Hopefully as a woman again."

"How do you plan on luring her to go with you?" inquires Damian. "Taking the girls isn't an option."

I chuckle at the reaper. "We won't be taking your females from you, boy. Just the wolf . . . by way of bribery—*hopefully*."

I look to my middle brother, and he shrugs and steels himself as he steps forward to kneel before Rhesa. The wolf pricks her ears and sizes him up halfheartedly, and Atlas extends his hand toward her as he coos her name and whispers a few encouraging commands to her. Then, after a moment, Rhesa steps forward and allows him to pet her. Something curls in my stomach at the sight, and I grit my teeth.

I don't like this.

"I need you to trust me again, little wolf," coos Atlas. "We're just gonna go on a little errand, and then we'll come back home, okay?"

Rhesa blinks at him but doesn't pull away. Atlas nods once, then stands back up and looks to us. I turn just as Alastair opens a conveyance, and moments later, we're striding through the tunnel and into the surrounding territory of the Four Pillars. Rhesa follows along behind Atlas quietly, and I often find myself glancing back at her to ensure she's still there. She stops every once in a while to sniff along the ground and snap at the bugs, but other than that, she trails behind us without much complaint.

"How long did you hide here?" inquires Alastair, his tone oddly more curious than accusing.

I scowl at his choice of words, then admit, "A few decades."

"And Siren never bothered to intervene and reclaim his name and *skin*?" asks Atlas.

"Evidently not."

"Did you murder him?" inquires Alastair again.

"No."

"Harm him in any way?" *Atlas.*

"No."

"Bargain?" *Alastair.*

"No."

"*Ah.* So you bribed him." *Atlas.*

"*N*—well, sort of . . . technically, yes." I halt and spin around to find them smirking at me, and the wolf cocks her head at me, too. "Wipe those fucking grins off your faces. You know I don't appreciate being tag-teamed and interrogated."

Alastair puts his hands up in mock surrender, but his eyes shine with satisfaction and mirth despite his resting scowl. "Just trying to figure out where you've been all this time, little brother."

I scoff, turning around again. "Why? You miss me that much?"

I hear Alastair's stride falter before he stops altogether behind me, and I turn to face him once more.

"What if I said yes?"

I blink at him, raising my brow. "What?"

"What if I said I did miss your company? What would you say to that?"

"I'd say you're a liar . . . and that your sense of humor has somehow gotten worse, since it was already shit to begin with."

He chuckles lowly, beginning to walk again. "Those letters Rhesa sent you two . . . what did she say?"

"Smooth segue," I quip. "And are you sure that's really any of your business?"

"Rhesa asked for my help, then called me a coward when I said no," admits Atlas, and I glare at him. He shrugs. "She said she was already in communication with you and that Alastair was with her, too."

Alastair dips his chin at Atlas. "What made you change your mind and decide to step in?"

"Finding her half dead in the desert . . . as a *wolf*."

Alastair chuckles. "Yeah, I'd imagine that's as good a motivation as any." He looks at me again.

Rolling my eyes, I reveal through clenched teeth, "She *provoked* me."

Atlas snorts. "I've found it's not hard to do."

I scowl. "Yeah, *well*. My many years of *hiding* have since made me a bit more tolerable to half-assed jabs and empty threats. A few years after the Great Betrayal when everyone exhaled and deemed it safe to start living again, you could say I was content to remain where I was. But even so, give or take a few centuries later, Rhesa's letters made me curious again."

"*Curious?*" inquires Alastair.

"Of the outside. Of the spheres. Of her . . . and whatever may have become of you two."

"I'm flattered," mocks Atlas.

"Don't be," I deadpan. "A large part of me was perfectly okay with learning you two had somehow kicked the bucket."

"*Alas*, we remain immortal," drawls Alastair. "And thus harder to kill than most."

"Much to my dismay, *yes*. How did *you* even acquire a place by her side as swiftly as you did, anyway?"

"Found her when I was playing hunter and searching for the Child on the First's behalf. At the time, I didn't know the extent of everyone's schemes, but I had a suspicion all the same. Rhesa and I bargained, and I, knowing *exactly* who she was, branded her so I could keep her close."

I grin. "Doubt you expected you'd ever want to be *this* close."

He meets my eyes, the silver there smoldering menacingly. "I wanted to kill her when I found her. Almost did, too. A few times afterward, I thought about it, as well."

"Then what stopped you?" inquires Atlas.

Alastair shrugs, a rare look of indecisiveness brewing in his silver eyes for a moment as he ponders the question. "Similarly to you, I suppose I could blame it on curiosity . . . but if I'm honest, I don't know. I just . . . didn't. *Couldn't.* I could hardly feel the forbidden power to begin with, and as I later learned, that's because she didn't have it at the time. But even so, she had enough for me to sense it . . . and then she woke up, and we conversed, and I quickly learned I wanted to learn everything. I wanted to know everything. *Know her.*"

"How romantic," I tease.

And yet I agree completely.

We're silent for another heartbeat as we walk on, until Alastair reveals quietly, "I know what became of the Reverie."

I whirl around to face him, sneering, "I never want to lay eyes on that fucking book ever again. Wherever it is, it can rot for all I care."

Alastair cocks his head, raising his brows as he drawls, "That was an impressively passionate declaration of your abhorrence on the matter. Is there perhaps something in there that Atlas or I have yet to read that you don't want us to?"

I restrain my growl, my eyes flickering over to Rhesa for a heartbeat before settling back on Alastair. She is busy sniffing some flowers and snapping at the butterflies, and from the side, Atlas watches us both with a steady gaze. I snarl very softly. "Let it lie, brother. The book means nothing to me, and it shouldn't mean anything to either of you . . . not anymore."

I don't wait for a reply as I turn on my heel to keep walking, and we continue on in silence once more.

Rhesa's low growling catches our attention then, and I dart my eyes toward her to find her hackles raised as she lowers herself to the ground. Looking forward, I can't help but mutter a quiet *fuck.*

Within the woodwork, a lone baku stands stock-still as he sizes up the dire wolf ahead of him. His eyes are unblinking and his body unmoving, and Rhesa sinks lower to the soil to prowl forward.

The baku bolts.

And Rhesa goes after him.

My brothers and I curse as we chase after her like *fucking imbeciles*, and Rhesa snarls and *barks* as she closes in on the fearful baku. Eventually, we near the proper gates and gardens of the Four Pillars, and while the baku is able to run straight into the courtyard of Draven's castle, Rhesa is immediately expelled by the wards and thus propelled backward.

She snarls and shakes her head as she rights herself on her paws again, and then she weaves back and forth before the gates as she sizes up the baku that taunts her from the other side.

"*Well*," drawls Draven from the other side of the gates. "That was entertaining."

My brothers and I come to stand beside Rhesa, and Atlas does his best to console the wolf as she whines and continues to growl.

Draven cocks his head at her, then glances between us as he says, "Tell me that isn't who I think it is."

I shrug. "We're not above lying if that'll make you feel better."

Draven scowls. "What are you doing here? And all *three of you* at that?" He chuckles darkly, lowly. "Stars only know what you're up to, as few good things tend to come about when all three of you converse nowadays."

"We find ourselves in need of your expertise," explains Alastair, ignoring the lord's attitude. "You *and* Wicker's."

Draven raises his brows, then glances down at Rhesa again. "If it's got anything to do with that demon-turned-wolf there, then I can only *dream* of what you've got planned."

"*Hilarious*," I snarl. "Will you help us or not?"

"Depends on what you three can do for me. Having all three deities indebted to me certainly has its perks."

"I won't remove your head from your body," threatens Atlas casually, quietly. "How's that for a bargain?"

I raise my brows to myself at his tone. Seems as though the brother bred for bloodshed is still somewhere in there, after all. And he's about ready to come out and *play*. I dare claim his time with our *little wolf* has been quite productive in reminding him of his better, more brutal nature, and I'll be curious to see just how he attempts to fight it. Assuming he even *can* now that Rhesamyre is involved.

Draven clicks his tongue in disapproval as he smirks a little. "See, now that's *not exactly* the positive motivation I'm looking for if I am to allow you access into my home."

"You let Rhesa in once already," claims Alastair. Ironically enough, he's the only one of us keeping things civilized. "What did you demand from her then?"

"I gave her a discount. But it was a once-in-a-lifetime invitation, and it doesn't extend to her bodyguards, boyfriends, or whatever else the *fuck* you three are playing at now."

"You just—" states Atlas, baffled. "You just *let her in*?"

Draven shrugs. "Her dreams were quite tasty and rather complex." He cocks his head at Alastair, grinning. "Or perhaps I should call them *your* dreams, Vengeance. They were your memories, after all."

Alastair growls. "If you won't do it for us, then do it for Rhesamyre. Tap into whatever curiosity you had the first time and recycle those emotions. I assure you, they'll be just as tasty this time, if not even more so. Especially when you learn of what we wish to do."

Draven's gaze darts to Rhesamyre again, and her ears prick forward at the attention he gives her.

"What's your plan?" he inquires, eyes still on the wolf.

"We believe getting Rhesa *angry*, for lack of a better term, will serve as enough motivation for another shift," explains Alastair. "Grief and rage drove her to shift in the first place, so perhaps another high-strung emotion will spur her power into doing it again. But we need to get inside her head to do it, which is where you and Wicker come in. For it can't just be a dream . . . it has to be something darker."

"You're hoping that if she fights the nightmare hard enough, her power will step in to turn her back into a woman."

"Precisely."

"That's quite ballsy."

"We're aware," mutters Atlas.

"And what if she doesn't fight as hard as she needs to?" His gaze flickers to study each of us again. "Perhaps you're overestimating your female's willpower. As well as her desire to return to you three and Hell in the first place. One without her beloved father and devil, though I doubt you need the reminder."

"You've spoken to her once already, Draven," I drawl. "So you tell us. Do *you* think she'll fight back?"

Draven chuckles, then commands his wards to lower so we may step forward into his courtyard.

"I'm willing to gamble a fair bit on her fighting back, yes. But it seems as though I have less to lose than you three at the moment. So my initial inquiry still stands. Are you three ready to own the repercussions of your actions? Looking back on history, I can't say with confidence that I trust that you are."

"Quit worrying over things that don't concern you, and get your neighbor over here," I demand.

Draven scowls. "He was your neighbor not that long ago, too."

I shrug. "I find myself in different company these days."

"So I've noticed."

Following Draven into his castle, he leads us into one of his larger dens where oversized hourglasses and grandfather clocks tick away. He commands a servant to send word to Wicker, and then he gathers whatever he needs from his cabinets and worktables, glancing at Rhesa often as she sniffs about. Most likely on the prowl for another one of his intrusive pet bakus.

My brothers and I separate ourselves to survey his many gadgets and artwork pertaining to star symbols and time, as well as observe the model system and maps of our Eight Living Spheres that revolve around the single sun that claims this space as its home within the vast darkness of the Starfall Sea. Hell is the closest to the sun and one of the larger spheres, followed by the West, the Midlands, the Forsaken Isles, the Four Pillars, the Hollow, the Celestial Cities, and then finally, the Forbidden Cities. And while most spheres only have a single moon, the Forsaken Isles have two, while the Celestial Cities have three.

The Umbra Mundi is said to coexist between the living spheres. A starry or dark place the living cannot see nor touch unless magic and spells are involved, which are often forbidden in nature.

"The Lord of Fear, my lord and majesties," calls the servant lad, thus drawing our attention to him and the arrival of Wicker.

The infamous Boogeyman waltzes in like he's overly familiar with the place and grins at Draven before glancing over at us and Rhesa. He chuckles, shaking his head as he sizes us up alongside the wolf. We do the same to him, and Rhesa bares her teeth.

"I almost didn't believe you, dream eyes," calls Wicker, striding toward Draven to hand him a leather pouch of some sort. "Yet here the three of them stand. With a wolf, no less. It sounds like the beginning of a shitty joke."

"*If only*," mutters Draven.

Alastair growls quietly, thus catching Rhesa's attention again. "If you two are quite finished, we'd like to know how you plan to accomplish the task at hand."

Wicker grins, but it is Draven who seems more willing to comply as he explains, "By mixing in a few of Wicker's properties, we'll be able to put her under the appropriate spell that will entice the emotions you three desire in order to get a rise out of her."

"What sort of properties?" inquires Atlas, kneeling beside Rhesa to rub her ears.

"Stardust, ground dream roots from my garden, and another powdered concoction containing Wicker's blood."

Draven grounds the rest of the ingredients into a bowl, then pours it out onto a thin sheet of paper.

"And how do you plan on getting that into her system?" I inquire.

"She just needs to inhale it, and that'll be enough," says Draven, walking toward Atlas and Rhesa. "I figure that's easier than subduing her and forcing it down her throat."

Atlas, ever so carefully, wraps his arms around Rhesa to keep her in place as Draven approaches. She struggles in Atlas's arms, beginning to snarl quietly as she bares her teeth, and Atlas's tatted muscles remain bulged and steeled around the wolf despite her best efforts to break free. Then he holds his breath when Draven bends down and blows the dusty concoction right onto her face.

Rhesa snarls and attempts to bite him, but then she sneezes and shakes her head violently, allowing a few whines to escape her throat. Atlas's arms loosen around her form, and although she attempts to take a step forward after Draven, her legs buckle beneath her. Atlas surges to catch her again, and she snarls pathetically at him.

"I know, my little wolf," he coos, picking her up now. He motions toward the sofa with his eyes, and Draven nods as he returns to Wicker's side.

Rhesa's body grows heavy in my brother's arms, and he takes a seat with her nestled against his lap as her growls begin to quiet down. She struggles to keep her eyes open, but finally, after a few moments, she stills completely.

"And now we wait," says Draven, moving to take a seat on the other sofa.

"For how long?" inquires Alastair, moving to sit beside her and run his hand through her silky fur, and I take a seat on the chair near Atlas.

Wicker shrugs now, beginning to order a drink from the nearest servant. "However long she needs."

"She took about an hour to sift through your memories," says Draven to Alastair, but then the lord shrugs. "Facing her fears in such a way, though . . . I've only studied the spellwork. Never have I tested the theory. Nonetheless, I would expect it'll take a while."

I curse angel names under my breath and pray to whoever or whatever will listen that it doesn't take long.

Atticus,

I would claim that the rules are simple:
Don't fall in love with me, but I'm afraid it's inevitable.
And as far as our bargain is concerned, I believe it will be simple in nature, too.
Although arrogant of me to assume, I would claim with near certainty that your existence has become boring at best, and thus redundant in nature.
Let's face the facts, shall we? You're withering away in that pillar, wearing a suit of tainted skin that does not belong to you. If you're honest with yourself, you crave something different. Unlike your middle brother, you're itching to get back into the fight again. And I am more than happy to provide you with the means to do so.
Swear yourself to me, or don't. I don't care. Just promise me one thing first.
Fight with me. You need not fight for me, as I have enough males doing that already. However, I still encourage you to fight alongside Hell and its allies.
Let's remind the spheres of why they call you the Deity of Chaos and Control, and why they will one day call me the Queen of Hell.

Best regards, Rhesamyre.

CHAPTER ELEVEN
RHESAMYRE

Gentle fingers trace the side of my face, tucking a strand of hair behind my ear before returning to rub my cheekbone gently. I open my eyes slowly, momentarily blinded by the sunlight that shines through the nearest window and casts rays over the luxurious, black bedsheets I lie on. After a heartbeat, I am finally able to focus and trace the dark tattoos upon the hand that caresses me gently, following them up his arm to the broad, tattooed form of a handsome male.

Alastair smiles at me gently, then leans down and presses his lips to my temple.

"Good morning, love," he husks, his silver eyes gleaming in the morning light as he showcases the tanned, inked skin on his torso since he's shirtless.

My hands twitch to reach out and trace the lines of his chiseled muscles, which appear to be very *lickable*, but I refrain. Then I slowly sit up, but find I am unable to get very far since another tatted arm wraps around my middle. I glance behind me to find . . . *Atticus* in bed with me. And from our positions, it seems as though he has been holding me while we slept.

Alastair chuckles, drawing my eyes back to his. "Wake him, will you? Atlas is downstairs already, preparing breakfast. Come down when you're ready. There's no rush."

He presses another gentle kiss to my forehead, and all I can do is mutter a quiet *okay* in response. Nodding, Alastair takes his leave, shutting the door quietly behind him as he goes. I glance around the bedchamber to find it embellished with silver, obsidian, and even hints of emeralds and rubies. Other doors are present that surely lead to the bathing chamber and closets, and a small loveseat is even nestled in the corner near the massive window that overlooks a garden and courtyard graced with hellion flora and architecture.

The arm slung around my middle tightens, and I find myself flipped onto my back as Atticus moves to completely lie on top of me. He sighs as he nestles his head against my chest, my *silver* nightgown rising upward as he bunches the soft material in his tatted hands. I take this moment to study his features and tattoos, which differ from Alastair's but are still similar as far as sigils and scriptures in Old Latin, skulls, antlers, and wicked mandalas are concerned. However, Atticus's ink seems to favor more chains and thorns rather than that of beasts and monsters. In addition, his dark hair is partially shaved, thus revealing the *entropy* scripture that is branded over his right ear.

"Admiring my beauty, *sweet sin*?"

I remain still as he opens his emerald eyes to watch me, and he quirks a brow at me.

"Or perhaps you're looking for another weakness to identify and stash in your arsenal to use later when it's more convenient to annoy me."

I cock my head at him, then quietly reply, "The latter."

The corner of his mouth tilts upward into a ridiculously attractive smirk, and he damn well knows it, too.

He leans forward to press his lips against my own, and I let him.

It feels like second nature to kiss him.

"Good morning, Rhesa," he says, smiling gently.

"Hello . . . Atticus."

"I believe we have breakfast waiting for us downstairs, yes? We'd do well not to keep Atlas waiting. We both know how irritable he can get when he believes his *hard work* is going to waste."

Not exactly understanding where the words come from, I reply, "He does claim to slave away for us to ensure we don't starve. Cause stars know *we would* if *you* were the one behind the stove."

Atticus scowls at me. "I burned your crepes *once*, Rhesa. You can't hold that against me forever, sweet sin."

"I can, and I will."

He chuckles, then pecks my lips again. "Very well, then I'll just spend the rest of my life making it up to you. I can't think of a better way to waste my time. Now, c'mon."

Atticus props himself up and pats my bare thigh, then removes himself completely from the bed. However, I refrain from following him at first as I stare down at my right thigh. Then, I glance at my inner right forearm, and then inside my nightgown to survey my *bare* skin.

Removing myself from the bed, I pad across the lush carpet to the floor-length mirror that hangs upon the wall by the entrance to the walk-in closet. Dropping my nightgown so it pools around my feet, I turn around to survey my back, which as I come to find, is void of any scars or *brandings*.

I cock my head at the sight, then turn to face myself and survey the rest of my body that is free of ink. My horns still remain, and while my hair is a little tangled from bed, it still remains as long and healthy as ever. My eyes and ears are my own, as are my painted nails. *And yet . . .*

"Rhesa?" calls Atticus, poking his head out from the bathing chamber to watch me. "You okay?"

I nod. "Yeah, I'm . . . I'm fine."

He furrows his brows at me but doesn't push it.

Shaking my head at my odd thoughts, I pull my nightgown back on to follow him into the bathing chamber. Trusting my body to know the routine even if my mind doesn't quite agree, Atticus and I freshen up and get ready for the day together. He pulls on casual slacks and a dark shirt that usually acts as the first layer of hellion leathers, while I slip on a black dress that is looser in nature, but allows for plenty of skin to show via slits and cutouts. The walk-in closet is littered with various gowns, jewels, shoes, and leathers that are all my size, and only a few sections contain male clothing.

Allowing Atticus to guide me, we stride hand in hand out of the bedchamber and into a grand hall fitted with hellion furnishings and more art. Plenty of murals and portraits hang upon the walls, and I recognize them all to be of my family and me, as well as a few of the deities and me, too. Oftentimes, I am sitting between the three of them in some luxurious gown as they stand at attention nearby. My horns are on full display while their hands are placed strategically over mine or on my shoulders while their wings are visible, too.

Atticus leads me down a grand staircase into a smaller dining room, and as we enter, so do Alastair and . . . *Atlas*, carrying a few trays of breakfast platters that will finish off the small feast already settled upon the table.

Atticus pulls out a chair for me, then takes a seat next to me while Atlas and Alastair occupy the seats across from us. Platters of breakfast meats, pastries, fruits, and stacked toast covered in powdered sugar sit before me, but I find it hard to focus on the food at first as I'm too busy glancing around at the spacious room. More windows line the wall straight ahead of me, giving me the perfect view of valleys and black mountains in the distance, as well as what appears to be the heart of Hell.

"I hope he didn't keep you up all night, Rhesa," says Atlas, and I slide my gaze over to meet his.

Pink eyes and yet another handsome face, more tattoos, and a delicate inscription that translates to *strength* near the bottom corner of his right eye.

"If anything," drawls Atticus, beginning to fill my plate for me, "our activities should've made her work up quite the appetite."

The Deity of Chaos and Control winks at me, and I just narrow my eyes at his cocky smirk.

"Are you sure?" I inquire before I can stop myself.

Atlas and Alastair chuckle while Atticus frowns, and I feel a sudden wave of satisfaction come over me at the sight.

"If you found my performance lacking and thus *unsatisfactory* in any way," quips Atticus, "I'd be more than happy to devote myself to new endeavors."

I take a bite of the stacked toast and fruit as I shrug. "Perhaps I'd be willing to indulge you. Though I haven't quite decided if you're deserving of a second chance yet."

Atticus doesn't smile, but his emerald eyes smolder with the promise of what I'm offering. And then slowly, he nods.

"I'll win you over again, you can count on that." He leans toward me, nipping my ear as he husks, "You'll be screaming my name again by the end of the day, I promise."

"Not unless I scream your brothers' names instead."

He leans away from me, the heat in his emerald gaze intensifying as he sizes me up, basking in the challenge I lay down between us. Then, he gives me a wicked grin.

"Challenge accepted, sweet sin."

The corner of my lip quirks up into a sly smirk, but I hide it by taking another bite of food.

"The first wave of guests will be arriving later this morning," informs Alastair, allowing a mortal servant to pour him more tea. The delicate teacup looks odd in his larger, tatted hand, and I almost smirk again at the ridiculous, tame sight. "Your family will be amongst them," he continues, and I meet his cool, silver gaze. "Then the rest of the lords and ladies of the court will be along in the afternoon before the evening officially begins."

Atlas reaches across the table to grab my left hand, then he presses a kiss to my knuckles, and I finally take notice of the glittering, black ring that's abruptly nestled itself upon my ring finger. It is elegant in nature with intricate braiding featuring three types of gems embedded into the obsidian and steel:

Diamonds. Rubies. And emeralds.

The main oval is obsidian in nature, and appears like that of a shining black mirror as I peer down at myself, not looking nearly as perplexed as I feel, which I am honestly grateful for. Years of training once again aid me in remaining stoic with a practiced, perfected poker face that apparently not even these deities can decipher.

"I do hope you're excited to host your first gala of the season," continues Atlas, rubbing my knuckles while a gentle smile graces his lips. "We had quite the extensive and *productive* honeymoon, but I suppose it's only right to return to society now," he teases.

"*Oh*, the *horror*," chuckles Alastair, giving me a rare grin. "We would much rather keep you cooped up in here all to ourselves, but *someone* insisted otherwise."

"I don't wish to grow tired of my—" I stop short.

Atticus chuckles, kissing my temple. "You can say husbands, sweet sin. No one's gonna jump you."

I nod my head, forcing myself to crack a grin for their sake.

I feel like screaming.

Clearing my throat, I segue. "So, my family will be arriving first?"

Atlas nods, finally releasing my hand. "Yep. Your uncles, lieutenants, and your father."

Once again, if it wasn't for my years of intensive training to conceal my emotions and expressions, I probably would've spit out my tea. Suddenly craving something stronger, I force out lightly, "My father?"

"Naturally," quips Atticus. "The last time you saw him was when he walked you down the aisle, then later, when you two danced before we stole you away. None of them have seen you in the few months we've been here and away, traveling."

"Speaking of which," drawls Alastair, his attention divided between his brothers. "Pollux and his brothers will be in attendance, after all."

"Good. They threw quite a bachelor party for us with the help of the assassins. I plan to pour them all a few glasses of our finer wines in thanks."

"Better let Atlas do the pouring, little brother. We all know you tend to have a heavy hand."

Atticus appears as if he wants to protest, thinks better of it, and then nods in agreement with a small grin. "Touché."

"Rhesa, you okay?" inquires Atlas.

I raise my eyes from my plate of half-eaten food and steel myself as I survey the deities' concerned gazes.

"I'm fine," I claim.

Alastair raises his brow, no doubt scenting the lie that rolls off my tongue with ease. "Is your power giving you trouble again?"

"No, no, I . . .," I sigh, getting frustrated with myself, though I don't quite know why. "Just . . . *tired*. If you'll excuse me, gents, I'm going for a stroll to clear my head."

They look amongst each other, then nod and shrug, appearing as though they're at a loss for words. I don't spare them another glance as I take my leave, allowing my instincts to guide me through this luxurious castle of hellion furnishings. Plenty of mortal servants run amuck, making final preparations for whatever gala is being held here tonight. They're quick to step aside out of my way, bowing slightly or curtsying with gentle smiles as they mutter quiet greetings.

I dip my head back in acknowledgment a few times and eventually find myself following one of the giggling maid clusters into a grand ballroom decorated in the silvers, blacks, greens, and reds that tastefully paint this household.

The regal, esteemed colors of the deities and myself . . . *husbands and wife.*

"Is everything to your liking, Princess?" inquires one of the older ladies as she saunters up to me politely.

I survey the space that is decorated with plenty of flower arrangements, dark garlands, gems, and delicate chains that drip from curtains, stairwells, and obsidian chandeliers.

Nodding, I reply softly, "It's lovely. You've done beautiful work."

The head maid smiles and nods enthusiastically. "You have a keen eye for beauty, Princess. It has been an honor to perfect your vision. *Oh!* And the rest of the guestrooms have been made up as well, per your request."

I nod again, wishing I knew this one's name. "Thank you."

Not wanting to linger here any longer, I excuse myself once more and take my leave, eventually finding myself outside in the gardens. The sunshine is pleasantly warm against my skin, and I tip my head back to feel it warm my cheeks as I inhale deeply to take in the scents around me. Dark roses bloom alongside other floral breeds, while ivy vines curl atop structures to create grand archways that lead into different areas of the vast grounds. Statues of beasts and a few winged beings dot the pathways, and I recognize many of them to be that of the deities and their late Sleipnir. There is even another grand statue of Mamba, as well as one of Orpheus, too.

Following the ivy-clad archway toward the ponds, I saunter up to the water to survey the dark lily pads and koi fish. However, as I near the water and gaze down at my reflection, I can't help the sudden response to look away just as swiftly.

What. The. Hell.

Steeling myself, I glance down at the water again to properly meet the eyes of the black, white-eyed wolf that stares back up at me. When I cock my head, so does the wolf. And when I snarl, so does the beast.

I reach down to smack the water with a growl, and when the ripples return to normal, my proper reflection is there. Womanly features, demon eyes, pointed ears, horns, and all.

My heartbeat is steady in my chest, and my gaze is steeled in the familiar, practiced fashion, but my mind races all the same.

Forcing myself to inhale and exhale slowly, I turn away from the water once more, and my eyes again snag on the nearby life-sized statue of Orpheus.

One thing is for certain: a ride has always succeeded in clearing my head. So, with little trouble, I go in search of the stables and my hell-horse.

Sirius is here, too. As well as a few other steeds that are demonic or angelic in nature, but I pay them no mind as I grab a few bribes for Orpheus, then head out to the vast pasture that lies next to the grand stables upon this estate.

Placing my fingers in my mouth, I whistle loudly, and seconds later, my hell-horse is galloping over the hill toward me, on a mission for snacks. I grin as he nickers and nears me, nosing my hands for his favorite volcanic coals. I oblige his cravings, then swing onto his back without bothering with tack or proper riding attire.

I stroke his mane and neck, feeling my nerves settle as his back reminds me of home.

"Good boy, Orpheus," I whisper. "Can you help me make sense of this, sweet boy?"

Orpheus slips into a steady trot and canter when I ask, and soon, we're heading straight for the perimeter fence. He slips over the rails and stone walls with ease and then settles into a gallop over the hillsides as we ride through the neighboring farmland that surrounds this estate.

He carries me wherever I choose for however long I desire as we explore the nearby forest and trails. Jumping hedges and logs, stepping across the few streams, and listening to the hollion critters scurry about as they flee from Orpheus's fiery hooves.

When he rests in another meadow littered with dark wildflowers, which he happily munches on, I mind my horns as I lean against his back to gaze up at the clouds above, listening to the chirps of insects and birds and scenting whatever the wind carries when it caresses my face and curls my hair teasingly. Allowing my hands to drop by my sides, I rub his hips and hindquarters gently, forever loving the warm feel of his dark fur beneath my palms.

"Something is amiss here, Orpheus," I mutter. "I can't quite explain it, handsome boy. But it is . . . and we both know better than to doubt our instincts."

I sit up again to stroke his mane and neck, and he raises his head to glance back at me.

"I'm going to get us home," I vow. Though I say the words with conviction, deep down, I am forced to admit to myself that I have no idea where to begin.

Feeling my power surge gently as the hairs upon my arms stand on end, I look back toward the estate as I feel its wards shudder in recognition of arriving guests. Sighing and steeling myself once more, I nudge Orpheus forward into another pleasant gallop back toward the manor. Soon enough, we're jumping over a perimeter hedge right onto the driveway where several carriages draw up.

The deities are there upon the stairsteps to greet our guests alongside a few servants, and plenty of them get to work unloading the carriages and tending to the horses.

"Ah! There she is!" calls Pride, grinning at me from where he stands amongst the Hellion Court. My family.

I allow a small smile to slip through my scowl as I dismount Orpheus, handing him over to another servant as I stride up to the assassins, generals, and lieutenants.

"You always did know how to make an appearance, lovely niece," teases Envy.

"I've learned from the best," I quip.

"Indeed you have."

I stop short at the sound of his velvety voice, and I almost have to force myself to step forward again and embrace my father as he approaches me, appearing as regal and handsome as ever.

He chuckles as he hugs me, pulling away to cup my cheeks as he smiles at me. "What's wrong? You look as though you've just seen a ghost."

I shake my head, forcing another smile for his benefit as I focus on the feeling of his warm hands upon my face.

"I'm just glad to see you again," I admit, then glance around at the rest of my family. "All of you."

Uncle War smiles, slinging his arm over my shoulders as he claims, "As are we, Rhesa. We trust the deities have been taking good care of you?"

I nod. "Yes. They've been quite accommodating."

Atticus snorts from where he stands nearby, and I glance at him. "I suppose that's one word for it," he teases.

"And it's the *only word* we'll be using when in the presence of her *family*, brother," quips Alastair.

Atticus grins, then winks at me. I narrow my eyes at him.

"Well," drawls Atlas. "If you'll follow us, we'll show you to your chambers so you all may settle in."

My family members follow the deities into the manor, but I remain behind for a moment since I spot the lieutenants hanging back near one of the carriages. I saunter up to them, and Silas is the first to greet me, sparing me a hug.

"Hello there, Princess," greets Damian next, and I pause at the sight of Feronia upon his arm.

"Fern?" I question.

The unshifted wendigo squeals before jumping forward to embrace me, and I catch her as she hugs me close.

"I'm so happy to see you again!" exclaims Fern, and though I hate to admit it, her excitement is nearly contagious, and I find myself smiling and laughing with her.

"You have *no idea* how *obnoxious* all these males have been without you around to keep them in check!" She continues, my hands in hers. "We've missed you terribly."

I raise my brow. "*We?*" I repeat.

"Rhesa?" calls Tallulah, grinning. "C'mon, girlfriend! I guess we should have a word with your husbands if they have indeed fucked you stupid."

I snarl lightly, though I laugh through the action as I pull Tally in for a hug. "I find I'm just a little overwhelmed is all. It's good to see you all the same, even if the first words you speak to me are an insult."

"Though I don't think you're complaining too much about getting *fucked stupid* by those gorgeous males," calls Althea, and I snap my eyes to her, watching Gage help her out of the carriage.

She remains a human woman, though I can tell she has since been adopted by hell's ways as she appears to have stopped aging like a mortal. However, what really catches my attention is the hand placed upon her *baby bump.*

"I know," says Thea, snickering gently as she rubs her pregnant belly. The obsidian gem upon her left hand shimmers in the sunlight with the action. "I'm finally starting to properly show."

I look at Gage, and he grins at me.

"You've been busy," I quip, smirking at my honorary brother.

He chuckles, wrapping his arm around Thea as he kisses her temple. *Husband and wife.*

"You'll be an aunt before you know it, Rhesa," he teases. "I can only *imagine* what sort of lessons *you'll* be responsible for."

My smirk widens into a proper grin. "Male or female, it won't matter. I'll be the best damned aunt there ever was."

The lieutenants smile and chuckle, and I realize with startling candor that *I want that to be true.*

I want this.

CHAPTER TWELVE
RHESAMYRE

The ballroom practically has a heartbeat of its own since there is so much magic and power pulsing through the air, with the entirety of the Hellion Court, the three deities, and seven archangels, alongside the rest of the many lords and ladies of both Hell and the Celestial Cities. The Zodiacs are not in attendance, nor are the mortal royals or many *others* from what I can tell from atop this balcony. Even so, it is strange to find those of Hell and the Heavens to be getting along as well as they are.

"I suppose this shouldn't surprise me," drawls Pollux as he comes to stand beside me. The Archangel of Perception is clad in silver and wears the iconic grin I have become so familiar with, the one he seems to reserve for only a select few.

"You hiding up here," he continues to tease. "Appearing as though you're already searching for the perfect escape route."

I spare him a grin. "Come now, Lux. You should know me better than that by now. I'm already aware of *several* escape routes."

He laughs. "I suppose I should have expected as much. Very well. Then may I inquire as to what you're really doing up here, darling?"

I turn to face him, my gown gently swaying with me as I do so. Obsidian jewels and silver chains cover my form, as the majority of my black gown is sheer lace in nature and adorned with plenty of cutouts to expose my skin and figure. Despite the circumstances of my temporary skepticism, I would be lying to myself if I said I didn't enjoy dressing for this occasion, ensuring all three deities are represented upon my accouter of choice by either way of makeup, painted nails, or jewelry.

Picking at my shimmering, ruby-red nails, I ask him instead, "What are *you* doing up here, Pollux?"

He raises his brow at me, then shrugs as he surveys the ballroom again. "Checking in, I suppose. A few of us have noticed you're a little . . . off your game tonight."

I snicker politely. "How eloquently put, Perception."

He spares me another calculated but gentle glance. "Are you truly all right, Rhesa?"

It feels as though everyone has been asking me that as of late, so the question doesn't catch me off guard. However, my lack of an answer does, and Pollux knows it, too.

He turns to face me again, his hand rising to gently trace my cheekbone as he cups my face. "What's got you down these days, darling?"

I shake my head, stepping away from him. His hand falls back to his side, and I could swear a flash of hurt and confusion crosses his face for a moment. However, he does his best to school his features back into gentle indifference, but I still don't miss the look of concern in his icy eyes as he surveys me.

His eyes get snagged on my lower belly, and I watch as his nostrils flare.

Before I can think better of it, my ring-clad hand is upon him. The resounding *slap* is loud in my ears, but thankfully not loud enough to draw any unnecessary attention. Pollux's head whips to the side.

"Don't. You. *Dare*," I seethe quietly.

He narrows his eyes at me. "*Well*," he drawls softly. "Should I take that as an admission that you are *in fact* with child?"

"No," I snarl. "I'm not."

"You're positive?"

"Certain of it."

Pollux sighs, nodding to himself and looking *almost* disappointed at the news. "Oh . . . and here I thought perhaps we all would have something else to celebrate. My apologies, Rhesamyre."

I raise my brow at him as I quip, "Sorry to disappoint."

He puts his hands up in surrender, softening his gaze again. "I didn't mean anything by it, Rhesa. We're just . . . worried, I guess."

"Who's *we*?"

He sighs. "Your immediate family, for starters. Me. And the majority of my brothers, too. You hide it well, but we all know you well enough to notice when something is wrong."

I raise my other brow at him this time, beginning to get tired of the action. "Your brothers?" I scoff a little. "I find that hard to believe."

Pollux furrows his brows, frowning. "Why? They've been a part of your life for as long as the rest of the Hellion Court have. Granted, not on a daily basis, but certainly often enough to know when something is up with you. We spend all our holidays together, after all."

I blink at him. "What?"

"I think Castor and Alto would be quite offended to learn you don't think as highly of them as they believed. After all, right next to me, they are your favorite angelic uncles."

Carefully, I nod. "Right . . . a shitty tease on my part. My mistake."

Pollux rolls his eyes, chuckling softly. "You've certainly been spending too much time with Alastair if that's your idea of *funny*."

I force out a smile and pray to whatever or whoever may be listening that Pollux doesn't notice how fake it is. He holds out his arm for me, and I take it, allowing him to guide me down the staircase, onto the ballroom floor, where couples twirl and dance to the grand, enchanted orchestra. Pollux spins me around, then allows my hands to slip from his own and into another's.

"Hello, my beautiful daughter," says my father.

I meet his eyes, and my hands tighten in his for a heartbeat as I gaze into the dead, black pools that lie where his usual, glittering obsidian eyes are. His form is drained of its tanner color, black wings broken and dull behind him, and a massive, bloody hole lies in his chest, staining his black suit with his blood as it drips onto the floor. I glance down, and I wish I hadn't, because there lies his heart with the Zodiac Blade firmly plunged inside it.

"Rhesa?"

I blink again, meeting his eyes, and everything appears perfect and pristine once more. No blood. No hearts. No death.

Willing my heartbeat to remain steady, I spare him a soft smile. "Hi, Dad."

The devil spares me a smile as we begin to twirl and dance with practiced, graceful ease, and I allow my instincts and training to guide me as my mind wanders about the ballroom to survey the many archangels in the room. They all laugh and chatter amongst themselves and other guests, including that of the Hellion Court. No resentment. No ulterior motives. No bloodshed. Not even between Apollo or Adriel as they laugh with a few of the assassins and Horsemen.

However, I can't help but narrow my eyes at the sight of *Lilith* and *Andrew* standing with Apollo. The golden angel's arms are around both his mate and son, and Lilith appears like that of a beautiful, young witch rather than an *ugly, old crone*. She seems to sense my gaze, then meets my eyes and smiles before waving at me kindly.

What. The. Hell.

"Your attention seems especially divided tonight, baby girl," notes my father. "What's on your mind?"

I have to force myself not to roll my eyes as I reply, "Just surveying the crowds, Father. Old habits die hard, I suppose."

He hums. "I suppose, though I don't quite know why you'd be so suspicious of this crowd. You know just about everyone here. Everyone of importance, that is."

I mimic his hum. "Pollux said something of the sort, too. However, I still can't help but cock my head at the sight of Apollo being so pleasant."

The devil chuckles. "I admit, Apollo can certainly be an asshole when he wants to be. However, I would claim he's been rather well-behaved these past years. I believe babysitting you when you were younger certainly helped in that regard. However, you and his son are practically cousins, and Andrew has always taken a liking to you, too. The boy was crushing *hard* when he was a teen."

I ignore that comment about Andrew, muttering, "It seems as though I've had a plethora of babysitters throughout the years."

My father shrugs. "Only when the Hellion Court wasn't readily available, which was rare. As uncommon as it may have been, sometimes they would be summoned to Ursa Major with me to report to the Zodiacs and Three Kings. From there, Pollux or one of my other brothers would look after you . . . or try to, at least. You've always been quite skilled at playing hide-and-seek. All sorts of nooks and crannies to hide in at the Celestial Palace."

Carefully, I nod along. "Right . . . and the Zodiacs and kings allowed a little demon to run amuck in their sacred halls?"

He smirks at me. "You may have horns, Rhesa, but it's no secret you're of celestial origins, thanks to the forbidden power that courses through your veins. Perhaps the only good thing that came out of Adam and Evelyn's failed revolt. We couldn't stop them from stealing the fruit, but we did stop them from harming you and everyone else within the spheres."

"*We*?"

My father nods. "Me, those of Hell, as well as the rest of my brothers and the deities. All of us." He cocks his head at me. "Don't tell me you've forgotten our history that quickly, baby girl," he teases. "Sloth would be quite disappointed. He thought for sure his lessons burrowed deep inside of you with no danger of ever being forgotten."

"I haven't forgotten," I claim, though I don't quite believe it.

And neither does my father evidently, as he simply hums again before explaining, "Then you'll also recall that it was the late King of Hell, Abaddon, that tricked Adam and Eve in the first place. Then once we removed them from the Spheres of the Living, the beasts and beings of Hell appointed me as their next king, and thus you as its princess and future queen."

I nod. "Naturally."

My father chuckles a little, albeit humorlessly. "*Naturally*," he repeats, though I know he doesn't believe me.

Hell. I don't even believe me. And I've always been taught and raised to believe that the secret to a good lie relies on the authenticity of the liar.

Honest schemers make for trusted confidants, and great liars breed better lies.

And right now, dare I say I am surrounded by liars and schemers. Some of whom seem better at playing this game than I am at the moment, and while I may not always admit it outright, I can at least admit this much to myself:

I'm a sore loser.

So game on, motherfuckers.

My father's fingers come to pinch my chin gently, thus drawing my gaze back up to his again and snapping me out of my scheming. His brows are furrowed as he studies me; his eyes rapidly rake over my features and form before they come to rest and find my gaze again.

"Will you take a walk with me?" he asks, and his voice sounds . . . *different* now. Huskier.

I dip my chin. "I could use some fresh air."

He nods, then leads me outside into the gardens and away from the crowded, noisy ballroom. I remain on his arm until we find ourselves in the middle of another patio adorned with stone statues of archangels and more flowers or trees in dark planters and pots.

"You're getting tired of answering, and I'm getting tired of asking," drawls my father, and I leave him to sit on one of the benches as I pace near the black roses and fountains, pretending to admire the statues of my claimed uncles.

I hum in acknowledgment, and my father only sighs.

"Rhesamyre."

I turn my eyes to him but don't approach. And he looks . . . *distraught.*

"Had I known giving your hand away to the Three Kings would cause you so much *grief*," he continues, "then I would have told them to go fuck themselves."

I can't help the snicker that escapes me, and my father smiles at the sound.

"There she is," he remarks, then pats the spot next to him.

Silently, I comply and take a seat next to him.

"It's not that," I admit slowly. "Alastair, Atlas, and Atticus . . . they love me. They treat me like the queen I am, and practically worship me as their own personal goddess."

And I do believe that. With all my heart. *That* at least is the truth. Perhaps the only truth here at the moment.

"Then what is it?" he inquires gently. "And don't lie to me again."

I spare him a smile, though even I know it to be a broken one. A pathetic excuse for happiness, and he knows it, and it isn't by any means going to buy it a second time.

"Something is . . . amiss here, Dad," I reveal softly. "I don't . . ." I sigh, looking away from him so I don't have to look into his dead eyes again. "I don't know how to explain it, but my gut just keeps telling me that something is *wrong*."

I watch him nod out of the corner of my eye as he inquires, "Can you try to narrow it down? Or is it too vague?"

I shrug. "Some things are more obvious than others."

"Such as?"

I meet his eyes again, and this time, I don't flinch at the sight of the blood that pours from his chest. "When I look at you, I see your corpse."

My father blinks at me in alarm, then furrows his brows. "Like a vision? Are you perhaps having a premonition of my demise?"

I shake my head. "I don't think so . . ." And then I whisper more to myself than to him, admitting to myself the truth I almost refuse to face, "I think you already *died* . . . and I couldn't save you."

Pity. That's pity I see in his eyes now. "Rhesa—"

"*No.*" I stop him, standing up again. "Don't *Rhesa* me, Dad . . . *please*, just *listen* to me when I say this isn't *right*. This place is *not* my home."

I can tell he's trying to listen. He's trying to piece together the pitiful, broken explanation that not even I completely understand at the moment.

"This place," he begins. "Meaning the manor? Hell?"

"No—*well*, at least . . . not this *version* of it," I growl to myself, then force myself to exhale before I lose my composure. "The splintered memories I have are not ones containing that of a family of demons *and* celestials. The few things and people I can recall are not all friendly with one another, nor are they considered allies of ours. Allies of Hell. From what I *can* recall, many of the beings in that ballroom are our enemies . . . and may even be responsible for your death, too."

My father doesn't look convinced, but he's still willing to listen to me, and that's more than I can ask for. I know how insane it sounds, and I know I'm not doing a very good job of convincing him otherwise. Hell, *I* barely know how to make sense of it, let alone convince someone else to believe me.

I shake my head at myself, snickering a little. "Never mind . . . I know how it sounds. For my sake, just forget I said anything. We should get back to the ballroom before one of my *husbands* comes sniffing around."

I twirl around to head back inside, and I hear my father rise behind me to follow my lead.

"*Myra.*"

I whirl around to face him once more, snarling softly, "*What* did you just call me?"

My father looks alarmed as he raises his brow and repeats, "Rhesa*myre*?"

I blink at him, nod once, and then leave him where he stands.

....

It wasn't easy, but nothing worth doing ever is.

Slipping heavy sedatives and sleeping spells into the last of everyone's drinks without anyone taking notice was an impressive feat in itself, considering how many guests were in attendance. Especially when I count how many high-ranking celestials and demons there are, too. However, what I'm even more proud of is not only getting the deities under my spell, but getting them away from the ballroom as a whole before they could take notice of guests dismissing themselves one by one at swift, and perhaps even considerably alarming rates, if one were to sniff deeper.

A few bats of my lashes, some well-constructed comments doubled as challenges, and some strategic flirting. Then even a few, well-placed hands or fingers upon the more sensitive feathers of their wings or the skin of their necks, teasing the tendrils of their hair or tracing their tattoos when no eyes were upon us, and I had all three of them stumbling up the staircase and chasing after me through the halls, back toward my bedchamber.

Laughing and grinning and teasing all the way as they fought each other to grab me first. One would kiss me passionately while another sought to aid me in ditching my dress, and then another would immediately growl and steal me away for more possessive kisses while the other two would attach themselves to my neck and other parts of my body. Playing with me in creative, sinful ways that felt far too good to end. Devouring me whole all at once. I figured I might as well enjoy the attention a little bit, and thus get some damned good orgasms out of their endeavors to please me.

Three mouths. Three sets of hands. Three pairs of eyes.

Three kings, and their queen.

But the best lies always taste the sweetest, and this one is no different. Tranquil and sinful in the most delicious of ways. Me, surrounded by friends and family and all three deities, who love me unconditionally, as they claimed over and over again as they took turns with me.

I'd be a fool if I lied to myself again and said a part of me didn't enjoy this. Didn't long for it . . . I could learn to love it. Love this version of them. All of them, including the archangels who happily claim the daughter of the devil as their lovely niece. A sphere where even Lilith and Andrew are accepted as a part of the family, and no one succeeds in betraying anyone else. A world where no ghosts haunt the deities' nightmares, and no regrets rest heavy on their minds, forcing their gazes to be steeled and jaded out of fear of another eruption. Their shoulders heavy with the weight of their wings and burdens.

And then there's my father . . .

I shake my head at the intrusive thoughts, then skillfully remove the many appendages that are tangled across my body. Alastair, Atlas, and Atticus remain sprawled around me, snoozing peacefully, both in thanks to the spells and the sexual satisfaction of fucking me a few times each.

My legs *wobble* when I stand, and I softly curse up a storm as I quietly pad around the room to retrieve new clothes from my closet. Dressing in my leathers and armed to the teeth with obsidian, I glance back at the three of them once more as I stand ready by the door, studying their *almost* too-familiar tattoos and features, each deity a lethal, gorgeous predator in his own right.

Concord. Control. And Devotion.

My power flares once, and a piercing headache stabs my mind and forces me to wince as the broken memories violently overtake my vision.

I shove the intrusive thoughts aside once more, then step out of the room and click the door shut behind me.

CHAPTER THIRTEEN
RHESAMYRE

Searching and skimming through the spell books and grimoires of this estate's library for a few hours has left me exhausted and *irritated* beyond reason. I've never minded research before; Sloth and I used to spend *days* holed up in the libraries of the Obsidian Palace together, reading books of all genres, both for pleasure and to further my education on all things that can be learned from the sacred pages of a book. Geography, history, mathematics, anthropology, and then the lovers' quarrels during daring adventures and passionate romances between anti-heroes and sworn enemies.

But searching for spells or records of memory loss or alternate realities within these limited tomes is proving to be nearly impossible.

I need a bigger library.

My power flares in warning, but I ignore it as I vaguely register the library door opening and closing softly.

"And here I'd hoped the sleeping spells and sedatives would last a bit longer," I remark from where I remain sprawled upon the carpet before the hearth, surrounded by open tomes. I glance up to meet her green eyes. "But I should've guessed a witch would know better."

Lilith surveys my form and the many open pages around me, then she crinkles her nose and quips, "You reek of sex."

I shrug, looking back down at my research notes. "Bite me."

She snickers. "No, thanks. I believe you've been bitten enough tonight by those feral beasts you call *husbands*, and we call *kings*. I hope you're prepared for the repercussions that are sure to follow drugging everyone. Your males seem to get quite *peeved* when you pull stunts like this without their knowledge."

I shrug, still ignoring her. "I can't quite find the energy to care at the moment."

"Because you don't believe any of them to be *your males*, right?"

I meet her calculated gaze, which is alight with humor and curiosity.

She smirks a little. "Don't look at me like that, little las. It's not hard to figure out what's going on in that pretty little head of yours when I spot what sort of books you have open before you." She bends down to pick one up, skimming through it before tossing it back onto the nearby table where a few more enchanted journals rest. "Though, I don't believe you'll find what you're looking for here."

"Then care to share where I might?"

Lilith shrugs again, then takes a seat at the table, crossing her legs. "Spellwork like this is highly convoluted and almost *nonexistent*. There are no rules when it comes to this sort of time manipulation because it's never before been put to practice." She gestures to all my research. "All of this is theory, not reality, so what makes you so certain you're in an alternate plane?"

I study her for a moment, weighing whether or not I should trust this version of the wicked witch. She doesn't smell malicious, nor does my power whir within me in warning of her presence. In this odd version of the spheres, the Lilith here is an ally. A friend. The true wife of Apollo, and her son is claimed as my cousin. Not only that, but she's *beautiful*. With bright green eyes and fiery red hair and an hourglass body built similarly to my own, though she is taller.

"My . . . " I drawl quietly, vaguely. "My memories don't quite match up with everyone else's. The history here is *different* than what I believe I have been taught before."

Lilith hums. "Well, there is only one spell that can be used for the most basic forms of time travel."

"The Reformation Spell."

"Yes, but it isn't an easy spell to complete by any means. Besides, you're not looking to jump backward or forward in time. You're looking to take a step sideways . . . which means you need time *altering*, not necessarily time *travel*."

I raise my brow at her but then lower my gaze as I contemplate her words. Time traveling back and forth is one thing, but to move sideways into an entirely different plane of existence is completely different magic.

According to the witch, anyway.

"Are you certain you're not dead? I hear the Umbra Mundi rewards those deserving of eternal peace with the most perfect of dreams. Everything the heart desires but couldn't have when beating in the Spheres of the Living. Even if the dead didn't know what they desired back then, they do by the time they enter their final resting place, and thus their eternal dreams."

I meet her eyes again, then sigh and shake my head. "I'm not dead."

"You sure?"

"Positive."

Lilith hums, and I ponder over her choice of words again. *Perfect dreams.*

I close my eyes. *Of fucking course.*

"You figured something out, didn't you?"

I spare Lilith another glance, only to find her head cocked at me curiously, but I don't answer her.

She lifts her shoulders, not seeming offended by my silence as she says, "Never mind. I won't pry. It's obvious you don't trust me, which must mean that you and I are not friends in your alternate version of reality . . . are we?"

Carefully, I shake my head.

Lilith nods again. "What a shame . . . you may not have the memories for it, but I do. Real or not, I can recall this plane's version of history. You and I could have been good friends in a different sphere . . . in this sphere, we are, anyway."

I dip my chin. "I agree."

She smiles gently, but then hesitates before inquiring, "Apollo and I . . . what are we like in your plane?"

Unsure I want to tell her the truth, but knowing better than to lie, I state, "You're madly in love. He only has eyes for you, and you for him. And your son is grown and successful, too . . . You would do anything for your child and mate, and Apollo would do anything for the two of you, as well."

And that is the truth. I've learned it firsthand

Lilith smiles at me, then rises from her chair and approaches me. She cups my face gently and bends down to place a kiss on my forehead. Then she mutters, "Get home safe, Rhesamyre."

She turns to leave, but before she can, I call out to her again. She pauses mid-step by the door but doesn't turn around to face me again.

"Thank you, Lilith."

She nods once and then disappears.

....

The Four Pillars at least look familiar and remain just as eerily beautiful as I recall.

Orpheus surveys the land ahead of us that rests just outside the Lords of Exile's wards, and after a moment of ensuring we aren't being watched or followed, we kick on toward the Tower of Dreams. The Sandman is sure to have the answers I seek, and if not him, then another will. I'm not above visiting the Hollow, either, as it is possible the Wise Men may be able to aid me in my quest to get home, too. They claim to have a copy of every book or spell in existence, after all. So perhaps they have what I need to snap out of this strange, spelled dreamscape I'm stuck in.

Dismounting Orpheus as we near the gates of the courtyard, I ignore the few bakus that prowl about the space, looking for trouble.

Feral cats, the lot of them.

However, before I can go knocking on Draven's castle door, the fine hairs upon my arms stand on end, and I whirl around with an obsidian dagger in hand. I clash with another's weaponry of dark steel, then command my power to rise and push the estranged, cloaked assailant backward.

He's fucking massive. And he does not carry a sword, but instead a double-edged battle-axe of obsidian. He's easily a few heads taller than the deities, and far broader, too. And from what I can tell, his legs and feet beneath his cloak are not that of human origins, but instead, they're *hooves.*

I meet his eyes through the darkness of his cloak, and *three* white eyes stare back at me.

"Hello, stranger," I drawl.

The monster chuckles, then uses one of his tatted, humanoid hands to pull his hood back to reveal the features of a bull with a man's proportions. A thick ring pierces his septum, and a few more gems line his fuzzy ears near his horns. His fur is black and dark brown, and he remains shirtless to reveal his hairy, but tatted chest of supernatural muscles.

I cock my head at him, but I don't dare lower my daggers. "I had once learned that the Lord of Sanity was a beast bred between the three-eyed bull and a banshee. Though I've never had the pleasure of ever meeting him until now . . . . Greetings, my lord. My name is Rhesamyre."

The minotaur chuckles again, then sheathes his axe upon his back as he crosses his meaty arms, now sizing me up. Those three eyes of his are rumored to be *all-seeing*, and they're all white and without proper pupils, and he looks more bull than man. More beast than banshee.

"You certainly don't waste much time, *Princess*," he drawls gruffly, though I catch a subtle, mocking tone in his statement that has me narrowing my eyes at him. "Though it is *here* of all planes and spheres, it is nice to finally make your acquaintance. I've seen and heard a great deal about you. You may call me Kure."

I raise my brow at him. "You've *seen* me?"

He nods. "I have. As have my underlings You remain their favorite player at the moment in this never-ending game of chess the spheres and planes play simultaneously. It's a convoluted, vast board, and while there are plenty of rules, there is a plethora of skilled cheaters."

I hum. "Your existence sounds exhausting. Especially if you're the keeper of the *prophets*. I've heard they tend to shapeshift sporadically in order to better fuck around with time."

"My troublesome creatures love to hide, yes. *Little shits.*"

I crack a grin, sheathing my daggers as I start toward the beast who bears the Sight. "Perhaps you're a better creature to question if I am dealing with alternate realities, then . . . . I had thought perhaps I was stuck in a dream. Hence the Sandman."

He shrugs. "You are. Something wicked that both Draven and Wicker concocted together on the outside. As per the request of your rightful Three Kings."

I hum, crossing my arms. "*Fantastic.*" I sigh. "So that means speaking with *this* Draven won't help me much, after all."

"Don't be so despondent. It was certainly a step in the right direction, but he would only be able to offer you less than half the advice I am about to give you now."

"Which is?"

"That getting out of this nightmare relies on your willpower to leave it."

I raise my brow again. "*Nightmare*?"

Kure inclines his head. "This place is meant to tempt you, Queen of Hell. But it is not strong enough to *keep* you here. As all things tend to do, it will turn sour soon enough. It is merely a question of *when*, and that timeline relies on you."

I growl quietly. "Unfortunately, I find myself at a loss of what to do next. Any suggestions?"

He shrugs. "Provoke them."

"Who?"

"*Everyone.*"

I nod, but then find myself inquiring, "Why are you helping me? And how come you didn't come to my aid sooner? I'm sure you're aware I was up to my horns in useless research."

"You had to come to me first. You have to be willing to take the initiative to free yourself. All has occurred how it was supposed to if I am to aid you, but even I know better than to push my limits in such an odd, alternate plane of reality. This place has not occurred naturally, and instead remains the convoluted creation of estranged spellwork that my neighbors are experimenting with. I dare say out of both boredom and obligation."

"Obligation . . . to whom?"

Kure grins, then inquires ominously in Old Latin, *"Do you remember yet?"*

I remain silent, then glance back at Draven's castle to survey the surrounding area once more. No baku roam about anymore, and the air remains scentless. I no longer feel the wards of the Four Pillars, and the castles themselves almost shimmer in the moon and starlight like odd mirages.

"Draven is not here . . . is he?"

Kure shrugs halfheartedly, appearing as though he doesn't quite know how to answer honestly. "He would be if you decided to speak with him again, but it wouldn't be the Draven you've become so familiar with. This plane continues to shift with your choices in order to keep up appearances and pretend to be real."

"They're all figments of my imagination . . . the perfect dream."

Kure nods.

"Then what are you doing here? How are you so self-aware?"

"That is my magic, my queen. I am the Lord of Sanity, and I have the Sight to see not only forward and backward in time, but also sideways all at once. As well as the necessary magic to shift through these different times or planes, and interact with the inhabitants in each."

"So there are more planes than even the one I call home? Lilith made it sound as though this magic didn't exist at all."

"That's because it isn't any of the witch's business, much to her dismay. And there are plenty more, but that is a conversation for another time, I'm afraid. *Their* return is imminent, Queen of Hell. And if we are to survive and win the war to come, or perhaps prevent it before it even begins, then we need you back home in your *proper* form."

I scowl at him, crossing my arms. "If you're so certain of what is to come, then why don't you warn everyone on my behalf?"

Kure shakes his head. "*No one remembers.* Sanity may be my namesake, but I am still considered *other* and therefore untrustworthy to the majority of the beings in these spheres that remain in power and wear the crowns that dictate what our plane is and is not. The spheres need you, *My—*"

My dagger glides past his head, thudding into the tree near his left ear. Carefully, he tips his head sideways away from my blade, and a droplet of blood drips from his ear.

"*Don't,*" I command softly. "That is not my name."

"It used to be."

"Long ago, maybe . . . but that is a time I can hardly recall now."

Kure dips his chin. "Your old spellwork is still in place, for the most part, but they are chipping away at it every time someone remembers them and schemes to bring them back. Even now, we're wasting precious seconds."

"*Who,* specifically? Who dares to utter their names after it was forbidden so long ago?"

He's quiet for a moment, until he says, "Come find me in reality, *Rhesamyre.* Then we may bargain."

I snarl and leap forward as Kure is enveloped by a shadowed conveyance, but before I can grab him, he disappears.

I growl and scream into the night, feeling my power surge and erupt forward. It devours a part of the courtyard and Draven's castle, and when I turn to survey the damage, only glittering shadows and odd miasma remain where the structure once stood.

A mirage. A dream. An illusion.

I glance back at Orpheus, but even he, too, has disappeared. This world or plane or *whatever the fuck it is*, is crumbling around me. Shattering into a million tiny shards, and I stand in the center of the broken mess, still debating whether or not I should pick up the pieces.

Nothing like this exists out there in reality. No peace without conflicts. No glory without bloodshed. It's a beautiful lie.

Inhaling and exhaling slowly, I steel myself as I flare my power once more so I may open a conveyance straight into the manor I've been residing in. I still sense a great number of beings resting in the many rooms of this house, but I only focus on three as I prowl up the grand staircase toward my bedchamber.

I open the door, ready to strike, but am forced to stop short as I gaze at the three of them casually laughing with one another. They bicker like the brothers they are, throwing pillows or clothing pieces at one another as they attempt to clean up the room.

"*Ah!* There you are!" calls Atticus, grinning at me from where he stands above Atlas with a pillow in hand, ready to strike.

Atlas tilts his head back to meet my eyes from where he lies on the floor, arms braced upward to defend himself against Atticus's pillow assault. Atlas smiles kindly at me, then kicks Atticus's legs out from underneath him so he may rise with little trouble.

"Where'd you run off to, little sin?" inquires Atlas, looking ridiculously handsome even with disheveled bed hair and wrinkled slacks, which hang low on his tatted hips.

I swallow thickly.

Focus. This isn't real. They are not real.

Steeling myself once more, I mutter, "Little wolf."

Atlas's smile falters as he asks, "What?"

"Your nickname for me . . . it's supposed to be *little wolf*."

He chuckles a little, glancing back at his brothers who look just as puzzled as he does. "Why would I call you that?"

"Because that's what I was when we met. When you saved my life in the desert of the West. I was a little wolf . . . *your little wolf.*"

Before Atlas can comment, I turn my gaze to Atticus. "And you're supposed to call me sweet spice . . . . We haven't officially spoken yet, but I would imagine the nickname comes from the letters you and I exchanged."

Atticus cocks his head with a perplexed expression, then tries to claim with a soft chuckle, "Rhesa, we've known each other for years. We've never exchanged letters."

I nod in agreement. "Not here, anyway. But out there, we have. We did . . . I still have your replies. Both of yours. They're in my bedside drawer with a few of Alastair's rings I stole when he wasn't paying attention."

This Alastair now furrows his brows, but before he can step in, I say, "None of you know this because none of you are *mine.*"

Glancing down at my left hand, I tug the beautiful ring off my finger, then melt it in my palm. The molten steel, obsidian, and gems pool in my palm, and I tip my hand sideways to allow the messy, melted cluster to fall to the floor. Then, when I meet the eyes of these males again, their gazes have gone cold. Steeled and *livid* predators that no longer bear the familiar marks that made them appealing and similar to *my* three deities.

Alastair *chuckles*, but when he speaks, his voice is not his own as he seethes, "You shouldn't have done that, *Rhesamyre.*"

Bracing myself, I narrowly avoid Alastair as he lunges for me. I sidestep him and dodge both Atlas and Atticus next, and the three of them skid through the open door or hit the walls on either side ungracefully since their bodies *shift* and implode from the inside out. They shriek and holler like banshees and wicked monsters as their wings rip outward from their backs, but when they attempt to use their feathers, they molt and break and bleed. Melting from skin and cartilage and bone and making a slippery mess upon the floor.

The three males' faces are soon in similar states as fangs lengthen and rip from their gums, and their tattoos glow and smolder upon their skin. The smell of burning flesh makes me crinkle my nose and snarl in disgust, and their bodies continue to morph into larger, cursed versions of themselves as they growl and attempt to grab me. I duck under their oncoming arms and claws, then command a sword to erupt from my own flames to defend myself against their cursed weaponry.

I slip in their melted skin and blood as I scurry out into the hall ungracefully, and the monsters behind me roar and scream my name. Barreling down the hallway, they slip and slide in their own mess as they trip over one another.

One of them shrieks and launches forward, and I twirl out of his way and jump onto the railing of the nearby staircase. The ugly, deformed beast barrels into another wall, shaking the entire mansion in the process. Then, before the other two can harm me, I flip off the railing and land on the first floor of the foyer. However, when I gaze at the marble beneath my hands and boots, I am startled to find everything is stained *red*.

Standing at attention to survey my surroundings, I find the walls are now *bleeding*. More blood seeps into the marble and woodwork, thanks to the bodies and gore that litter the floor, all of which belong to my family and the archangels. Even Lilith and Andrew are among them, their skin peeled off to reveal their tendons and broken bones while their guts spill over the sides of their torsos.

Ripped to shreds. *Butchered.*

"Rhe-Rhesa?"

I whirl around to face Althea as she sputters and coughs up more blood, her body already broken in a million ways as blood pools beneath her. Her hands remain stained a glossy red as she clutches the contents of her stomach, attempting to hide or save what *used* to grow inside her.

"W-Why?" she questions weakly, coughing again as red tears line her eyes. "Weren't you *happy*? WHY WOULD YOU DO THIS TO US?" she screams, sobbing.

Steeling myself, I command another sword to erupt in my hand, and I prowl toward the woman who carries—*carried*—Gage's child. Then, as she gapes at me with wide, bloodshot eyes, I plunge my sword straight through her chest and into her pathetically beating heart.

"Because you're not real," I mutter softly, stepping back from her and leaving my sword in her body.

"It could have been, though," coos one of the monsters, appearing a few steps ahead of me. This one used to be Atlas, but he isn't anymore. Not since he appears as a heap of fatty, bloody skin and claws and horns and too many eyes that blink at different times. The foul monster grins with a mouth of edged and broken teeth. "But instead, you've chosen death."

I stand at attention as the deformed bodies of Alastair and Atticus reveal themselves once more, and even a few of my fallen family members rise again as corpses, too, my father once again amongst them. I size them all up, counting how many now stand next to the three monsters.

Twelve.

I bark a sudden laugh, and before I know it, I'm full-on *cackling* like a *fucking witch* as I survey their forms. I can tell they're pissed and unamused at my inside joke and revelation, but I don't quite care at the moment.

Wiping the humored tears from my eyes with bloody hands, I sigh and re-compose myself with a feral grin, relishing the burn of my tattoos that once again brand my skin. My back tingles with a pleasant heat from my bargain with Mamba, and my chest and thigh glow through my torn leathers as Alastair's original designs re-mark my skin, claiming me as his. In addition to his *trouvaille* tattoo, another inscription marks my inner left forearm in a mirrored fashion:

Sarang.

"You're right," I drawl, glancing up from my brands to glower at my enemies again. "I've chosen death."

The twelve of them launch toward me, shrieking with weapons raised and magic ready to murder and tear me limb from limb.

I erupt.

CHAPTER FOURTEEN
RHESAMYRE

"—myre, my love?"

"She's coming out of it, but be prepared for the backlash. Her magic has risen to the surface and has yet to settle back down."

A scoff. "That's nothing new, but it seems as though your little dreamscape was a success, after all."

"So it would seem."

"Our queen is quite remarkable. How long was that, dream eyes?"

"Thirty-six hours."

A chuckle. "Are you surprised?"

"By her? Always."

I both hear and feel shuffling around and above me, and my power rises and falls with my erratic breathing as I slowly register the varying scents and powers surrounding me. Fingers slowly trace my jawbone and brush the hair away from my face, and I lean into his familiar touch.

"*Alastair*," I murmur with my eyes still closed.

"I'm here, love," he coos with his hands on me, not straying far. "*We're* right here."

Slowly, I crack my eyes open as my blurry gaze remains off to the side. Blinking away the sleep and haziness, I slowly draw my eyes upward, mesmerized by the ink that glows upon the already tatted skin of his inner left forearm. The pattern of Old Latin smolders like a fresh brand, translating to *sarang*.

My eyes continue their sweep, and I meet his pink gaze.

Atlas smiles gently at me. "Hello, little wolf."

Fingers gently pinch my chin, drawing my gaze to Alistair's gentle expression. His silver eyes glow as he surveys my form, and he grins at me. His thumbs come to sweep under my eyes as his hands rest upon my cheeks, and I realize with a start that I'm *crying*.

Seeming to sense or see where my thoughts have gone, Alastair commands softly, "Don't panic. It's just your magic and emotions trying to catch up with your shift again. You . . . haven't quite been yourself for a bit."

"And by that," drawls another male with a familiar, accented voice, and I glance over to peer at the back of the couch where Atticus stands. His arms are crossed, and his expression is hard, but I'd be a blind fool not to pick up on the *relief* that shines in his emerald eyes. "He means you've been a temperamental beast who's been quick to bite first and ask questions later." He smirks at me, shrugging tauntingly. "But then again. I wouldn't quite call that out of character for you, either."

Alastair and Atlas growl in warning at their brother, but I simply cock my head at him. Then mutter—*nearly croak*, "You like it when I bite."

Atticus's grin widens, and he purrs, "I believe I do . . . . *Hello, sweet spice.*"

With help from Alastair, I move to sit up on the couch; the blanket they laid overtop me shifts with the motion, thus revealing my inked chest when I glance down the gap. Slowly, I trace my intricate and *beautiful* branding, my gaze still low until Draven speaks up from the corner where he stands beside Wicker.

"That was one of your first clues," he muses, and I meet his violet eyes.

The Sandman smiles gently at me, though I dare say the action is forced as something new brews in his gaze as he surveys me from beside the Boogeyman. I can't quite place the look right now, but whatever it is, it remains a subtle shine in Wicker's eyes, too.

Something akin to apprehension or recognition, I believe. Though, as to what changed between the way they're looking at me now versus how they used to, I'm not—

Oh.

They saw everything in that nightmare—*dream*, whatever the *fuck it was* they concocted. Thus, they know a good number of the rest of my secrets now, too.

I incline my head at Draven. "I sensed something was off the minute I awoke there. But you're right. My lack of ink was certainly a *clue*."

Draven nods, then glances at the deities as he says, "You have what you came for."

Atticus chuckles. "Fret not, *Sandy*," he teases, thus drawing a scowl from Draven and a growl from Wicker. "We'll be out of your hair shortly."

Atlas and Alastair are there beside me to offer their hands, and I take both of them with the blanket still securely wrapped around me. My knees buckle at first, but Alastair is quick to scoop me up into his arms.

"Put. Me. Down," I command quietly, though my voice lacks the usual vigor I need to successfully get my point across to stubborn, territorial, and overprotective males who often think they know better.

As expected, Alastair ignores me.

"Don't pout," teases Atticus, and I glare at him.

"*Atticus*," warns Atlas, and the youngest brother merely rolls his eyes.

"We *appreciate* your cooperation, gents," drawls Alastair as he begins to take his leave.

"Don't mention it," calls Wicker, his eyes on me once again. "Consider it a show of good faith."

Alastair halts, as do Atlas and Atticus, thus giving the lords another moment to explain themselves. And though I remain bundled up in Alastair's arms, I convey with daggers in my eyes that they had better keep their mouths *shut* if they fancy having their tongues intact.

And because they're not *stupid*, Draven and Wicker pick up on my promise of pain, and Draven explains for his . . . *whatever Fear is to him*, "We stand with Hell and are loyal to its queen and her court."

Alastair nods, then continues on his way as his brothers flank us. We're silent as we exit the castle and outer wards, sauntering far enough away to open a conveyance back home.

Back to Hell. The real one, this time.

"How are you feeling?" inquires Atlas. "And don't lie to us."

Us. I want to laugh but refrain from doing so. "I'm fine . . . a little disoriented at the moment, but none the worse for wear."

Atticus snorts at that, muttering, "Yeah. We'll see about that."

I growl at him, but Alastair draws my attention to him once more when he sighs and moves to put me down. His hands remain on my waist to steady me, and he dips his head to better meet my eyes as his gaze skips between my own. Seeming satisfied with whatever he finds, he finally asks, "What do you want to do first?"

I raise my brow at him, then quip, "Getting some proper clothes would be a good start."

"I'm not complaining," snipes Atticus, and Atlas goes to whack him upside the head, but the youngest brother dodges the attack with ease.

Rolling his eyes and taking a deep breath to calm himself, Alastair clenches his jaw as he drawls, "We have some options here at our disposal, love. We can take you back home to be with your family and friends, or we can take you somewhere else."

Slowly, I inquire, "Somewhere . . . *else*?"

He nods, tucking a stray curl behind my pointed ear. "Anywhere you want. We can even go be recluses in the mountains if that's what you so desire. With all of us, one of us, or none of us. It's up to you."

I narrow my eyes at him, surveying him and his brothers suspiciously. None of them move or quip any more witty remarks. They just watch me as I watch them.

"*Oh* . . . you're actually serious," I deadpan. Then despite myself, I huff a quiet laugh, though I don't find this situation to be all that amusing, and neither do they. I exhale slowly. "I want to know what happened."

"That can wait—"

"No. *It can't*," I cut Atticus off, and he snarls at me. I ignore him as I cross my arms and settle my gaze on Alastair again. "Tell me what happened after . . . how many days has it been?"

Alastair doesn't appear as though he's going to give in that easily, but as soon as I open my mouth to sass him, he sighs and concedes. "Weeks."

I raise my brow, repeating slowly, "*Weeks.*"

He nods. "You erupted after Samael was slain, and we weren't able to locate you in your wolf form until a few days later. Then, you were captured by Lilith and Apollo, escaped, and then wound up with Atlas in the West for a bit until Pollux tracked you down.

From there, you remained a wolf within the confines of the Obsidian Palace."

"Until we got sick of your attitude and sought other means to change you back," quips Atticus.

I cock my head at him. "That reminds me. What the hell are *you* doing here, *Siren*?"

Atticus grins. "Such pathetic name-calling is beneath you, sweet spice. And you know very well what I'm doing here. You summoned me, remember?"

I scoff. "*Hardly.* More like I insulted you enough that you felt the need to come defend your honor in person. How's that going, by the way? Piss anyone off recently?"

"Including you, *plenty*," he snarls, stepping forward around Alastair despite his brother's warning growls. Then, with a surprisingly gentle hand that is at odds with the way his emerald eyes smolder, he grasps my chin to tip my head back as he stands chest to chest with me. "Nonetheless, you asked for my presence, *Princess*. So here I am."

I raise my head higher despite his close proximity. "Queen."

He cocks his head.

"You will refer to me as *queen*."

Atticus spares me a feral grin, which is borderline wolfish as his eyes shine with mirth and . . . *pride*.

Pride. And, dare I say, a mixed potion of adoration and admiration.

"*Indeed you are*," he mutters. Then he nods. "You are my queen, sweet spice. Rest assured, I won't be making that mistake *ever* again."

I remain stock still as he leans forward and presses a kiss to my forehead, but I half-expect him to *steal* a kiss since he's here and could manage to obtain one before his brothers tackle him.

Atticus seems to sense my shift in thoughts, and he merely grins again as he whispers only loud enough for me to hear, "Trust me. When I kiss you, it won't be in mixed company. Instead, it will be when we're alone, and I have you at my mercy. *Begging* for it."

"We'll see," I mutter. "Two can play that game, Atticus. We'll see who's *begging* for it first."

Atticus smirks and winks at me, then finally backs away before Atlas stabs him or Alastair erupts again. He glances at his brothers, then shrugs nonchalantly.

Steeling myself, I survey the other two deities once again. My eyes catch on Atlas's familiar form, but I don't allow my gaze to linger for long as I inquire, "Is that all?"

Alastair nods. "The rest we can fill you in on later . . . . If I may inquire, what do *you* remember?"

I don't answer immediately and instead give myself a moment to better ponder how I want to do so in the first place. "I remember enough." My eyes fall to Atlas again. "I remember you."

Though he hides it well, I can tell he almost *buckles* in relief at the news. But with a steeled gaze, he just nods and admits, "I'm pleased to hear that, little wolf. And what of your time under the spellwork of Fear and Dreams?"

Now *that* is certainly *not* something I want to discuss at the moment, so instead, I segue with, "You said you would take me anywhere?"

Alastair raises his brow at my pitiful evasion of Atlas's question, but still, he obliges me. "Anywhere you want, for however long, and with *whomever* you choose."

I nod. "Then take me home."

This time, both Atlas and Atticus raise their brows, too. However, before any of them can further second guess me, I command, "Take me home . . . *please*. Take me back to Hell."

The brothers look at each other one last time, then nod and open a conveyance straight into the throne room. And with a blanket as my only attire, I stride through the glittering tunnel and pad onto the marble floors with bare feet. Not even two seconds later, the doors burst open to reveal a good portion of the court, as well as my girlfriends, who lead the charge toward me and nearly crash into me while exclaiming my name with tears in their eyes. Fern, Thea, and Tally embrace me all at once, and I can't help the unintentional *giggle* of relief that leaves me as I hug them back.

"Hell below, Rhesa!" exclaims Althea. "You scared the living *shit* out of us!"

I smile sheepishly. "My apologies." My gaze then swiftly skips to Tallulah, and while I'm happy to see the ex-genie here, I can't help my inner curiosity.

Tally seems to sense the question in my gaze, and she shrugs as she explains with a grin, "Alastair's been crashing in your room. He caught me the day you disappeared."

I raise my brow at the deity in question, and he just shrugs at me, not looking the least bit remorseful.

Rolling my eyes, I focus on embracing my girls again, and then my brothers. Then one by one, I am bombarded with hugs from the rest of my family. The Four Horsemen and the Seven Deadly Assassins, and then Pollux appear in my line of sight.

I stop short at the sight of the archangel, and he dips his head at me with a gentle smile.

"Good to see you again, Rhesa," he drawls.

Cocking my head at him, I slowly approach him and allow him to embrace me. His wings encircle me, tickling my calves, and I feel him release a careful sigh as his arms tighten around my form.

"I know we have much to discuss—"

"*Hush*," he mutters quietly, laying his cheek on my head while nuzzling my hair, minding my horns. "Our problems aren't going anywhere. Our enemies have waited this long. They can wait a damn bit longer." He pulls back to meet my eyes, his hand coming to cup my cheek as he gives me one of his dazzling smiles. He winks at me. "Glad to have you back, darling."

I smile gently, nodding as I feel a lump form in my throat. Pollux knows it, too, then glances over my head and makes eye contact with someone. Next thing I know, the girls are beside me once more, and all four of us are disappearing down the hall and into my private chambers.

"*Ugh*, you weren't kidding," I remark as I enter my bedroom with Tally and Fern on either side of me, Althea behind me. "It does reek of Alastair in here."

Though, I know I'd be lying to myself if I said I didn't like the smell at least a *little* bit.

Tallulah giggles, then goes to sit on the edge of my bed as she glances around. "Yes, he and the others were quite *worried*."

"That's putting it mildly," quips Althea.

"More like *politely*," claims Feronia, coming near me once more to grab both my hands in hers. "Please, for our sake and everyone's sanity, *never* do that again."

I smile and wink at the unshifted wendigo. "As you wish, milady."

Fern rolls her eyes, then pulls me toward the bathing chamber and gets to work preparing a bath for me while I pull off the blanket. My eyes snag on my reflection in the mirror, and I take a minute to appreciate the multiple brandings upon my forearms, chest, thigh, and spine.

"We'll keep the males out for as long as you want," claims Althea by the doorway with Tally. "So take as long as you need."

"Surely I don't smell *that* bad?" I inquire playfully, sinking into the luxurious tub full of bubbles and petals.

"You don't," agrees Thea. "But that's only because we managed to bathe you when you had *paws*."

I flick water at the three girls, and they grin at me. However, before they run off, I admit softly, "I don't quite want to be left alone yet . . . if you three don't mind staying? I'd love to hear what you've been up to since I was otherwise occupied with *paws*."

The three of them glance at one another, then pull up stools to remain nearby. Feronia even takes up residence behind my head, beginning to run a brush through my tangled hair while massaging shampoo and conditioner into the strands. Althea and Tally sit on either side of me, explaining in enthusiastic detail the simpler things I've missed. Such as all three of them getting closer to three of the four lieutenants, too. Learning of Hell's culture and language, and indulging in self-defense training, as well as other luxuries.

"This tattoo is new," notes Althea, my left hand in hers as she fixes my nails.

I hum, glancing down at the brand I now share with Atlas. "I believe it marks where Atlas and I imprinted on one another."

Tally nods from my other side, her own attention divided between telling stories and painting my nails black and silver, too. "The court did say your bond with him was imperative in bringing you back as a woman. If you don't mind sharing, what did they really end up doing? We were aware of the gist of it, but . . ."

I sigh quietly. "Then I'm sure it's as they explained. They needed to provoke my power into surging again, thus forcing me to shift from a wolf back into a woman. And so they did."

Fern hums from behind me, her hands still busy with my hair. "You dreamed of something, right?"

"I did."

"But obviously," drawls Althea, "it wasn't a very *sweet dream* if it caused such a spike in power."

I don't mean to hesitate in answering, but I know the girls have no ulterior motives in asking me any of this. I trust that they're not asking on the males' behalf; they're just worried for me.

"It was . . . for a little bit, at least," I admit softly. "It certainly had its moments. But by the end of it, when I realized all was not right . . . no . . . it became the nightmare they needed—*that I needed*—to break free from my wolf form."

My eyes drop to Althea's plump waist, her belly no longer rounded in the way that suggests a new life may be growing within her.

I look away.

Sensing a new conversation must be had—*and I silently thank her for it*—Fern taps the delicate, sharp points of my horns as she inquires, "Do these ever get caught on anything?"

"All the fucking time." I grin, snickering gently. "For the most part, I'm pretty mindful of them . . . unless I'm drunk."

Tally grins at me. "Now *that's* a sight I would certainly pay to see."

"Pay for the first dozen drinks, and you just might," I quip.

The girls' eyes sparkle with mischief, and I find myself genuinely smiling at the sight.

CHAPTER FIFTEEN
RHESAMYRE

Surrounded by dawn's light while blood pools at my feet and a dark storm rages overhead. I stand alone with a nearly forgotten and foreign weight upon my back. My battle leathers are dark with soot and stained red, and my swords clatter to the muddy soil since my hands shake so much, thanks to my magic, adrenaline, and truthfully, my ut-ter exhaustion.

The slaughtered forms of angelic and demonic foot soldiers litter the ground, creating literal mounds *of bodies around me. Then ahead, another body twitches and rises once again. The being is like that of a highbred predator, but he bears leather wings instead of feathers. No demonic horns rip from his skull, but cursed black magic still crackles around him as he sizes me up from across the battlefield.*

"Your forces have fallen, Myra," the stranger coos, grinning. "Some Champion *you are."*

"I am not finished," I reply, though I don't quite recognize my voice. "We end this here, Apostle."

He cackles like a warlock, then raises his sword and points it at me. "Then let the stars bear witness to your fall from grace!"

I raise my chin, commanding another sword to erupt from white flames into my hands. I raise it forward and ready myself to strike as I snarl. "Your blood will stain this soil before the day is done. I vow to see it through, even if it costs me my soul."

"It will cost you a great deal more than that, little feather.*"*

....

Startling awake, I do my best not to jolt too harshly since I feel the girls still sleeping around me. They all piled into my bed last night to continue their stories, and then we eventually crashed after eating dinner on my bed, indulging in sweets, and finishing the few smutty books they had started reading to me when I was a wolf.

Slowly, I slip from the bed and do my best not to jostle their bodies too much so I can leave without them taking notice. Silently, I grab my robe and slip it over my nightgown, then exit my room and continue down the hall.

The windows are still dark as the land outside is alight with only stars and moonlight, as well as the few fires or streetlights of the city. And while the enchanted candelabras of the hallways are few and far between, I have no trouble finding my way to the throne room, where Mamba slumbers. The massive, obsidian serpent slithers awake as I pad across the polished floor toward him, and he pokes his head around the throne to watch me.

I saunter up the stairs to stroke his scales, and he leans into my touch with a gentle hiss.

"You remained a trusted friend and protector once again," I mutter. "Even though my memories are foggy at best, I remember you, too, Mamba. I'm only sorry I forgot about our friendship."

I press my forehead against his own, then sigh as I feel the hairs upon my arms stand on end as my magic flares.

"I trust you found somewhere suitable to rest since the girls and I reclaimed my bedroom?"

I glance back over my shoulder to face Alastair, who casually strides up to stand nearby with his hands stuffed inside the pockets of his loungewear. He nods at me, watching me carefully as I remain by the ancient snake.

"Your shirt's inside out," I remark, studying the seams.

He glances down at himself, then shakes his head as a corner of his lip twitches upward.

"I'll admit," he drawls lowly, "I put it on with some *haste*."

I smirk, then turn around to face him head-on with my arms crossed as I lean against the throne. I raise my brow at him. "Afraid I'll run off in the middle of the night again?" I look around the room, making a show of it. "I'm surprised to find you here alone."

"It took some convincing . . . and quite a few threats. But rest assured, my brothers are elsewhere and not eavesdropping."

I nod at him, and a heartbeat later, he begins to prowl toward me, his eyes searching for, dare I say *permission*. And when I say and do nothing in response, he takes his place directly in front of me as his hands rise to cup my cheeks. His thumbs trace my cheekbones gently as his eyes slowly trail up and down my body. However, his gaze does not burn with lust. Desire, yes, but above all, I simply observe a male who studies me as if I may disappear in front of his very eyes again. His silver gaze catches on every tiny nick or scar that paints my otherwise flawless skin, and he takes extra care to study the tattoos I bear, too. Both his own that he can see, and Atlas's.

I close my eyes, inhaling slowly to breathe him in. I hold his scent captive in my lungs and raise my hands to cup his knuckles. My skin prickles where it touches his, as though I couldn't feel anything at all prior to him.

"I'm *here*, Alastair," I mutter.

The deity named king *shutters* and takes a step closer and dips his head to press his lips against mine. Slowly at first, but as he continues to taste and feel me, his body temperature and power begin to rise. His hands move lower to grasp my waist, and he moves us until my back is against the side of the throne. His mouth devours mine, tongue tangling with mine and leading the dance despite my growls as I attempt to regain control. He snarls lightly in return, the sound all animal, while his fangs graze my lips before moving down my jaw, latching onto my neck. He sucks and nips my skin hard, then moves upward again to slip his tongue back into my mouth as if he wasn't satisfied with it the first time.

And his *scent*. While a part of me is annoyed that it lingers all around my room now, *hell below*, he smells *incredible*.

"I missed you," he husks, cursing angel names under his breath. "Fucking hell, *I missed you so much*, Rhesamyre . . . and I didn't quite realize I would until you were gone."

I grasp his cheeks to make him stop and look at me, and I smile gently before leaning forward to kiss his eyelids and the corner of his mouth. His hands tug me against him, pulling me tighter as he embraces me, and I find myself wrapping my hands around his neck and shoulders to better embrace him, too. I bury my head into his chest and inhale a few times to steady my racing heart and the magic that coils within me in need of him. My core clenches, and everything aches because all I want is to devour him, and in turn, let him devour me.

Raw. Powerful. And *mine*.

"I don't quite know what this is yet, Alastair, but I will not deny it. I won't deny myself nor you of whatever it is. Whatever we could be." I steel myself. "I want you. I want to claim you as mine."

He tenses, then pulls back to meet my eyes, the silver in them molten and swirling with magic and devotion.

"Mine," I repeat, placing my hand on his cheek again. "Whatever that may entail. Whatever may come of it. You. Are. *Mine.* Dare I say, you have been since the moment you pulled me from the river. Before then, even . . . but I wasn't completely aware of it until . . ."

"Until your dream," he supplies, cocking his head at me gently. "You . . . *dreamt of me*?"

I roll my eyes, teasing, "Is that so hard to believe?"

He shrugs a little, but he still doesn't smile. "While a part of me had hoped that may be the case, my next question would have to be what turned it into a *nightmare*?"

I open my mouth to reply, but then find myself *hesitating* again. "I dreamt of you . . . and I realized immediately what I wanted . . . but I also quickly found that it wasn't *just* you."

He furrows his brows, but thankfully, his hands don't loosen on my waist.

"I just have to remind myself now, with every step I take, that it *wasn't real*. But is it so wrong that I wanted it to be? It wasn't a nightmare at first. In the beginning, it was nearly . . . *perfect* . . . the *four* of us."

Softly, he inquires, "Do you love them?"

There is no accusation in his tone, just simple curiosity. However, I'd be a fool to miss the way he has to force himself to ask it without growling. Not *at* me, but instead, just at the *idea*.

I believe the deity is less than keen on *sharing*.

"I hardly even *know* them, Alastair," I conclude. "But a part of me, something feral and primal just *wants* them, too. But not if it means losing you. I could *never*—"

"My love," he begins, cutting me off from my inevitable rambling, and I silently thank him for it. He smiles at me gently, then presses his lips to my forehead before meeting my eyes again. "I would be lying if I said a part of me didn't expect this to happen. Whether I want to admit it or not, the four of us are connected by powers out of our control. Be it thanks to the very magic that fuels us, or something greater and stronger, I don't quite know. But you are who you are, and I would never seek to change anything about you."

A corner of his mouth quirks up. "While you may drive me absolutely *fucking* insane sometimes, I want you, too. Dare I say, I've wanted to claim you as mine since the moment I realized I no longer wanted to drive a knife through your heart, and even back then, I think I was in denial. So if keeping you happy, safe, and by my side means having my brothers nearby, too, then I suppose I can learn to *share*."

I shake my head. "But what about *your* happiness?"

He spares me a sincere smile this time, his silver eyes shining with an intimate warmth, one which I've never seen until now. "I'm speaking to her right now."

My heart does something strange in my chest, and then I smile at him. Something genuine and tender, softer in nature, which is usually not *my* nature, nor his.

"I don't know what I've done in this life to deserve you," I mutter, my fingers teasing the seam of his collar, which is still inside-out, and I can't help but smirk again at the sight.

"I have *yet* to deserve you, Rhesamyre." He grabs my hands, then presses gentle kisses to the tips of my fingers, and his eyes flare with something strange when he peers at the silver tips of my black nails. "But I vow to earn your desire every day, my queen." He spares me another look. Devious, devoted, and *dark*. "Starting now, if you'll let me."

I quirk a brow at him, but I don't stop him as he sinks to his knees. His hands grasp my thighs as he moves my nightgown out of his way, thus giving him complete access to my bare core, which seems to have a heartbeat of its own now. It has begun to *ache*, throbbing with a rhythm that sounds like a prayer, and Alastair is the name on my lips. He presses a kiss to my clit, then licks it with the tip of his tongue as he grins at me.

And then he eats me like a man starved.

"*Oh*—fuck me, *Alastair*," I snarl, my hands flying to his hair as my fingers thread through his silky, dark strands.

The devious male chuckles, lapping at me gently. His tongue is a sin in itself as he moves it between my folds, flicking my clit and fucking my entrance. He kisses and sucks on me, tugging gently with his teeth and nibbling on my clit before lapping away the sting of his antics.

"That is the plan, my love," he husks, but I honestly can't even recall what I had said earlier that demanded a reply.

He doesn't stop his assault until I've come at least twice on his tongue, incorporating his thick fingers to stroke my inner walls that flutter and flex around his thick digits. Then he finally rises again to pull down his trousers, line his hard length up with my entrance, and sink deep inside me. He's slow on purpose, letting me feel and appreciate the stretch and fullness, and once he's fully seated inside, he growls and pulls out once more, before slamming all the way to the hilt. A growl tears from his lips, and I clench down on his cock as it throbs deep inside of me.

I inhale swiftly when he hoists me up by my thighs, further pressing me against the throne and nearly over the entirety of the seat as he thrusts into me. I reach back to brace myself against the armrest, ready to match his pace and give him as much pleasure as he is me. His growls and groans fill the otherwise silent room, and my little gasps and moans seem to only encourage him.

"Mine," he snarls in Old Latin, thrusting harder to punctuate his claim. *"Mine."*

I smile, kissing him as our hips move in sync. *"Yours,"* I snarl, nipping at his lip and sucking on the blood I draw.

He comes with a roar, and I tumble over the edge of pleasure not long after him.

....

"You were a picky eater as a wolf," drawls Atlas gently, sitting across from me while sipping his tea and watching me devour a multitude of goodies for breakfast. A strange look passes over his eyes, and I can't tell if it's intrigue or irritation. "It was often a challenge to get you to eat, to say the least."

Atticus chuckles quietly, nearly scoffing as he quips under his breath, "Obviously that's not the case now. *Glutton.*"

From somewhere further down the table, Gluttony releases a low growl in warning. Meanwhile, I just glare at the youngest deity from over my plate, shoving another forkful of stuffed crepes into my mouth. I throw my butter knife at him, and the damn deity catches it. Then proceeds to use it to smear strawberry jam onto his biscuit.

I'm about to launch across the table at him, but Alastair's hand on my thigh reminds me to stay seated. His fingers weave between my skirts to delicately trace the fern pattern that brands my skin, and his hand flexes on my thigh, pinching the meat there in warning.

The Hellion Court's table in the dining hall is full of my uncles, as well as my brothers and the girls, too. Plus, while Alastair sits next to me, Pollux occupies my other side, thus leaving Atticus and Atlas to sit in front of me. The hall is loud with the chatter of other demons, all of whom were both startled and relieved to see me stride in this morning on Alastair's arm, dressed in one of my favorite gowns and properly armed to the teeth with obsidian.

Plenty have come up to me this morning to welcome me home, including Dexter, as well as share their sympathies and condolences for the passing of our late king.

Dad.

Slowly, I place down my fork and wipe my mouth gracefully, losing my appetite at the thought of him. Most of my family members clock the action but say nothing and continue with their own individual conversations across the table.

Clearing his throat, Alastair drawls from beside me, "When you're ready, I have a surprise for you."

I quirk a brow at him, smirking as I mock, "A *surprise*?"

He shrugs. "Well, I believe you'll certainly *be surprised* when you see them, anyway."

I raise my other brow at him this time, and he chuckles quietly. Rising from his chair, he extends his hand for me. I take it, and none of my immediate family members say anything as he leads me away, nor do they seem to care too much, knowing I'm safe with him. However, I don't miss the way Atlas and Atticus tense as I take my leave. The former simply takes another sip from his teacup, though I notice his tatted knuckles are whiter than usual. The latter, however, nearly breaks the stone table because he's gripping it so hard.

Someone chuckles at the sight—Pollux, I believe.

I ignore them, continuing out of the room on Alastair's arm as he leads me down the halls. Then eventually, he leads me *down* into the lower caverns, where a few of our *nicer* prison cells lie. Before I can question him, we halt in front of the bars of our largest confines, and I blink in surprise at the sight of five dire wolves, which slumber on straw mats on top of one another.

"The Soldiers of Sorrow," I muse. "They didn't shift back when I did."

Alastair shakes his head, and the wolves begin to stir awake at the sound of my voice. They whine and approach the bars when they spot me, and I kneel down to rub the darkest wolf's ears as he sits and studies me silently.

"I would suspect since they weren't caught up in your second show of power, they remained in this form instead of shifting back with you."

I nod. "I suppose that makes enough sense. Though, they weren't quite *anything* beforehand, either."

Alastair shrugs. "Merely the embodiments of grief and ancient power. Magic, which is similar in nature to yours. You are their master now."

I hum. "I do recall them following me around. What of the rest of the wolves and hellhounds I acquired when I had *paws*?"

"Cerberus and Orthrus have since returned to their rightful posts, as have the rest of the pack you gathered, and you gathered *a lot*. Or, I suppose, it would be more accurate to say they gathered around *you*."

I lift my shoulders. "I would love to give you an explanation as to why, but unfortunately, even I'm at a loss for that one. My memories of my time as a *dog* are . . . *suspect*. I remember most of it, but some incidents stick out more than others. Such as Atlas . . . and Lilith."

"Do you remember your time with the witch and archangels?"

I exhale quietly. "Would you prefer it if I said yes or no?"

"I would prefer the truth. Assuming you're willing to give it to me."

I glance back over my shoulder to meet his steeled gaze while I'm still crouched before the wolves. "I remember what they did to me, and in turn, what Atlas had to do in order to heal me. Pollux's brothers didn't agree with Apollo's methods. They wanted to save me, but I snapped before they could."

Alastair dips his chin. "Pollux mentioned as much."

"I killed Lilith."

He nods.

"And when I erupted before that. Adriel, too."

Another nod.

"Apollo still lives, despite my best efforts."

"Rest assured, love. When you're ready, he won't be living for much longer."

I dip my chin. Then turn my gaze back to the wolves as I sigh and rise to stand beside Alastair again. "Well, what should we do with them now?"

"That remains up to you. To be honest, I am unsure if they can even be *slain*. As I mentioned beforehand, they are derived from raw magic, and it is thanks to both of our states of mind at the times of our eruptions that they were given such forms. First warriors, and now wolves."

I hum in agreement. "Then perhaps they can merely bo *repurposed* again. They seem keen to follow my orders."

"I agree."

Nodding, I step forward to place my hand against the cell's door in order to unlock it. After muttering commands, it swings open, and the wolves stand at attention as they watch Alastair and I warily.

"Then for now," I conclude, "I believe it only fitting to introduce them to the court as proper members. *Guard dogs,* if you will. We can never have too many of those running around. Beasts loyal to Hell and my court alone, and ready to butcher our enemies on my command."

Alastair chuckles. "An enticing purpose, indeed."

"Do they have names?"

"Not unless you consider what *grief* is as their names."

I shake my head. "Denial, anger, bargaining, depression, and acceptance." I wink at my mate. "I do believe we can do better than that."

Crouching again and holding my hand out to the nearest wolf once more, the dark beast prowls forward cautiously to sniff my hand, and then he licks my fingers and whines. All five of them share the same silver eyes that shine with something supernatural and primal, but their fur colors range from ebony to shades of light gray.

This one is completely black, and I name him *Veto.*

The next is a sooty dark gray, and he becomes *Vex.*

The third *Barter*, and the fourth *Dolor.*

The fifth is the lightest in color, nearly white, and I name him *Embrace.*

"Rhesa, your *hand.*"

I glance down at my left hand, noticing the five delicate paw prints that now brand my knuckles directly on top of my fingers and thumb. Looking at the wolves again, they watch me just as intently as their eyes change color. Now, one of their eyes remains silver, while the other changes to obsidian.

Rhesamyre,

Very well, sweet spice.
Then remind them, I shall.
I hope for your sake you don't regret this. You think
you're a challenging creature to get along with? I hold
the fucking record. You'll be no different than the
rest, I'm afraid. And I look forward to proving as
much.
But a promise is a promise, so with that said, I believe
I'll be seeing you sooner rather than later.

Until then,
Atticus

CHAPTER SIXTEEN
RHESAMYRE

"Are you ready?"

Glancing at Althea through my vanity's mirror, I nod at her, Fern, and Tally.

Steeling myself, I quip, "I was born ready."

The girls smirk at me, then step to the side and bow their heads. Though I would never expect them to, nor demand it, they know when to overshow their respect for not only me, but my title. One which will be made official and well-known throughout all the spheres today.

We're dressed to the nines in hellion garments and gowns, and I don my own obsidian gown, jewels, and blades, too. Dressed both to kill and to rule.

The girls follow my lead out of my bedchamber where the lieutenants stand on guard in the hall to escort us to the throne room. Each of their black leathers and weaponry is polished to perfection, and while their gazes are steeled, the lingering glow of excitement behind their eyes is easy to spot when they study us walking toward them.

We strut down the hallways that are lined with hellion foot soldiers, and upon entering the throne room, all chatter ceases immediately. Subjects and soldiers of hell crowd the space, and I don't miss the way a few lords and ladies make an attempt to size me up. I *almost* grin. And as I strut in my heels, I allow my power to prowl forward ahead of me.

Many fall to their knees with the first wave, and I don't bother to stifle my feral grin at that.

My family stands upon the steps of the dais, staggered in heights, along with Pollux and the deities, before the Obsidian Throne, where Mamba slithers, head raised above the back of the chair to watch me as I approach, his beady eyes revealing nothing. As I near the stairs, the lieutenants and our girls veer off to take their places by the sides near my newest wolves, and I halt just before the first step.

Gracefully, I kneel before Mamba and the throne, then lower my head and horns out of respect for the ancient predator. A steady stride clicks across the floor toward me, and polished shoes come into my line of sight as a delicate but honorable weight is placed upon my head.

The Obsidian Crown, freshly forged to mimic the late king's.

"Rise, Queen Rhesamyre of Hell," begins General Death. "Rightful Heir to the Obsidian Throne, Daughter of the Devil, and Protector of the First Sphere. May your reign be of fire and obsidian. Justice and truth. And may our enemies know the strength of Hell's wrath when you invoke your fury upon them."

I rise as instructed, stroll up the dais, and take my rightful place upon the Obsidian Throne.

"All hail, Queen Rhesamyre!" shouts General War. "Queen of Hell! Long live the queen!"

The entire throne room echoes War's chant while either throwing their fists up or placing their hands against their chests and hearts. My family does the same, as do Pollux and my deities, joyous, feral grins outshining their scowls and steeled gazes as pride stakes a claim in all of their eyes, even that of Atticus, though I know he'll never admit it.

With impeccable posture and crackling, dark magic, I'm aware of my wicked smirk as I survey my court and many subjects kneeling before me. Outside the windows and balconies of the throne room, the rest of my kingdom rejoices as I am finally crowned their queen.

....

The crypt below the palace is not grungy by any means but is instead polished and alight with enchanted candelabras atop many of the plaques and columbarium spaces. Tombs line the walls and inner rooms, revealing family names and graves of hellion origins that date back thousands of centuries ago. No flowers bloom down here as they would in proper cemeteries, but offerings still line the walls and shelves where the dead may be honored all the same.

I stop before the vast mouth of the cavern, where a mighty stone snake curls around the next entrance. Then, with a steady heart, I stride through to observe the tomb where my father rests.

His sarcophagus shines in the enchanted lights like black magic, and atop the black stone are numerous inscriptions in Old Latin depicting his greatest achievements in history, his namesakes, familial ties, and even how he was slain.

I slide my eyes away from the elegant coffin and peer upward at the life-sized stone statue that watches over his eternal resting place. His wings are raised at his back, leathers and weapons are on display, and a familiar dagger is clutched in his interlocked hands. Atop his head, his own crown glitters in the lights, with gems of obsidian embedded into the stone. Mine is far more delicate in nature than his, but just as luxurious, perhaps even more so since it's littered with more gems and spikes than his was.

"You may have named me your heir," I murmur, "but this crown was never meant to find a permanent home atop my head. At least, certainly not this soon."

Silence remains my only answer, and I will my heart not to ache with the lack of a reply.

"I will rule," I continue. "But don't expect me to be happy about it. Not when you were supposed to remain king for a great deal longer than this. Perhaps even for all of eternity."

Without having a reason behind my actions, I stroke his stone face. "*Traitor.*"

My chest *hurts*, and there's a lump in my throat that causes my voice to ache. I back away from his silent statue, trailing my fingers upon the stone of his coffin as I turn away.

Uncle Death is there to greet me.

"The coronation festivities are still in full swing," he drawls, brows furrowed as he watches me with pensive, dark eyes. "Everyone wondered where you ran off to but knew better than to follow. Which is saying quite a lot. I hope you're proud."

I shrug gracefully, ignoring his comment, which is no doubt about the Three Kings. "I had yet to come down here. Would you think it weak of me to admit I wasn't ready?"

He shakes his head, pushing off the wall to stand before me in just a few strides. "Never. But if I may inquire, why now?"

My fingers still dance over the inscriptions upon his tomb, tracing Samael's name. "He was the king, and now I'm the queen. It felt as good a time as any. One crown exchanged for another as I take a seat upon his throne, preparing to rule a kingdom he called his own for a few centuries." I meet my uncle's soft gaze, and I'm thankful when I don't find any judgment or pity in his eyes. "Can you . . . " I swallow hard. "Is he at peace wherever he is?"

Death sighs quietly, raising his hand to brush my cheek gently. "You know as well as I that I am forbidden from revealing the whereabouts of the dead."

"You've done it for me before."

He nods. "I've allowed them temporary passage back to this sphere in order to commune with those you and I chose, but they were lighter souls. Know that he dreams of you, Rhesa. Of us and Hell. *That* is his peace. His eternal dream. And though difficult, it would be wiser to leave him be."

Death's thumbs brush under my eyes gently, gathering the unshed tears there. "He loved you beyond reason, baby girl. And he . . ." Death stalls, and while I knew Sam's death had hit them all like an arrow to the heart, watching Death struggle to form words only proves that he was much beloved and will be dearly missed. "When I ferried his soul to the other side, he made me promise once again to always protect you. To remain by your side." Death chuckles, though the sound is strained and grim. "Foolish male. I would have done it anyway without the order. We all would have, and we will continue to do so for as long as we are able."

I nod. "I know." And I do. I trust them all with my life and more. I steel myself. "When I was in that place, that near-perfect dream, he was alive again. He and the entire court were there, as well as the archangels and a few others I consider enemies. But Dad, though a figment of my imagination, called me something else. A name I had once forgotten. I didn't will that to fruition. Maybe deep down, I did unintentionally, but if it was meant to be the perfect world, then I never would've wanted to hear that ancient name uttered aloud again. *Never* . . . never did I want to be called that again."

I meet Death's gaze, and his steeled expression is that of professionalism. He is both the general and the lord. A Horseman. The Grim Reaper.

"How would that have been possible, Death?" I inquire, the accusation thick on my tongue.

His tone is cautious. "Even in death, your father remains the best at bargaining. At finding compromises . . . It could stand to reason that through some odd and ancient spellwork, he found a way to communicate with you as you dreamed. Perhaps because your dream was a mirror image of his own."

"But the only way he would have been able to bargain to see me again, even in death, would be by *bargaining* with *you* . . . so tell me you didn't."

That cursed silence settles between us once more, and I take a step back until my hip hits the side of the coffin. I raise my chin. "You can no longer communicate with him because he no longer remains in the Umbra Mundi. So where is my dad, *our king*, Death?"

He sets his jaw, a muscle fluttering there. "He has since returned to where he once derived from. In order to see you one last time, he bargained to give up his place in the afterlife. He did it to aid you in getting out of your entrapment."

"*And you let him?*" I snarl. "What did you demand in return?"

"His soul was a heavy one. I refused him at first, but then he offered up something greater that even I couldn't refuse, and the *damned male knew it.*"

I raise my brow at him, and Death sighs quietly, nearly snarling as he replies, "*The truth.*"

I blink at him.

"The truth about *you*, Rhesamyre," he stresses, sounding exhausted. "He offered me the memories he had only just recovered since *dying*. When his life flashed before him one final time, it came back complete and intact, and I have since been made aware of who and *what* you truly are again. What and who you once were to *all* the spheres. Whatever cursed spellwork you once used has since fallen away from my own mind again, *and I remember you*."

He takes a step toward me, but whatever he finds in my eyes makes him think better of it, and he stands back again.

"My next question would have to be who else knows?" he inquires.

I'm silent for a heartbeat, my gaze unyielding. "Pollux figured it out long ago, no doubt thanks to his own abilities and allies. And Draven and Wicker have since been made aware, as has Kure."

Death nods. "But the deities still don't know."

"No."

"And how long do you plan to keep it that way?"

"I'm afraid for not much longer. Time seems to be of the essence now, and I'm running out of it. I need to gather allies once again. An *army*."

"You *have* one. You command the entirety of the hellion militia."

I shake my head. "It won't be enough. It was barely enough the first time, and most of the foot soldiers then merely served as monster fodder for the Apostles' cursed regiments. I barely had enough time to . . ."

He narrows his eyes at me. "Sacrifice yourself for our survival?" he drawls darkly.

I incline my head, teeth clenched. "So it would seem. Samael has since returned to the origin of the archangels. Somewhere so far into the Yonder Star that not even you can track him down now, is that what you're telling me?"

Death nods once more, finally stepping up to me. He doesn't touch me again, though I know he wants to. Original memories or not, I've still been raised by this male for the past few centuries. I've called him and the others my uncles and family, and that's not about to change now.

Our bonds are stronger now.

Seeming to sense my shift in thoughts, Death gently grasps my face and inclines his head. "This does not change who you are *now*. Who you have since become to me. *Us.* Hell still belongs to you, as does its court. We're still family, Rhesa . . . assuming you still prefer to be called that."

I place my hands over his, offering him a gentle smile. "I do. I want to keep the name Samael gave me."

Death nods. "Then keep it, you shall. You'll keep it all. Everything he gave you and left for you. I know he doesn't regret anything, Rhesamyre. His conscious was clear."

I dip my chin, finding that I'm truly grateful to hear that. Death leans forward and kisses my forehead, and when he leans back again, his eyes are clear with resolve.

Needing a segue, I ask, "Whatever happened to the Zodiac Blade?"

"We buried it with him. And the chalice and mirror are safe in our vaults, too."

I raise my brow at that but then nod along in agreement. "Perhaps that is for the best, considering the circumstances to come. And even afterward, I believe the phenomenon is referred to as *mutually assured destruction.* Never mind the mirror and cup, but if we keep the blade in rotation, then it could end up in the wrong hands again. Be it an archangel's . . . or an Apostle's."

Death nods. "How long do we have?"

I shrug. "To be honest, I'm not sure. Most likely not long enough, but if we want a better idea, then Kure will be the one we want to speak with. He's another one that infiltrated my dreamscape to aid me in freeing myself."

"If you'll let me, I would like to speak to him on your behalf."

I go to argue, but Death cuts me off. "This is the job of your council and court, my queen. Please, let me do this for you, as you have other pressing matters to address, such as informing everyone else of the situation at hand. The threats upon the horizon."

Despite where we are, I allow a soft snicker to slip through. "As usual, Uncle, your reasoning is sound."

Death merely grins at me, but as I recall what else has occurred, I find it hard to return the smile.

"We need to discuss the *other one*," I prompt.

"We do, though I don't exactly know who or *what* it is. I have a suspicion, but nothing more. Nothing to back up my findings, even with my original memories of what happened long before."

"It spoke to Alastair in Ursa Major."

"He mentioned as much. And it spoke to Atlas, too."

I hum. "From what I recall of the interaction between Alastair and *it*, it claims that the deities and I are carved from the same sun. The same source of magic. Our souls seek solace with one another."

Death nods. "That is what we've gathered, as well. When it would pop up here and there when you were younger—*well*, as a child in our care—it would seek to know you were safe with us. Once satisfied with our vows, it would disappear again. No names or schemes exchanged, only unyielding loyalty."

I inhale carefully. "I think I know what it is. It has hinted at it a few times now. First to Alastair, and then to Atlas, too. It *knows* things. It called me its *Champion*."

He nods again. "I know."

"Then do we dare utter its name?"

He hesitates, but then slowly shakes his head. "I don't believe we should. It is a raw magic I have very little knowledge of. And we know better than to trifle with such powers that we have no understanding of. There is a reason it was once called *forbidden*."

I nod, exhaling a breath I hadn't realized I had been holding. "It doesn't seek to harm me, nor any of you. Only our enemies."

"That, too, is something I have gathered. And though I hate it for you, I believe we are safe from whatever prowls beneath your skin. It has rested there since you were reborn and appears as though it shall remain."

"I agree."

"Then we shall let it lie still."

"We shall."

Uncle Death bows his head, then reaches for me. And with one final glance at my father's statue, I take my leave on Death's arm.

·················

Heading back to my bedchamber alone, I slowly start to pull my jewelry from my hair and ears as my heels hang from my fingers, thus leaving me barefoot and silent. Alastair has promised he'd be along, but I know better than to pull him away from the fun he is having with the rest of the court, playing drinking games. Though he'll probably never admit it, I know he is enjoying himself with the Horsemen and assassins despite his scowl.

The lieutenants ran off with the girls earlier in the evening, hitting the town, which still rejoices and celebrates my coronation. Although Malcolm has yet to claim a female of his own, he still enjoys his time with his boys and soldiers. It wouldn't surprise me if he's balls deep in one of the pleasure houses at this moment, as he's always been a favorite amongst the whores.

I don't blame the females, either. Malcolm is quite the lovemaker.

Turning down my hallway, I stop short when my power flares in warning, and I spin around with a dagger in hand to swipe at the intruder.

He chuckles, clashing steel with obsidian as he quips, "I'm surprised you can still manage to twirl like that. Considering how *drunk* you are."

I snarl at Atticus. "And I suppose the only time you have the *balls* to approach me *alone* is when *you're* drunk."

Atticus grins at me, then knocks my dagger out of my hand and reaches out to grab me. I spin out of his reach, but he catches me around my waist again. Growling when he laughs, I elbow him in the ribs, then spin again to pull my knee up to his crotch. With startling ease, he catches my knee and then proceeds to back me into the nearest wall. I slap him, my rings cutting his cheek in the process as his head snaps to the side. His jaw works as he reins in his rising power, and his emerald eyes *smolder* with hostility as he sizes me up.

"*Let. Go,*" I seethe. "Otherwise, a cut cheek will be the least of your concerns."

"We need to have a little chat, *my queen.*"

"Whatever it is, it can damn well wait till morning. I'm exhausted and need my beauty sleep."

"It's hard enough as it is. I don't need you to get any *prettier.*"

I blink at him. "*What?*"

He scowls at me. "Don't get all modest on me now, Your Majesty."

"Modesty is the last thing I concern myself with." I attempt to free myself again, but he catches my hands and presses them into the wall above my head. I growl. He grins. "*Fine.* My attention is all yours, *Chaos.* What do you want?"

"Such a convoluted question to answer, so let's address your first statement, shall we? The issue here, aside from you basically *ignoring* me, is that your attention is *not* all *mine.*"

I grin, leaning forward to whisper against his lips. "*Jealous?*"

"A *bit,*" he snarls. "Which now brings us to what I *want . . . .*" Some of that ferocity leaves his gaze as he stares at me, his eyes shifting all over my face as he studies the shape of my lips, horns, and ears.

In turn, I do the same to him and note the way he braids half his hair since the other half remains shaved off to better reveal his *entropy* brand above his right ear. The inscription is surrounded by the rest of his tattoos, which feature chains, thorns, and wicked mandala patterns, too. All three deities' tattoos are similar in nature and design, but each has a subtle difference about them that is nearly nonexistent at first glance.

"And what do you want, Atticus?" I inquire softly, meeting his gaze again.

He's silent for a heartbeat. "What would you do if I said *you?*"

"I would say that the prospect is undoubtedly tempting and can certainly be up for discussion. Though I would like us to be *sober* if at all possible."

"My resolve has never been clearer."

I hum. "I think I believe you. Very well. Why should I entertain the idea of an *us?* Especially since I already have your older brother to warm my bed? In addition to Atlas's unyielding loyalty, as well."

He ignores my taunt and raises his hand to trail his fingers over my cheekbone and down to my lips, then he grasps my chin gently to better press his thumb against my bottom lip. He forces his thumb into my mouth and over my tongue, and I swallow hard as my core clenches at his show of dominance.

"Alastair is certainly a proper gentleman and will remain loyal and *yours* until you kick him to the streets," he drawls huskily, his gaze transfixed on his thumb in my mouth as his nostrils flare, no doubt scenting my arousal. "And even then, he'll stay close by for a few decades to ensure you're safe. He's steady, far more cool-headed than I am. And a powerful wall that will always be at your back. He's . . . your *faith,* if you will."

"Meanwhile, Atlas remains softer in nature, but that mother-fucker will *absolutely tear someone apart* in a *heartbeat* if it means keeping you safe. I dare say you've already seen a glimpse of that underlying *ruthlessness* firsthand. The one he tries so hard in vain to hide nowadays, because he fears admitting to himself once again just how much he actually enjoys the bloodshed. He's the gentle one. Until he isn't. The kinder hand you often need without realizing it. And though you'll never admit it, you need him around when you feel vulnerable, because he's your *strength*. And he'll always be by your side, whether you want him there or not."

Atticus gives me a devilish grin. "But you have two sides, sweet spice. And if you'll entertain the idea for at least a little while, then I would like to occupy that other side. For I can serve as whatever you may need. Be it a friend, a lover, or an outlet. On the days you need to rage and rant, I'm happy to listen or brawl. Other times, should you find yourself in need of another male to *warm your bed*, then I am happy to fill that role, too." His thumb presses down harder on my tongue. "I'm happy to fill *you*."

He cocks his head at me, his gaze surprisingly gentle despite the underlying threat that often occupies his tone of voice. "I can be whatever you need me to be, Rhesa. In my own way, to the best of my ability, I will fulfill the duties bestowed upon me. And then when you come to trust me, and perhaps even *love* me, then we can discuss just how truly different I am from my brothers when it comes to *pleasure*."

He pulls his thumb from my mouth, and I inhale deeply, capturing his scent.

"*Pleasure*?" I breathe.

He smirks. "Yes, sweet spice. The pleasure I want to give you will be like *nothing* you've ever felt before. Alastair may play rough, but he doesn't enjoy the same wide range of *pleasantries* that I do, and Atlas is far too *vanilla* for his own good. Though with you, I would suspect that may change."

He leans closer to my ear, licking the pointed shell of it as he husks, "I want you to show me your chaos, but surrender your control."

I can't help the primal *shiver* that races down my spine at the raw *promise* in his words, and my core clenches and throbs again. Atticus leans back to meet my gaze once more, and a handsome, wicked smirk plays on his lips as he no doubt senses and scents where my thoughts have drifted.

"May I seduce you, sweet spice?" he teases, leaning down so he may lick my lips.

Finding my voice, I mutter, "You can try."

Atticus grins and then presses his lips against mine.

His kiss is different than Alastair's. While Alastair is just as dominating and commanding when he kisses, Atticus feels as though he's attempting to suck my soul from my body. Not to mention, just as his scent is different, he tastes different, too. Alastair is smokier in nature, but Atticus is almost *tart*. However, there is still a thick sweetness that cuts back the sour, and it's molten and addicting and unholy and just *lovely*.

He wraps his hand around my throat, pressing on my pulse points just enough to have me gasping against his mouth as he positions my head where he wants it. His tongue explores my mouth, poking my cheeks and running along my fangs to cut himself so his blood mingles with our breaths.

Then after feeling satisfied that he's tasted every inch of my mouth, he pulls away. No sly grin adorns his handsome features. And instead of a teasing glint in his eyes, I only find *lust*, but the beast is barely caged and nearly *unhinged*.

"That's going to be addictive," he husks.

I nod, breathing deeply. "I agree, but before you become an addict for me," I drawl, and his eyes brighten again at the underlying promise of *more* that I lay between us, "I would like to use you for a personal side quest of mine."

He cocks his head at me, and I can almost physically see when he sobers up from the lustful haze that had staked a claim over his eyes and mind. "What do you need, sweet spice?"

"You're probably not going to like it."

"Out with it, Rhesamyre."

I almost grin. "I would like to retrieve something that once belonged to you and your brothers, though while I know *where* it is, I don't exactly know *what* it is."

"Does *it* have a name?"

"The Reverie."

Atticus leans away from me, that familiar, playful glint in his eye completely extinguished now. And it dawns on me that his hand is still wrapped around my throat, and he squeezes gently before seeming to realize the same thing.

He drops his hand.

"How do you know of that? Why do you want it?" He almost snarls but seems to catch himself before he does.

"It once belonged to you and your brothers, and I learned of its whereabouts through Andrew with Alastair. Your brother seems to entertain the notion of getting it back." I narrow my eyes. "But evidently, you don't."

"I don't see the appeal in having it back."

"And what exactly *is it*?"

Atticus doesn't appear as though he's going to answer at first, but I don't yield.

"An enchanted tome that my brothers and I once shared before and during the Wild Hunt. We could write journal entries into it from anywhere within the spheres, and it served as a . . . *peace offering* between the three of us. A reminder that we were still blood even if we were fighting on different fronts, sometimes against each other. It was a way for us to be honest with ourselves and each other. To voice what we were seeing and doing no matter how . . . *horrendous*."

I nod carefully, keeping ahold of his gaze. "Alastair mentioned it was stolen."

He dips his chin, his hand rising once more, this time resting on my cheek as he gently cups the side of my face. "Like most things, it happened after the Great Betrayal. Only a few beings knew of its existence and sought to steal it in order to find a potential weakness of ours that would kill us. But the Reverie doesn't actually hold such information, and I would imagine it was discarded somewhere and left to rot."

"It lies in the arachnid's den."

Atticus raises his brow, nodding carefully. "And retrieving it . . . would that make you happy?"

I shrug gracefully. "Admittedly, I was hoping it would make Alastair, you, and Atlas happy. Though judging by your reaction, I'm thinking now it would do more harm than good."

"I have my own issues with the Reverie, but I do not believe my brothers share the same sentiments. And though they may not admit it, I do believe they would appreciate having it back. Alastair already mentioned he knew where it was, though he didn't mention *how* or that you knew of it, too. If this is something you wish to pursue, then I would rather go with you than have you face the arachnid alone."

I offer him an appreciative smile, and he smirks at me.

"Then we best get going," he claims, then *winks*. "Let's make it a bloody date, sweet spice."

I laugh, and his eyes brighten again as he watches me smile.

CHAPTER SEVENTEEN
RHESAMYRE

The arachnid's den isn't found in the Forbidden Cities like one would suspect. Instead, the overgrown spider lives in the intricate, twisted cave systems of the Hollow, hunting and feasting on those who attempt to break into the heavily warded castles of the Wise Men. The tunnels weave and bend beneath the structures, and the arachnid's webbing plagues the mouth of the closest cave that we stand a few feet ahead of.

We opened a conveyance as close as we could to the den without setting off the wards, and now Atticus and I crouch in the woodwork, watching the cave and listening for the monster that calls it home. Darkness encompasses all the land as stars flicker overhead, but thanks to our magic, Atticus and I can spy on the cave with little trouble.

"Have you ever dealt with this monster before?" inquires Atticus quietly.

"Nope. You?"

"Nope."

"Spectacular."

He spares me a sly grin. "Still time to turn back, my queen."

I rise from my crouch, my hellion leathers hugging my curves as I prowl forward. He huffs a quiet laugh from behind me, murmuring an *okay, then.*

He keeps pace beside me with ease, and we're mindful of the layers of webbing that stretch across the ground below our boots as we enter the cave. The darkness is all-consuming, but we know better than to reach out to touch the walls for balance and direction, lest we desire to attract the arachnid by tripping one of its many silk lines.

"Do you know how to locate it?" I inquire softly, prowling forward with my daggers ready.

"I'm homing in on it as we speak," he mutters just as quietly.

Nodding, I slow my pace to let him take the lead, and he brushes my side gently as he passes me. All is silent as we continue through the cave littered with sticky webbing, and a few smaller spiders crawl and watch us with their many eyes, too. Some are no bigger than my fingernail, while others are closer in size to my whole hand or my head. All range in colors and breeds, but I'm sure they all have one thing in common:

They're underlings of the arachnid.

Another line of defense on top of the webbing and wards.

Atticus halts when we come to a fork in the tunnels, and he cocks his head for a moment as if listening for something. I turn my back to his, pressing against him as I watch our six, and I can swear the spiders are drawing nearer. Then, I feel him reach back and tap my side, and I turn again when he starts walking once more.

Larger lumps in the webbing begin to line the walls or hang from the ceiling, and I would suspect them to be *bodies*. Foolish hunters who attempted to break into the Hollow by way of these tunnels, only to be met with a horrifying, gruesome death by way of the arachnid.

Some look more like egg sacks, though.

Atticus halts again, and I stop right behind him. He glances back over his shoulder at me, then points to his ear and presses a finger against his lips. I nod and listen, and a heartbeat later, I hear it.

The near-silent shuffling of limbs. Very *large* limbs.

Willing my heartbeat to stay quiet and steady, we continue on, raising our knees higher to step over the bundled bodies that litter the ground. Atticus holds his arm out for me, and I don't bother arguing with him as I use him to balance and climb over a larger lump. Truthfully, I need the hand, as his legs are much longer than mine, and that particular lump of webbing was much bigger than the rest.

I can only imagine what sort of other monsters have fallen victim to the arachnid.

However, before Atticus proceeds onward, he stands directly in front of me as I halt before him. I cock my head at him, but then my vision refocuses, and I watch as an overgrown black widow descends between us on a thin line of silk. We both watch it as it just hangs between us, swaying gently before scurrying back up to the ceiling. We track it, and I nearly *shutter* at the sight of the thousands of spiders that cover and crawl across the ceiling. Little legs tangle and twitch, and everything is *furry*.

I look at Atticus, and with a steeled expression, he just nods and turns around again. I clench my jaw and stay close, following him into yet another open cavern littered with dozens more tunnels that lie within the walls and ceiling. However, while I scan our surroundings, Atticus keeps his attention on the floor as he searches the thick webbing. Then finally, he seems to home in on the Reverie and crouches to better see it between the few lumps of other bodies and objects that are covered in the sticky threads.

I take note of the other egg sacks and web-covered skeletons belonging to people and other animals, but as I trail my eyes upward toward the ceiling again, I still as I meet the multiple eyes of the arachnid. It just sits up there, watching us as its fangs twitch, and *fucking hell*, that is a *big-ass spider.*

Easily bigger than Orpheus, those eight fuzzy legs are equipped with barbs and claws, too. Carefully, I place my hand back on Atticus's shoulder, and he stills beneath my hand before rising at my back.

I feel his tense chest brush against my shoulders, but out of the corner of my eye, I also know he pockets the Reverie into an inner pouch of his leathers. Then slowly, he puts pressure on my lower back, and I take a careful step forward.

That seems to greatly insult the arachnid, and the massive spider shrieks before dropping from the ceiling. Atticus roars at me to *fucking run*, and not needing to be told twice, I bolt. He keeps pace with me right on my heels as we book it through the tunnels, and I'm thankful I memorized the way since I'm in front now, leaping over lumps and sacks and dodging falling spiders as they drop onto my shoulders and hair. I brush them off, running faster as I hear Atticus snarl and growl a few commands of fire alchemy.

Whatever he does back there seems to royally piss off the arachnid, and as it screeches again, the tunnels shudder and quake as if they're about to close in on us. I finally catch sight of the exit ahead, though I no longer feel Atticus at my back.

Risking a glance behind me, I find that he has slowed a step, his leathers torn near his ribs as blood drips from a fresh wound, and his breathing already sounds labored.

Shit.

Spinning on my heel, I turn back for him, and I'm faced with why the arachnid is now so enraged.

He set it on *fucking fire.*

I slide up beside him and grab his arm to wrap it around my shoulders as the arachnid gains on us again, and we hobble toward the exit, his entire weight pressing on me and slowing us down, but I don't stop. Not until I feel the arachnid's breath as it reaches for me, and trusting Atticus to remain upright for a heartbeat, I spin and kick outward, successfully startling the arachnid and making it pause to avoid getting hit by my feet and the daggers I throw at it.

That's all the time I need to haul Atticus out of the creepy-crawly cave and back out into the open again. The arachnid doesn't follow much further once we're in the woods, and I spin just in time to watch it lurk in the mouth of the cave, snarling and twitching before receding into the darkness completely.

Not trusting it to stay there, I pull Atticus with me as we pass the last of the wards, and then I open a conveyance back into the woods of Hell since I—*selfishly*—don't feel like explaining this to his brothers quite yet.

Atticus finally collapses, sensing we're out of danger, and I attempt to catch him and lean him against the nearest tree. He winces and does his best to suppress his groans of pain, and I get to work surveying the extent of his injury. Pulling his leathers up, I find the slash on his lower ribs isn't too deep, but I'm more concerned about the venom now coursing through his veins.

So, with a calm breath, I lean toward the bloody wound and begin to mutter my commands to heal him and draw out the venom. However, the venom will need somewhere to go first if I am to magically draw it out of him, so I open my mouth, ready to devour his pain.

Weakly, he presses on my shoulders to get me to stop, muttering my name in a pain-filled haze, but I ignore him as I press my lips to his wound to lick, suck, and command his and my magic to heal him despite the venom's paralyzing effects. The vile taste of his infected blood assaults my tongue, and I nearly gag, but I gather it all into my mouth before spitting it out. Then again, I repeat the process until he is free of pain and nothing but an inscription remains over and intertwined within the already tatted skin of his lower ribs.

A familiar burn begins to prickle across my left hip bone, and I would imagine the word *truculent* now brands my skin, symbolizing the bargain I made with his magic to heal him and expel the venom I took from him.

On my hands and knees, I crawl away from him, allowing myself to breathe heavily and heave up the contents of my own stomach as my gag reflex takes over from tasting the venom. A steady hand rubs along my back, coming to rest on the nape of my neck, and I glance over to meet Atticus's emerald eyes. His chest still rises and falls deeply, but his eyes are clear and free of pain as he surveys my form.

I offer him a small smile.

"You didn't have to do that," he says.

"And you didn't have to come with me."

I lean back on my heels, then sit down and lean against the same tree as him. Wiping my mouth, I lean my head back against the trunk, then reach for the small flask of water I carry in one of the pouches of my leathers. I swish out my mouth, spit, and then take a few gulps before handing it over to Atticus, whose eyes have yet to leave me.

"Thanks," he says, taking a swig. "For this and the quick healing, though it *was* ridiculously reckless of you."

I laugh a little. "I should be saying that to you." I meet his eyes. "You took a venomous arachnid barb to the chest for me. I *know* you did. And we retrieved the Reverie."

He nods, handing back my flask before pulling out the journal from within his leathers. The leather-bound tome is all black and marked with a familiar dagger and wing pattern on the front, and I feel the weight of it in my hands while I run my thumb along the edges of the hundreds of pages.

"I hope it was worth it," he says.

I nod. "I believe it will be."

I tuck the journal away into my leathers, then look at Atticus again.

"Sorry I branded you," I mutter.

He smirks at me, raising his hand to cup my cheek, his thumb sweeping over my cheekbone. "No apologies necessary, sweet spice. I know it was necessary to heal me, and once again, I thank you for that." He surveys my leather-clad form, his eyes seeming to search for something. "If I may inquire, where is yours?"

I sit forward and stand up to shift around and pull my leathers down, and his eyes dart to the fresh inscription that brands my left hip bone. Carefully, he raises his hand to trace the pattern, and a pleasurable, searing caress slithers across my skin, and I *shiver*.

Atticus stills, then glances up to meet my eyes, his thumb still pressed against the brand.

"What was that?" he inquires lowly, his eyes hooded as he watches me.

"They . . . tend to do that."

He hums a little, sounding intrigued. "I've never had a brand cause *that* sort of reaction before."

"You've never shared a brand with *me*."

Slowly, he grins, studying the inscription again. "No, I haven't."

With swift movements, Atticus is on his knees with his hands grasping my waist, forcing me back against the tree he had just been resting against. I inhale sharply, watching intently as he gently presses his lips to my fresh ink. The brand buzzes warmly with need and desire, as if it has a mind of its own, and another wave of searing pleasure shoots across my skin and settles deep within my core. Everything throbs and pulses, and I moan softly.

"A-Atticus," I *quiver* as his tongue begins to lap at the glowing ink gently before sucking and nibbling on each individual letter.

His hands move lower on my body, pulling my leathers down as he goes to grasp my thighs, thus baring my soaking wet core to him. His fingers trace the outside of my heat, and he chuckles darkly as he all but growls, "You're not wearing any *panties*?"

I blink down at him. "Evidently not."

"Do you *always* parade around bare?"

"What will you do if I say yes?"

He chuckles again, kissing my brand once more. "I would say that you were tempting beforehand, Rhesamyre. But now, you're nearly *mouthwatering*."

"You sound as if you want to eat me."

"I do. And I will."

"Shameless."

He gives me a shameless, feral grin to match before turning his attention back to my soaked core, and he moves forward to lick me from entrance to clit. Moaning deeply at the taste of me, he husks against my mound, "Indeed I am. Perhaps even more so now that I have you in my clutches."

"You're forgetting the rules of our initial bargain again."

"*Fuck the rules.*"

I raise my brow at him, then release a ridiculous whimpering sound as he licks me again. Slowly, teasingly, as if he's tasting a sample of the meal before devouring it. Devouring *me*. His tongue glides through my slick folds, and he nibbles and sucks on my clit, growling lowly.

"If you don't want this," he strains, "tell me to stop."

Slowly, I lower my hands to thread my fingers through his hair, as well as trace the tattoos on his scalp with my nails.

"Don't stop," I command.

Atticus grins and then dives in as if I am the feast and he is a starving man. His tongue flicks and fucks, massaging my folds and exploring every inch of my smooth, soft, and most sensitive skin both inside and out. His hands grasp my hips and thighs to pull me against his face, all while his thumb rubs the *truculent* brand in tandem with his tongue on my clit, thus drawing out sinful noises from me that I wasn't even aware I could make.

And finally, he commands me to come, and I do. *Hard.*

With heavy breaths, I watch as he presses a final kiss against my sensitive clit before rising to his full height again to meet my eyes. He straightens out my leathers for me, smirking.

"Quite the tease," he drawls. "But I plan on savoring you. So we should run along now, *sweetness,* before my brothers realize you're gone. Though last I saw them, they were still quite drunk at the party."

I glance down at his bulge, inquiring softly, "What about you?"

"I'll take care of it myself, but you can rest assured. I'll be thinking of *you* when I do."

CHAPTER EIGHTEEN
RHESAMYRE

The war drums echo in the distance as thunder still rolls through dark, cursed clouds overhead, but I pay the noises no mind as I survey what remains of the troops.

Both celestial, demonic, and even a few others *and mortals. Only a few hundred are left now, and not even half of that are our winged regiments. The celestial alicorns have taken the heaviest toll, littering the battlefields.*

It isn't enough.

"Convoluted spellwork it was, but I think I found what you're looking for."

I turn to face the beloved Witch Queen of our ranks; the gorgeous female is dressed in dark battle leathers with her red hair immaculately braided away from her face, but her green eyes have since dulled over the past years as the war has raged on for far too long.

I dare say, her only saving grace has been Apollo.

Lilith hands me a parchment littered with alchemic schematics and inscriptions of black magic, and I scan the text thoroughly despite her inquisitive, intrusive gaze.

"What?" I inquire, finally meeting her eyes.

Her lips form a thin line as she shakes her head. "Just . . . are you sure this is the way?"

I sigh. "I'm afraid this is the only *way, my friend."*

Lilith nods. "Well . . . in that case, I suppose now is as good a time as any to say it's been an honor, Myra, Champion of the Yonder Star."

....

Flinching awake, I watch as the world outside my window lights up with the lightning of the thunderstorm that has rolled over Hell throughout the night. Alastair's arm is casually slung over my middle, his breathing still and even behind me as he sleeps peacefully, and I'm thankful I didn't wake him with my restless dreaming.

More like careless memories that now seek to haunt me every time I close my eyes.

If Alastair could scent Atticus on me when he returned to my side last night, *which I know he did*, then he didn't show it or mention anything of it. He already gave me his blessing on the matter, but even so, half of me expected him to *stake a claim.*

Though, he *was* quite drunk and sought to snuggle with me rather than fuck me. He isn't an angry drunk like I thought he might be. Instead, he's a cuddler.

He was out within minutes of lying down behind me.

What troubles you, little wolf?

I raise my brows at the silent inquisition, which echoes in my head hoarsely as if he only just stirred awake from a deep slumber, thanks to my restlessness.

Settling back against Alastair again, I reply silently to Atlas, *Sorry I woke you.*

That isn't what I asked.

My imprinted brand with Atlas begins to itch, and I stroke it gently to ease the annoyance.

Please don't do that, he strains.

I smirk a little. *My apologies, Atlas. Sometimes it slips my mind.*

Liar. A heartbeat of silence. *Why are you awake?*

Thunder booms across the sky again, nearly shaking the palace as I feel my bones rattle with it.

Ah, notes Atlas, though his tone isn't teasing by any means. Merely noteworthy. *Thunder confused and frightened you as a wolf, too.*

I roll my eyes. *I'm not frightened—*

Then what would you call it?

I . . . just had a harmless nightmare. Nothing more.

Another lie.

I growl, and from behind me, Alastair stirs slightly, his arm tightening around my middle momentarily before relaxing again.

Careful not to wake the beast, little wolf.

He's your *brother.*

And your *lover . . . one of them, anyway.*

Do my ears deceive me, or do you sound jealous, *Atlas?*

You would do well to recall that it was only a short week ago that I *was the one to embrace you.*

I was a lapdog, I deadpan.

He chuckles. *Perhaps, but it was still* my *lap, now, wasn't it?*

So you are *jealous.*

If one of us is to assume the burden of honesty, then yes, *Rhesamyre. I'm jealous.*

I hum quietly.

Well, he drawls. *Since we're both awake now, do you fancy a midnight meetup? I have something I'd like to give you.*

What is it?

I can nearly feel him mentally check out of the conversation, so I take that as my cue to slip away from Alastair unnoticed, don my sheer robe, exit my room, and silently pad down the hall toward Atlas's chambers. Upon arrival, his door is unlocked, so I stride in with little difficulty to find him on his balcony, staring out at my kingdom.

Sauntering up next to him, I place my hands on the railing as I inhale the petrichor that drenches the city since the larger part of the storm has moved on over the distant mountains. He stands quietly next to me, shirtless and tatted up with a height that is about two to three heads taller than me, much like his brothers, as well as the rest of the males in my life, for that matter.

"What did you dream of?" he inquires softly, his hand sliding down the railing until his pinky finger gently touches mine.

I watch our hands for a heartbeat before I reply. "A memory."

He hums. "Then it wasn't a pleasant one, I take it."

"*It . . .*" I exhale. "Might have been. Could have been under different circumstances, I suppose." I shrug. "I don't quite know, to be honest."

He hums again, then commands gently, "Wait here."

I do as he says, my gaze straying from the heart of Hell for a moment in order to observe the tattoos that brand his back and thus the silhouette of wings there that are formed from inscriptions and prayers in a similar manner to Alastair's, and most likely Atticus's, too.

Turning my gaze back to my kingdom, I lean against the railing as I watch little fires and lights flicker upon quiet streets.

When Atlas returns to my side, I turn to face him as he holds out a velvet box. I take it gently, finding a band of white steel that is littered with delicate rubies embedded into the center line.

"Atlas . . ."

"Think of it as a promise ring," he supplies, taking the ring to slip it over my right ring finger.

I study the ring closely, watching in awe as it shifts into a smaller version of itself to better fit my finger, admiring its beauty and the raw *power* that wafts off it in waves.

"I assumed our imprint and brand satisfied the need for such promises," I muse, meeting his pink eyes again.

He shrugs. "Then think of this as a secondary security measure . . . for my sake. To preserve my sanity, it would mean a great deal to me if you accepted it."

I nod. "Of course, I accept it, Atlas, but I'll admit, I'm just a little surprised that it's *this* ring. The Ring of Rubies was your gift from the Yonder Star and Evergreen Fern. Your *weapon* on top of your powers."

He dips his chin. "It was a necessary power in our quest for peace. I wasn't as skilled in combat as my brothers and often preferred training my brain over my body. I was capable of protecting myself with a blade, but I never desired to take up arms against others. It was often my job to outthink them, not overpower them. The ring gave me the skill set necessary to survive, and now I'm giving it to you. Use it if you want, or wear it as a fashion statement; I don't quite care so long as you have it."

With my hand that now bears the weight of his ring, I stroke his cheek, and he leans into my touch as he studies me with gentle but calculating eyes.

"Is it correct to assume that you are now active with both of my brothers?" he inquires softly.

"Alastair and I have been for a while, but the relationship with Atticus is still new."

Atlas nods again, then steps around me to maneuver my back against the railing; his arms rest on either side of me as he cages me in, his head dipping lower to better meet my eyes.

And my lips . . . if he so chooses to.

"Alastair and Atticus are . . . *okay* with it. With the prospect of an *us*, but where do *you* stand on the matter? I suppose it's quite unfair that I haven't asked you until now."

"You will do as you choose, Rhesa, and I know that. And while my brothers and I have not been close for centuries, I know that you want them. And I also know that when you love, you love passionately. Wholly. It may take some time, but you give your-self completely to those who have earned your love and trust. You're fiercely loyal and a force to be reckoned with, and I pity anyone who dares tell you what you can and cannot do. Who you can and cannot be with."

He dips his head lower, his breath fanning over my lips. "There is far too much violence in the world, and I would be a fool to dissuade you from loving us. *Being* with us."

"*Us*?" I breathe.

Atlas closes the distance, kissing me gently, sweetly. Far gen-tler than what I am used to, but the sugary taste isn't unwelcome by any means. And when he does add tongue, he asks for permis-sion first by licking my lips and pressing forward without forcing his way in.

"*Finally*," he murmurs, angling his head to kiss me deeper, his tongue like silk against mine.

I smile into the kiss, and somehow, I manage to push him backward into the bedroom. More like he lets me move him, and when the backs of his knees hit the bed, he sits and pulls me onto his lap.

I break the kiss, meeting his eyes. "If I ask you to fuck me, will you?"

His pink eyes glow with an intensity I've never seen on him before, but his hands remain gentle as they rub up and down my back.

"How do you want it?" he inquires, pressing featherlight kisses to my neck and jaw that cause sweet shivers to race across my skin.

I hum. "I want you to love me however you see fit, Atlas. Gentle, rough, I don't care. So long as it is you, and it remains *your* choice."

He hums, or maybe it's more of a groan as I rub my core against his bulge.

"Then stand up for a moment and strip," he commands gently.

I do as he instructs, stepping back onto my feet to pull Alastair's shirt over my head and horns. Atlas pulls down his trousers, then shuffles back against the headboard. I crawl onto the bed toward him, straddling him to rub my bare core against his hard length. The tight cords of his muscles bulge and strain, and he inhales sharply. I swear, if I could bottle up the sound and inhale it when in need of a pick-me-up, I would.

His hands rest on my waist as he studies my nude form, and he notes with a low moan, "You're marked up."

I trace Alastair's ink that brands my chest. "He had to when he healed me from the Soldiers of Sorrow. I was stabbed with half-light."

Atlas growls, the sound more monster than man. And he glances down to spot Atticus's more recent claim that brands my left hip bone. "And it appears as though Atticus didn't want to be left out, either."

I snicker quietly, then raise my left forearm to lick the *sarang* brand I share with Atlas, and he curses under his breath as his cock twitches beneath me, which is soaked with my arousal.

I rise above him slowly, then line his length up with my wet entrance, and lower myself until he is completely seated inside of me. His hands twitch on my waist, squeezing me as I begin to move.

Grabbing his hands, I pull them together before making them overlap on his tatted chest, and I press down on them as I roll my hips and shift forward to share my pleasure with him. His groans and twitches only fuel my need for him, and he gives me the reins and full freedom to do whatever I please—steal my pleasure however I choose.

"I think I quite like this view," he husks, thrusting his hips upward, driving his cock deeper inside of me until I gasp. I can feel him everywhere, and my skin prickles as our shared brand flares in pleasure. His cock drives home with every thrust, and my walls clench when he strokes that sensitive spot inside of me.

"Me, too," I reply, letting go of his hands to lean back on his thighs, tossing my head back. "*Harder.*"

He chuckles darkly. "You make the rules, little wolf."

He obeys my request and grabs my hips again to slam upward so far inside that I'm nearly seeing stars with every thrust. His growls echo throughout the otherwise quiet room as his fingers dig into my hips, surely leaving bruises, and I welcome the pain as he snarls. I match his pace, flexing with every muscle I've got as my core clenches.

"Almost there, little wolf," he growls, his thrusts getting sloppier. "Come all over me, my queen."

I moan something incoherent, and then I shatter completely when he presses on my clit with his thumb. He tumbles over the edge right after me, his cock pulsing and twitching deep inside as his seed spills like hot ribbons as I milk him. It warms me from the inside out, and I shiver on his lap. He leans forward and catches my mouth, and I whimper around his tongue as he rolls us over. He pulls out gently, and his seed spills from my entrance as soon as his cock is free.

"If you impregnate me, I'll stab you in your sleep," I snarl, snuggling against him.

Atlas chuckles, pulling me close while trapping me with his limbs. He presses a kiss to my forehead, then mutters something in Old Latin so softly I can hardly hear him.

But later in the night, my sex-hazed brain finally makes sense of it.

Finally, we are whole again.

....

When dawn comes around, I find myself waking up in Atlas's arms. My chest is practically on top of his as I use him instead of the mattress, but his arms are still around me while our legs tangle, so I know he probably prefers it this way.

Good morning, he mutters in my mind, his breathing changing its nature as he shifts awake beneath me.

Pink eyes meet mine, and I reply, "Good morning."

"Sleep well?" he inquires.

I nod.

He smiles at me, then leans forward and pecks my lips. "Glad to hear it. Shall we head down to breakfast?"

Again, I nod.

Atlas raises his brow at me, but before he can question me, I maneuver off his chest and pad over to his bathing chamber to freshen up for the day. He joins me after a moment, and it feels alarmingly natural to be near him in this platonic routine.

"I suppose I should either sneak back to my bedchamber or call a maid to deliver a dress," I remark, brushing my hair.

Atlas meets my gaze through the mirror as he washes his face. "Or I can lend you one of my shirts."

I can't help but take a moment to appreciate the harmless sight before me, nearly grinning at him. Here stands this centuries-old predator, *who is anything but harmless*, with disheveled bed hair, crooked cotton pants, and eyes slightly puffy from sleep.

He furrows his brows. "What?"

I shake my head, doing a poor job of hiding my smile. "Nothing, and though tempting, I don't believe parading around in one of your shirts will give people the appropriate impression of their new *queen*."

He shrugs again. "What's the point of being queen if you can't wear what you want whenever you want to?"

I open my mouth to argue, but come up empty. I huff quietly. "*Fair enough*, but my answer is still *no*."

He smirks. "Fair enough."

I roll my eyes, then do as I said I would, and summon a maid to retrieve a dress from my bedchamber. However, what I don't expect when I open the door again a few minutes later is to find Alastair standing there instead, with my gown, shoes, and necessities in hand.

A corner of his mouth tilts up at the sight of me. "Good morning, love."

I lean against the doorframe and cross my arms. "Did you scare off my servant?"

He looks offended as he replies, "I'll have you know that I did nothing of the sort. I simply offered to bring this to you, and she agreed . . . albeit *hesitantly* at first."

I quirk my brow at him, and from somewhere behind me, Atlas quips, "I believe your presence alone was enough to scare the poor girl, brother. No threats necessary."

Alastair scowls, and I grin at the sight.

Snickering, I grab his hand to pull him inside, and Alastair follows wordlessly as he hands me my gown and jewels. Disappearing from sight, I leave the two males alone to get dressed in peace without having them eye-fuck me the entire time, *because I know they would.*

Hell, I'd do the same to them in a heartbeat.

It is silent for a moment before I hear an awkward *good morning* from Atlas.

"Hello, brother," replies Alastair.

I smirk to myself at the sound of their bizarre discomfort, fixing my earrings and horn ornaments perhaps a bit too slowly in order to draw it out.

"I'll confess," drawls Alastair with a low rumble in his chest. "I didn't quite expect to wake up alone this morning."

"She and I needed to speak with one another, and I didn't seek to invoke your wrath by waking you up mid-slumber."

"Undoubtedly wise. Does that ring on her finger have anything to do with your *conversation*?"

I poke my head around the bathing chamber doorway. "I *can* hear you."

I strut toward them, and both brothers do a doubletake at the sight of me. Stopping before them with my hands on my hips, I raise my brow. "We can be civilized about this, yes?"

They glance at one another, and then Atlas shrugs before bending down to slip my feet into my heels for me. Using Alastair to balance, I meet his silver gaze as he surveys my form with a steeled expression.

I tilt my head at him. "What?"

He shakes his head, the corner of his mouth quirking up again. "If you think we're bad, wait till Atticus hears of us *bonding* without him."

I roll my eyes, letting go of his arms as Atlas rises once more. I'm of course taller now, thanks to my heels, but these males forever tower over me no matter the stilettos.

"Well," I drawl. "Shall we head to breakfast, gentlemen?"

With each arm interlocked with one of their own, we stride out of Atlas's chambers as a single unit toward the dining hall, passing a few guards or other lords and ladies of the court as we go, but we pay them no mind. And aside from the polite bows or curtsies, they don't pay us much mind, either.

"So I've been thinking," I drawl, and both males now watch me out of the corners of their eyes. I'd be a fool not to notice the way they look almost *alarmed* at my introduction into a new conversation. I ignore them.

"I believe it is time I come up with my own pet names for you three, no? Each of you has one for me, after all. I believe it only fair."

"Knowing your indeterminable vocabulary," drawls Alastair, "I can only *imagine* what sort of wicked things you'd like to call us, love. Be it a term of endearment or an insult."

Nodding, Atlas agrees. "You are the creative type, little wolf. For better or worse."

Scowling, I slip my arms from theirs and halt before them. They both raise their brows at me in mirrored fashions, and I almost laugh again at the sight. I point my finger at Alastair and then Atlas.

"Asshole number one and asshole number two." I grin, nodding. "Atticus will serve as asshole number three."

Atlas raises his hand like a child.

"You may speak, asshole number two."

"*Thanks.* Do we get a say in our names?" he inquires.

"Unfortunately, the topic is not up for discussion at the moment, but perhaps a promotion could be arranged. It all depends upon your commendable services, of course."

"*Figures*," quips Alastair, scowling *harder.*

"Have I mentioned how beautiful you are today, my little wolf?" inquires Atlas, grinning.

I match his smile, sauntering up to him to kiss the corner of his mouth. "Not yet, but the day is young. You're quite handsome, too. Though I do think you're an ass-kisser."

"For you, absolutely," he admits.

"How is that any better than *asshole*?" growls Alastair.

I shrug, smirking as Atlas's hands wind around my waist. "I don't know. What do you prefer? Asshole, or clingy bastard?"

Alastair growls, ripping me out of Atlas's embrace as he takes me by my throat and presses his lips to mine, nipping gently.

"I'd prefer something *sweeter*," he all but snarls, though I can still distinguish the hilarity over the hostility that swirls in his silver eyes.

"But I'm not sweet," I argue, pouting.

"*Oh*, but you *are*, my love," he husks. Then he whispers closer to my ear, his breath tickling the pointed shell of it, "I never realized I could have such a sweet tooth before *tasting* you."

I gawk at him, my body heating up at the insinuations behind his words, and my core clenches.

"*Hey*! That's cheating!" snaps Atlas.

Alastair gives me a rare grin. "Shall we continue to breakfast, love? Although, you do look a bit flushed now. Perhaps you're coming down with something."

I snarl at him, then spin on my heel as I quip, "We'll see who's laughing later, *sweet tooth*."

Alastair chuckles, muttering to himself, "*That's more like it.*"

I roll my eyes, ignoring him as I turn the corner to head into the dining room. However, before I can get much further, my magic bristles, thus giving me enough time to command a dagger into my palm as I clash with steel.

"We should really stop meeting like this, sweet spice."

I roll my eyes even *harder*, lowering my dagger again as it disappears from sight, and I cross my arms. "Dare I say you *like* my violence, you shameless flirt."

Atticus smiles at me, not looking the least apologetic. "And I dare say that I agree with you."

He interlocks his arm with mine, and we stride into the dining hall together.

CHAPTER NINETEEN
RHES AMYRE

Sitting at the center of the dining table so I may observe the entirety of the hall is nothing new; however, having all three deities, plus Pollux, in my line of sight or right next to me will certainly take some getting used to.

I sip from my chalice of blood slowly, surveying the many tables of chattering demons, as well as the rest of my family, too. I smile at the sight of my girls sitting next to their rightful lieutenants, as well as the Wolves of Woe that lounge about or beg the girls for table scraps. However, my smile soon fades when my eyes snag on a mortal servant man as he approaches with a sealed letter in hand, and the messenger proceeds to step up the dais and present it to Atlas.

Atlas hides his puzzlement well, but I can pick out the perplexity in his pink eyes with ease, and that intense, steeled gaze only grows more complex as he surveys the seal upon the parchment.

Is everything okay? I inquire.

Without missing a beat, he breaks the seal with a butter knife as he replies to me, *A seal from a friend in the West. Do you recall the clinic we visited?*

The one run by a witch doctor?

That's the one. Her name is Imani. It seems as though that, once again, things in the West have taken another turn for the worse.

In what way? More raiders?

Something of the sort. Imani is requesting aid since she has learned of your coronation. She was always somewhat privy to your identity, and through the grapevine, I'm sure she's learned of my true identity, too.

Hell has always been an ally of the Hussars in the West. It would stand to reason that since our attention has been divided in recent weeks, the raiders have taken this opportunity to stake a claim upon the desert territories once more.

I agree . . . . Is it overstepping my place if I ask that we intervene, Your Majesty?

I meet Atlas's gaze. *You need not ever be afraid of asking, Atlas. You are a part of this court now, and your experience, mind, and magic are all of great value to me.* You *are of great value to me.*

He spares me a smirk, then passes the letter across the table to me.

Sawbones,

Assuming you can still even be called that.

The West remains a wasteland, and the Hussars need assistance with replenishing their ranks. As you are familiar with the recently crowned queen of Hell, I ask that you speak to her on my behalf. The people of the West need external aid if they are to survive and reclaim their freedom and homes from the raiders, and as Hell has often supplied warriors and riders to the cause, it seems only fitting to write to you now.

I do not know the formalities of armies and treaties. I only know that families are suffering, and assuming my memories have not betrayed me, then

__I think it correct to presume that Queen Rhesamyre will respond as needed.__

__If her reputation is to be believed, then I trust her. And I still trust you.__

__Sincerely,__
__Imani of the West__

I pass the letter to the rest of my family members and the other two deities, believing it faster to let them come to their own conclusions than attempting to explain everything.

Once all of them have read it, and the rest of the dining room clears out to leave us alone, I start.

"I recall Imani. Fierce woman and an intelligent witch doctor. She's passionate about helping people." I shrug. "At least, that's what I gathered as a wolf, anyway."

Atlas nods. "You're correct. Imani is all that and more. She ran that clinic with my help and funding for a long time, helping those in town as well as the migrant families that passed through due to the raiders' terrors."

"*Sawbones*?" inquires Atticus, raising a brow at his brother. "You peddled about as a *doctor*?"

Atlas shrugs. "Better than being balls deep in whores day in and day out. You fuck anything that *breathes*, brother. I'd be curious to know if there's anyone or *thing* you haven't done yet."

Atticus glances at me, and I scowl at him. "*I dare you*," I mutter.

He chuckles. "No, thanks. I quite like having my *balls* where they are." He glances around the table, muttering, "Because you wouldn't be the only one to take offense to that."

Atticus downs the rest of whatever the hell he's drinking, and I know better than to believe it isn't alcoholic. I narrow my eyes at him.

Sighing, Pollux crosses his arms. "I do believe we discussed such matters when you were away, Your Majesty. We had come to the conclusion that the matters of the West would have to be put on hold until you returned and claimed your place as queen. Now that you have, we can proceed in whatever manner you choose."

"That's easy enough," I quip. "I choose to fight. And just as our late king did, we will provide the Hussars with whatever tools, weapons, or warriors they need to reclaim the West."

Uncle War nods from his place down the table. "I concur. We'll gather the numbers needed for a full-scale, spherical invasion, and we can be ready to move out by the end of the day. We'll send word to the Hussars." He looks to Atlas. "Send word to Imani. See what she can do to ensure the people of the West stay out of our way. The last thing we need is for the raiders to start using civilians as shields."

Atlas nods, and just like that, the deities, Horsemen, their lieutenants, and the assassins begin scheming and talking battle tactics. I tip my head back to finish the last of the blood in my chalice, then rise to approach my girls and see if they want any part of this. They have yet to begin their tactical training outside of basic self-defense, so they won't be on the frontlines. However, they still have skills that may be of use to me if properly exploited.

However, before I can get to them, Pollux appears by my side and murmurs into my ear, "Walk with me?"

I nod, and he leads me out of the dining hall and away from any listening ears or prying eyes. Then, once he's satisfied on another balcony that hangs off the throne room, he sighs and turns to face me.

"You recall what lies in the West, correct?" he inquires.

With my eyes trained on the heart of Hell, I nod. "I do."

"Then what are you going to do about it?"

"Nothing. Not until we get the West back under control."

"Everyone deserves the truth, darling."

"I agree. But the truth can wait a damn minute longer. We have more pressing matters to attend to at the moment."

He scoffs a little. *"Debatable."*

Slowly, I turn to face him, and there's not a trace of humor in his icy eyes, the predator's scowl once again taking precedence.

"If we are to battle the Apostles once again and keep *him* from returning," I explain, "we're going to need all the assistance we can gather, and the Western territories are a part of that plan, just as they were back then. And I doubt you need the reminder that we barely had enough allies to win last time."

His wings grow heavy behind him as they lower, and his professional scowl cracks. *"We didn't win, Rhesamyre . . . .* You sacrificed yourself to save what remained of the Ten Spheres, and you succeeded in doing so, yes, but I wouldn't dare call that a *win."*

"Call it whatever you want, Pollux. The spell held on for thousands of centuries, and would have held on for longer had it not been for the First's interference with the Tree of Creation."

That predator's rage is back in full swing as he seethes, *"They robbed your fucking grave!"*

"Not making excuses, but to be fair, they didn't know it was my grave—"

"MYRA!"

I can tell he regrets it as soon as he shouts it, but that remorseful, pitiful look in his eyes doesn't stop me from raising my head, but lowering my voice as I drawl, "You think I'm not *aware* of what's at *risk*, Pollux? I *know* what we have to lose. Dare I say, I have even *more* to lose now. *And I remember everything.* I'm haunted by memories every night, and tormented by the regrets and mistakes we made back then. *I know what's at stake*, but it will be *my* decision to make everyone privy to the dangers ahead. And I will . . . I just need to find the appropriate time to do so. And gearing up to storm the entirety of the West is *not* the appropriate time!"

He's silent for a heartbeat. "Lord Death approached me . . . said you told him that three of the four Lords of Exile are now aware of what's to come. And that Sam . . . Sam was reminded of it when he died, too."

I nod. "He was. Which is how Death has been made privy to the information now, as well." I sigh, allowing my anger to lessen as my magic settles down again. "*I'm* . . .*" I want to laugh at my loss for words, but I don't. "I don't know what I am, Pollux. I thought I knew who I was, but dare I say . . . I don't think I do anymore."

Pollux steps forward to place his hands on my shoulders gently, dipping his head to better meet my eyes. "I never wanted this for you. I believe I can at least relate to you when you find yourself torn. On one hand, I'm ecstatic to remember and relearn who you and I once were to one another, and who we can be again . . . but at the same time—"

"I wasn't supposed to come back," I supply, but I hardly recognize my own voice as it *cracks*. "You weren't *supposed* to *remember* me . . . . The fact that I'm here now means that we didn't . . . *win*. It means that I *failed*."

"No. *No*, darling," he coos, drawing me to his chest and warm embrace. He rests his chin on my head, minding my horns as he strokes my hair and holds me tighter than he ever has before. And I let him. I hug him back, wrapping my arms around his middle and pressing my face into his chest, inhaling his familiar scent of mint and smoke.

"You were right when you said before that everything held for as long as it could. You did succeed, Myra. We that remained were the imbeciles who couldn't keep the peace you once sacrificed yourself for. And we allowed two unruly mortals to steal the forbidden fruit. The one the deities were charged with protecting at all costs." He leans back to grasp my cheeks and meet my eyes. *"None of this is your fault."*

I nod, and I do believe him. While unfortunate, I know I had no control over anything that happened after I died. "A part of me is still happy to be here, though . . . despite what it means."

"I know. And please understand that you shouldn't feel guilty."

"I don't," I vow. And that is the truth.

He nods, seeming satisfied with that.

"I will tell them, Pollux. Soon."

He nods again, leaning forward to kiss my forehead. "And I'll be there right beside you when you do. But do you mind if I inquire if it is at all possible to restore everyone else's memories? Perhaps all at once?"

I shrug. "Lilith and I didn't create the spell with remembrance in mind, but I would have been a fool to not have any contingencies in place."

"You're no fool now, and you were no fool back then, either."

I smirk a little. "I think the answers I need lie in the West."

He nods. "So then, to the West we will travel."

....

Hellion troops camp across a grand portion of the Western Desert, their fires crackling steadily in a similar manner to the stars above. A sea of sand paints the landscape for miles between here and the next territory of civilization, one the raiders have claimed as their own. However, on the other side of that territory lies more hellion regiments commanded by War, Silas, and a few of the assassins. Then, elsewhere, to cover all four battlefronts of this sphere, Death, Famine, and Conquest lead their troops with their rightful lieutenants and the rest of the assassins scattered amongst them.

Naturally, someone had to remain behind to watch over the throne while we're away, and that responsibility fell to Sloth and Mamba. The former only protested once before agreeing, but Mamba had no complaints about being left alone to nap in peace.

Standing in the center of the Hussars' base of operations in hellion battle leathers, I survey the maps and war table situated before myself, Pollux, the deities, and the handful of field masters that command the Hussar calvary.

"We've received confirmation from all four generals," informs Ardust in butchered Babel—the only woman in leadership but not the only female among the equestrian ranks—"that everyone is in place, Your Majesty. We await your orders."

Nodding, I trail my fingers along the maps where miniature figurines sit in display of our scattered ranks.

"Did we ever hear back from the raiders?" I inquire, glancing up to survey the Western-bred masters before me.

While their ranks are made up of demons, mortals, and some *others*, the field masters themselves are supernatural natives of the West. If one is to assume the stories are true, then those of Hussar command ride with equine blood in their veins. Born from the wild horses that once ran across these deserts, untamed and untouched before mingling with other supernatural creatures and beasts. Somewhere down the line, mortal blood was introduced, and thus these horses were given human forms.

Ardust is beautiful and lithe in nature, like that of a high-bred hell-horse of the royal and regal bloodlines. Meanwhile, Hocks, Flint, Rice, and Waze are stockier and built with strength in mind over speed. Nonetheless, all five are not to be trifled with and have been around for a very long time.

The five of them look amongst each other at my inquiry, and I raise my brow at their antics.

"What?" I demand.

"We heard back," answers Hocks, albeit hesitantly. "They don't desire a ceasefire. They won't be surrendering anything or anyone."

I cock my head at his tone. "And where's the proof of this disagreement?"

"In pieces," answers Ardust. "It wasn't a formal reply. More like a show of force."

"Show me."

"My queen," starts Rice. "I highly protest—"

"*Show. Her*," commands Atticus, his tone far more hostile and demanding than usual. And that's saying *a lot*.

Obliging, Ardust nods and mutters, "This way." We follow her through the camp toward an established perimeter guarded by horses and riders, and it's thanks to both my training and overall comfort in all things bloody and violent that I don't stall at the sight of the butchered horses and humans situated ahead of me on bloodstained blankets. Hussars attempt to sort through the carnage and bloodshed, but it's obvious they're having trouble distinguishing between the dismembered *parts*.

"*Well*," I drawl humorlessly. "I suppose that is one way to tell us *no*."

"These are only a few of the captives they held," supplies Ardust. "Five different heads, and two pack ponies."

"Innocents caught on the road trying to flee, I take it."

She nods, and I turn my gaze to Atlas. "What of Imani? Was she able to secure a safe haven for those who could reach it in time with the few soldiers and supplies we sent to aid her?"

"I received confirmation from the squad that they reached the town and found a few more survivors," replies Atlas. "Though no word on Imani."

I furrow my brows, then turn to Pollux. "Can you find her?"

Pollux nods. "Give me a moment, and I'll have a location."

The archangel steps away to go about contacting his informants, and I look to the slaughtered innocents again. Men, women, and children. *A family.*

"We have our answer," snarls Waze, and I meet the master's livid golden eyes. His pupils are horizontal in shape, like an equine's. "We have the numbers now, as well as every location of raider outposts. What are we waiting for?"

"It is not my intention to spill any more innocent blood," I drawl.

"You already made the mistake of waiting once, *Your Majesty*," Rice spits. "Giving the raiders a chance to surrender? *A fool's wish.* And this family's blood is on *your* hands."

I cock my head, but I don't have to lift a *bloodstained finger* to ensure Rice's throat is nearly crushed to the point of no return.

Because Atticus does it for me.

"That doesn't sound like gratitude to me," drawls the deity, his voice eerily calm and even. "Would you like the *chance* to try again?"

"You have the numbers and firepower now *because* of our generous queen," growls Alastair as he stands at my back, and I can only imagine what sort of glare he's giving these commanders to make them nearly *shit* themselves.

The first to recover is Ardust, since she steps forward and glowers at her male counterparts. "My apologies, my queen . . . we're just concerned for our home."

I dip my chin. "I'm aware, but I will not tolerate disrespect and insubordination to any degree from anyone. Do you understand, Master Ardust?"

She nods, bowing slightly. "I do, my queen."

"Good. Then let it lie."

I snap my gaze back to Pollux as he returns, his eyes grim despite his scowl firmly in place.

"More bad news, I take it?" inquires Atticus, his arms crossed and eyes bored as if he didn't just nearly choke a man to death two seconds ago.

"There was another attack," explains Pollux. "Imani was caught in the crossfire."

Atlas steps forward. "Where?"

Pollux shakes his head. "Somewhere in the middle of the *fucking desert*. She strayed from her clinic in town to get as many as she could to safety."

"Take me there. Now."

Pollux glances at me, and I place my hand on Atlas's shoulder, my eyes still on the archangel. "Can you take *us*?"

With a clenched jaw, the archangel nods as he opens a conveyance. Atticus and Alastair stay behind with the Hussars, while the three of us step through the glittering tunnel onto a sandstone ground splattered with blood and gore. I survey the carnage, mulling over the lost caravan of supplies, livestock, and families.

"Imani!" shouts Atlas, stepping through the mess to find his friend.

"She could open conveyances, too," says Pollux, surveying the tipped-over wagons, raided barrels, empty crates, and multiple bodies of people and animals that line the road. "She had been using tracking spells to find caravans like this and then lead them to safety."

I nod. "Good woman . . . I do hope she isn't dead."

"As do I, though I don't believe we're that lucky."

"Neither do I."

I step forward with Pollux to find where Atlas ran off to, nudging bodies gently with my boot as I go to ensure these folks are indeed deceased. Pollux bends down next to a few, studying their wounds with furrowed brows. However, I don't have time to question him on his antics since I round the edge of a busted wagon. And there on the ground, I find Atlas holding a bloody and *dying* Imani in his arms. The dark-skinned woman murmurs to him with tears in her eyes as she clutches her bloody chest with one of Atlas's hands overtop hers.

Then, her gaze slides over to me, and she mutters, "*The wolf.*"

Carefully, I step forward to kneel by the Western witch, and I take her hand in mine. "You have my eternal gratitude and respect, Imani of the West. I'm sorry I was late."

She smiles at me. "Don't be, young lady. It was a pleasure to meet you as a wolf then, and it's a pleasure to meet you as a woman now."

I offer her a sad smile, but before we can exchange any more words, she stops breathing.

I let her hand slip from my own.

"I tried to heal her," mutters Atlas. "*It didn't work in time.*"

Pollux curses demon names under his breath. "*As I suspected,*" he snarls.

I raise my brow at him, then glance down at Imani again and remove her hands from her wound. Tasting her blood, I immediately spit it out again with a snarl. "*Poison*. Like the crone's work."

"Lilith is dead," states Atlas. "You made sure of that, little wolf. Besides, I find it hard to believe Imani would willingly ingest poison."

"I agree." I rise back onto my booted feet. "Perhaps the late crone left enough ingredients for someone else to manufacture the poison on her behalf. Witchcraft could be considered *cookbook material* with simpler spells, so long as someone knows how to follow the instructions step-by-step. And the poison could have just as easily been poured onto the weapon, or even forged with it if done properly." I make eye contact with Pollux. "We'd be looking for someone who has a knack for such schemes   and has the means of distributing the final product."

Pollux's wings tense as he growls to himself. "*The Pantomath*."

Atlas furrows his brows, looking between us. "Lilith and Apollo's bastard?"

"The one and only," I quip. "And this would further explain how the raiders have been able to not only multiply as quickly as they have, but also kill off the Hussars' ranks easier, too."

"They've struck a deal with Andrew's fleet," finishes Pollux. "And are most likely splitting the profits of livestock, supplies, and slaves."

"Shady bastard," growls Atlas. "If Andrew is involved, this changes things."

"Andrew can go fuck himself," I bite. "This changes nothing. We stick to the plan, and we'll just give our troops a heads-up not to get *stabbed*. If Andrew wants to play this game, then so be it. I'll destroy him *and* the entire *fucking board* while I'm at it."

The males exchange a wary glance with one another before nodding, and Atlas merely sighs and closes Imani's eyes for her.

"First things first," says Atlas, rising to stand beside me. "We need to find Bellatrix."

I quirk a brow at him, and he drawls, "Imani's daughter."

CHAPTER TWENTY
RHESAMYRE

Ash falls from the sky as the West goes up in flames, and I get a sudden rush of déjà vu at the sight.

Shaking myself from the memory, I focus once more on the task at hand:

Infiltrate the enemy stronghold. Find Bellatrix. Save the rest of the captives. And murder every fucking raider that gets in my way.

Simple enough.

"Steady as we go, men," calls Ardust beside me from atop her faithful steed. "Any moment now."

I stroke Orpheus's neck as I study the raiders' main outpost from behind the spelled cloak that keeps us hidden from their sights, and I can practically *feel* the adrenaline of the Hussars and their horses behind me. The entirety of the Western Sphere has now fallen to the mercy of the hellion regiments and my generals as we attack the raiders all at once across multiple battlefronts. Pollux and the deities are among them, picking up the slack and opening conveyances wherever they may be needed most to evacuate the wounded and fight alongside our warriors.

And finally, from the chaos of the battle ahead that commences over this raiders' outpost, which has been established within a town they *stole*, light and fire alchemy flash across the darkened sky as flares shoot through the smoke, serving as our signal to enter the fray.

Backed by the battle cry of over a hundred riders, Orpheus and I surge forward with Ardust and the Wolves of Woe into battle. I release the spellwork that keeps us hidden just as we trample the first wave of raiders, and none of them have enough time to retaliate as we strike them down dozens at a time. With a sword in hand and a stallion beneath me, I slaughter raiders left and right as I ride straight into the fray, clouded by ash, smoke, and the nearly overwhelming scents of bodily waste, blood, and poison.

Plenty of the raiders charge toward us on horseback, too, while others remain posted up higher on rooftops to pick off Hussars one by one with their arrows and bolts.

Commanding various forms of alchemy is easy enough, but I've always been partial to fire. Thus, flames coat both myself and my horse as we set ourselves aflame to burn raiders when they get too close. In addition, rapid commands roll off my tongue to drop plenty of enemies where they stand, turning them to ash, burning them alive from the inside out, or halting their movements long enough for a wolf to maul them or another Hussar to drive a sword through their chests or chop off their heads.

Plenty of arrows and bolts whir past me, and the few that come directly at me, I either catch or deflect. However, when I find myself to be the center of attention all of a sudden, I recognize that I have to make myself swifter and smaller.

So, with a heavy heart, I leap off Orpheus and tackle another raider off his own mount. Slitting his throat with his own sword, I rise and duck again just in time to avoid another mounted raider's sword. Slashing his horse out from underneath him, he tumbles and is crushed to death immediately, and I command another sword of obsidian to erupt from flames into my palm so I may clash weapons with yet another raider.

Spinning away from him to kick his legs out and stab him, I shove him back into another and move to stab that one, too, evading swords, arrows, horses, and friendly fire in the process. I wear their blood splatters like warpaint as dust and sand cling to my skin, coating me in more gore, as well as what has essentially become mud, thanks to all the blood and fluids lost as more soldiers, Hussars, horses, and raiders fall.

I duck under another's sword as he swings it at me with a snarl, then go for his middle; however, before I can, a rogue horse crushes him, and I'm left reeling and nearly tripping backward over another corpse in order to avoid getting trampled, too. With myself off balance, I barely have the time to dodge an incoming arrow, and the poisoned steel slices my cheek.

I hiss and set my sights on where it came from, and the archer just nocks another and lets it fly. Catching this one, I snap it in half and command a bow and arrow to erupt from flames into my hands so I can put the little fucker out of his misery. I shoot multiple arrows at a time, targeting the raiders that line the rooftops while my wolves circle me, ensuring no raiders get near me on foot while I'm otherwise occupied.

Eventually forced to ditch the bow as I roll forward through the gore to avoid another falling horse, I grab a foreign sword of poisoned steel to slice through a few more enemies. However, one manages to grab me when he falls, and we trip over more bodies in an attempt to gain control. My magic and power flare nonstop as it warns me of everything coming my way, but even that may not be enough to give me the upper hand against this male who now straddles me. He wraps his hands around my throat, growling and spitting in my face, and I snarl back at him with bared fangs as I use my supernatural strength to buck my hips and twist us around.

Driving one of my daggers into his eye, I leave him there as I flip backward to avoid another barrage of arrows.

Pain shoots through me as something pierces my lower leg, and I release an impressively loud snarl when I detach the hand that holds the sword from whoever dared to stab me. The pathetic male screams as he reels backward, tripping over more corpses in an attempt to get away from me, but he doesn't get very far since I use his own sword to decapitate him.

You're injured.

I growl at Atlas's prying as I twirl and kill two more raiders, replying, *Worry about your own damn battle.*

I can multitask. Where are you?

Winning my front. What about you?

He chuckles. *We're about finished here. We'll be coming to you shortly.*

Don't. You. Dare, I seethe.

It isn't up for discussion.

That's not your decision.

Too late. We've already decided. We'll see you soon.

Snarling again as I feel him mentally check out, I snap the neck of another raider while commanding more forms of Alchemy, thus allowing me to shift through conveyances and slice through more enemies at a swifter pace, killing dozens at a time alongside my soldiers and wolves.

My shared brandings burn and glow the entire time I fight, but I ignore them. Especially when I finally allow myself to partially erupt in order to rid our battlefield of the rest of our enemies.

Screams grow louder as bodies burst from the inside out and melt away, and then the screams cease altogether.

Huffing gently as I stand in the center of the carnage, I glance over every nook and cranny for more raiders that may have survived my final assault. When I find none, only then do I allow my power to settle back down deep within me, simmering quietly and ready to erupt again when necessary.

"You couldn't have done that earlier?" inquires Ardust, limping toward me as she spits some blood from her mouth, keeping pressure on her bloodied side.

I shrug, glancing down to survey the mess that is my right calf. *Bloody hell*, it fucking *stings*. Damn poison and black magic.

"I wouldn't have been much use to you had I done it too early," I admit. "It's not exactly forgiving magic. I needed to weed out a few more to lessen the blow to my own reserves."

Ardust shrugs, standing near me as she surely takes count of all those we lost here today. I cough quietly into my hand, ignoring the blood that coats my mouth and my gloved palm, rubbing it off on my thigh without a second thought.

"Bloody mess." She sighs.

I nod, then grin and wink at her. "But we won."

At what cost, though? I think to myself.

She snickers, raising her hand to slap it against mine in triumph. However, both of us wince at the action, then either laugh or cough again, I'm not entirely sure.

"I'd better find and contact my fellow field masters, assuming they haven't been slain," she prompts, beginning to limp off. "We'll rendezvous again soon."

I incline my head, watching her go for a moment before turning to observe the fallen around me once more. My wolves whine and return to my sides again, and I bend down to wipe some of the blood and grime off their faces as I keep surveying the slaughterhouse I stand in. However, instead of studying the faces of men and demons alike, I glance over the dozens of fallen horses to look for Orpheus.

Before I can find him, my power flares again, and I turn back around to find another conveyance that reveals my deities and Pollux. I release a breath I didn't realize I was holding, and while each of their leathers is splattered with blood, dirt, and gore in a similar manner as my own, they look none the worse for wear at first glance. At least, there won't be any *permanent* damage. The poison may stunt our supernatural healing abilities, but unlike getting harmed by half-light, we can still recover, albeit slowly.

Pollux doesn't have any scrapes on him, and Alastair only has a few. Atticus is sporting a few deep gashes across his torso, while Atlas's arms have certainly seen better days.

"You lot look like *shit*," I quip, limping up to them. Then I crinkle my nose. "And you smell like it, too."

Alastair grabs me first, pulling me off my wounded leg, relieving the pressure there as he holds me close.

However, it is Atticus who reaches for my face to stroke the scrapes that mar my cheeks, and he snarls. "Those *motherfuckers—*"

"Are all dead," I say softly, placing my hand on his cheek. "I'll heal."

He sighs, nodding and closing his eyes for a moment. I smile gently, then glance at Atlas and Pollux next. Pollux offers me a gentle smirk as he bows his head, while Atlas steps forward to rub my other cheek in an attempt to get rid of whatever soot, grime, or blood paints me.

"What of the others?" I inquire.

"Success on all fronts," supplies Alastair, his hands still around my waist. "Plenty of casualties among the footmen, but none between your family members. And I believe all the field masters came out with their lives intact, too."

I nod, feeling my heart lighten again at the news. "Good. Then I suppose we should initiate cleaning this shit up . . . and I need to find my horse."

The four of them nod and step over the fallen corpses of both our enemies and allies as we go. Alastair remains by my side to help me walk toward the building that once served as this town's meetinghouse.

<hr/>

My face and hands are finally clean at least, but the rest of me is still impressively splattered with dried blood and sand that clings to every crevice of my leathers and strand of my hair.

Orpheus's coat doesn't fare much better, either.

"You'll get the pampering of a lifetime," I promise him, holding his jaws as I nuzzle my cheek against the velvet of his nose. "We both will. You can guarantee that much, handsome boy."

"*See*?" quips Alastair, raising his brow while leaning against the nearby fence post where we tie the horses. "Now how come you can't come up with a nickname like that for us? That one is sweet, no?"

I scowl at him, kissing Orpheus's muzzle. Alastair frowns at me, and I grin at the sight.

"Don't be so uptight," I tease. "Getting jealous over a *horse* is beneath you, my almighty deity."

He rolls his eyes, then reaches for me when I start toward him. My limp is barely noticeable now, but a twinge of pain still accompanies every step.

"Are you okay?" he inquires softly.

"I'm fine, Alastair. Are *you* okay? No hidden injuries I need to know about?"

A corner of his mouth tilts up. "You're welcome to search."

I roll my eyes. "I'll take that as a sign that you are indeed *fine*."

"Rhesa!"

Alastair and I look forward to find Damian jogging toward us, the reaper in a similar state of dishevelment.

"Damian," I greet.

He spares me a smile, then sobers up and remembers to be professional. "We found her."

I blink at him, then command softly, "Lead the way, lieutenant."

He nods, leading Alastair and me toward one of the back barns where a few Hussars and hellion soldiers keep watch outside.

"We've been clearing all the buildings," explains Damian, opening the doors for us. "Found her down below with some other slaves in hiding. They claim she's the one who led them all to safety when the battle began. However, she had been held captive by the raiders for some time beforehand. Held at knifepoint and forced to heal their wounded."

I smile at that. "Despite her circumstances, she sounds like her mother."

Atlas and Atticus are already inside, and Alastair remains behind me as I step between his brothers to survey the survivors who had been slaves to the raiders. Plenty of them are laid out on cots as a dark-skinned woman treats their shallow wounds. Her figure is curvy, but not as thick as Althea's, and her skin is far lighter than her mother's was. However, she shares similar facial markings, and her eyes are of the same bewitching golden color, too.

"Bellatrix," I call.

The beautiful, Western-bred female whirls around at the sound of her name, and her attention snags on me, then my deities, *who are no doubt scowling at her*, and then me again. She attempts to size me up, and I almost smirk at the sight, then opt to spare her a kinder smile instead as I approach her with my hand outstretched to shake hers.

"My name is Rhesamyre."

She cocks her head at me, hesitantly placing her hand in mine. "Would that be *Queen* Rhesamyre?" she asks, her Western accent thick.

I nod. "It would be, but it can be quite the mouthful. So please, just call me Rhesa."

She nods, shaking my hand firmly before releasing it. "I'm under the impression we have you to thank for the aid?"

"The Hussars may have needed an extra set of hands, but it was their war."

"You just helped them win it."

I shrug. "My soldiers fought alongside their own, and plenty died on both sides. All that matters is the West is free again and back under the protection of the Hussars with Hell to back them."

Bellatrix nods, but before she can say anything more, I ask, "Will you take a walk with me, please?"

She hesitates again, glancing back at the wounded she was tending to.

"We won't stray far," I add. "Please, there are some things I would like to discuss with you."

Finally, she nods, then strides forward to walk with me away from the barn, and thus my deities. We take a path that is free of carnage and end up on the backside of town, which allows us to overlook a large portion of the desert and observe where Hussars and hellion foot soldiers tend to the wounded and dead and are gathering supplies to eventually return home.

Carefully, Bellatrix takes a breath to no doubt steel herself. "Dare I ask . . . I have a feeling this has to do with my mom?"

I dip my chin. "Her final wish was for you. To ensure you were found safe and unharmed. I promised her I would."

"And now you have." She inhales deeply, though her breath isn't even. "So what now?"

I shrug at her, meeting her teary eyes. "Now it is up to you." I cock my head. "From what I've seen and heard, you're a talented witch doctor like your mom. And you've helped a great number of people here in the West, both innocent and not. Of course, you can keep up the good fight here . . . or you can start over somewhere else."

"Somewhere . . . like Hell?"

"That's certainly one option."

"This isn't some weird *sell my soul* business, is it?"

I can't help but laugh a little. "No. No, not at all. This is simply me offering you a new place to call home. A new beginning, I suppose. After everything you and the others have been through, there is nothing else to do but start anew. Rebuild either here or elsewhere. Forgive me if I'm overstepping, but how did you know your mom had passed?"

Bellatrix smiles gently, then pulls out a necklace from within her bodice. I raise my brow at the red crystal tied to a black string, a few beads adorning it on either side.

"A heart rock," I note. "One of the gentler forms of witchcraft. Passionate spellwork, but simple in nature."

Bellatrix's smile broadens as she admires the red gem littered with faint runes in her palm. "My mom and I shared one. So when she died . . ."

"You could feel it."

She nods again, then stuffs it back into her grimy shirt once more. Taking a few breaths to rein in her emotions, she meets my eyes again. "You're right. I don't want to stay here. I was born in the West, but . . . dare I say it's never quite been a real home to me. Mom and I moved around a lot and often couldn't practice out of fear of being caught by the wrong folks. Slavers are everywhere out here, or they *were*, anyway. And while everything will be rebuilt, and people will have homes again, all I can think is that my mom won't be here to rebuild with me."

She sniffles, then snickers a little as she dabs at her eyes. "You probably think I'm some fool or weak-minded—"

"I don't," I vow. "I don't think anything other than that you just survived a great ordeal and need somewhere to rest for now. Somewhere safe and warm that can offer you sanctuary for as long as you choose. And Hell will not burn you at the stake for what you are, either." I shrug, smirking at her. "You're a witch, Bella. Own it."

She laughs. "And you're *sure* there's no ulterior motive or selling of souls going on here?"

I grin. "*Well*, I may or may not want to set you up with a male friend of mine, but that can come later." I grab her hands in mine, squeezing gently. "I'm not after anything other than your company and friendship, and even then, you can come and go as you please. You can be whoever you want to be in Hell, be it a witch, a warrior, or even a whore if you want. No one will bother you ever again, and you will *never* be a slave. Not while I reign."

Bellatrix smiles and takes a few breaths to steady her heart again. "Okay, but I have one request in return."

"Name it."

"My mother called me Bella. So do you mind calling me something else?"

I soften my smirk, winking. "Not at all, *Trix*."

CHAPTER TWENTY ONE
RHESAMYRE

"I believe we're ready to return home, my queen," claims Famine, waltzing up to my side as I survey the last of our troops that march through conveyances back into the heart of Hell. "The Hussars have control of the situation from here, and as you requested, the remaining raiders will be returning with us for *questioning*. In addition, the damage wasn't as extensive as we expected. Only a few dozen of our soldiers lost, but a few hundred are wounded and need extended time to heal due to the poison."

I nod. "Then they shall be gifted that time. Luckily, plenty of them will have a few days off already, thanks to the approaching holiday."

Famine blinks at me, then chuckles, "*Ah* I nearly forgot that All Hallow's Eve will soon be upon us. I suppose that is good timing."

I smile at the Horseman, placing my hand on his shoulder. "Return home with our troops and family, Uncle. And please, get some rest yourself."

He furrows his brows at me. "Why do you sound as if you're not coming with us?"

"Because I'm not. I have some unfinished business here that I need to tend to with my deities. As well as Pollux, too, but you needn't worry. I'll be home soon."

Famine looks as if he wants to argue or interrogate me further, but then seems to think better of it as he sighs and bows his head. "Very well. The males have proven themselves capable of watching your back. We will await your return with commendable restraint."

"Thank you."

He nods again, then takes his leave to join the rest of my family as they tie up loose ends with the Hussars. I also spot Dexter leading Orpheus home in the mix, and I smile at the sight. My smirk only widens when I spy Malcolm looking after Bellatrix, and the wolves accompany them, too.

"So," drawls Alastair as he finds a home at my side. "Where are we off to now, my love?"

I turn my eyes up to his, then glance behind us to find Atticus, Atlas, and Pollux standing nearby.

"Now," I drawl, though I'll be honest, I don't quite know *how*. "Now we go somewhere more private. I have something I want to show all of you."

Atticus crosses his arms and narrows his eyes, jerking his chin at Pollux. "And *his* presence is necessary because . . .?"

"Because I want him there," I deadpan, leaving no room for argument.

Atticus *scoffs*. "I'm going to need a little bit more than that, *darling*."

I raise my brows at him, then mutter a quiet, "*Oh.*" I level him with a look. "I get it now."

"*You get it now*?" he repeats slowly, nearly *snarling*.

I raise my chin. "I do. But you're mistaken, Atticus."

"*Doubtful.* Especially after hearing that conversation you two shared on the balcony."

I cock my head at him, unsure of how he heard that conversation without me, or at least Pollux, sensing him. "First of all, that conversation was none of your business. Hence why it didn't include you. And second of all, you obviously didn't hear *all* of it and are basing this conversation off false information. Not to mention, this is not the place to be speaking of this."

"Then where would you like us to take you, little wolf?" inquires Atlas softly, though his eyes are hard.

I will my heart not to hurt at that fact and steel myself once more as I command a conveyance to open beside me. Then I step through it wordlessly, not even glancing back to ensure they follow. I know they do.

My conveyance deposits us in the middle of the desert, and I hear Atticus mutter a few curses at this fact. Ignoring him and the others, I spread my arms out beside me to better feel the aerial patterns of the otherwise stagnant heat around us, then drop to a knee to brush away the sand beneath my boots. The males watch me wordlessly as I dig, but I sense them step closer when my fingers scrape against stone, and I push the sand further away to reveal angelic inscriptions, sigils, and seals.

"What the hell is *that* doing out here? In the middle of *nowhere*?" inquires Atlas.

"It wasn't always the middle of nowhere," replies Pollux quietly, his tone reminiscent of something I know he regrets forgetting about.

Stepping back again, I mutter a few alchemic commands to move the stone and sandy soil beneath our boots, and a moment later, the ground is trembling and parting to reveal an in-ground staircase that winds further into the earth.

"Despite my best efforts," I drawl, "it seems as though the spheres never forgot. The West kept it hidden for me."

Atticus moves to step forward and place his hand on me, but I step out of his grasp as I begin my descent into the darkness. Silently, the males follow, and as we continue, the entire structure below the sandy surface seems to shudder awake. Enchanted candelabras flicker to life on the walls, and as we finally reach the ground level, the ceiling expands with glittering chandeliers that hang from the painted rafters, which feature angels, wild beasts, and monsters.

Grand tapestries depicting archangels, and angelic symbols and runes hang from the walls near the blacked-out windows. And while the stone floor is littered with sand and dust, the marble and glass mosaics still make an attempt to glow with every step I take. Statues of *all* the archangels in their armored glory are situated near the windows against the walls, including that of Samael before he left and claimed the titles of *Devil* and *King of Hell.*

I halt before one of those very statues, staring up at a female archangel. She's beautiful, with fierce eyes, a steeled expression, and vast wings that rise behind her as if she's mid-flight and fighting. With a sword in hand, she commands respect and power, and though she no longer exists here in this state, she still commands it from the males behind me as they all halt and go eerily still and quiet.

With calculated steps, I turn to face them, leaning back against her statue as I cross my arms and meet the gazes of all three deities. Pollux stands off to the side, surveying the other statues and architecture around him with a scowl.

But his eyes are almost *sad.*

I steel myself. "Pollux should be the least of your concerns since I'm not particularly interested in entering romantic relationships with one of my blood brothers, and thus *fucking* him as I would you three."

Their eyes are wide, and their emotions are laid bare before me like never before. Jaws clenched shut, muscles pulled taut, and wild gazes that flicker between me and the statue of the winged female at my back. I would laugh at the sight if not for the circumstances.

"Her name was Myra," I explain. "She was the youngest of the archangels and was not born with a namesake like her brothers. She had to earn hers when the Ten Spheres needed a savior to free them from the tyranny of a foreign and self-proclaimed god, whose own twisted arrogance and prejudiced sense of self-righteousness caused the spheres to *burn*, while his closest followers, his Twelve Apostles, wreaked havoc upon the lands as they raped, pillaged, and murdered all species by the *hundreds*. However, despite the spherical carnage that poisoned all territories alike, none of the leaders could ban together and put their own prejudices aside to defeat their common enemy.

"Myra, however, *ever the rebellious spirit*, refused to follow protocol and sought out various warriors, monsters, and beasts that were willing to bargain and fight alongside her against their common foe. Thus, she was approached by the Yonder Star and Evergreen Fern and was given abilities like no other, making her their Champion. Her reign and command became indisputable as she swiftly gained a respectable reputation that ensured victory and peace as she drove the Apostles back.

"She commanded armies consisting of all bloodlines and beasts for *years*, but it still wasn't enough. Not when Lucifer and his Apostles still had access to the stolen and forbidden acts of magic that relied on *souls*. Both the living and the dead suffered at his hand because he acquired the spellwork and cursed ability to harvest souls and prematurely recycle them as energy, gaining knowledge and archaic magic in the process and thus, immortality.

"As the years dragged on and the bodies piled up, Myra understood there was only one way to drive him back into the sphere from whence he came. *For good.* So she concocted a spell to do just that, but the magic and sacrifice it required would mean the end of the Champion. And just to add insult to injury, after she succeeded, no one would remember her. Not her blood brothers, nor her brothers in arms, nor the friends she had made along the way despite the war raging around them. She had to give herself up completely to drive Lucifer and the Apostles back into Purgatory, the Tenth Sphere. But while she may have been forgotten, they would be, too, thus ensuring none of his other tormented followers would ever seek to free him once more. He would be trapped for eternity, and the spheres would be safe from his tyranny.

"Myra's sacrifice and body grew the Tree of Creation. The forbidden fruit containing her power had to be recycled into something pure as the raw magic could not be trusted to run amuck without a container within the remaining Nine Spheres. Nor could it return to the origins of all life and power within the Great Star and Fern.

"Thousands of centuries passed, and the Spheres once again found themselves in disarray. However, instead of a lone, rebellious archangel to bridge the gap between beasts, Three Kings were chosen instead. Gifted with tools and magic to use as weapons of peace, they led the Wild Hunt to bring tranquility to all spheres. And for a long time, this peace did last, until two mortals sought to steal the forbidden fruit.

"In doing so, Myra's convoluted spellwork faltered, thus allowing some to recall what was once lost and forgotten. And with the information of Lucifer and his Apostles in the wrong minds, discord has since returned across the spheres as those wrong minds seek to free him from the Tenth Sphere once more. And they have just about all they need to tip the scales back in their favor."

Silence is my only answer for a few heartbeats as my deities absorb the burden of my words, and Pollux still remains off to the side. His head is in his hands as he sits at the base of Samael's statue, his wings heavy, and his shoulders *shake.*

I make an attempt to swallow the lump in my throat, but the action merely succeeds in making it hurt more as the backs of my eyes burn, and tears prick along my lashes. I inhale a shaky breath.

"*Please* . . . say *something,*" I command quietly.

Alastair raises his head, but his scowl isn't as steeled as it usually is, and his silver eyes are polluted by raw anguish as he stares at me. Gently, he shakes his head, seemingly at a loss for words, much like his brothers.

"I thought," drawls Atticus, but his voice is quiet and nearly *weak.* "I thought archangels were supposed to be indestructible . . . yet you've been injured."

Carefully, I nod. "Because I'm not an archangel. At least, not anymore. I was born again to mortal parents. Re-gifted my immortality and magic, thanks to the forbidden fruit, but as I was claimed and shaped by Hell when I was only minutes old, it would stand to reason that I have since traded my wings for horns."

"An archangel's power," muses Atlas softly, his eyes meeting mine. "But a demon's body."

I nod again. "I'm not . . ." I almost choke. "*I'm not her.* I have her memories and magic, yes, but Myra died sacrificing herself to save the spheres she once called home." I steel myself again, squaring my shoulders. "I am Rhesamyre. The Queen of Hell, Daughter of the Devil, and mate to the Three Kings who rightfully claim and *deserve* their titles as deities. You are the ones who prayed and fought *tooth and* fucking *nail* to save and protect those who needed help, thus reestablishing the peace Myra wanted and worked so hard for. What she fought and died for."

They're silent again at that, until Alastair carefully bows his head before his gaze shifts to meet mine once more. He prowls toward me with renewed vigor swirling in the silver of his steeled gaze, reaching me in a few long, calculated strides before reaching out to clutch my waist. One hand rests on my hip, while the other rises to gently brush the tears from my eyes.

"After the battles ceased and the war was won, and all we had left to remember it by were the scars and trauma we collected," he drawls with a gentle rasp, "I once allowed my grief to swallow me whole when that power was stolen. It settled deep within me, drowning me. And for a long time, I let it. I sank to the bottom of that power and allowed it to consume everything I was and could be again . . . but you . . ." He shakes his head, gritting his teeth. "You make me want to *fight it.* To swim out of the depths that I have become content with. For you, I think I would be willing to try my hand at finding something to live for once again."

He presses his forehead against mine. "You are more than my *mate*, love. You are my *everything.* You are my *bride.* I wish to make you my wife, assuming you'll have me."

A choked sob escapes my lips, and my knees buckle. Alastair catches me effortlessly, and we lower to the floor together as he holds me against his chest. He presses his cheek against the top of my head, minding my horns as his arms pull taut around me like steel bands as he mutters sweet nothings to me softly.

Another's fingers trace my cheekbone, and I turn my head to meet Atticus's gentle gaze. He's crouched next to me, and he offers me a soft smile that is so at odds with the casual, playful scowl he often prefers.

"Declarations of loyalty and promises to be together for eternity are foolish in my eyes," he whispers. "For I have made plenty of them, and I've broken plenty more. Oaths, bargains, promises, and the trust placed in me by the subjects of the spheres, as well as those I once fought beside and called *brother*." He inhales sharply. "And yet here I *kneel*, willing to lower myself onto a proper knee and promise my heart to you. Promise my mind and my sword and, should you want it, my whole life. It is broken and battered, but it is yours to do with whatever you wish. And until you, I never thought it worth much, but you have proven me wrong because you claim it means something to you. My only regret now is that Alastair beat me to the question of asking for your hand, sweetness."

I laugh a little, sniffling as he takes my hand and presses kisses to my palm and fingers. His lips linger on the pulse point of my wrist as my fingers skim along his jaw, and I glance past him to meet Atlas's eyes.

He offers me another one of his kind smiles. "I left my brothers and the spheres when they needed a king the most. I abandoned all those who had placed their faith in us and hid away like a coward. Waiting for something or someone else to solve our problems for us. And then I met you. And you called me out for what I was. *A fucking coward.* You've reminded me once again what it could mean to fight for something. For *someone*. For *you*, I will fight. Either by your side as your king or as a foolish foot soldier, I don't care, so long as it is you I am fighting for. I'd be willing to pick up arms again. I already gave you my ring, little wolf . . . you've been mine since the day I found you in that desert."

I grin at him, then offer him my other hand to pull him closer to me. He obliges me, sitting nearby and rubbing my back as I remain in Alastair's arms. Steady strides echo across the floor, and my eyes search for Pollux's gaze as he nears us. His eyes are red around the edges, but his expression remains steeled once more as he watches me.

He inclines his head softly. "I'll see you around, darling."

I nod at him. "We'll talk again soon, Lux."

His eyes soften at the use of his old nickname, and then he opens a conveyance and disappears from view, thus leaving me alone with my deities in what remains of my old estate. A home away from home. The one I often fled to when *Myra* was feeling rebellious, long before the West became the wasteland it is today.

Long before the war against Lucifer and his Apostles. Long before it was forced into ruin when the rivers dried up and the forests and fields shriveled into nothing.

Long before the deities ever came into existence.

....

Prowling forward through the bloody mess of my ranks, I slice my palm open with the newly acquired Blade of Zodiacs. Forged from the light of the Yonder Star, which is emitted from the Twelve Zodiacs when they reveal their true forms and take the shape of their namesakes and constellations. Forms which we have needed in order to counteract the forbidden magic that Lucifer has commanded by turning raw souls into energy. Both from the living and those safely tucked away within the Umbra Mundi. He has robbed them all of eternity.

The Sacred Cities crumble around me, but I pay the damage no mind as I set my sights on Lucifer's disheveled form. He stands captive in Mamba's embrace, the obsidian serpent hissing and tightening his scales around Lucifer to ensure the corrupt male is unable to escape.

Lucifer groans from nearly being crushed to death, chuckling darkly as he snarls. "Quite the elaborate trap you set. My Apostles still fight the majority of your forces in the West, but here you have managed to trick me." He spits his blood at my boots, grinning. "Well, what will you do with me now, Champion?"

"Whatever may be necessary to ensure that you are thoroughly destroyed."

He clicks his forked tongue at me, a disgrace and insult to serpents everywhere, and Mamba releases another menacing hiss at the sight of it.

The supernatural male before me isn't as handsome as he used to be, as the cursed power of harnessing innocent souls through mass genocide has since corrupted his figure and face. Scars and dark lines trace his veins, and his eyes have become bloodshot and sickly yellow while his complexion grows pale. Rotten gums and black teeth and thin hair that falls out and leaves him riddled with bald patches. He's nearly all skin and bone since the magic has taken its toll, but his strength and mind have yet to waver. He remains a powerful enemy and an even more remarkable strategist that has put even Pollux, Conquest, and War's schemes to the test.

"Much like I shall do to you," he drawls, but his eyes flicker to the blade in my hand that drips with my blood. "Though, it seems as though you've tipped the scales in my favor with the creation of such a weapon. Foolish girl."

I cock my head, stalking toward him to grab him roughly by the jaw and keep his head steady to trace blood runes on his cheeks and forehead.

"We'll see," I muse, stepping back again.

He snarls at me. "What are you up to, little feather?"

....

I'm thankful when I don't jolt awake in his arms this time, but I still flinch a little all the same. I glance behind me to find Atlas spooning me, then look up from where I lie with him upon thick blankets on the floor before the burning hearth to spot Alastair snoozing on the sofa. The damn male's legs are too long to fit on the whole thing, so his feet hang off the edge of the armrest. His arms are crossed over his chest, and he seems comfortable enough. However, as I continue my sweep of the den, I fail to spot Atticus.

Carefully, I sit up and climb out of Atlas's arms, minding the books and journals that are strewn about the floor where each of

us had been reading of the spheres I was born into with a different name.

Thousands of centuries ago.

Atticus had the balls to call me *old*.

This hidden estate has acted as a tomb for all these centuries,
protecting the truth of what happened back then below our very
noses. Plenty of the journals belonged to me, as well as other foot
soldiers of all bloodlines. Diaries, medical records, descriptions of
the battles, and the dead accounted for in each. They span across
years, and I vaguely recall I had collected them over the course
of the war when the owners passed on with no family or friends
remaining to claim their belongings. It felt wrong to destroy so
many stories, so I found a way to keep them safe.

My three *fiancés* sought to read as many of the accounts as
they could. Reading not only about the fallen men and monsters
that fought against Lucifer and his Apostles, but also the winged
general and *Champion* that commanded them.

The one that could be said to have led them to their deaths.

I ignore the intrusive thoughts and memories, then set my jaw
and allow my senses and power to prowl forward in order to find
Atticus. Picking up his scent quickly enough, I pad out of the den
and down one of the hallways, then into another sitting room
adorned with artwork of people, places, and even objects. Still-
lifes, landscapes, portraits, and even the occasional abstract piece
that better encapsulates the bloody chaos that was the war.

I stride up to Atticus, my arm brushing against his as I stand
beside him, turning my gaze up to admire the oil painting of a
seated young woman and a handsome winged male standing at
attention behind her.

"Lilith was beautiful," he admits softly.

I hum, nodding. "She was. And she was a remarkable witch. We didn't suffer nearly as many losses after she and her coven came to our aid, healing and saving all those they could. That's how she met Apollo. The first time, anyway. He was a warrior first, of course, but he was the Archangel of Healing, too . . . *still technically is, I suppose*," I mutter. I take a breath. "Myra entrusted the Zodiac Blade to him after she was through with it, believing she could trust him to only use it for the greater good. He may have forgotten that vow, but his magic didn't, and he came to hold it by way of destiny after she was gone."

Atticus hums. "But even with Lilith's help, the body count is quite remarkable."

"It is, but believe it or not, Lilith *did* make a difference."

"I do believe it. I was once fortunate enough to meet and interact with Lilith before she became the crone. She was beautiful then, too. Though, it seems that she and Apollo's relationship was a better kept secret in my time than when they were together in yours."

I shrug. "No one was safe. No one was guaranteed a *tomorrow*, so people put their differences and prejudices aside to finally enjoy themselves. A witch and an archangel. Dare I say their love story has transcended time itself. For they were given chances to meet and love each other all over again, and they did. I'm not entirely sure how life proceeded after Myra died, but I would imagine plenty forgot they had ever met each other, seeing as how most friends and lovers met on the battlefield. Lilith and Apollo were no different."

Atticus hums, then turns to face me. He cups my cheek gently, his thumb tracing my cheekbone. "I owe you an apology, Rhesa."

I furrow my brows, placing my hand over his. "For what?"

"For using my power to eavesdrop on your conversation, first of all. And then jumping to conclusions about you and Pollux."

I offer him a small smile. "While I'll admit, the eavesdropping pissed me off, you have nothing to apologize for, Atticus. If anything, I owe you and your brothers an apology . . . I didn't mean to keep this from you. I just—"

"You need not explain yourself, sweetness. It was a heavy secret to bear, and we're just grateful you trusted us enough to share that burden. You're not alone in this anymore."

I nod, then lean up onto my toes to kiss him. Atticus wastes no time in hoisting me up, and I wrap my legs around his waist as he presses me against the closest wall. His mouth opens to devour mine, sucking my lips and tongue into his as one hand grasps my neck, and the other sneaks between us so he can rub my clit. We all ditched our battle leathers and armor long ago, and now parade around in the base layers that hug our bodies and leave very little to the imagination.

Atticus *rips* my shirt and then my pants as he keeps me pinned to the wall to kiss and taste me everywhere he can possibly latch his mouth onto. Often nibbling and biting gently to mark me as his, lapping at my blood whenever he pierces my flesh too roughly. My snarls and moans mix as one, and he chuckles at the sounds I give him before he devours those, too.

Then he flips us around, and I suddenly find myself on my own feet again as he presses my front against the nearby table. His hands grope me and fondle my ass as he sinks his teeth into my shoulder, then he trails his tongue down the center of my spine, licking the brand I received from Mamba. I feel him tease my soaked entrance with the tip of his cock, and he grabs me by my *horns* to pull my head up.

I meet his feral gaze through the dusty mirror that hangs upon the wall for decorative purposes straight ahead of us, and he bares his teeth at me, grinning as he husks, "Watch closely now, sweet spice."

He doesn't give me a chance to reply as he bucks his hips to enter me in one successful, swift movement. Nor does he give me much time to adjust to his size as he starts thrusting. My eyes roll backward from the force of it, but he doesn't allow my gaze to stray far from the mirror as one of his hands keeps a firm hold of my horns. The other finds a home upon my left hip, and his fingers are long enough to stroke both my *truculent* brand and my clit at the same time.

Holy hell.

He teases my sensitive bundle of nerves in addition to the individual letters of my brand, and a mixed, nearly knee-buckling sensation of lust and desire floods my system. It's overwhelming in itself and makes my vision blur with pleasure as all my thoughts are consumed with him. *By him.* Allowing him to please me as he uses my body to please himself. His length stretches me and rubs my spongy, tight inner walls, and I'm so *wet* for him it's nearly ridiculous, but the sounds of our sex only seem to egg him on.

And then I realize with a start that these emotions are not only mine, but *his*. That somehow, through our brand, I can now feel him *everywhere*. His entire existence wraps around my mind in a gentle caress, and his lust, rage, need, jealousy, and undeniable, *unyielding,* and *startling loyalty* and love for me nearly overwhelm me. And nothing else matters but his hands on me and his cock inside me. Right now. Him and I as *one*. Mine. *He's mine.*

"A-Atticus," I moan.

He shushes me in mock sympathy, arching his hips to go *deeper*, which I didn't even believe was possible. His thrusts are powerful as he hits that pleasurable spot within me with every stroke, his moans and groans filling my ears and sending me to the brink of my pleasure.

"I want you to remember this sight," he husks. *Thrust.* "Every time you touch yourself." *Thrust.* "Remember that this feeling is the one I give you every time you pleasure yourself."

He licks the pointed shell of my ear, snarling softly, "*Because I certainly will.*"

I *shatter*.

....

Standing with my toes in the desert sand wearing only Atticus's shirt since he *ripped* mine, I watch as the soil swallows the entrance to my old estate once more.

"It stood for thousands of years after Myra left," drawls Atlas. "I believe it correct to assume it'll stand for a thousand more after the spheres reset themselves again. If such a phenomenon repeats, that is. Long after all of us are gone."

"Let's pray to whatever the *fuck* will listen that *that* won't be the case," mutters Atticus.

I nod. "*Let's* . . . this place protected all her secrets in the process, and serves as the only memorial for many of the soldiers that have since been forgotten with her."

Alastair places his hands on my shoulders, drawing me into his chest as he presses a kiss to my temple. "It'll be here whenever you want to return to it, love. We don't have to abandon it if you don't want to."

I shrug. "We'll see. For now, let's go home."

The Three Kings nod, then open a conveyance to do as I've requested.

Atlas,

We're all tired of fighting.
But I know you and your brothers are exhausted, and I would
never reach out if it were not of grave importance. And I
believe you know that.
With that said, I will let it lie. It remains your choice, of course,
but I would encourage you to return. The spheres need you.
I've come to realize that I need you. But more importantly,
your brothers need you.
Don't believe me? Come see for yourself.

Best regards,
Rhesamyre.

CHAPTER TWENTY TWO
RHESAMYRE

Strolling forward in my crown and leathers, I allow Greed and Envy to prowl ahead of me by just a stride. The two of them dress in menacing, blacked-out suits, and their scowls are firmly in place as they size up the hellion military outpost and prison camp before us known as Castle Blackstone. By far, it's the most forbidding of our slave camps where sinners mine the obsidian ore of the Blackened Mountain Range under the watchful eye of hellhounds and sadistic guards alike.

The slaves here have proven themselves incapable of earning and deserving second chances to lessen their punishments, and thus have been assigned to mine these dark caves for all of eternity until the Yonder Star above is satisfied with their pathetic souls, and seeks to free them upon its own accord and allow them eternal rest and peace within the proper confines of the Umbra Mundi.

The Devil may have been the one to bargain and allow the sinful, spiteful creatures a chance at power, but it is ultimately the Great Star and Fern above, using Death as their dagger, that allow the souls to be placed where we see fit when sinners sign their names and choose to damn themselves. It was always a sensitive, convoluted arrangement between us of Hell and the powers that be, but the Devil was, and arguably still remains, the best of us when it came to bargains. He ensured all was fair and just when delivering punishments that fit the crimes, and I strive to follow in his footsteps.

Hence why I am visiting such an infamous hellion entrapment now, guarded by two of the assassins as we observe the courtyard that reeks of vile, *evil* souls that have yet to feel remorseful for whatever atrocities they committed elsewhere—commonly rape or the mass murder of innocents, and then naturally whatever they agreed to when bargaining with the Devil himself.

Guards stand at attention upon the walls and catwalks that stretch across the lawn of the castle, and plenty of cages and cells that hang or are embedded into the stone structures sit facing the yard and thus open to the elements, while more rows of posts and hanging manacles litter the open archways, and slaves rot away in shackles or behind bars. They often snivel and curse up a storm at the guards, each other, and even me when they spot me, spitting and snarling at me with hateful gazes. I smirk at the sight, ignoring the way my boots splash in the questionable liquids that puddle near the cells.

Hellhounds prowl the outer perimeters of the wards and walls, often taking it upon themselves to punish the slaves as they see fit when the sinners step out of line, thus losing fingers in the process as their other appendages are mauled to the bone and devoured. Hellhounds have always been aggressive chewers, after all, and they often keep teething well into their final decades of life.

Other lines of shackled slaves march in and out of the mines carrying sacks or pushing wagons of raw obsidian, while the guards on duty bark orders and crack their whips ruthlessly. Many of these lower-bred demons are favored for such command and often desire the outlets of overseeing slavery and torturing evil souls to relieve their own tensions of magic and sin that coil within their blood and bodies.

Hellion nature at its finest.

"Apologies. We were not made aware of your arrival until the last minute."

I glance to the side to survey the heavyset demon that strides toward me. He's burly in nature with a potbelly protruding from his torn and stained leathers, and his common face reminds me of a bat's proportions. Blue horns twist forward from his forehead, and his dull black hair sits tied in a low tail. His blue-tinted skin is flushed pink as if he's always out of breath, and a healthy beard grows from his jaw and sits in a few braids. I glance at his choices of weaponry: a few daggers, his trusted whip, and a standard short sword.

"Warden Bael," I drawl. "A pleasure to see you again."

"Likewise, my queen."

The warden extends his clawed appendage to reach for mine, and I allow the slimy male to kiss my knuckles. I don't miss the way his eyes brighten at the sight of the rings I wear. First, the Ring of Rubies gifted by Atlas that rests upon my right hand, and then his eyes flick down to the obsidian stone upon my left hand that features diamonds, emeralds, and rubies embedded into the twisting silver braids that surround the main radiant cut of black stone.

My engagement ring. Gifted to me by the deities just this morning before I left to attend to my queenly duties. All three on their knees before me was quite the sight, and I let them slide that ring onto my finger before letting them slide their cocks into me one at a time, each one waiting with barely restrained patience as they readied themselves to individually fuck me and once again declare their love for me over and over again. Moaning and muttering my name like a prayer as they brought me to climax on their cocks something fierce.

"And might I add," continues Bael with a sleazy grin. "You have grown into quite the beauty, my queen. Our late king only allowed you to visit a handful of times, and even back then, he kept you nearby. Never in my wildest dreams would I have ever expected you to look like . . . well . . . *you.*"

"What you lack in imagination you thankfully make up for in your torture skills, warden. And the Devil was smart to keep me close, seeing as how most of your slaves here are rapists of the worst and cruelest calibers."

He chuckles. "Indeed they are." He makes a show of looking outward at his operation. Glancing over the cages full of slaves and whipping posts where males and females sit chained with bloody lines running down their backs, splitting their already torn and stained shirts. "And I do hope Castle Blackstone is to your liking."

I hum, ignoring him. "And what of the mines themselves? The obsidian veins are holding strong, I presume?"

"As strong as ever. The mountains remain as plentiful as the day we carved into them centuries ago."

I nod. "And I assume you have all you need here to continue contributing to Hell? What of your men stationed here? Do they desire anything as far as accommodations are concerned?"

The warden looks taken aback by my inquisition, blinking once before he stutters, "T-The men are satisfied."

I raise my brow at him. "*Satisfied?* You sound unsure of yourself, warden."

"I will see to it that my men have all they need and want to continue serving you and our kingdom to the best of their ability, my queen."

He says that very slowly, as though he still isn't all that sure of himself. I almost want to laugh.

I hum again. "Very well, warden. Then I believe that concludes our *last-minute* visit."

He nods, bowing slightly. I turn on my heel and take my leave, Envy and Greed remaining by my sides as we stride down the staircase into the courtyard once more.

"He seems as clueless as ever," I quip quietly, eyeing the slaves chained to the walls nearby.

"Brain cells are not always required to be cruel, Your Majesty," supplies Envy. "He is skilled in the art of torture, but that doesn't mean he has the means to *interrogate* these prisoners. He is simply a sadist who fell into leadership seamlessly under the early years of your father's reign."

"He is loyal to Hell, and that is all that matters. And what of the guards and hounds here? Are we sure there are no complaints on their end? It would be a hassle to deal with a mutiny over the approaching holiday."

Envy chuckles quietly. "We'll be sure to guarantee all is well with the demons stationed here, Your Majesty."

I smirk back at him, mounting Orpheus near the portcullis. "Good." I grin at my uncles. "I do hope you enjoyed watching the warden squirm as much as I did."

Greed chuckles now, mounting his stallion in sync with Envy. "Perhaps a bit too much, my queen."

I wink at him, and the three of us move our horses off the castle grounds so we may open a conveyance to our next destination.

The rest of the day is spent playing politics with the lords and ladies across Hell, as well as the common folk and soldiers within the outlying towns and outposts. Throughout the visits, the generals and assassins switch places with each other to both accompany and guard my sides, coffee housing with our levels of leadership as we bounce between forts and villages well into the evening. And while I know my deities would have loved to join me, I find it best to have my proper court join me for these errands.

Especially since I desire the individual time with each of them to reveal what I really am, as well as who I once was as far as wings and wars are concerned.

Needless to say, they were all quite stunned into silence as I paraded around on the arms of other lords and leaders, making small talk and masking my anxiety over my family's reactions to the truth with a professional scowl or smile for pleasantries and schemes to better the lives of hellion soldiers and civilians alike, in addition to a few slaves-turned-servants while I'm at it. We discuss the matters of altered punishments and contracts as rewards for continued loyalty and good behavior over the past centuries.

Returning to the Obsidian Palace, I part ways with Lust and Gluttony as I make my way toward the court's private training arenas where I sense the lieutenants and my girls roughhousing. Stroking the pawprints upon my left knuckles, I summon the Wolves of Woe as I halt in the archway that leads into the training mats, surveying the scene of the lieutenants laughing with the girls as they all spar with one another. My honorary brothers are no doubt teaching the girls how to better defend themselves, and then getting into a pissing contest amongst each other in the process, too.

"You've gotten fucking sloppy, my friend," teases Gage as he twirls his twin knives, sizing up Damian.

Damian points his spear at the hybrid demon of wolfish origins, grinning in a manner that is all things reckless and feral.

"Careful not to trip over that fluffy tail of yours, wolf. Lest you desire me to chop it off and feed it to the hounds."

I roll my eyes at the two of them, then grin at the sight of Tally, Fern, Thea, and Trix all cheering quietly and watching the match with trained eyes as Mal and Silas explain what's happening and who has the upper hand every time the reaper and wolf clash. All of them are dressed in lightweight training fabrics, thus showcasing a fair bit of skin, which gleams with sweat from their activities. The girls' ponytails and braids are damp as strands cling to their shoulders and foreheads, and I can clearly see the red lines caused by safety wraps still fresh on their wrists and arms.

Meanwhile, the males opt to remain shirtless, thus revealing their toned muscles and inked torsos that are similar in design to one another since the tattoos and hellion sigils indicate their shared brands with their generals. By far, these four males are the least tatted up when compared to the rest of the hellion court, and have yet to branch out and receive any more tattoos on their own accord. Seems as though the smoky patterns and mandala prints are enough to satisfy their desires.

And as far as I know of the girls, only Feronia has ink. Her love for the sun and ocean is printed down her spine in a single, line-art pattern.

A wet nose rubs against my palm, and I raise my hand to rub the ears of one of my wolves. The other four stand casually behind me, sniffing about as they wait for my commands.

I stride forward and make my presence known. "Can I have his tail when you chop it off, Dami?"

The reaper grins at me, dodging a kick from Gage as he replies, "Why, of course, my queen."

I smile and wink at him, coming to stand by the others while the wolves trail behind me, watching the fight with impressively honed focus that finds most predators of their caliber.

Tally tips forward to meet my gaze around Silas's chest, and it appears as though she's going to tease me about something until she catches sight of my eyes, and the corners of her lips turn downward.

"Hell below, Rhesa," she drawls softly. "You look *exhausted*."

I place my hands on my hips as the rest come to study me. "Well, that's rude."

Tally straightens again, coming closer. "No, no. I mean no offense, really. It's just an observation."

"Old habits die hard, I suppose," quips Trix. "Being an ex-genie and all. But she isn't wrong. You *do* look tired."

I huff a quiet laugh. "Well, it has been a rather *long* day."

"And why does it sound as though it isn't over for you yet?" inquires Silas, raising his brow at me.

I shrug. "Because it isn't. Being queen has plenty of perks, sure. But the workload has certainly doubled."

"Have you eaten dinner yet?" asks Mal. "Actually, have you eaten *anything* today?"

I go to say yes or at least explain myself, but come up short, and opt to segue as I turn to Dami and Gage again. "You two. Quit fooling around and get over here. I have something for you eight. Well, more specifically the girls, but it appears as though you lot are quickly becoming a *package deal*."

"Would this *something* have anything to do with those wolves of yours?" inquires Gage, sheathing his knives.

I nod, then call my five dire wolves of suspicious origins over, and they quickly sit nearby at attention. I make eye contact with each of my girls as they stand near the male they have swiftly taken a liking to, and I smile at the sight.

"It would do my heart good to know you four have an extra layer of protection in addition to the lieutenants, so I'm gifting each of you a wolf."

"*Whoa*," says Thea, eyeing the massive canines, her blue eyes sparkling in awe. "Really?"

I nod, smirking again as I repeat, "Really. So, Thea, you'll take responsibility of Vex."

Said soot-gray wolf saunters up to the woman, and Thea bends down to better pet and kiss the menacing dire wolf with teeth made of half-light steel rather than bone.

Continuing down the line, I give the black one, Veto, to Feronia.

Between the two grays, Barter now belongs to Trix, and Dolor belongs to Tally.

"And I'll keep ahold of Embrace," I say, rubbing the white wolf's ears as he sits next to me.

The girls look more than pleased with their new *pets* as they swiftly crouch to give the canines well-deserved belly scratches and kisses, and the lieutenants also seem thankful with the added layer of protection.

I nod my head at each of them before taking my leave again, strolling down the hallways toward my office, *which used to be Samael's*, so I can get some last-minute desk work done before I turn in for the evening. Embrace is by my side as I enter the room, and he goes straight to the settee settled before the windows to lie down for a nap. I, however, am not that lucky, and promptly take a seat at my desk to get to work on signing documents, reviewing forms and letters, as well as reading over the recent reports from the Hussars and Artemis, in addition to the rest of

Hell's stocks, food supply, and the overall financial state of my kingdom.

My mind often wanders to the deities, but I do my best not to get all hot and bothered as memories from this morning flood my mind, and instead, I try to focus on my work.

Keyword: *try*.

Such as how to deal with the approaching dangers of Lucifer and his Apostles, as well as Apollo, Andrew, and the rest of the Zodiacs and archangels, too. Revealing everything to the rest of my family has left me emotionally drained, but considering what I told them, they all seemed to have taken it as well as possible.

Though none of them were all that happy about it. Quite pissed, actually, but I don't believe it is *at me*. Just at our situation as a whole.

Seven devils, I'm fucking *tired*.

Not to mention, horny as fuck again and in need of a nap. But *wow*, sleep-deprived and amorous as hell may just shape up to be a deliciously dangerous and satisfying combination.

CHAPTER TWENTY-THREE
ATLAS

"*Ugh*. You three without Rhesamyre is just depressing as fuck. Not to mention *obnoxious* as hell."

Alastair growls lowly at Pollux from where he sits with Atticus, a game of chess between them. Atticus is winning, and it's pissing Alastair off again.

Meanwhile, I bide my time with reading and researching the oldest spells we know of, as far as memories and minds are concerned. Odds are that whatever we need to finish lifting the veil of Myra and Lilith's old spellwork will be found in her buried estate in the West, but I figured it would be worth a shot to skim through the hellion texts again. It certainly beats just waiting and wandering around aimlessly for Rhesa to return from being *queen* all day.

The Horsemen and assassins have alternated going with her to visit every possible outpost, fort, and city across Hell, and every time they return, they come straight to those of us who were already aware of *Myra*, demanding answers and inquiring about what the *fuck* we're going to do now.

We all seem to be at a loss as far as that is concerned, as not even my little wolf has voiced what she wants to do yet. General Death has since been busy fraternizing with the Lord of Sanity, and as far as I know, Pollux has been busy keeping an eye on those in the Celestial Cities, too. Keeping his ears open for any chatter regarding *their* impending return.

Sloth sighs next to me on the sofa, tossing his head back to rub his eyes with a tatted hand. "*We're fucked*," he mutters, then meets my eyes through the crack in his ring-clad fingers. "I've got nothing, and I've read every book in this damn palace at least *thrice*. If the answers were here, we'd already have them. At least *that* I am certain of."

I find myself nodding in agreement. "Perhaps the Western estate would be the better option."

"Or the Hollow," adds Envy absentmindedly from across the table settled on the other side of the den. One tatted hand is busy twirling a dagger while the other grasps some hellion parchments pertaining to the kingdom's current wellbeing.

"*Fuck the Wise Men*," growls Wrath, a cue stick in hand as he plays with War and Conquest. He lines up his shot, then sinks the ball he had aimed at before taking a swig from his glass of glittering whiskey. "They're useless fucks and would never *lower themselves* to fraternize with . . . *well* . . . *anyone* who isn't *them*."

"And you've tried breaking and entering?" inquires Alastair, quirking a brow.

"Don't even get me *fucking* started," snarls Pride, throwing daggers. "Been there, done that. *Fucking impenetrable*."

I nod along. "I honestly don't recall ever even *meeting* any of the Wise Men. Received plenty of letters and documents, but I've never had a proper conversation with them."

"Trust us," drawls Death. "You're not missing out on much."

"Imagine a bunch of fickle old men who believe they know everything because they read it in a book somewhere," adds Conquest. "Then you apply the theatrics of a dramatic actor, the theoretical mindset of a scholar who's never practiced what he preaches, and then the integral belief of a busybody who thinks everything is *their* business."

"Sounds like a nightmare," snarls Alastair, resetting the chess board since Atticus beat him. *Again.*

"Worse," admits Famine. "Much, *much worse.*"

We all fall silent again, then turn our gazes to the last two to arrive, having since just returned from traversing the kingdom with Rhesamyre, greeting every*one* or *thing* fucking imaginable in her quest to *play politics.* Quite commendable and necessary, but I feel as though she rushed to get it all done in a single day. Then to top it all off, revealing her past to the rest of her family?

I shake my head at the thought, then reach out through our imprint to speak with her. However, when I stroke her mental shields, she doesn't let up. She may be so mentally checked out that she doesn't even realize I'm knocking, but I know better than to stroke our shared *sarang* brand, even though it has begun to itch, meaning I am at least a *minor* thought in her head at the moment. However, unlike my brothers, I am content to leave her be and give her the space she so obviously desires if she isn't actively seeking us out at this very moment.

Gluttony and Lust stride in and go straight for the bar, pouring themselves some whiskey with heavy hands before settling down somewhere and setting their dark gazes on us.

"So," drawls Lust. "Seems as though we've all finally been made aware of *Myra* now."

"Go easy," warns Pollux, his gaze cool despite the obvious threat lacing his tone. "*Rhesamyre* has trusted us with this knowledge, and we would all do well to remember how expensive that trust has proven to be."

Gluttony narrows his eyes at the archangel. "I was under the impression *you* were the one to remind *her.*"

I flick my eyes to Pollux again, watching the muscles in his jaw tense before he replies smoothly, "I was this time around, but once upon a time, my *sister* came to me with her concerns. As well as the knowledge of her newly acquired abilities and title as *Champion*. She trusted me back then, and she still trusts me now. And all of *you* would do well to try and recall on your own accord what happened back then." He meets my eyes, then glances at my brothers as he mutters, "Well, *most of you*, anyway."

Death sighs, and the release of breath sounds thousands of years old. "Look, it doesn't matter who amongst *our court* has re-called *Myra* first. What does matter is who else has recalled her, and therefore the evils involved. We know that Kure, Draven, and Wicker have all been made privy to the knowledge of what is to come, and having spoken with all three of them, I can guarantee and vouch for them. They will stand with Hell and Rhesa, just as they once stood with Myra all those centuries ago. Evidently, fucking around with Lucifer's mood swings isn't a goal of theirs, as they wish to keep their lives *and* eternal souls."

Atticus nods. "That's reassuring at least, and I would imagine it is also safe to say that the majority of Hell's current allies will still stand behind Rhesa, too. Including that of the Hussars and Artemis. Though the mortal kingdom is still in disarray and will most likely be caught in the crossfires if we're completely honest with ourselves."

"Don't count on the celestials, either," adds Pollux.

War raises his brow. "What of your brethren?"

Pollux doesn't answer, and that seems to serve as an answer in itself. *Don't count on the celestials.*

"Very well," continues Atticus. "Though, from Rhesa's stories and your collective knowledge of the events back then, I am un-der the impression that what we have now won't be enough to defeat them."

"Yes and no," admits Conquest, glancing between my brothers and me. "We may not have the combined strength of angels, monsters, demons, and men fighting against the Apostles and Lucifer, but we do have you three."

"That's right," adds Famine, his eyes lighter with the reminder, but not by much. "Like Rhesamyre, you three have magic directly derived from the Great Star and Fern. Not just bloodline power, but raw, gifted energy. Hopefully, that will serve as enough weight to tip the scales in our favor."

"*Hopefully*," mutters Pollux again, taking a long, slow sip from his whiskey. "Where is our lovely queen, anyway?"

"She claimed to have other matters to attend to," answers Lust. "We parted ways once we got back."

I glance down at my *sarang* brand, feeling the ink flare for a moment. Alastair and Atticus seem to glance down at themselves, too, as if feeling the same itch I did. And once again, I reach out to Rhesa through our bond, but she doesn't respond immediately.

"She's fucking exhausted," claims Atticus, rubbing his own eyes as if he suddenly feels drained, too. "And hungry, and . . ." Atticus cocks his head, then slowly rises from his seat.

I narrow my eyes at the sight of how *strained* he looks all of a sudden, then reach out to Rhesamyre once more in another vain attempt to get her attention before my brothers do.

Little wolf?

A heartbeat of silence, and then, *Atlas?*

I raise my brows at her *tone*. She sounds as if I just woke her up from a deep sleep, but at the same time, she's nearly *breathless* as she mutters my name. Her voice is a gentle caress that wraps itself around my mind and slithers down my spine, leaving delightful shivers in its wake. Most of which shoot straight to my cock like a fucking waterfall.

"*Wait a damn minute*," drawls Pride, narrowing his eyes on Atticus and then me. "Can you *feel* her exhaustion and hunger?"

Atticus nods slowly, then lifts his shirt to reveal the tail end of a recent brand that flares and pulses like a heartbeat upon his ribs.

Pollux barks a sudden laugh, cursing demon names under his breath. "You can feel her emotions." He looks at me. "And you can read her mind."

I'm not about to correct him that it's more like mentally communicating and focus instead on what Atticus must be feeling. Because if she sounded like *that* . . .

Oh.

A wry grin dares to split Atticus's face, and I believe most of us are taken aback by the sight of it at first.

"Well, if you'll excuse me, gentlemen," he quips. "I best turn in for the evening."

"*Bullshit*," snarls Alastair, rising to his feet because he no doubt *knows*, or at least *senses*, what our brother is about to get up to. *Who* he's about to *do*.

So, while my brothers busy themselves with confronting one another, I slip out unnoticed and prowl down the hall toward Rhesamyre's study. Without bothering to knock, I stride in silently, then immediately take notice of the slumbering white wolf on the settee, and then Rhesa slumped over her desk straight ahead of me. She raises her head just enough to meet my gaze, and while her eyes certainly look tired, her hellfire gaze is still sharp enough to pierce right through me.

I stride forward and round the desk, then carefully pull her chair out and crouch right in front of her, immediately cupping her cheeks in my hands so I can find her eyes again.

"Atlas," she murmurs, leaning into my palms and almost tipping forward in the process.

"Hey there, my little wolf." I rub my thumbs over her eyes, and she hums as she closes them. "You need to eat something, and going to bed would be a good idea, too."

She hums again, and I allow my senses to open once more so I can *scent* her.

Fucking hell.

My eyes snap to where her legs barely part, and though her leggings are dark, I can still scent how *wet* she is. Her arousal is sweet and makes the air heavy with lust, and I slowly raise my eyes to meet hers again. She's already looking at me.

It won't stop, she mutters into my mind.

"What won't stop, little wolf?"

It has a heartbeat of its own, she continues, nearly whining. *I . . . I tried to take care of it myself, but I'm so* fucking *tired, Atlas, I—*

"Shh, *shh*, little wolf," I coo, rising back onto my feet to pull her to my chest. I pick her up gently, and she clings to me immediately by wrapping her legs around my waist as her hands slide around my neck. Her face buries into my shoulder, and she trails her nose up the side of my neck as she inhales my scent, and then she *licks* me.

I groan, my cock already rock fucking hard and straining against my pants. Then with ease, I walk over to the larger sofa embedded into the bookcase and take a seat with her on my lap just as she begins to grind on me. Her core is warm and welcoming and *so fucking wet.*

With great difficulty, I pry her face away from my neck where she had been nibbling and sucking gently and hold her chin between my thumb and forefinger as I search her hellfire eyes, finding nothing there but a hazy gaze that seems to have trouble focusing on me.

"Rhesamyre?"

She hums, her eyelids heavy, as are her breaths; her chest begins to heave as she lowers her eyes to rake up and down my form. I squeeze her chin harder in warning, and she snaps her eyes upward to meet mine again. The exhaustion is obviously making her vulnerable, while the *bonds* are making her clingy and horny as hell.

"You're exhausted. You haven't eaten all day for whatever *fucking reason* that we won't get into right now. And you're not quite in your right mind at the moment."

She *pouts* at me, and fuck me if it isn't *adorable*.

So you don't want to fuck me? she inquires silently again.

"I don't want to fuck you when you're not quite in control of your own actions right now," I admit softly.

She growls quietly, though the sound is halfhearted at best and not nearly as threatening as her usual snarls. Then she slowly moves to get off me, her limbs almost *trembling*, but I snatch her by the waist and spin her around so her back is pressed against my front. She gasps quietly at the action, and I trail my nose up the side of her neck as one of my hands splays across the flat of her stomach, and the other sinks lower to cup her heat. Her thighs twitch, and she attempts to hump my hand, but I raise it just enough so she's incapable of getting the friction she desires.

"Now *where* do you think you're going?" I inquire softly, almost *snarling*.

She blinks up at me, narrowing her eyes as she replies silently, *To find a deity that* will *fuck me.*

I chuckle lowly. "They wouldn't while you're in this state, either."

Debatable, she replies.

I stop myself from agreeing since I have a point to make here, and instead shake my head, muttering her name repeatedly as I trail my nose up the side of her neck again while kissing her skin gently. She shudders in my arms, and I lower my hand again to press my thumb against her clit gently, and she bucks her hips against my palm.

"After I make you come," I husk, licking the shell of her pointed ear before taking the entire lobe into my mouth, "you're going to eat a proper meal, and then you're going to soak in the bath before I take you to bed to sleep. *Just. Sleep.* Do we have a deal, my little wolf?"

She nods her head gently, and I stay mindful of her horns as I hug her tighter to my chest, dipping my head to rest in the crook of her neck as my hand slips inside her leggings so I can stroke her bare, *sopping*-wet core. She whimpers as she bucks her hips again, grinding against my palm, and I let her as I rub her clit for her. Splaying my fingers, I dip further into her entrance to gather the wetness pooled there, then spread it over her sensitive bud and through her folds.

A-Atlas, she moans straight into my mind, and my dick twitches at the sound. Then she glances back at me and mutters, "Fuck me properly, or don't fuck me at all."

I raise my brow at her, then slowly slip my hand from her heat. And before she can open that smart mouth of hers again, I grab her by the waist and spin us around so her back is bouncing against the sofa, and I'm left kneeling in front of her. I tug her leggings down, then latch my mouth onto her core and suck and lick until she's writhing and clenching the sides of my head with her thighs while her fingers thread through my hair.

I flatten my tongue over her folds before flexing it to penetrate her, my hands groping her ass and massaging up and down her thighs. Then, once I feel her begin to tighten as if she's going to come, I lean back and observe her for a moment. Her hands fall away from me as she tries to finish herself off, but I grab her wrists gently and press them against her stomach.

"Hands to yourself, little wolf," I chide, and she whines and snarls softly at me, her eyes hooded with lust and fatigue. "You'll come; I promise. But on *my* terms. You demanded I fuck you properly, so the only thing you'll be coming on tonight is my cock, *hmm*?"

She nods her head at me vigorously, her mouth agape and thus revealing her extended fangs, and I'm once again reminded that she's most likely starving. I lower my gaze again but am forced to pause and take in the sight of her clenching core as more wetness seeps out of her, flowing all the way down to her *secondary hole*. And before I can stop myself, I reach forward and gather her wetness again, then slide my fingers down to swirl her back entrance, prodding gently and teasingly, then daring to press forward to the first knuckle when she tenses and relaxes again.

"I'm surprised," she mumbles, and I meet her weary gaze again. "I figured at least one of you might, but I didn't think it'd be *you* . . . my bets were on Atticus."

I chuckle darkly. "Just so you know, I take it as a challenge when you say my brother's name when *I'm* the one fucking you. And I'll admit, I'm surprised, too . . . I find all of you tempting, Rhesamyre, and thus I want to fuck you everywhere I can. In any way I can, all the time."

"That's . . . *promising*."

I grin, standing up again to undo my pants and fuck her the way she wants me to. "I'm glad you think so." I drop my trousers, and my hard-on springs outward. Then leaning forward, I brace my hands on either side of her head upon the back of the sofa, kissing her gently as my tip teases her entrance. "I am completely enamored with you, Rhesamyre. All of you. Everywhere. *All the fucking time.*"

I slide into her slowly, and she gasps gently at the intrusion. Then once I'm completely seated inside of her all the way to the hilt, I groan deeply, and then pull out just as slowly.

A-Atlas . . . please, she fucking begs.

I can't help my grin, then I grip the back of the sofa harder and roll my hips forward, giving her the motion and friction she so desires, and when she goes to rub her clit on her own accord, I don't stop her this time. We find our pleasure together, rolling into a rocking rhythm that isn't slow by any means, but somehow more sensual than our usual fucking. Her tight, wet walls hug my cock perfectly, nearly strangling me, and I groan at how tight and wet she is for me. And soon enough, we're finding our climaxes in sync, too. Feeling her walls clench around my cock is probably as close to heaven as I'll ever get, and once we're both satisfied, I slowly pull out of her again, my seed seeping from her core as her heat twitches.

She slumps against the back of the sofa, breathing heavily as she closes her eyes, and I watch with an awed sense of satisfaction while I stuff myself back into my pants. Her chest heaves up and down a few more times before settling down into a steadier rhythm, but her eyes remain closed even as I lean forward to grab her from under her knees and back. Disregarding her clothes on the floor, I hold her close as I prowl out of the office and toward her bedroom, which is thankfully in the same wing.

"Rhesa?" I coo softly, and it takes her a minute before she's humming in reply. "You remember our deal, right, little wolf? You need to eat something."

I'm not hungry, I barely hear her mumble. Then she snuggles closer into my shoulder. *Sleep.*

"Not yet. You need sustenance and a bath."

Are you saying I smell?

I chuckle. "Never, but I'm sure soaking in a warm bath with your favorite herb infusions will help you sleep better, no?"

She shrugs halfheartedly, and I finally reach her bedroom. She remains in my arms the entire way to her bathing chamber, and I place her on her feet just long enough to fiddle with the faucets.

"Will you fall over if I take my hand off you?" I inquire, watching her fucking *sway*.

She doesn't reply, and her eyes are still fucking closed. So, with a careful breath, I keep one hand on her waist the entire time I prep her bath. And once the tub is full and steaming, I pick her up again and gently lower her into the dark petals and bubbles. She hums a little, and in record time, I'm stripped bare and climbing in behind her. I glide my hands over her slick skin, tracing soapy circles as I go while unbraiding and washing her hair for her, kissing a few of the strands as I go.

"You still need to eat, little wolf," I whisper into her ear, and she barely opens her eyes to look at me now.

You.

I raise my brow. "Me?"

She nods a little. *I'll be satisfied with just you.*

Nodding in understanding, I raise my wrist to her mouth where her fangs extend, poking out from behind her perfect lips.

Her nose twitches once when she scents my vein nearby, and she opens her eyes, then grasps my arm gently and brings it closer to her teeth.

I wince a little at the initial bite, but then relax again as she hums and sucks on my blood. I rest my chin atop her wet hair, minding her horns as my other hand rests on her right hip bone, rubbing gently.

"I love you," I say.

She pauses in her drinking for a moment, but then settles against me once more and resumes as she repeats, *I love you.*

I smile, kissing the top of her head.

Eventually, she drinks her fill, and I pull my wrist away from her gently; the wound swiftly closes. She lays her head back against my shoulder, and it's once again on me to maneuver us both out of the bath, towel us dry, and then carry her to bed.

I slip into the sheets naked with her, resting chest to chest as she snuggles into me, my arm slung around her middle, pressing against her lower back to keep her close.

When her breathing evens out the rest of the way, I breathe a sigh of relief myself and just take a moment to study this stubborn, beautiful woman that lies in my arms.

Demon and archangel.

I hold her tighter at the thought, vowing that no one will harm her. *Lucifer can go fuck himself.* And his Apostles . . . I can't help but grin a little, feeling a piece of my power I thought I had buried long ago flare to life again at the thought of *slaughtering* the Apostles. Butchering and torturing and eviscerating them so thoroughly that *nothing* remains of them this time around.

Speaking of buried power, I feel another piece of my magic being tugged on as if a foreign ward is being agitated, and I warily open the mental door I once locked decades ago.

Is she okay? inquires Alastair, straight to the point. Never mind the fact that we haven't used this old bond as a way to mentally communicate in *centuries.*

She's finally asleep, I reply. *And it wasn't fucking easy by any means.*

Lucky bastard, growls Atticus. *I was on my way to her, then you had to sneak off and steal my girl.*

Your girl? Repeats Alastair.

Our woman, *brothers,* I amend. *And yes. While you two were having your pathetic pissing contest, I went ahead and aided Rhesa when she needed some* assistance *. . . although, it does alarm me that she was so exhausted. Not to mention, she refused to eat at first.*

What did you end up feeding her, then? inquires Atticus.

My blood. She seemed to prefer it.

Alastair hums. *She can sustain her magic and strength on blood alone in dire situations, though she does know better. And I would claim her running amuck all day across the kingdom took a bigger toll on her than she was expecting. Then there is also the matter of her explaining to her court the situation we have found ourselves in as far as* Myra *is concerned. That was no doubt mentally draining, as well.*

Makes sense to me, quips Atticus. Then a heartbeat later, he inquires again, *So she's all right now?*

I smile to myself. *She's fine, brothers. You can reclaim her in the morning. For tonight, she's mine.*

And I close the proverbial door once more, leaving our conversation there for the evening as I snuggle closer to Rhesamyre.

CHAPTER TWENTY FOUR
RHESAMYRE

Feeling a sudden rush of ecstasy spasm throughout my body, I gasp awake as my back arches in pleasure. My thighs tremble as my core clenches, and my breathing hitches, but when I go to move my arms, I'm startled by the feeling of soft restraints around my wrists, forcing my arms to stretch outward above my head.

"You were dead to the world this morning," drawls Atticus, and I snap my eyes south to spot the deity between my legs. His emerald eyes are bright with lust and hilarity as he wipes his mouth of my *wetness*. He grins at me, nuzzling my inner thigh as I come down from my high. "Perfectly sated, thanks to Atlas's endeavors to soothe you last night. He got to you before I could, so this morning, I kicked him out and claimed you as *mine.*"

I glance back up at my wrists, which are tied to opposite ends of the headboard with black satin ropes, which are surely enchanted to ensure I cannot break them as easily. I look back at my deity, and he shuffles upward so he may kiss my toned stomach and hug my middle, resting his chin on my navel as he smirks at me.

Fucking hell, he's gorgeous.

"You tied me up."

His smile widens again. "I did. Couldn't risk you spoiling my fun before I had you coming *at least* once. What a brilliant way to greet the morning sun, *no?*"

I raise my brow at him. "Well, then. I believe I've only come once so far, right?"

"You have.

I nod. "Then you still have some work left to finish, Chaos."

He growls, nipping at the flesh of my stomach again. "So demanding, sweet spice. But I find myself inclined to follow your instructions. Even if *you* are the one *tied up*."

He lowers his head between my thighs again, licking up the length of my slit before sucking and nibbling on my clit.

The morning lasts forever.

··················

Grinning from ear to ear with a drink of champagne in hand, I watch from my place on the palace steps as my girls order the lieutenants and footmen to decorate the courtyard to their liking. All Hallow's Eve wreaths and ornaments adorn the entirety of Heart, while more streamers, flower arrangements, and offerings for the dead cluster along the walls, where the people of Hell pay their respects to the old ways. All of the city is in uproar for the coming celebration, which often lasts a few days at a minimum. A nonstop party of drinking, live music, plays, games for the children, and open vendors that crowd the streets to sell their merchandise and artisan crafts.

Taking another sip from my flute, I lean back against Alastair's legs since he stands behind me, while my dire wolf, Embrace, lays his fluffy head on my lap so I may keep rubbing his ears the way he likes.

"I rarely see you drink champagne," Alastair notes.

I tip my head back to meet his eyes, then grin at him.

However, before I can reply with a witty response, Pride calls from nearby, "Bubbles make her smile at everyone more and threaten us less. She tends to save champagne for special occasions."

"Yeah," adds Envy, grinning. "Watch this."

Envy prowls over and crouches right in front of me, his eyes glittering with mischievous mirth. I narrow my eyes at him, not breaking eye contact, but a corner of my lip quirks upward despite my best efforts to scowl.

"What do you call a dog with one cock, but three heads?"

I blink at him.

"Cerberus."

I *giggle*.

"What the fuck did you do?" shouts Atticus in disbelief.

"Aw, *c'mon*! That wasn't even a good one!" shouts Atlas.

"I'm both entertained and almost disappointed that you laughed at that, love," complains Alastair.

"*Hush it*!" I growl, swatting his thigh while still grinning because *I can't help it*.

"Told you," quips Envy, looking all too proud of himself.

He really shouldn't be. That was a terrible joke at *best*.

"It was always a drinking game of ours to see who could get her laughing the hardest," adds Lust, smiling at me, even though I glare at him halfheartedly. "As it turns out, her humor goes to shit when she gets a few dozen glasses in her."

"Shitty puns are the go-to," adds Wrath. "Gluttony holds the record. He got her to *snort* once."

"I don't appreciate this harassment," I snarl, but I'm still *smiling*.

"I've seen warriors and monsters *shit themselves* when you smile and make threats at the same time, darling," quips Pollux. "But, dare I say, that was almost *cute*."

"Now this I've got to try," quips Atticus, sparing me a shit-eating grin.

"You will do no such thing," I command.

"It won't be much of a competition, brother," remarks Alastair, a corner of his mouth turned up. "You're entire existence is laughable."

That sends me just about *roaring*.

"I'm almost concerned," drawls Atlas, but he, too, is smiling.

"*Nah*, don't be," says Greed. "They come in waves. This hysterical state of hers will pass soon enough."

Getting my giggles back under control, I down the rest of my glass. Then without looking at any of my deities in particular, I hold it up. "It seems I'm in need of a refill. Be a good fiancé and get me another glass, would you?"

I'm not even sure which one of them grabs it from me, nor do I care to see which two of them growl at the third. Instead, I stand from the stairs and strut over to the girls.

Fern, Tally, Thea, and Trix all stand off to the side with beverages and clipboards in hand as they survey the tasteful décor that adorns every inch of the courtyard. The gates of the palace remain open for the entirety of the celebration, and I've always done my best in the past to ensure the soldiers are rotated through their working hours so that everyone has a chance to enjoy the festivities. This year will be no different, but it seems as though the lieutenants will have their hands full with not only protecting my girls, but pleasing them, too.

Pussy-whipped, the lot of them. Dami took a liking to Fern the moment he saw her, and I'm fairly certain Gage got a hard-on watching Thea defend my cottage back in Soulton. Mal and Trix have been getting along great so far, and Silas is fascinated by Tally something fierce.

"I hope this task remains enjoyable for you four, and not as taxing as it appears," I drawl as I approach.

Fern grins at me, her attention split between me and her newly acquired dire wolf, Veto, as he drags over another box of décor for her to sift through.

"Yes, this will do," she says, thanking him by rubbing his ears as she looks at me again. "I quite enjoy it."

"Only because we're the visionaries," says Thea, with Vex sitting by her feet patiently. "We get to boss *them* around."

"And that is *certainly* enjoyable," quips Tally, feeding Dolor some snacks off her plate of hors d'oeuvres as she clinks her champagne flute against Thea's.

I smile, then glance at Barter as he stands near Bellatrix, whose eyes remain trained on Malcolm's form, though Conquest's lieutenant is too busy arguing with Damian about how to best present and hang the wreaths upon the spikes of the walls to notice her gaze.

I nudge her shoulder, and she spares me a sheepish smile at being caught in the act of ogling my honorary brother.

"Enjoying the view?" I tease.

She laughs a little. "Hell is certainly a beautiful place."

I roll my eyes. "That isn't what I'm referring to, and you know it."

She shrugs. "Your grand scheme to hook me up with Malcolm has proven . . ."

"*Successful*, I hope?"

"That is . . . one word for it, I suppose."

I grin at her. "Do you like him?"

"I like looking at him . . . especially when he's shirtless."

"And pantless?"

"Perhaps."

"You fucked him yet?"

She raises her brow at me, huffing another gentle laugh. "Is that any of your business?"

"No, but I've always loved the smutty details."

"Understatement of the fucking year," quips Tally.

Trix laughs again at my expense, then admits quietly, "He does this trick with his *hips,* where he'll flip you mid-fuck, and hit that spot deep within you where it's like, *whoa,* didn't know it could feel like *that.*"

I nod enthusiastically. "He has since perfected the skill it seems."

She narrows her eyes at me. "Have *you* fucked him?"

I purse my lips. "Not important."

"*Rhesa.*"

"A long, *long* time ago . . . I fucked all of them."

"At *once?*" whispers Fern, her eyes wide but tone more curious than accusatory.

I shrug. "Like I said, it was a *very long* time ago. They've since become better at fucking since then, and so have I, but without using each other for practice, I might add. We were each other's firsts, and that's where it ended. I had a cherry to pop, no strings attached."

"*Oh,*" remarks Thea. "Now *we* need the smutty details of *that* adventure."

"There wasn't much to it," I admit. "We literally just fucked around. There wasn't a lot of true passion or care involved. None of us knew what the hell we were doing. Even with Lust's advice on the matter. We just did what felt good."

Bellatrix hums. "Nothing like what you have now with your *Three* Kings?"

"It isn't even a comparison."

She nods firmly. "Good."

"*Anyway*," I segue. "Trix, I actually need to ask a favor of you."

"Oh. What's up?"

"Walk with me?"

She nods, and we leave the other girls to dictate where the décor goes. Barter and Embrace follow us, and soon enough, Trix and I are in the gardens and away from the prying eyes of the common folk.

Pulling out a folded piece of parchment, I hand it over to her as I take a seat on one of the stone benches, Embrace once again putting his head on my lap to encourage me to pet him, and I do.

"This is . . ." she drawls, studying the paper. "Rhesa, what am I looking at?"

Trix takes a seat next to me as she rakes her gaze over the runes and convoluted spellwork once created by Myra and Lilith, and I keep my attention on my hands as I bury my fingers in Embrace's white fur.

"It was designed by a skilled witch, who was once a queen in her own right."

"And where is she now?"

I look at her. "I killed her."

Trix looks taken aback at my answer, then nods. "*Okay* . . . so what exactly do you want me to do with this?"

I shrug. "Whatever you can. Understand it, study it. Perhaps find a way to break or reverse it."

"*Break it*? Why me?"

"Because you're a witch."

She scoffs a little. "*Hardly*. My mother and I were barely able to practice our craft out of fear, you know that. So my schooling and knowledge of my heritage is primary at best."

"It's in your blood, Trix. Unlike mine, your eyes can make better sense of these alchemic patterns. I understand a few of the runes and what they entail, but there are some in there that I didn't—*that I don't know of.*"

Trix doesn't look convinced, but thankfully doesn't seem to pick up on my slip-up. Instead, she just releases a calculated breath. "I'll do my best, but I can't promise anything."

"I know."

"Some are easy enough to decipher at first glance, such as the runes for protection and spherical impact, as well as the ones for . . ." Trix meets my eyes again, cocking her head. "Why is this spellwork riddled with memory -ltering runes, Rhesa?"

I purse my lips. I don't like lying to her, or any of my girls for that matter. They've quickly become a part of my family and have nestled their way into my brothers' hearts, too.

"That's a complicated question to answer," I reply slowly.

"Well, are you going to answer it?"

"At the moment? No. Probably not."

"But you will eventually?"

"Eventually."

Trix watches me for a moment, then sighs and pockets the parchment. "I'll get to it when I can, and see what I can make of it. But like I said, no promises."

I spare her a smile, nodding again. "I truly appreciate it, Trix."

. . . .

Twirling around the town square with Tally to the live band, my dancing has certainly seen better days. However, the bubbles have *absolutely* gone to my head, and Tally doesn't fare much better as we spin together. Our champagne spills over the sides of our flutes as we laugh and dance, grinding on one another with hands that aren't afraid to travel south.

Fern, Thea, and Trix surround the two of us once more, and our drinks spill again when the five of us throw our hands toward the stars to sing along to the chorus of the song the band plays. A hellion favorite, which is more than obvious since every citizen and soldier within earshot sings along, too. The heart of Hell erupts into vocals as dozens of free demons, common folk, and lords and ladies forget the politics of our spheres, and just *sing*. Gems, jewels, and costumes glitter in the hanging lights and bulbs as stars twinkle far overhead, and enchanted spellwork leaves plenty of lanterns to float above us without the need for strings and cables.

The lieutenants appear behind their appropriate females again, grabbing them by their waists, hips, hands, and necks to sway and spin them around while their boots stomp to the rhythm of the beat. However, before I can slip away so as not to be a hindrance to their moments, I feel hands slip around my own waist, successfully pulling me into a solid chest, and I waste no time in pressing my ass into his crotch.

Atlas hisses. "Please don't do that, little wolf," he husks into my ear.

I spin around to face him, leaning over him drunkenly as I inquire, "Why not? Don't you want me?"

"More than you'll ever know, and if you have to ask, then that means I must not be loving you hard enough."

I grin, then tip my champagne flute back to pour what remains of my drink onto my neck and down my chest. Atlas's pink eyes flash as he tracks the movement of the droplets, which fall into my cleavage tauntingly as my dress's neckline allows for an exaggerated dip. He's quick to grab my waist again, his tatted hands bunching up the dark fabric to pull me closer as he dips his head toward my neck. His tongue glides up my chest toward my neck, lapping up the champagne, and he nips my skin to draw blood, then moans at the taste of me.

I drop my glass, and it shatters to the ground as I thread my fingers through his hair. He lifts his head again, grinning at me as he kisses me passionately, our tongues tangling as he swipes it against my own, and only one word comes to mind when he does:

Possessive.

Somehow, Atlas manages to toe the line of gentle and unfathomably, ridiculously dominating. It is a reminder that while he may be softer-spoken than his two brothers, he is nothing short of a powerful predator and beast. A king. One who is hellbent on loving his queen in whatever manner she may desire or need.

Alastair wants to eat me body and soul, while Atticus wants to tie me up and tease me until I'm a writhing, wet mess.

But Atlas wants to savor me. Devour me whole *slowly* and completely until I'm utterly gone and all that remains is what he craves the most. Then, *and only then*, will he fuck me like the animal I know he can be, saving the good parts for last.

"Can I take you somewhere more private?" he inquires. "Or would you like me to eat you out here within the crowd?"

"I don't believe I can keep quiet."

"I wouldn't dare ask you to. Those noises belong to me and my brothers, but should you want to share—"

I growl. "There will be no *sharing*. Take me somewhere quiet and fuck me, Atlas. Just as you did last night."

He grins, picking me up so I can wrap my legs around his waist.

"Yes, my queen," he husks.

I smile, leaning forward to kiss him again, swiping my tongue against his while threading my fingers through his hair, my nails scraping his scalp and massaging him. He groans, grinding his concealed cock against my heat, and I vaguely register us moving into another dark alley away from the party. My back is pressed against a wall, and Atlas allows his hands to drop from my shoulders to grasp my breasts, kneading my hardened nipples through the thin fabric of my dress.

He tweaks a nipple, forcing a gasp from me, and he uses my momentary distraction to remove his tongue from my mouth and replace it with his fingers.

"Suck them for me, little wolf," he husks, his eyes hooded as I do as he commands, swirling my tongue over the pads of his two fingers while sucking them as I would his cock. "You'll need to get them nice and wet for me if I am to have my way with your ass tonight."

I feel my core tighten in desire at the sound of the raw need in his dirty promise, and his eyes brighten as his nostrils flare, no doubt scenting the new flood of arousal that seeps out of me. When he seems satisfied with his fingers in my mouth, he allows them to slip from my lips and dip lower toward my rear, hiking up my dress in the process. His other hand had been busy playing with my wet folds and clit, leaving me to lean back against the wall with my legs still firmly wrapped around his middle to ensure I don't fall.

Removing his hand from my heat for a moment so he can pull his trousers down, I watch in awe as his cock springs free. He strokes himself a few times, coating it in pre-cum, and I drop one of my legs from around his waist to find a better position so he can enter me with little resistance; his other hand still firmly grasps my ass, wet fingers twirling and teasing my rear hole.

Atlas lines himself up with my soaked heat and pushes in with ease, growling lowly with every inch until he is completely seated inside of me. His hand once again comes to settle on my hip as his thumb presses against my clit, and I arch into him as I feel his other finger prod and stretch the muscles of my ass. He rubs my clit gently as he pumps his finger a few times, watching me with hooded eyes as he listens to my little moans and how my breath hitches for him. His cock is firmly nestled inside of me, twitching often, but he doesn't move it yet. Not until he presses a second finger into my ass, scissoring and stretching and rubbing his own length through the wall of sensitive skin that separates my two holes. My eyes go cross-eyed with the pleasure, and I struggle to keep his gaze as I toss my head back and moan his name.

"Give me your screams, little wolf," he drawls huskily, breath hitching as he starts to pump his cock into me in tandem with his fingers in my ass. "*I want everything*," he snarls quietly.

"You can have it all," I whine, pressing my forehead into his shoulder as his thrusts picks up, rocking me between the wall and his chest. He remains the only thing holding me up now as my moans grow louder. "You can have all of me, Atlas. I'm yours. All of me. *Yours*."

"Say it again," he growls, biting my neck as his cock and fingers work faster, his hips nearly slapping against my own as his moans grow louder, too. Rough and breathless and full of need and desire for *me*.

Seven devils, I can feel him *everywhere*. The pleasure builds swiftly and coils tight in my lower belly like molten heat as shivers slither up and down my spine from him rubbing my clit and the inner walls of my ass altogether.

"All yours," I repeat. "All I have to give. You can have everything, Atlas."

His thrusting becomes sloppy, and he sends me over the edge before tumbling right behind me, coming with a roar as I *scream*. He covers my mouth with his own, swallowing the sound as his hips thrust independently to shoot his release deep inside of me. My inner walls convulse and milk him for all he's worth, and my ass squeezes his fingers so hard it's a wonder how he can even get them out.

His kiss turns gentle before he slowly pulls away, meeting my eyes as his chest heaves up and down in a similar manner to my own, and he keeps eye contact with me as he pulls both his cock and fingers out of me in tandem. I *shudder* at the feeling, my knees nearly buckling as I find my feet, but Atlas doesn't hesitate to keep his hands on me until I'm steady.

"Fucking hell," he mumbles in Old Latin, his accent deep. He presses his forehead against mine. "You're magnificent, Rhesamyre."

I smile at him, pecking his lips. "We should play rough more often, Atlas. I quite like it when you come undone for me. Lost in your own lust and instincts to claim me as yours."

He spares me a handsome grin. "Whatever you want, little wolf. You can have all of me in whatever way you want. In whatever way you may need. I'm yours."

I kiss him again, grinning against his lips.

CHAPTER TWENTY FIVE
RHESAMYRE

Atlas and I return to the lieutenants' table hand in hand, and my deity pulls out a chair for himself, then promptly sits me on his lap.

My legs are still *trembling*, my knees threatening to buckle as my core recovers from Atlas's sexual endeavors.

Damian spares me a shit-eating grin. "Done already?"

Nosy reaper. I scowl at him, kicking him under the table while pouring myself and Atlas a glass of wine. Then I return his grin from behind my drink. "I could ask you lot the same thing."

Silas smirks. "The girls still wanted to party some more. And they've been running in and out of shops, hunting for sales for the past hour. We finally found a neutral spot to relax while they use our paychecks to fund their shopping sprees."

"Such good mates you four are. I'm so proud."

Malcolm chuckles. "We know how to court females, Rhesa. We've spent enough time with our generals and the assassins to know who to avoid and what *not* to do."

I snicker, and Atlas inquires from behind me, "None of them have settled down yet?"

"It isn't really in their nature, to be honest," I reply. "Plenty of them have shared partners in the past and fucked around with males and females of all breeds, but I wouldn't dare call any of those conquests *mates*."

Atlas hums. "Do you think they ever will?"

I shrug, and the lieutenants and I look amongst each other and seem to come to the same conclusion.

"Probably not," admits Gage. "I think switching up partners and traveling for work keeps their lives interesting. Eternity is an awfully long time."

"It has remained their choice," I add. "They've all had plenty of partners that have spanned across decades, playing the role of bedwarmer, whore, or housewife, but I've only met them in passing. Never have any of my uncles officially introduced the women to court and sought my father's blessing."

"And your father never did either, it seems," notes Atlas.

"Same thing. I know he had interests and lovers, but none of them ever earned the title of *queen*. And I assume he was the same when you knew him as an archangel?"

Atlas nods, then says to me silently, *And he was the same when you called him brother?*

I take a slow sip from my wine, and Atlas's hands massage my sides gently.

"Besides," I continue. "If we're honest with ourselves, it usually isn't in hellion nature as a whole to settle down with a single partner. To limit one's choices and capabilities for love is almost considered forbidden, not to mention not *nearly* as much fun. The possibilities of pleasure and passion are endless with several mates, and thus polyamorous relationships are common among us demon folk. Not to mention, I think the hesitancy with most demons and matrimony stems from their memories of how it was under the Cruel One's rule. When mortals used to summon demons to do their dirty work, but Abaddon never ensured proper contracts were signed, nor justice when promises were broken. Plenty of demons were shackled to mortals and their familial bloodlines for centuries before my father put an end to the injustice and misuse of our bargains."

Atlas hums from behind me again. "Makes sense to me."

The lieutenants all nod, too, and Damian makes a show of glancing around before he inquires, "Where are the other two?"

"No idea. I seem to have misplaced two of my mates, which is quite impressive in itself."

"I'll say," agrees Silas, chuckling.

"Actually," drawls Atlas. "I think I do recall Alastair mentioning something about stepping into a ring?"

"Oh, fuck me," I groan. "He's gonna kill someone."

Atlas chuckles. "Don't fret. Atticus went with him."

"That's not comforting."

Atlas laughs again, then leans forward to press a kiss to my bare shoulder.

"I'm sure they'll be fine," says Mal. "Anyway, Trixie mentioned something to me today that I thought you would find interesting."

I meet his eyes. "Oh, *hell below*. What did she tell you?"

He raises his brow at me. "She mentioned wanting to learn how to ride a hell-horse." He furrows his brows now, tilting his head with a sly grin. "What did *you* think she was going to mention?"

I shrug. "Evidently, nothing that concerns you. So please, *continue*."

Malcolm doesn't look convinced but ends up putting the matter aside for now. "*Anyway*. I think it's about time she and the girls take up a more permanent place within the court. Study up on our history a bit more, train their minds and bodies, just as you saw yesterday, and get acquainted with riding, too."

I nod. "I agree. Except for one minor detail."

"Okay?"

"Obviously, it remains their choice. However, I was thinking of something with wings rather than hooves. At least for Althea, and perhaps Feronia, too."

"*Wyverns?*" inquires Damian, brows shooting to his hairline in disbelief.

"Maybe, but only for Althea. Fern is better suited for a *rhayven,* I believe."

"It slipped my mind for a moment that the winged regiments of Hell consist of both," notes Atlas. "But if I may inquire. Why?"

I shrug. "Why not? Trix rode with the Hussars for a bit before she was captured by the raiders, so she'll more than likely be more comfortable with a hell-horse. And Tally strikes me as a horse girl, too. However, with Thea's thicker build, she'll be strong enough to tame and ride a wyvern, while Fern remains thin and thus lightweight and swift enough to fly with a stealthier rhayven."

Silas nods. "Sound enough argument for me. I'm in."

"In for what?" inquires Tally as she skips up to our table.

She plants a kiss on Silas's lips as she places down her *many* bags, then promptly takes a seat on his lap in a similar manner to how I sit on Atlas. A moment later, Thea, Trix, and Fern arrive, sitting on or next to their appropriate lieutenants, too.

"We were discussing potential mounts for you four," I inform them. "And if you're interested, Fern, Thea, I was thinking the two of you would benefit from something a little bigger than a hell-horse."

"Such as?" inquires Fern, leaning back against Damian.

"A rhayven for you and a wyvern for Thea." I look between Tally and Trix. "I figured you two would be more comfortable with hell-horses."

Trix nods. "I had a mortal horse back in the West." She laughs awkwardly. "I don't believe I'm built for flying."

"It's been a long time, but I have ridden a horse before," says Tally. "Though, it wasn't demonic by any means."

"A rhayven? Really?" inquires Fern, looking awestruck at the thought of flight. "I can still shoot, right?"

I grin. "Absolutely."

"Oh, yeah," remarks Silas, grinning. "That's right. You are claimed to be quite the marksman, aren't you?"

Fern smirks. "I believe some say I am."

"The Artemis are fools to refuse you," quips Trix. "From what little I've seen of your abilities, you're better than all of them combined."

Silas's shit-eating grin widens. "Care for a friendly wager, wendigo?"

Fern raises her brow. "I believe we're both quite impaired at the moment."

He waves her off, lifting Tally off his lap as he stands, and the ex-genie pouts at him. He gives her a kiss, and she smiles again. "Nonsense. That just makes it all the more entertaining."

Fern still looks uncertain, that is until I stand up and grab one of the mini cakes from the platter that is situated between all of us.

"Whatever you're about to do, *please*," drawls Atlas. "*Don't*."

Situating the cake on top of my head, I back up a few yards until I'm against the nearest wall.

"Just don't tell your brothers, and it'll be fine," I quip.

"You want me to *lie* to them?"

"Only if they ask why I have cake crumbles in my hair. Is that a problem?"

"*No*, but that isn't the point here."

"Your concern is noted. Now hush so my friends can concentrate on *not* hitting me."

Atlas growls to himself, while Silas and Feronia each command a bow and arrow to erupt into their outstretched hands.

Taking up his stance first, I can tell Silas has had perhaps a few too many drinks since he needs Tally's help to steady himself at first, but he doesn't let that stop him as he takes aim and fires.

His arrow pierces the air and slices into the cake's center.

He bows mockingly, his bow disappearing from view as he grins at Fern. "Your turn, milady."

Fern rolls her eyes, then squares up. She makes a show of narrowing her eyes at the cake upon my head, then glances over her shoulder at Silas and *winks* at him, then lets her arrow fly. It slices through the air, and someone, I think Thea, inhales sharply when it hits its mark.

Carefully, I duck beneath the cake as it crumbles away and turn to face the arrows embedded into the wall.

Fern's pierces the very center of Silas's, thus splitting it in a similar manner to how she did my own arrow back in Aftermath when I first met her.

I grin at my friends, and the males waste no time whistling and congratulating Fern.

"And *that's* why she's a part of my court," I quip.

"That and my *spectacular* personality," adds Fern, flipping her hair dramatically.

"I believe that came afterward," says Damian, grabbing her by the waist. "Rhesa usually prioritizes opportunity first and friendship second."

"Well then, what do *you* prioritize, Dami?" she purrs.

Damian grins at his mate, then kisses her passionately, and there is nothing appropriate about the action.

"I prioritize *you*," quips the reaper.

....

Walking hand in hand again, Atlas and I find ourselves heading to one of the underground boxing rings within a hellion speakeasy owned by Wrath in search of Atticus and Alastair. The crowd is loud and rambunctious as we enter the fray, but Atlas leads me through the people and toward a private balcony with ease. Plenty of demons part to let us through once they see us, but I pay them no mind as I keep my eyes trained on the cage fight in the center of the room.

Alastair prowls around his opponent in a circular motion, his shirt off to reveal his tanned and tatted rippling muscles that glisten with sweat as he sizes up the other fighter in the ring with him. My eyes track every single one of those droplets of sweat, and I vaguely register Atlas moving me around, pressing me against the balcony railing so he can stand behind me to watch his brother over my head.

Alastair raises his arms again, gearing up to spar once more, and I finally slide my eyes away from him to spot his opponent.

I raise my brows at the sight of Dexter. The male is shirtless and ripped with his own tight muscles, and I spot a few tattoos littering his torso, too. Some appear to have been from when he was originally with the Mortal Suns, but I spy plenty of fresher designs that are of hellion art.

My magic whirs within me in recognition and pleasure of a familiar scent, and I slide my eyes away from the fight to face Atticus as he approaches Atlas and me. He smirks scanning me from head to toe, and I narrow my eyes at him.

"Seems as though my brother has been *thoroughly* enjoying your company, sweet spice," he quips.

"You could be, too, if you weren't off fooling around," replies Atlas cooly. "What are you two even doing down here?"

Atticus raises his brow at his brother, grinning as he shrugs. "It's a party, is it not? I am allowed to mess around however I choose, no?"

"And you and Alastair have chosen to fight and toy with my footmen?" I drawl. "Why not spar with my uncles who would actually provide a challenge?"

He meets my eyes again, the mirth in his emerald gaze never faltering as he surveys my form in satisfaction. "We did."

I quirk a brow at him. "Oh? Who won?"

He shrugs, grabbing my hand to pull me from Atlas to hold me against his own chest. "We all basically tied with each other, and then Alastair took to teaching when the crowds formed."

"*Teaching*?" I repeat incredulously.

I feel Atlas press against my back as he says, "Alastair, while he'll most likely deny it, actually enjoys giving instruction and helping others learn combat and fighting techniques. He's the one who often taught the townsfolk how to defend themselves when we were younger. Before we claimed our magic and titles, that is. Back in the day when we were proper boys with too much energy and a passion for brawling."

I hum, my gaze drifting toward Alastair again as he oversees Dexter and another demon taking each other to the mat; Dexter is currently winning. However, the deity's silver eyes are already on me, surveying my form that is still sandwiched between his brothers.

I cock my head at him, allowing my eyes to trail down his tatted body again, appreciating every dip and curve.

Atticus chuckles against me, his arms tightening around my body, and I snap my eyes up to meet his again. He gives me another sultry grin. "I can feel not only your lust, sweet spice, but my dear brother just flashed us a fantastical vision of taking you on those mats. Your skin glistening with sweat as wetness pools between your legs. All of our brands on display as we make love to you. Pumping our cocks above your naked body and letting our scents mingle with your own. Smothering you in our essence."

I gape at him, then narrow my eyes, even though desire begins to coil tight in my lower belly again. Ignoring the vivid imagery, I simply inquire, "You three can communicate via mindscapes?"

Atticus quirks his brow at me, obviously caught off guard that *that's* what I chose to comment on first. He chuckles a little. "You didn't know that? *Huh*, I guess we forgot to mention that. But yes, the three of us can communicate in a similar manner to how you and Atlas can."

I nod, looking back down at Alastair again. "*Well*, then tell your brother to get his fine ass up here so he can make good on that promise he just laid between us four. I'm flattered that I'm your fantasy. So let me help you make it a reality."

Atticus grins, and I feel Atlas press closer. And from the dangerous smirk that begins to split Alastair's face, I can tell Atticus has done as I've requested. The deity below us mutters his goodbyes and claims he's finished for the evening, and more fights resume again once he's clear of the ring, prowling up the staircase and stalking toward the three of us with a deadly gaze that is primarily set on me.

He saunters up to me, cupping my face gently as he purrs, "Hello, love."

I tip my head back, quirking a brow at him in a sultry manner as I quip, "I hear I've been on your mind again."

"You consume my every *fucking* thought, Rhesamyre." He chuckles deeply, darkly. "But yes, my love. You're once again *on my mind*."

He makes a show of lowering his gaze to survey my gown, as well as where his brothers' hands grip me by my waist and hips. Then, just as slowly, he brings his silver gaze back up to meet mine, as if he's teasing and edging himself with just the mere thought of fucking me senseless.

"Well, then," I drawl. "What are you waiting for, *my loves*?"

With a snarl, though I'm not entirely sure which one it came from, I'm hoisted upward as all four of us are consumed by a glittering conveyance. Then I'm thrown down onto a bed that is not my own, and I bounce a little with the force of the action. Smirking up at my three deities, I watch in awe as they start to strip.

"Strip out of that gown, sweet spice," orders Atticus. "Lest you desire us to *rip it* off you."

I cock my head at him, my hands moving to untie the thin straps of my gown and slip out of it *oh so slowly*. Then, seeming to sense and see the challenge in my gaze, Alastair growls, and when I blink again, he is upon me. His lips are on mine, leaving me with no room nor time to dominate the kiss as he all but devours me.

Nipping my lips, he pulls away and husks gently, "I'm going to fuck that attitude right out of you. Starting with this little mouth of yours, love."

"Promise?" I quip with a grin.

He *rips* my gown off my body, threads snapping and tearing across my skin in the process, but before I can snarl at him, his mouth is on mine again. I moan into his kiss as his fingers find my throbbing clit, and he rubs me harshly before dipping them lower to find my soaked heat. He presses his fingers inside of me, finding little resistance despite my hot channel being as tight as it is, and Alastair hisses against my mouth, sucking my tongue into his mouth and swallowing all the noises I can possibly make.

I've never been vocal during sex. Not until these three.

Then in a blink, I'm shifted and tossed around on the bed so that my head is hanging off the edge. My back arches as I feel Alastair's mouth attach itself to my clit, sucking and tugging and biting and chewing, and I'm a writhing mess on my back as my thighs attempt to clench around his head. He keeps my legs spread with his big hands as he feasts, my knees bent, and his grip remains bruising and strong as he slows his endeavors to lap at me teasingly, gently, savoring everything I have to give.

He chuckles, slapping my inner thigh as he husks, "Now be a good girl and open that pretty mouth for my brother."

I tilt my head backward off the bed, finding Atticus right above me, fapping his hard length as he watches me with hooded, emerald eyes that glow with lust and desire. He taps his tip against my lips, and I open my mouth for him, tasting him on my tongue. He slides into my mouth, groaning as he goes, hitting the back of my throat before pulling out and thrusting forward again. I suck and gag on him, and then I feel Alastair lower his mouth to my core to suck and lick. One of his hands cups my ass and prods at my rear entrance gently before sinking his finger inside all the way to his knuckle, and his tongue moves in tandem with his fingers in both my ass and heat, and I'm left moaning around Atticus's cock and twitching and bucking against their endeavors.

Atticus swells in my mouth, one hand tangling in my hair near my horn while the other comes to rest on the column of my throat where he can feel himself thrusting inside of me, and I moan again at the lack of air and the overwhelming pleasure I feel, thanks to both Alastair's tongue and Atticus's brand. Everything flares and pulses with pleasure, and I shudder.

You're a vision, little wolf, says Atlas through our bond, and I know he's somewhere in the room, masturbating to the sight of me on my back between his brothers. *Yes, I am,* he agrees, and I can hear him moaning my name aloud as the bed dips next to me.

I reach outward blindly, and Atlas acknowledges my request as he wraps my hand around his hard cock, and the two of us glide up and down his slick length together.

Rhesa, Rhesa, Rhesa, he chants, his thrusts growing harder as he moans my name silently and out loud.

I whimper and moan around Atticus's cock again, which has also grown sloppier and harder, and his pleasure and need for me floods my mind and forces another deluge of wetness to gush out of me. Alastair laps it up greedily, licking me from slit to clit over and over again as he presses another finger into my ass, pumping deeply.

Atticus and Atlas roar as they come, and I shatter and writhe as Atticus spills his release down my throat. I vaguely register Atlas's seed spilling across my chest, and Alastair growls again as he flicks his tongue into my entrance, fucking me with it through my climax.

And then I'm no longer seeing the underside of Atticus. Instead, I'm looking at myself as my chest heaves, nipples hard and covered in cum as Atticus and Atlas finish themselves off by using me as their muse. A growl shudders through Alastair, and my cherry taste floods his mouth as well as my own as his vision shifts to look down at the creamy mess between my thighs again. He focuses on where his fingers still fuck me, rubbing my clit with his thumb as he scrapes the spongy insides of both my core and ass at the same time. Wetness coats his entire hand as he cups me.

A second climax swiftly claims me before I can recover from the first, and I am jostled back into my own body to feel it crash into me. Atticus pulls out of my mouth, and I can barely see him through the tears in my eyes as he watches me with an intense, lewd gaze.

"What did she just do?" I barely hear Atlas ask one of his brothers. "I felt her . . . *leave*."

A chuckle sounds from between my thighs as Alastair kisses my mound, slowly pulling his fingers from my holes, and I whimper at the feeling of *emptiness* that settles inside my satisfied but sore lower half.

"She fucking astral projected," growls Alastair, and he chuckles darkly again. "She enjoyed watching us fuck her from a different vantage point."

"I suppose we have your brand to thank for that," quips Atticus, sounding pleased as he cups my sore jaws. "Pretty little thing . . . our perfect fuck toy."

"I trust you also did your part to loosen her up back here, little brother?" inquires Alastair, swirling my wetness around my ass again.

"I did," agrees Atlas, and I can hear the smile in his tone. "Though, she's a tight one."

"We like her tight. Get her on her fucking hands and knees."

I'm flipped around onto all fours as requested, and I feel Alastair's hands circle me from behind. He wraps one hand around my throat, while the other goes to rub my overstimulated clit again. I whimper and moan his name, and he shushes me in mock sympathy as the tip of his cock prods my back entrance. Slowly, he drives forward inch by torturous inch, pulling in and out until I am stretched around him to his liking, his fingers playing with my clit and wet folds again as his hand tightens around my throat.

I moan and snarl softly, attempting to rock back on his cock and take more, but he growls, and the hand that was holding my throat comes down on my ass with a harsh *slap*.

"You don't call the shots here, love," he husks, rocking forward, and I have to reposition my hands in front of myself so as not to fall forward. "We might call you queen out there, but in here, you're our fucking *whore*."

I moan something incoherent again as his thrusting picks up, and then his hand is around my throat again, and he's pulling me back against his chest. I lift one arm to wrap it back around his head, fingers tugging at the strands of his dark hair as he thrusts upward into my ass. And through my blurry, lust-hazed vision, I recognize Atlas prowling toward me again and rising onto the bed to position his cock at the entrance of my core. He grips my hips and slides into me, thrusting upward as Alastair pulls out, and they work in conjunction to steal their pleasure by using my body to do it.

And I fucking let them.

I wrap my other arm around Atlas's shoulders, and he kisses me deeply as he thrusts in tandem with his brother. One of his hands pinch and pull at my nipple, and I gasp and whine again as Alastair keeps rubbing my clit.

And then my *truculent* brand begins to simmer and hum in pleasure, and I glance over to find Atticus lounging on the settee, watching us. His legs are spread wide before him as he pleasures himself while rubbing along our shared *truculent* tattoo that brands his lower ribs. His eyes are hooded, mouth agape as he gets off on my moans and pleasure, and *seven devils*, is it a beautiful sight. Hot and lewd and unholy.

The sight is enough to throw me over another edge, and Atlas and Alastair's thrusts grow sloppy as they near their own releases. I scream when I come, and both Atlas and Alastair roar and sink their teeth into my neck and shoulder as they pump their cum into me.

Mine. Mine. Mine, I chant breathlessly to Atlas, and I may have said it aloud, too, though I'm honestly not quite sure at the moment since I'm nothing but a whiny, twitchy mess when they both pull out at the same time. Their release spills out of me with their synced actions, thus making a sticky mess between my thighs.

I slump forward, and Atlas catches me effortlessly and tucks me against his chest as he picks me up. He presses his lips to my sweaty forehead as he carries me away from the bedroom, and the next thing I know, we're both in a bathtub teeming with hot water and luxurious hellion scents.

I sigh in contentment as I lie back against him, letting him hold me and massage soap onto my skin. With clearer eyes, I watch as Alastair and Atticus enter the chamber, too. The former heads into the glass shower to clean up, while Atticus strides over to crouch in front of me. He grabs my chin gently, looking into my eyes, seeming to search for something.

I lean forward, and he smirks a little and meets me halfway, kissing me sweetly before murmuring against my lips, "We love you, Rhesamyre."

I smile. "I love you." I glance back at Atlas, and he offers me a gentle smile. "All of you."

Atticus pinches my chin, drawing my gaze back to his as he leans forward to kiss my forehead, muttering again, "Our beautiful queen."

"I thought I was your *whore*," I quip, grinning.

Alastair laughs from within the shower.

Atticus rolls his eyes, nipping at my lips as he replies, "You can be both, sweet spice. We'll all take turns acting as your throne if you want. You can sit your fine ass down right here." He taps his nose. "That way we can have our bloody way with that sweet sex of yours whenever we want while you command your kingdom."

I gape at him, and Atlas's chest rumbles behind me as he chuckles. I smile and laugh, leaning forward to kiss Atticus's nose as I quip, "I believe you'd make a fine throne, my king."

CHAPTER TWENTY SIX
ALASTAIR

Feeling my power flare, I slowly shift awake and reach for Rhesamyre out of instinct.

I don't feel her.

Snapping my eyes open, I sit up and look around my bed for her, but only find Atticus sleeping soundly on the other side, a warm gap between us where she had been sleeping soundly, nestled between us while Atlas chose to sleep in his own bedroom across the hall.

Grabbing a nearby pillow, I fling it onto my brother's face with a satisfying *thump* as I climb out of bed. He springs up and growls, then narrows his eyes at me tiredly and sputters, "Wh-*What*? What the *fuck*, Ala—"

"*Hush it*, Atticus. Rhesa's missing."

That sobers him up, and he blinks at me before steeling himself as he looks down at the bed. He feels where she had been sleeping, claiming, "The bed is still warm. She hasn't been gone long."

"I figured not. I woke up when my magic startled awake with her."

He hums, moving out of bed. Both of us had dressed in loungewear last night after cleaning up with Rhesa, and she had promptly fallen asleep in the bath with Atlas. So after changing out our sheets, Atticus and I stole her from our brother and promptly sandwiched her between us. Atlas merely sighed with a smile, said goodnight, and then bid us farewell.

"I sense her moving about, too," says Atticus, heading for the door. "Though, I can't sense a purpose behind her prowling yet. She's just . . . wandering aimlessly."

I furrow my brows. "That doesn't seem like a *Rhesa* thing to do."

"I agree. Let's go."

As we depart my room, we run into Atlas leaving his room, too. He meets our eyes, his door clicking shut behind him as he looks up and down the dark hall with narrowed eyes.

"I take it you two sensed her get up, too?" inquires my middle brother, quirking his brow at us.

I nod, and the three of us continue down the hall, following Rhesa's scent toward the throne room. As we get closer, we run into the rest of the Hellion Court, too. Most of them look hungover or still half-asleep, but they're quick to sober up with every step they take toward their queen, especially when they spot us coming. Pollux is swift to join, as well.

The Horsemen and Seven all look amongst each other and us, and then stride into the throne room.

We stop at the sight of Rhesa sitting on the throne, picking at her nails with one of her daggers, her legs crossed in regal grace as she struts about in one of my shirts that hangs off her like a dress. Mamba slithers about restlessly, still curled around the throne, but his head is reared back as he watches Rhesa with perplexed, calculating eyes. I swear there is a darkness in his gaze, one that spans across voids of time, existing long before the stars winked to life across the skies.

Rhesa raises her head, and we're met with the glimmering white eyes that belong to the *other one*.

Atticus steps forward, his voice low, "If the obsidian serpent is wary of you, then I would imagine that doesn't bode well for the rest of us." He cocks his head at this one, grinning without humor; the action is merely a baring of his teeth. "Yet I'm more pissed than fearful. You're parading around in something that belongs to my brothers and me, and as history has proven, we don't take too kindly to *thieves.*"

This one cocks its head, then purrs in Old Latin, *"She belonged to another* first, *Control, and I have since re-gifted her to you. Do not take my kindness for granted, boy."*

I step forward to stand with my youngest brother. *"Rhesamyre would be quite insulted to learn she has been* given away. *I believe she would seek to rebel against loving us at that knowledge."*

"Best not to let her know then, Concord."

I nod carefully. *"Why are you here this time?"*

"And perhaps this time," drawls Death. "You'd like to properly introduce yourself." He gives it a pointed look, dark eyes full of challenge. "Lest you desire me to do it for you."

This one peels back her lips, baring Rhesa's fangs as she seethes, *"You dare utter my name, Death?"*

Death cocks his head, a menacing scowl in place as he sizes up the creature that prowls beneath Rhesa's skin. "I would like my niece back."

"Niece?" It repeats incredulously. *"You still call her such a thing after your memories have returned to you? After* all *your memories have returned to you?"* It clicks its tongue, looking between the Hellion Court and Pollux. *"Intriguing. I knew the old sigils still marked your skin, hence how I could summon you as I did, but I didn't think your bonds and loyalties would evolve in such a manner. You're stronger now. Familial ties are certainly . . .* fascinating. *Yet her blood brothers, save for that of Perception and, once upon a time, Retribu-*

tion, were never so loyal. Certainly not now, either. Healing seeks to end her life, and Loyalty already tried, but he is no longer of these spheres since he failed in touching what is mine." It looks to my brothers and me again. *"What is ours."*

Atlas steps forward to stand on my other side. "Ours. Yes. And similarly to you, we seek to protect her. We know you mean her no harm, and though you bare *her* teeth, you make empty threats. You will not harm her allies."

Pollux nods in agreement, chuckling lowly. "He's got you there, *Yonder*."

It goes still at the name, and all of us tense in preparation for whatever backlash may come our way thanks to Pollux's taunting. However, the archangel merely grins smugly, rocking back and forth on his heels as he drawls, "You give yourself away with all your territorial *bullshit* over your beloved *Champion*. For not even Evergreen was ever so blatantly obvious in its utter possessiveness over Myra, and now Rhesamyre. Your old spells are fading as we speak." He snarls and mocks, *"Vows of silence*, right?"

I watch this one cock its head at Pollux, and then it grins. However, the action merely succeeds in setting me further on edge rather than relieving my anxieties of it still possessing Rhesamyre. And from the tense forms of the demons and my brothers around me, I know they're feeling the same hesitancies in entertaining it, too. And although Pollux smiles, it doesn't reach his eyes.

"You were always a favorite of mine," it coos. *"Myra loved you and Samael dearly."*

Pollux nods carefully. "I know."

The *Yonder Star* hums, then glances at where Mamba slithers about warily. *"You're one of Evergreen's immortal beasts, hence why you are so hesitant to approach me. Have you forgotten your voice after all these centuries, too, snake?"*

Mamba growls, and the sound shakes the entire palace. Chandeliers rattle above us, and the floor nearly quakes and cracks beneath our feet, many of us still barefoot. And then a regal, deep voice hisses in Old Latin, *"I do not like you in her skin."*

What. The. Fuck.

I glance over at some of the Seven and Horsemen, and through their scowls, they appear as awestruck as my brothers and I do. Even Pollux looks impressively startled by the sound of the obsidian serpent *speaking*.

Mamba slithers closer, unhinging his jaw as he snarls and growls again. *"Give me back the queen of this sphere. You do not belong in her skin, so shed it, you* self-righteous coward. *Find another body to torment us with, and be gone from here, Yonder. You are not welcome here."*

Using Rhesa's features, the Yonder Star looks impressively insulted and enraged as it stands from the Obsidian Throne. It cocks its head again, then glances at us once more as it drawls, *"I have something for you."*

"Then get on with it," snarls Atticus. "Our patience is wearing thin."

Scoffing, this one struts down the dais and comes to stand before my brothers and me. Mamba tracks its movements as it nears us, slithering closer, and the rest of the Hellion Court and Pollux strategically place themselves around my brothers and me, and therefore it.

This one clocks the movements, almost smirking to itself as it says to my brothers and me, *"If you wish to be rid of Lucifer and his Apostles once more, for good this time, I have what you need to do so."*

"Which is?" inquires Atlas.

"A memory."

"One of Myra's?" asks Atticus.

This one cocks its head at my brother now. *"One of mine."*

Yonder raises Rhesa's hand toward us, and my brothers and I glance between each other before placing our hands on Rhesa's skin. I suck in a harsh breath as I am astral projected elsewhere, and a strange wasteland of a sphere materializes before me.

The Tenth Sphere serves as Purgatory for many of the monsters and men of the other Eight Living Spheres. When the souls of the dead are ferried to me by Death's reapers, if they are not claimed by the bargains of hell or worthy of going straight to heaven, then they often come here first if I have any questions of their purity. I sort through the monsters and creatures that crave blood at my leisure, allowing some of the men who find themselves here a chance to fight their way out, though it often takes an eternity to do so.

I enjoy watching them suffer. These monstrosities cannot harm the Nine Spheres anymore. They will rot here where the ground splinters to reveal the rivers of bubbling magma that race between the deep caverns and crevasses that litter the dry land. The sky is a smoky, ash-filled mess of clouds and dry lightning, and the land stretches on for miles; covered in the corpses of monsters. More beasts and creatures fight one another atop the rest of the bodies, all of them searching for a way out.

But the only way out is the one I provide, and they will not have it.

"Please, I know you are listening," prays one of the monsters that hides beneath human skin. This one is named Lucifer. *"I do not understand why I was born in this carnage. Why hasn't it ended?"*

Ah. One of the few who was unfortunate enough to be born here. Born in Blood, I call them. A rare native of Purgatory.

Years pass of this creature praying to me. Praying for powers, answers, or a way out. But I sense darkness in his heart, and he shall not have my gifts. He has been corrupted by this sphere, but that is not my doing. The monsters here sought to **breed,** *and thus Lucifer was born. Their choices. Not mine.*

Lucifer listens to a few of the men who find themselves trapped here. Listening to their stories of spheres unlike this one that is not as thoroughly coated in blood, Lucifer longs for it. Longs to make those spheres his own. And the men that find themselves here foolishly believe that he can. They believe he has the answers they desire, acting as though he is the one who can grant them freedom, but he is not. Only I can free them, but they seem to have forgotten their prayers, and now they call him their **god.**

Using his monstrous lineage, he learns how to consume their souls and all the magic, power, and knowledge that accompanies them. He swallows them up greedily and grows in power, his heart darkening to a poisonous degree as his own soul rots in his body. Then, he dares to build an **altar.** *Claiming the souls are for me, but I refuse them.*

Lucifer is insulted, and then he manages to swallow the soul of a powerful witch, thus gaining the ability to open a conveyance out of this sphere and into the others, allowing a way through for the monsters he brutally shackled to do his bidding.

He swallows souls and devours lands and cultures, and grows and grows and grows. Fueling his altar, claiming them as offerings to me, but I continue to refuse them. The altar hums with energy. Hums with stolen, forbidden power he collected by reaping raw souls before it was their time. And then he robs the Umbra Mundi, claiming souls that were already mine to have.

He is a thief.

He will be punished. He will be defeated. Myra will see to it that he is. Myra will destroy him. The youngest of the archangels. A gift to the others to cherish and look after. She had not been born with powers like the rest of them, as her only reason for existence was to entertain the warriors. Care for them and play with them as a younger sibling would. Allow their souls solace from the carnage and blood-shed that often plague the spheres from time to time, even before Lucifer crossed the threshold into their homes. Myra was born from light to be their *light, and she remains the only one holy and worthy enough to receive my blessing of magic. A kernel of myself. A lover to the son. Where her brothers refused to aid in the fight against Lu-cifer, and commanded that she stay away from the bloodshed, Myra refused and rebelled.*

Born without blood magic, but born into a greater role than even I could have ever foretold. She is my Champion.

Myra. Myra. Myra . . .

I rip my hand and mind away from the Yonder Star's clutches, my brothers doing the same as we reel backward and snarl at the scowling god that wears Rhesa's flesh.

"You sent a *child* to do your dirty work for you," snarls Atticus, his emerald eyes alight with wrath and promising death. *"You're a coward,"* he seethes in Old Latin.

"The altar," drawls Atlas, scowling with barely reined-in aggres-sion. "It is how he stores and fuels his magic, and you refuse to consume the souls he gathers because of *how* they were gath-ered in the first place, thus leaving him to use the souls as his own power source instead. If it is the key to destroying him, why didn't Myra do so?"

"Because she didn't know of it," snarls Mamba, closer now. *"Be-cause* this one *did not warn its dear* Champion. *It withheld infor-mation and sought to be done with it swiftly, but not permanently. Throwing beasts and beings and creatures at Lucifer rather than strategizing with Myra on how to get to the altar and destroy it perma-*

nently. Sacrificing Myra and countless others in the process. Relying on her to figure it out, and considering what little information Myra had to depend on, she did a damn good job of banishing him for a few hundred-thousand years."

Mamba *roars*, snapping his jaws at this one, but not daring to get much closer so as not to harm Rhesa. He snarls and seethes, smoke pouring from his nostrils as he glares at the Yonder Star that *hides* inside Rhesamyre.

"You sent her to her death because you couldn't bring yourself to admit you were wrong," seethes the obsidian serpent. *"You still refuse to show yourself and claim accountability for the countless lives lost then and now. You allowed Lucifer to gain strength. To obtain the knowledge necessary to learn how to escape the Tenth Sphere he was born into. You allowed him to step through a con-veyance into the unsuspecting Midlands and wreak* insurmountable *havoc. You gave Myra powerful magic to fight him, yes, but it cost her* everything. *And then you allowed those foolish mortals to get close to her grave, stealing the forbidden magic and thus weakening Myra's spell that has kept the fucker at bay all this time."*

Mamba is nose to nose with this one now, baring his fangs. *"This. Is. Your. Fault. And you sent a child to do a god's work."*

"She was nineteen," mutters Pollux. He scowls at the god again. "Myra was nineteen when she went to war. The rest of us already had close to a century of life on her and had borne witness to both peace and civil war over the course of many decades. We had grown blind to many of the atrocities the com-mon people of the spheres were facing." He shakes his head, pain flashing in his eyes. "But not Myra. She was young, new, and born into a decade of peace, but she understood what was at stake. She knew Lucifer was a different breed of danger. And she was the first to acknowledge him as something that could destroy us, and he nearly did. He would have much sooner if not for Myra."

"With your abilities," drawls Atticus quietly, "I would have thought you able to inquire about him and come to understand the danger he posed on your own accord."

Pollux nods, his eyes hardened by the memories and loss of his little sister. "I should have been more diligent. I should have done a lot of things differently than I did. But I was a cocky bastard and too confident in my own abilities. So blinded by my own arrogance that I didn't bother to properly inquire about Lucifer until Myra revealed to me that she had been approached by the Yonder Star and blessed with its power. Only then did I take the threat of Lucifer seriously . . . and what I found . . ."

He shakes his head again. "To inquire about him killed off my genies. A dozen of them dove into the wells of knowledge headfirst, and only one resurfaced long enough to warn me of what he was capable of. She didn't have time to inform me of the altar or much else about the Tenth Sphere, only that it was a bloodstained battlefield where the monsters and beasts we once slayed roamed with vengeance on their brains and poison on their tongues. I later came to learn that Lucifer had spelled himself and his Apostles with his soul-rendering magic to be immune to my antics and my genies, and thus I wasn't equipped with the knowledge of how to properly defeat him. To permanently be rid of him."

"Myra had concocted that dangerous spell with the help of Lilith at the time," says Conquest. "She had kept it a secret from us all, knowing we wouldn't allow her to sacrifice herself, Then she went and did it anyway. To save us at the cost of her life and our memories of her. The spheres became darker that day. The threat was gone. The war that none of us could recall was over. And yet the Nine Spheres felt so . . . *empty*."

"We had gaps in our memories," adds Pride. "We could tell something was amiss, though none of us could pinpoint exactly *what* . . . or *who*. Life resumed. Time passed. And we just *forgot*. History was erased, and everything that was Myra's or had Myra imprinted upon it just *vanished*. Claimed by the spheres and the Hollow, no doubt."

"She crafted the Zodiac Blade so she could gain access to her blood to create the runes and sigils necessary for the spell," says War. "When all was said and done, the blade found a home upon Apollo's side."

"There was carnage and destruction everywhere," drawls Death. "The spheres were painted red. Stained with blood. However, there were no souls left to reap from the bodies. Nothing left to ferry by that point, so we couldn't read their memories. We just . . . assumed another fight had broken out between the bloodlines and breeds, and that was all that was left. All who had died in the war, we could not recall. Thus, the family members and friends that were left behind believed them to be missing people. No one knew they were already dead."

"Blissful ignorance," quips Envy, chuckling darkly despite a lack of humor as he shakes his head. "Fools, the lot of us."

Looking between their crestfallen scowls, I settle my gaze on Mamba once more as I drawl, "And why didn't you ever say anything?"

Mamba's lips curl back again, and he seethes at the Yonder Star, *"I tried. But* it *silenced me. It silenced all the greater beasts of these spheres to keep us quiet about the secrets and schemes of higher powers and gods. And then it slaughtered others."*

Using Rhesa's features, the god scowls again, but it is Atlas who inquires, "Is that true?"

It snaps its gaze to Atlas. *"Myra was enough."*

"No," I claim. "Evidently, she fucking *wasn't.*"

"I do not have to explain myself to you, boy—"

"Will you hide away again?" inquires Mamba, cocking his head and cutting off the god. A daring action, and I applaud the snake for it. *"You have split yourself four ways this time. Is that all the accountability you will assume? All the aid you will give?"*

The god snarls, then reluctantly reveals, *"You must travel there by way of the passage that Lucifer tore open to get here. It has since been sealed shut. It is not like a common conveyance, and the voyage is not for the faint of heart. It is not like the Umbra Mundi where souls rest. Purgatory is a Living Sphere, and you must travel there with bodies and souls intact. Lucifer created the spell from scratch to escape, and it is the same spell you must use now. Myra concocted a similar version of it, but she had to sacrifice her entire life and memory to complete it. Lucifer sacrificed hundreds of thousands of souls. So what are you willing to sacrifice?"*

"The passage you speak of is no longer sealed as thoroughly as it once was," claims Pollux. "Not since the Great Betrayal. Our enemies chip away at it from this side, while Lucifer and his Apostles chip away at it from the other side. When they meet in the middle, the rest will fall apart, and Myra's spellwork will completely crumble as the spheres are once again reminded of what happened back then. And fortunately but tragically, it will provide us with the only means to reach the altar."

Perception cocks his head at the god. "In order to be rid of Lucifer, we must first free him so we may use his forbidden passageway to gain access to the altar, but that's not all . . . . Why didn't you inform Myra of the altar, Yonder?"

"Because it requires a greater sacrifice to destroy such a raw source of energy," provides Mamba, accusing and hissing. *"The altar has since taken on a life of its own, and the only way to be rid of it now is to use an abundance of magic that none of us are capable of wielding in these binding forms. Only a few beings in existence have access to it. The very* Beings of Existence *and their* Sons . . . *and the Yonder Star refuses to sacrifice itself and Evergreen to see it through."*

Atticus snarls, seething, "So you would rather sacrifice *us*? You'd rather sacrifice your Champion again? How do you expect us to destroy such a power?"

"You wield my magic now, boy. All four of you do. It should be enough."

"Should be?" repeats Pollux incredulously, scoffing. "And what if it isn't? And you've sacrificed your only weapons in the coming war against Lucifer. If the deities and your Champion fall, so will everything and everyone else. You're setting us up for failure!"

"You thought Myra would be enough, and you were wrong," I avow. "You believe Rhesamyre and the three of us will be enough now, and you will be proven wrong again." I shake my head, huffing a humorless laugh as I size up the god that *hides* inside the woman I love. "You'd rather send us to our deaths than face the consequences of your own actions. You are full of regret and are deceiving yourself into a false sense of security thinking we will solve your problems for you. *You* created the monster that is Lucifer, and then you created a warrior to fight him in your stead. *Then she died.* And here you are, trying to reclaim what is left of your Champion in order to repeat history. So it is as the snake said. You are a coward."

The Yonder Star inhales and exhales slowly, reining in the power that prowls beneath Rhesa's skin. Lights flicker around us, and the ground splinters beneath Rhesa's bare feet. Then it drawls, *"Think what you will of me, Vengeance. I am a being capable of great turmoil and atrocities, and I do not lose sleep over what has happened in the past. I am power. I am blood. I am god. And I do not yield to the likes of you. You have the magic and knowledge necessary to fight and defeat Lucifer. Do with it what you will."*

The white eyes of the Yonder Star recede, and Rhesa's hellfire eyes flash to the forefront before rolling backward as her knees buckle. I surge forward to catch her, and she slumps into my arms softly. The Hellion Court draws nearer, as do Pollux and my brothers, and I kneel on the ground with her in my arms. Her breathing is even, heartbeat steady, and she sleeps soundlessly, dreamlessly. Unaware of what just occurred and all that was revealed.

Mamba slithers closer, sniffing over her and pressing his nose against her gently; his huffs of warm breath move her hair out of her face, and he licks her cheek gently.

The obsidian serpent meets my eyes, then retreats to the throne once more to return to his slumber, silenced by the Yonder Star once more.

"What the hell are we going to do now?" inquires Wrath softly, his eyes downcast as he peers down at Rhesa with a sullen scowl.

I shake my head, surveying her peaceful, beautiful face as she lies in my arms, safe and warm and satisfied and loved. "I don't know," I reply quietly before I sigh and press my forehead against hers. "I don't know," I repeat again, and I feel my brothers place their hands on my shoulders, squeezing gently as if to say *we are here, and we will figure it out and fight together.*

CHAPTER TWENTY SEVEN
RHESAMYRE

Brushing down Orpheus, my hell-horse practically ignores me since Althea stands before him with his favorite cinnamon treats in hand. Thea giggles as Orpheus takes them from her gently, nickering softly.

"I missed you, too, pretty boy," says Thea, stroking his dark face. "And might I say, you are much more handsome in your proper form. Far more regal and menacing."

"Glad you think so," I agree. "I will admit, for a bit, I was worried you'd be frightened of him."

Althea shakes her head, brushing her hands off on her leather-clad thighs before meeting my eyes. "He doesn't scare me, Rhesa . . . and neither do you." She lifts her shoulder. "I'll admit, you would startle me from time to time, but I've never feared you." She huffs a quiet laugh. "I don't know if that makes me stupid or foolishly brave, as you have proven to be someone worth fearing."

I smile gently at her, coming to her side to bump her hip with my own. "It makes me happy to hear that. I don't want you or any of the girls to ever be scared of me. Whether it's to come to me for help, or just in general. You're my best friends. Truly, my only girlfriends, and I've come to treasure you four greatly."

Althea grins. "We love you, too. As do the lieutenants. I know it to be more platonic than romantic, but those males would commit grand atrocities to protect you."

"They would for you four, too. You know that, right?"

She nods, then giggles a little. "So I've come to learn . . . Gage is a blushing flirt when he gets drunk."

I grin. "*Oh*, I know. The wolf can't hold his liquor for shit."

"And he . . . he's made it quite clear what his intentions are with me."

I raise my brows. "Oh?"

"He calls me *his* . . . and to gain the favor of a demon seems like something worth coveting."

"It certainly is. Are you comfortable with him? I know he can be a little . . . *rough* sometimes."

She shrugs, her eyes inquisitive as she admits softly, "His touch doesn't . . . *scald* me like other men—*boys*—of my past have. I don't feel like ripping my skin off when he embraces me. When he makes love to me, it's quite nice. *Electric*, even. Gage is respectful of my boundaries and is willing to go at my pace. In fact, we didn't fuck at all when he was drunk last night. He just listened to me talk and tell him of my life as a mortal woman. His eyes were alight with drunken wonder the entire time as he played with my hair or rubbed my sides, kissing my scars and stretch marks while telling me how beautiful I am . . . . I think I'm falling in love with him."

I take her hands in mine, sparing her a genuine smile. "I am so, *so* happy for you, Thea. My brother is a good male. And I can already see that you make him happy, and in turn, he to you. He deserves you, and you him. And I know you don't need my blessing on the matter, but I still want you to know that there is no other female I would ever feel comfortable with claiming Gage as hers. A few have come and gone, and while he is a warrior and bloodstained wolf through and through, he loves wholly. He's a protector and caretaker, and I'm ecstatic that you see it, too. That you can see past *his scars*, as well. Many of his courtships in the past could not, and they remain shallow, heartless *cunts*. You are everything but."

Althea smiles, her eyes almost wet as she nods and squeezes my hands. "Having your friendship and honesty mean so much to me, my queen. *You* mean so much to me, Rhesa. Even back in Soulton, I guess deep down I knew you were someone special. Something *other*, yes . . . but potentially *mine* all the same. And our friends, Gage, this entire place . . . Hell is my home, and Gage is my partner," she vows. "And to know that I have a place in your court is more than I could have ever asked for. Something I never thought I would ever dream of or desire, yet here I am. Dressed in obsidian battle leathers, prepping to travel to the winged regiments of the hellion military to learn how to ride a *wyvern*."

I grin at her again. "Fascinating how time flies, isn't it?"

She nods again, but then her eyes catch on something behind me, and her smile falters. I don't bother looking; I know who's there.

"They seem . . . *tense* this morning," she notes under her breath. "More so than usual . . . did something happen?"

I sigh, letting my hands slip from Thea's as I turn back to Orpheus to finish tacking him up. Ever since waking up this morning in Alastair's tight embrace, my three deities have refused to let me out of their sights. I attempted to inquire as to what was wrong, but all they did was shake their heads and hold me tighter, passing me between the three of them all morning and having me in their presence or upon one of their laps at breakfast. And even now, all three of them lounge at the other end of the barn aisle just a few strides away from me, watching my every move. Every breath I take, their eyes are locked on the movement of my chest as I inhale and exhale. Their gazes often glance up at my eyes, though when I attempt to catch their attention, I don't believe them to be looking at *me*.

Something must have happened last night with the *other one*. Something that included the rest of my family, as well. As many of them, even Pollux, seemed out of it this morning. At least, that is what I gathered from the few that actually showed up for breakfast, as a little over half of them didn't even bother to eat with the rest of us.

That rarely happens.

I sigh. "I don't exactly know," I tell her, and that's the truth.

Thea hums, not pushing the matter, and a heartbeat later, we're leading Orpheus out to the barnyard where the lieutenants, Tally, Fern, and Trix wait patiently, with the Wolves of Woe sitting by their feet. Embrace pads behind me, too, and remains by my side as I hoist myself onto my stallion. Thea saunters up to Gage and Embers, feeding the nightmare the last of her cinnamon treats before Gage grabs her by the waist to place her gently onto his saddle with little difficulty.

Silas is already situated upon Ignite, standing at attention next to Tally and her new nightmare, Hesperia, while Damian and Fern sit upon Blaze. Malcolm gives Trix a leg up onto her new hellhorse, Rhombus, the stallion's forehead painted with an uncommon white star in the center. Then, once Mal is mounted upon Cinders with Thea, I turn my gaze to my deities as they appear in my line of sight.

"You needn't come with us," I say, and Alastair draws closer to place his tatted hand on my thigh. "We'll only be gone for the day. We'll be back this evening, though probably after dinner. And I have . . . some things I would like to discuss with the eight of them."

Alastair nods, his steeled, silver eyes flickering all over my form. He squeezes my thigh as though to remind himself what I feel like. "And we won't breathe down your neck the entire time. Go. Be with your friends. The spheres and their problems can wait another day. Just be safe, Rhesa."

I furrow my brows at him, placing my hand over his to squeeze it in reassurance. "I do hope that by the time I return, you three are ready to inform me of what's been ailing you all morning."

He inclines his head, his scowl firmly in place, revealing very little of what he's feeling. Even Atticus's emotions are locked down tight, as is my bond with Atlas.

"You have my word, love," he husks. "We'll talk of schemes and secrets when you return."

He removes his palm from my thigh, and I just nod after him. I meet Atlas's and Atticus's gazes next, and then I turn away from them.

Following my brothers and girlfriends, Orpheus and I take up the rear position as Dami and Mal open a conveyance in the middle of the barnyard that will lead from the heart of Hell into the hellion military fort, Black Wing. The special units here consist of both jockeys that ride the rhayvens and wyverns within the ranks of my military. Very few infantry footmen patrol here, as Black Wing caters only to flyers and wranglers.

A proud castle stands in the center of the valley surrounded by smaller tents and stone barns, and overhead, the sound of flapping wings echoes between the clouds as leather and feathers soar in the navy sky. Silhouettes of wyvern and rhayven patrols dot the skyline, and plenty can be seen resting on the ground or upon their stone perches across the camp, too. Their demonic riders are clad in obsidian flight leathers and armed with aerial weaponry rather than the swords and staffs of close-quarter and hand-to-hand combat.

"*Wow*," breathes Fern. Her wide, awed gaze skipps all across the camp and sky above. "They're magnificent."

"And fucking *massive*," quips Trix. "Yeah. I'm fine with a horse, *thank you very much*."

I smile as I ride forward, taking point as we continue down the path into camp. Hellion soldiers march or run by in their squads, but plenty more care for their weaponry of bows and crossbows, leathers, and beasts off to the side while others spar or lift weights and train. Most are demons of varying bloodlines and appendages, but something they all have in common is their two builds:

Wranglers are often built taller and broader than the flyers, as the wranglers need more upper body strength to ride and command the scaly, leathery beasts we call wyverns. The creatures vary in a darker array of colors: from blacks, navy, burgundies, and grays. They only have two hind legs adorned with massive claws, while their front appendages are attached to their leather wings, and their scaled torsos are heavily muscled. Their necks are long with heads full of spikes, scales, and horns. Long tails swish behind them dangerously, sporting dagger tips that are often coated in venom like their fangs and claws.

While the rhayvens bear a striking resemblance to the smaller birds that claim crows as cousins, these black-feathered beasts are much, *much* bigger. Lithe and swift with sleek, obsidian feathers, mighty, arched beaks, beady eyes, and two feet riddled with larger talons. Thus, the flyers that find homes upon their backs must be lighter and lithe in nature, too.

Both winged beasts are a little bigger than our horses, and the many that we pass either growl or snarl softly or bare their teeth or click their beaks in warning. Orpheus releases a low, rumbling nicker in challenge, and plenty of the beasts quit their complaining about the newcomers as they size me up next. Their partnered riders either bow their heads or place an appendage over their hearts in acknowledgment, and I dip my head to them in return, winking at a few of the females as I pass. They grin at me, and the males gawk at them.

"Queen Rhesamyre," calls a demon from ahead of us situated near the portcullis of the castle, flanked by two other demons. He's built like a wrangler but resembles a lion; however, although he is armed to the teeth with obsidian and is nothing but a wall of muscle, his gray eyes are kind as he watches us approach.

I smile at him, dismounting Orpheus so I can saunter up to the massive male and embrace him. He chuckles as he squeezes me, grabbing me by my shoulders so he can peer down at my form and get a better look at me.

"My, my," he drawls. "Would you look at that? The crown and title of queen are certainly becoming of you. How have you been, little mama?"

"Been just fine, General Haidar. Thank you for taking the time to entertain me."

He laughs, the sound booming and strong just like him. "I could never deny my favorite princess a visit, now my favorite *queen*. Have you finally decided to ditch your hooves for wings?"

I grin. "Unfortunately not. However, I do have some friends of mine who I believe would benefit from taking up the flight leathers. One a potential wrangler and the other a flyer."

His eyes light up at the promise of new riders, and he glances over my head to no doubt observe Thea and Fern as they approach. I back up a few steps so that I am in line with them, and

I gesture to Althea on my left as I introduce her. And then Fern on my right.

"Althea here is a mortal turned hellion friend of mine," I say. "And just by looking at her, I'm sure you can guess she's our wrangler-to-be."

Haidar nods appreciatively, surveying Althea and sizing her up, and to her credit, she doesn't flinch under his scrutinizing gaze. And at the sight of her strength, he grins and whistles. "She's a strong one. Got some spirit in her, I can see it. Mortal, you say?" He chuckles. "You wouldn't think it looking at her now. Your weight and curves will be your saving grace here, mama. Be thankful for the potential of your size, as it will guarantee you are not *thrown* so easily."

Althea raises her brows at that, but then nods a little as her lips turn up at the edges into a delicate smile. And then, seeming to recall her strength, she downright gives the general a shit-eating grin. Haidar laughs again and then turns his eyes to Feronia next.

"Feronia is extremely skilled with a bow," I quip. "Can even give Silas a run for his money, though she was turned down by the Artemis. I'm sure you can gamble as to why."

Haidar grunts at the mention of the Artemis. "I'm sure they thought her too *pretty*."

Feronia cocks her head. Then nods. "They did. They called me an anorexic cunt who would be better suited to spreading my legs than shooting."

I raise my brows to myself at this new slice of information, tucking it away for now.

Haidar grunts again. "And I hope you took your arrows and promptly plunged them through their eyes."

She shakes her head, but a smile tugs at the corners of her mouth all the same. "No . . . though I did steal all their fish."

Haidar grins. "That'll do, little mama. And like your friend here, your size is ideal for the rhayvens. They cannot carry as much weight as the wyverns and rely on their speed and the skills of their rider to keep up with them. I believe you'll make a fine flyer."

"Thank you, sir."

He grins at me again, clapping his hands. "Well, then, shall we head out to the fields?"

I nod, and the three of us mount back up on our horses while Haidar looks to the sky. I follow his gaze, watching as the silhouette of one of the wyverns that had been circling high overhead begins to make its descent toward us at a swift pace. The leather beat of its wings draws nearer as it flares them outward to land upon the castle wall, its dagger tail swishing back and forth for balance as it scales the wall and lands beside Haidar. This one is larger in size and of a dark blue color with shimmering black scales around its joints and head. It cocks its head and snarls softly at us before turning its head to Haidar.

"Hello, my beautiful," he says, rubbing the wyvern's scales.

He walks around her head and neck to grab the leather straps of the flight saddle, which is situated at the base of her neck just before her wings, and he swings onto her back with practiced ease. Assuming I recall her name correctly, I believe the beast's name is *Ciel*. Haidar grins at me, pulls his flight goggles over his eyes, and then launches into the sky, stirring up dust and sand as he goes.

"Well," I drawl. "We best get galloping if we don't wish to be late meeting him out there."

The lieutenants roll their eyes, and the girls smile and snicker softly as we kick on with the Wolves of Woe flanking us as we ride out to one of the flight fields littered with flyers, wranglers, and a plethora of saddled and wild wyverns and rhayvens.

Not surprisingly, Haidar beat us here, and he stands with his wyvern proudly presented behind him as he watches us near. Ciel watches us approach with black eyes, sizing us up as either potential snacks or threats, I'm not entirely sure. Probably both.

"All the wyvern and rhayvens here have been handled before," explains General Haidar. "Not necessarily trained, but like our horses, we can break them in and teach them to get used to saddles, riders, and flying in formations. All the ones lounging out here without saddles are unclaimed and, similarly to your hell-horses, unnamed. In addition, as you already know, those of hellion breeds must choose *us* to be their partners just as we choose them. However, when compared to getting turned down by these winged beasts, hell-horses are considered tame and polite about the action. For if your horses tell you no, they simply kick, bite, or run off. Wyverns and rhayvens will not hesitate to take your life and gobble you up whole if they find anything about you to be lacking. They allow us to fit them into saddles and guide them as they grow, but only a worthy candidate may name them and take a permanent seat upon their backs."

He levels his gaze onto Fern, then Thea, and then he grins. "So, which of you ladies would like to go first?"

I watch as Damian squeezes his little wendigo before helping her slide off his horse, and Feronia takes a few steadying breaths before approaching the general. However, before she gets very far, I call out to her. She turns around, meeting my gaze, and while her sea-green eyes shine with bravery, I can tell she is still nervous about approaching one of the overgrown, murderous birds.

I smile gently at her, hoping the action conveys my encouragement. "Don't let that old lion scare you. Approaching the rhayvens is dangerous work, yes, but recall that *you* are dangerous, too, my little wendigo. You are as much *other* as they are, and your blood is powerful, your aim deadly accurate, and your pure heart worthy of bonding with one of the obsidian birds of my kingdom. You are a member of the queen's court, and the rhayvens will sense your intentions and allegiances. Loyalty is an ally, and you are my friend. I saw your potential the moment I laid eyes on you on that beach, and the rhayven are no fools. Be true to yourself, be brave, and take aim. You will not miss, Feronia."

Fern blinks at me, then nods with a small smirk as she turns on her heel and tosses over her shoulder, "As you command, my queen."

I grin at her fleeting form, watching as she struts up to the nearby *unkindness,* her shoulders back and obsidian knives gleaming on her thighs as a bow and quiver rest upon her back. Sun-kissed hair is braided with hellion rings into a crown around her head, and while she remains thin, the wendigo is all muscles.

"Thank you," murmurs Damian next to me.

"I didn't do it for you," I reply softly.

I can hear the smile in his voice as he says, "I know."

"*Wendigo,* huh?" inquires General Haidar, crossing his arms at me. "I thought they were all extinct."

I shrug gracefully. "And you'll keep thinking that."

He chuckles. "Indeed I will, Your Majesty. She has nothing to fear from the rhayven, and you already knew that even before you gave her your pep talk. I've seen grown warriors and demons *shit themselves* when facing down the rhayven and wyvern alike, yet your little wendigo shows no fear in her gait. However, I dare say her faith in you to not lead her astray is far greater than her fear of potentially being *eaten*. She trusts you with her life, and thus, the rhayven will trust *her*."

I nod along. "There are certainly worse traits to have. And there are certainly worse ways to feel about me, too."

"I know."

I finally peel my eyes away from Fern to glance at Haidar, and both the general and his wyvern are already looking at me. He offers me a gentle smile.

"Your father would be proud of the woman you have become, my queen. You've always been regal and confident . . . but seeing you now . . ." He shakes his head, huffing a quiet laugh. "You were so little when you came here to visit and train with me decades ago. No bigger than the pigs and goats we feed to our winged beasts, and yet you marched out there to the center of the flight field when you thought no one was watching, and the rhayven and wyvern *let* you. I've seen them devour children, men, women, and demons alike, yet they never harmed you."

"They *bowed*," I breathe, recalling the memory. I was smaller, as he stated, and surrounded by giant birds and scales and tails and wings, yet I never felt scared of the beautiful beasts. I just wanted to see what their feathers and scales felt like, and they let me pet them. Some even purred under my palms, nudging me and cuddling me just as Orpheus and Mamba have done before.

Haidar nods, and I feel the others' eyes on me now, too, glancing between me and Fern to keep an eye on her, as well.

"Yes," he agrees. "They bowed, and I remember thinking to myself, *finally. Here stands someone worthy of riding the wings.* Yet you never climbed onto their backs. You simply whispered to them words I still do not know and went on your way back to your father after he called your name. The damn male nearly had a heart attack when he realized where you were, yet you were not in danger." He glances over to Fern again, smirking a little. "I see your smaller frame when I watch that wendigo brave the wings."

I look out at Feronia again, and a rhayven has approached her. The beastly bird flares his wings and rears his head back, and I feel Damian tense beside me, his muscles tightening as if he is going to gallop out there to rescue her. However, he needn't waste his time, because the rhayven releases a mighty shriek, but the sound is of a sing-song manner. Not that of a shrill battle cry, but instead a song that claims Feronia as *his*.

The rhayven lowers his head to her, and I watch with pride as she pets his sharp beak and glides her hands through his feathers as she walks toward his back. Then with little hesitation, she swings onto him bareback and grasps whatever she can find as the rhayven flaps his wings, hops forward, and launches into the sky. I can see her struggle to remain seated at first as they climb, but once they level out within the clouds, soaring high above, she appears more at ease as she learns to fly with her new partner.

I turn my gaze to Althea, grinning. "Your turn, Thea."

•••••••••••••

The fire crackles between us as we lounge before the flames within the obsidian forest underneath the moon and stars. The evening air is warm, but the breeze provides the perfect chill and temperature for a fire.

I lean back against Orpheus as he lies down behind me, and Embrace has once again situated his head upon my lap as my hand absentmindedly rubs his furry ears. Bellatrix and Malcolm sit with each other and Barter in a similar manner, as do Tally and Silas with Dolor. However, Damian and Gage remain seated alone with Veto and Vex since their girls busy themselves with caring for their winged beasts.

Althea had claimed a wyvern with similar ease as Feronia and her rhayven companion, and the two of them spent the entire day learning the simplest of flight maneuvers and getting fitted for their saddles, extra gear, and flight leathers. Now, Feronia cares for Branwen, while Althea looks after the mahogany-colored female wyvern, Edana.

I smile as I watch them return to the fire and finally settle down with their restless males, their winged beasts slumbering quietly and keeping watch near the rest of the horses we tied to a line. Damian and Gage busy themselves with cooking the rabbits we shot over the fire, and I begin to mentally steel myself for what I am about to tell them. My honorary brothers are already partially aware of a part of the story that has to do with the Great Betrayal and Child, but they don't know of Myra yet.

So, as the girls settle down from the high of flying as they bite into their meals of rabbit, I nibble on my meat slowly before feeding most of it to Embrace.

Gently, Trix calls out to me, "Not a fan of rabbit?"

I moot the witch's teasing gaze, and it draws a small smirk to my lips before I let it drop again. "The rabbit is fine . . . it's the coming conversation that I find myself hesitating on."

"Conversation?" inquires Tally.

Everyone is listening intently now, and I could swear even Branwen and Edana watch me more closely, too.

"Does this . . . *conversation* . . . have anything to do with that odd spellwork you gave me?" asks Trix.

I nod. "It does . . . . What did you learn from it?"

She shrugs, picking at her rabbit now before offering it up to Barter as I did Embrace; Malcolm scowls at her, though she can't see his frown since her attention is split between me and her wolf.

"From what I could read and gather," she says, "it was a convoluted memory-wiping spell that also doubled as a banishing command. One which relied on a heavy sacrifice, powerful commands that are nearly forbidden in nature, and a *shit-ton* of magic. Most of which I am unfamiliar with, and the amount needed to complete the spell . . ." She shakes her head, meeting my eyes. "Aside from the deities, I don't know who or *what* would have access to that kind of power. And that *much* of it, nonetheless."

I dip my chin. "And were you able to read any of the names involved?"

"Just one, but I don't know if I translated it correctly since it was written with Enochian letters . . . *Myra*."

Tally tenses in Silas's arms, and she looks between Trix and me with wide, calculating eyes. Silas quirks a brow at her, but her attention remains solely on me as she drawls, "The wells of information I once had access to as a genie . . . it would whisper a name every once in a while, . . . *Myra, Myra* . . . but the accent was so thick, I had thought it was actually saying *mirror, mirror*." She narrows her eyes at me. "But it wasn't. It really was calling a name . . . dare I say, the magic was calling *your* name."

I remain silent, and that seems to be answer enough.

"Tell us," prompts Damian softly. The reaper swallows thickly, his eyes steeled, but his voice remains soft as he commands, "Tell us why you once answered to an *Enochian* name."

I inhale slowly to steel myself again, and then I tell them.

CHAPTER TWENTY EIGHT
RHESAMYRE

Sheathing my obsidian daggers in place upon my thighs, I steel myself as I survey my leather-clad form in the mirror of my closet. Hellion features and horns and hellfire eyes, yet once upon a time, I claimed wings and an Enochian accent.

"The other one paid us a visit last night," Alastair had said when I returned with my girls and lieutenants with a new rhayven and wyvern in tow. All of them were made aware of Myra and the dangers she once faced—the same dangers we may face yet again.

"I figured it was something of that nature," I had replied. *"But this interaction seems to have rattled you and your brothers. Rattled my entire court, for that matter. Even Pollux."*

He nodded and then proceeded to tell me all that *Yonder* had revealed to them, as well as what *Mamba* had *said*, too.

I couldn't reply at first. I didn't know how. Alastair didn't pressure me for a plan, either. He and his brothers just held me throughout the night as I remained silent and still in their arms. And I clutched them just as tightly, inhaling their scents and running my hands over their tattoos absentmindedly. Feeling them, but not teasing them. Just needing the reassurance of their presence and existence as a whole.

I close my eyes, and a heartbeat later, I feel his hands circling my waist as he presses his chest into my back, his chin settling on my shoulder as he squeezes me.

I open my eyes, meeting deep emeralds that belong to Atticus. His expression isn't steeled nor that of a scowl, just emotionlessly blank as he surveys my form in the mirror.

"We don't have to—"

"We have to deal with him first," I cut him off, but he doesn't snap at me. Merely listens. "We can't have any loose ends if we are to go to war with either the celestials or Lucifer . . . or possibly both. Andrew needs to either stand with us or stand aside. I cannot have him threatening my crown and kingdom any longer, and I will not stand for it if he comes after any of you next."

Atticus nods, then spins me around so we're vis-à-vis. He grasps my chin gently between his fingers, his gaze skipping all over my face before he settles on my eyes again. Whatever he finds there makes him frown.

Grabbing his hand, I clutch it to my heart. "If you could go anywhere in the spheres, where would you go?"

He quirks his brow at me, but then reveals softly, "When I was a boy, I would spend my sleepless nights staring up at the stars. Naming the constellations and watching as shooting stars and ships crossed the Starfall Sea. Guided by old-fashioned star maps and enchanted devices that stellar-kissed pirates used to smuggle their goods and arms between the spheres without the use of conveyances. And then I fell in love with the stories that would come from sailing those seas. Interactions with the peri or the starfish and stellar-cetacean. Thus, I believe that cruising amongst the stars on a luxury ship would be quite astonishing. As the Starfall Sea is one of the few places I have yet to traverse."

That brings a smile to my lips. "I've never been one for sailing. I can count on one hand the number of times I've been on a *boat*."

He pulls me closer, dipping his head to husk against my mouth, "It wouldn't just be a *boat*, sweetness. It would be a luxury class frigate. A cruise ship where you and I never have to work the sails or polish the rails . . . . How do you fancy a floating palace amongst the stars?"

He kisses me gently, and his tongue barely slides against mine before he pulls away to rest his forehead against my own.

I hum. "I believe I could learn to love it. Will you take me one day? Will you take me sailing across the stars, Atticus?"

He smiles at me. "Yes, sweet spice. There, and everywhere else we may wish to go."

I nod, inhaling deeply to capture his scent and keep it there until I feel my lungs burn with the need to breathe. And when I exhale, I open my eyes and steel myself once more. Atticus appears to have done the same, and we stride hand in hand out of my chambers toward the throne room, where my family and court await.

All of us are armed to the teeth in hellion leathers and obsidian, and I study all their forms until I settle my eyes on Atlas and Alastair, and then I slide my gaze to Pollux next. Leaving Atticus's side, I stride up to my brother and halt before him. He looks down at me, cocking his head at whatever he sees in my eyes. And for a moment, I just let myself study his icy eyes and familiar, handsome face. The way he holds his white wings behind him, and how he has begun to pull the top half of his hair back into a bun with hellion rings and coils braided into a few of the strands now.

For some reason, I want to cry when I spot the additional ornaments. It's such a transparent show of trust and loyalty that I find it hard to swallow for a moment, and slowly, Pollux's hand comes to cup my cheek as he narrows his eyes at me, his gaze forever calculating.

I grasp his hand, nuzzling into his large palm just like I used to when I was a young archangel.

"Not you, Pollux," I say softly, nearly whispering.

His eyes harden, and he quirks a brow at me. "Excuse me?"

I step away from his hand, and it falls back to his side like a dead weight. "I gave it some thought last night, and I need you to go to your—*our* brothers, and try to reason with them. I don't know if Apollo will listen, but surely the others will. We need to give them a chance to make the right choice. To stand with Hell. *With me* . . . I doubt the Zodiacs will listen, either, but surely our brothers will at least hear you out."

Pollux studies me for a few heartbeats, and I let him. Until finally, he nods gently and steps forward again, pressing his lips to my forehead as he murmurs, "As you wish, little feather."

"Thank you," I breathe.

He ducks his head to better meet my eyes. "You needn't thank me for this, baby sister. I am your big brother, and I will protect you." He pauses, pursing his lips, and I can see the raw anguish in his gaze. "I've failed you once before. I won't let it happen again."

I inhale carefully, doing my best to hide the way my lungs want to quake at the action, and all I can muster is a simple, pitiful nod in return. Pollux bows his head, then steps away from me and says a few farewells to my court and deities, and then he strides out in order to begin the trek toward the Celestial Cities, opening a conveyance as close as he can to Ursa Major since they have removed his runes within the wards of the palace.

I can't bring myself to survey his retreating form, and I don't turn around until I hear the doors click shut. Steeling myself, I raise my head and turn around to face my court and deities.

"The lieutenants and girls will stay here with Mamba to look after the throne," I claim, meeting each of their eyes. "The girls are not yet battle-ready, and the lieutenants can defend Hell with the soldiers posted here long enough for us to return, should anything occur while we're away dealing with the Pantomath. We take no prisoners. Andrew's fleet will either yield or sink, and we will not leave any survivors should they pose a threat to us. Whether they are alive in our cells, or out there, we leave nothing but carnage. This is the consequence of fraternizing with our enemies and scheming against Hell, and it is due time we remind the rest of the spheres what it means to stand against us. If they seek to raise their swords, let them be aware of what sort of demons they're attempting to slay."

All of the Hellion Court nods, and we open a conveyance just outside Silver Spoon with a battalion of hellion soldiers at our backs. And we lay waste to Andrew's fleet of pirates.

....

Driving my sword through one of the last pirates, I rip it out of him just as swiftly so I may stalk forward, stepping over other bodies of pirates and sailors that wear Andrew's colors as I go. Ahead of me, Atlas and Atticus stand with Andrew firmly clutched between them. The bastard-bred angel is on his knees with his head bowed as blood collects beneath him, dripping from his mouth and broken nose and other injuries inflicted upon him when he attempted to flee.

Alastair cut him down in the sky, and he fell to the ground with broken wings.

I reach for him, tipping his head back by grasping his chin roughly to jostle him awake. Green eyes that belong to his crone of a mother glare daggers at me, and he goes to spit at me, but I clamp a hand over his mouth and nose before he can.

"You brought this on yourself, Andrew," I drawl, and when I'm sure I have his attention and he won't try anything foolish again, I release his mouth and nose. He inhales sharply, his chest rattling with the sound, and he coughs up more blood at the action.

"We are presented with an opportunity here, Pantomath," I continue. "War is not my goal, Andrew. It never has been. But I could not allow your conspiracy to go unpunished. You were providing poisoned weaponry to the raiders and rapists of the West. Murdering innocents and hellion allies in cold blood, and their blood is on your hands. *I wonder if you can feel it*," I mutter. "The *stains* it leaves behind. The weight of your actions and choices. Do you hear their screams at night? The screams of women and children being slaughtered and raped and butchered? I would think it to be a sound you couldn't unhear, but I suppose you never stepped foot in the West to survey the aftermath of your carnage, did you? You were too caught up in drinking and gambling away within the safety of your ports with your filthy pirates. Speaking of schemes and secrets in the hopes that no one would overhear."

I lean forward, gripping him by his hair to make him meet my eyes again since he begins to glance down.

"*But we heard you*," I snarl. "And we came for you. And we have destroyed *everything* that you own. Freed every slave you had claimed from the West and elsewhere. Slaughtered your captains and burned your ships. Set fire to your banners and claimed your weapons and riches as collateral. You are *nothing* now. Nothing but a broken bastard bred between a traitorous, conniving archangel and a wicked crone."

Andrew widens his green eyes at me, and I toss his head back roughly before backing away from him.

"You figured it out when we first met, didn't you?" he inquires, coughing again. "From the minute you saw me, you *knew*."

"At the time of our meeting, I only realized that Lilith was your mother. I didn't put it together that Apollo had sired you until later. All I can ask now is *why*? What made you think coming after what is mine was a good idea to begin with? And what made you believe you'd get away with it?"

"I was reassured that you wouldn't get this far. That what my father had planned in the event that my mother failed would already be in the works. His *contingencies*. I was to play my part, and he promised I'd be safe from you and what was to come."

"He lied to you, Andrew."

He nods. "I see that now. By the end of it, he just used me like he used my mother. Even now, he still leaves me at your mercy as everything I built with my own hands comes crashing down around me. *Burning* like witches at the stake." He meets my eyes again, and I see they have begun to glaze over. "Be done with it, Queen of Hell. All I ask is that you make it quick."

I nod my head, raising my sword. "Maybe in another life, you and I could have been something closer to family. Friends, cousins . . . *or even my baby nephew*," I whisper

His eyes flicker brighter at that, but then I plunge my sword deep into his chest, and they dull just as swiftly.

"I'm sorry, Andrew," I murmur into his ear, and I mean it.

I'm sorry.

Atlas and Atticus allow his body to slump forward, and I back up a step to avoid him as he goes down onto the blood-splattered bricks.

I raise my eyes, surveying my three deities and the members of my court, all of us splattered with the blood of slain pirates. "Apollo may have let me slay his son, but he will still come for me with vengeance in mind. Using it to fuel his rage as he justifies bringing Lucifer and his Apostles back. He'll do everything he can to make me the villain, and perhaps I am." I steel myself. "And if that is the case, then I will wear the blood splatters I gained when murdering his son as warpaint. And I will stride through the grand halls of his palace in my heels with a sword stained with the blood of his angels. And I will rob him of the Zodiac Blade I once created, and I will carve out his heart with it just as Adriel did to Samael."

Atlas steps forward, cupping my cheeks as he kisses me gently despite the blood coating the both of us.

"And we will stand by you when you do," he vows. "All of us."

I nod. "We are one. Our magic and powers are of the same sun, and you claim my thoughts, Atlas." I look to his brothers. "Alastair, my heart. And Atticus owns my soul."

"And we will continue to cherish and covet them until we are nothing more than dust," Atticus promises.

"We claim your eternity, Rhesamyre," avows Alastair. "For however long it may be. You are ours, and we are yours. And we will follow you anywhere. Even if that means back into the *fucking* cowardly Yonder Star itself."

I can't help my grin, and I reach forward to embrace all three of my deities despite the bodies and bloodshed that surround us on all sides.

. . . .

I survey the slumbering forms of my three kings as they all lounge about in different areas of my bedroom. Atlas and Atticus had been the ones to cuddle me to sleep last night after we washed the blood off our skin and out of our hair after returning from Silver Spoon; and Alastair claimed the couch while his brothers claimed me.

Now, I hope my little sleeping spell holds while I disappear for the evening. Dressed in my leathers once again, I step through a conveyance straight out of my bedroom, landing just before the outermost wards of the Four Pillars. Then I trek down the trail under cover of darkness, stars and moonlight illuminating the path ahead, and through the woodwork, I can spot various eyes blinking at me.

Draven's baku.

I ignore the feral dream-eaters, continuing on my way toward the Lord of Sanity's castle and tower. Uncle Death had claimed to be communicating with Kure, but the minotaur once requested that I find him in *reality* to bargain.

Well, here I am.

I stride through his wards and gates with no issue, then prowl up the steps of his castle and enter without knocking. Odds are he already knows I'm here, or at least on my way, so skipping formalities doesn't feel ridiculous considering the circumstances.

"Kure!" I shout into the vast antechamber of his home where dust collects along the bookshelves and the various artwork all around me.

From the looks of things, he doesn't have a set aesthetic like that of his neighbors. Instead, objects and artifacts of varying origins and cultures clutter the many shelves, collecting more dust, while various pieces of artwork hang upon the walls haphazardly. Some just lean against each other upright on the floor, while others are scattered in broken piles across the tiles and in the corners. Windows are vast but clouded, and tapestries and curtains are torn at the seams and riddled with moth holes.

"Kure!" I call again, throwing my hands up in exasperation. "I'm here now as you once requested! The least you could do is have an audience with your queen. I came all this way to see you, after all."

A low growl sounds from the limited light ahead of me, and a heartbeat later, Kure waltzes out of another set of rooms, his hooves clicking along the tile flooring as he strides toward me.

Scowling, I steel myself and cross my arms. "There has to be another way," I say, my voice oddly calm despite my inner rage and turmoil.

Kure halts a few paces ahead of me, folding his arms over his burly, furry chest as he shakes his head slowly. "There is not."

"There *has* to be," I snarl. "*We* . . ." I take another breath to steady myself. "We cannot just sacrifice ourselves. There has to be an alternative. There has to be a better spell or scheme that we just haven't thought of yet."

"I'm afraid not, my queen. A sacrifice must be made."

I release a quiet breath, shaking my head. "How are you so calm? Knowing all that you know, how do you keep it together? When all that we know is about to be ripped out from under us, you're the epitome of patience and grace. I'm quite envious, to be honest. As I have tried for years to appear as put together as you are in the face of danger, yet I'm never sure if I quite succeed in doing so."

He nods. "You have. You may not trust me when I say it, but you have. And as to how I do it . . ." He shrugs. "Our reality has been upturned plenty of times before, and even after you and I are both gone, whether it is due to sacrifice or being slain, reality is liable to change again. Whether we are prepared for it or not, that will once again be the question. I just learned to quit asking it and do my best to answer what I can. The rest is not up to me."

"When we spoke last, you made it sound as though I could stop this from happening. Is that still true? Was it *ever* true? Or were you just saying that to get me to fight and return to those who needed me most? Were you just telling me what I wanted to hear? What I *needed* to hear?"

He nods again, carefully and slower this time. "It could have been prevented, yes. But it truthfully wouldn't have been you who made that difference. Apollo chose a long, long time ago which side he wanted to be on this time. And unfortunately, he made that choice even long before you first bargained with the crone. He set everything in motion when he activated the old sigils and runes worked into the Zodiacs' bodies, placed there by the Twelve Apostles before you killed and banished them back into the Tenth Sphere. It was a contingency plan of Lucifer's. In the event that they could return, he sought to ensure *vessels* would be waiting here for his Apostles. He kept ahold of their souls in his altar and didn't let the Yonder Star consume them . . . not like it would have, but even so, he had every intention of stuffing them into the Zodiacs. Possessing them if you will."

I remind myself to breathe. "How long . . ." I swallow thickly. "How long have the Apostles been inside the Zodiacs?"

"Since before you attended that banquet in Ursa Major. It was not Taurus you insulted and conversed with. It was one of the Apostles."

"Apollo let that aswang into the palace. He still wanted Lilith's plan to work. He still wanted the Reformation Spell to be their first course of action, but when it failed, he already had the Apostles here waiting and lurking in the wings . . . . *How*? I thought the passageway was still sealed. Breaking and chipping away, maybe, but still intact nonetheless, no?"

"It remains closed off to the *whole* of a physical body and matter coming through, but the Apostles were already dead when you banished Lucifer's soul and body back into Purgatory. Thus, with some convoluted spellwork in place and a forbidden summoning ritual, Apollo was able to get the Apostles' *souls* here and inside the Zodiacs, as only those who know the way may travel by way of souls. The rest must be consumed body and all."

"*Pollux*—how did Pollux *not*—"

"The Archangel of Perception, much like many of the immortal and original beasts, was spelled into secrecy by Yonder. He *could not* speak of the matter. It was never a vow. In addition, he learned his lesson long ago that inquiring too much about Lucifer and the Apostles led to near-certain death. Searching for the information killed his genies by the *dozens* once upon a time, and he was almost killed when his bonds and bargains nearly dragged him into the depths of endless magic with them. He had to snap his tethers to them quite viciously if he wanted to keep his life, hence why he has since taken to only keeping a few genies at a time. Treading lightly when it comes to using them so as not to repeat history."

"Why . . . why did Apollo . . .?"

"After the Great Betrayal, Pollux was the first to begin to recall you. Apollo was next, but he had more at stake this time. He had Lilith again, as well as Andrew to consider. He first wanted the Reformation Spell to work, as you suspected. But in the event that it failed, he learned how to communicate with Lucifer, and he bargained with the self-proclaimed god that if he aided in getting him and his Apostles here, then Lilith and Andrew would be safe. And they could claim the Obsidian Throne as their own. Claim *Hell* as their own, safe from Lucifer and his tyranny."

"Why would he believe that? He had to have known that Lucifer would *lie*."

Kure nods. "You would think that, yes, but Apollo was desperate. *Is* desperate. He wanted to save his family."

"*I* was his family! Pollux and Samael and the rest of my brothers, including Adriel . . . but he's sacrificing us all. He couldn't save Lilith, and he didn't even *try* to save Andrew . . . he doesn't care anymore."

"I would believe that fraternizing with Lucifer and ensuring the Apostles are *comfortable* in their new *accommodations* has taken its toll on his mind and magic. Apollo is not the brother you remember."

"And somewhere, deep inside, I believe a piece of my heart does break for him, but he has damned us all. Apollo was *selfish*."

Kure nods again. "I know, and therein also lies the origins of the Great Betrayal. Others were selfish, as well."

I snarl. "Adam and Eve have made a mess of things."

Kure neither confirms nor denies it, and I cock my head at him. However, I am robbed of the chance to question him on the matter of *betrayals* as I am left hissing in pain, feeling my shared brands begin to burn and simmer as if my arms are being sliced open. I glance down to find *sarang* and *trouvaille* glowing like white steel. Then pulling down my leathers to reveal my left hip bone, I find *truculent* is also glowing and burning white hot. And just to add insult to injury, at the same time, I feel my wards within the Obsidian Palace shudder and growl before *shrieking* in rage.

I meet Kure's gaze again, my eyes flicking between all three of his white eyes as I seethe, "*What have they done*?"

Kure's scowl is solemn as he stares at me, replying softly, "What they believe will save you."

"But it won't," I whisper.

He shakes his head. "It won't," he concurs.

I turn on my heel. "I have to go."

A faint wind moves a tendril of my hair, and Kure grasps my arm gently. I glare at him over my shoulder, tugging on my arm, but he doesn't release me.

"Let. *Go*," I growl, ready to conjure my magic.

"If you go now," he says carefully, slowly, as if speaking to a child, "there is a high probability we will not be able to get you out again for a long time."

I try to yank my arm back again, but his grip merely tightens with the action. "I don't care," I claim. "They are my *family*. I will not leave them at the mercy of my enemies."

Kure bows his head, his hand falling away from my arm. "I know. And you should know this, Queen of Hell. Never forget that we remember you, Myra. *Rhesamyre*. We will stand by you again, just as we did back then. You have allies waiting in the wings for you, Champion. And we will come when you call."

I nod, whispering, "Thank you."

And then I flee the safety of his castle, opening a conveyance as soon as I can straight into the chaos and carnage within the Obsidian Palace.

. . . .

Grasping my sword, I press my back into the wall of the hallway as I peek around the corner. The sounds and screams of hellion foot soldiers, servants, slaves, common folk, and the angels we slaughter echo across the entirety of the heart of Hell. The Obsidian Palace is a bloodbath, stained with the blood of fallen demons and angels alike as bodies litter the luxurious halls. I don't know where my court is, but I can't bring myself to focus on that right now as I size up another wave of angels prowling through an open conveyance that is situated in the center of the hallway at one of the crossroads between the wings.

Outside, steel rings as swords clash, and flares light up the night sky while the shrieks and roars of wyverns and rhayvens alike echo throughout the stars while hellhounds howl all throughout Heart. My footmen contain the carnage to the palace as best they can, but we were caught off guard, and our numbers are wavering as angelic conveyances open all throughout my capital and slaughter my people no matter what their affiliation is with the crown.

My magic growls within me, my power returning once more since I already partially erupted a few times to slaughter angels by the hundreds and slam their conveyances shut, cutting some angels in half in the process.

Covered in blood and gore, I stalk forward and pulse my power once again, ripping these angels to shreds and shutting their conveyance down as I have done the others. Commands for various forms of alchemy roll off my tongue as I twirl between my enemies, wielding my sword of obsidian and cutting down wings and limbs and slicing through their ranks. They all fall at my feet, and I keep prowling forward through my halls to find my court.

I've lost contact with my deities.

I snarl and scream as I stab and twist my sword through another angel, whirling around to block another attack before pulsing my magic again to erupt once more. Bodies fly backward and crash into the walls or through windows as the entire palace *shutters*, but I keep stalking onward. Magic and power roll off me in waves as the blood of my enemies splatters my entire body from head to toe. I can taste their blood on my lips, and thankfully, I don't taste any poison on my tongue. However, as I get near the throne room, something in the air shifts, and the miasma and smoke thickens to a near-suffocating degree.

I command hellion soldiers to look after and protect the people. Evacuate them out of Heart if at all possible, and they're quick to follow my commands to the best of their abilities as they fight their way out of the palace and into the streets where the chaos and carnage grow to an alarming rate.

My power simmers within me in a familiar manner, and I slip into the shadows before a patrol of angels can sense and see me. Opening up the hidden entrance within the wall, I disappear into the servants' halls and am immediately met with the wide eyes of Damian. He grasps me by my shoulders as he surveys my form with a calculating gaze, his own leathers and handsome face splattered with blood and gore, as well.

"The girls—"

"*Are safe,*" he says, his white eyes meeting mine. "They came so quickly. Ripped apart our wards and tore them to *shreds* as if they were *nothing.* This isn't angelic magic. It's dark and forbidden. Something vile and *evil* in nature, Rhesa."

"I know. The Apostles live within the Zodiacs, and Apollo is looking to open the passageway to bring Lucifer here. The magic they command is not something we trifle with, and for good reason. What of the rest of the court?"

He purses his lips, shaking his head. "There is another one here, Rhesa. The court went after him, recognizing his name, but they haven't come back. Just after we got our girls to safety, Mal, Gage, Silas, and I all geared up to go after them, but then our generals slammed the walls down on our bonds. We can't access the power that comes with their sigils anymore. They're shielding themselves. Blocking us out as if—"

"*They've been captured,*" I breathe, trying to keep ahold of my wits despite my worst fears coming to life. "They clamped down on your connections to protect you four, to ensure you wouldn't come for them, and so you can't be tracked. They wouldn't do that unless they were robbed of options. What name did they recognize, Damian?"

"*Abaddon.*"

I rear my head back at that. "The Cruel One is dead."

"Not the king. The prince. His *son.*"

"Abaddon never had an heir."

"Evidently, he did. And once the court caught wind of a *second one,* they ordered us to get out with your girls and evacuate as many of the people as we could."

I shake my head, cursing angel names under my breath. Then, I take a breath. Once, twice, and I steel myself as I order Death's lieutenant, "Get out of here, Damian. Flee with our brothers and girls with the wolves and their beasts, and *do not come back.*"

He reels backward, grasping my shoulders tighter as he snarls, "*I am not leaving you here!*"

"Yes. You are. You *have* to keep them safe, Damian. *Keep each other safe.* Find Kure, Wicker, and Draven and flee to my old estate in the West. *Hide, Damian. You must hide.* Until I call for you again, keep my girls safe and train them for war. Conspire with the lords and be ready when I call for you again. Find our allies or make new ones. You'll have to bargain."

"*Come with us,* Rhesamyre. We stick together!"

I shake my head, grasping him by the back of the neck as I feel tears begin to line my eyes. "I *can't.* They will never stop hunting me, which means you'll never be safe if I go with you. If you respect me as your rightful queen, then obey this final command. *Run.* Hide until I find you again, *and I will.* We *will* be together again, Damian. *All of us.*"

I'm almost sobbing now, grasping his face, and wiping his cheeks that are now wet with his own tears. He nods, leaning forward to press his forehead against my own as he mutters, "We love you, Rhesa. We always have and always will. We will see you again. We'll be ready for you when you call, my queen."

And then he's gone. Opening a conveyance and stepping through it, disappearing into the safety of the darkness. I lean back against the wall, my hands pressed firmly over my mouth as I sob into my palms, doing my best to keep as quiet as I can. And then once I regain control of my breathing, I dry my tears and steel myself, then stalk back out into the hall toward the throne room.

Using my power, I bang the doors open so violently that they bend and break off the hinges, and I release a low, territorial growl as I prowl into the room. More bodies of demons and angels litter the floor, and standing upon the stairsteps of the dais are my family. The Seven and Horsemen stand stock still with blank expressions and glazed-over eyes while thorn collars riddled with black magic wrap around their throats. Mamba is nowhere in sight.

And seated upon *my* throne is a demonic male with red skin and obsidian, bloodshot eyes. He's built lean and dressed in *clean* white battle leathers, and black horns protrude from his forehead and curl upward out of his dark hair. Angelic and hellion brands and sigils paint his red skin, and his facial features remind me of a reptile, thanks to the shimmering scales that coat his cheekbones and other patches of skin.

Stopping in the center of the room, I drawl, "I'll admit, my studies didn't reveal the fact that the Cruel One ever had a son. I don't even recall your existence from my memories of *before*."

The male peels back his cracked lips to grin at me, his fangs gleaming in the light as he says in a heavy *Enochian* accent while speaking perfect Babel, "I was a well-kept secret of my father's.

Nobody knew except for a select few, and Apollo sought me out with the intention of putting me back on my rightful throne. He's looked after me all these years. Grooming me to reclaim my crown."

"And groomed you have been, but you are a pawn, *Abaddon the Second.*"

He cocks his head at me. "Well, then. What does that make you? For you have played right into his hands, too. Granted, you thrashed and kicked and screamed the entire time like some feral beast, throwing a kink into a few of his plans. But nonetheless, here we both are."

I nod. "Here we both are, but you're in my seat."

He leans forward, grinning. "Am I?" He chuckles, then drawls, "Well, if this throne is to be yours, *then fucking prove it.* Unless, of course, you don't think you deserve it?"

I raise my sword, glancing at each of my uncles. Not an ounce of recognition flickers in their eyes, and the collars around their throats squeeze and glow darkly, drawing blood as the thorns pierce their skin and poison their blood while simultaneously drawing power from them to fuel whatever curse has been placed over their minds and bodies.

"They didn't know, in case you were wondering," says Abaddon. "My father didn't use them in his court like yours did . . . *well,* he wasn't really *your father,* though, was he? No matter. The point is, these Seven and Horsemen were not aware of my existence until it was too late. They heard whispers of the name *Abaddon* and didn't realize it was the *son* until they came after me. But it was already over before it began. Once they crossed the threshold, I had them in my clutches. Hence the collars. And now, they are *mine.*"

My uncles step forward as a single unit, their powers wafting off them and commanding me to kneel, but I refuse. Their magic crackles around their forms as the collars burn into their throats, and they claim their weapons as they draw nearer and begin to circle me like sharks.

Predators. Each and every one of them. But so am I.

Roaring and growling, my uncles come at me, and I raise my sword higher and pulse my power to defend myself against the very men who raised me as *Rhesamyre* and taught me how to fight as a demon and princess of Hell. How to be lethal and bare my teeth and spit my blood and go absolutely, *bloody fucking feral* when my magic demands bloodshed.

And so I go feral.

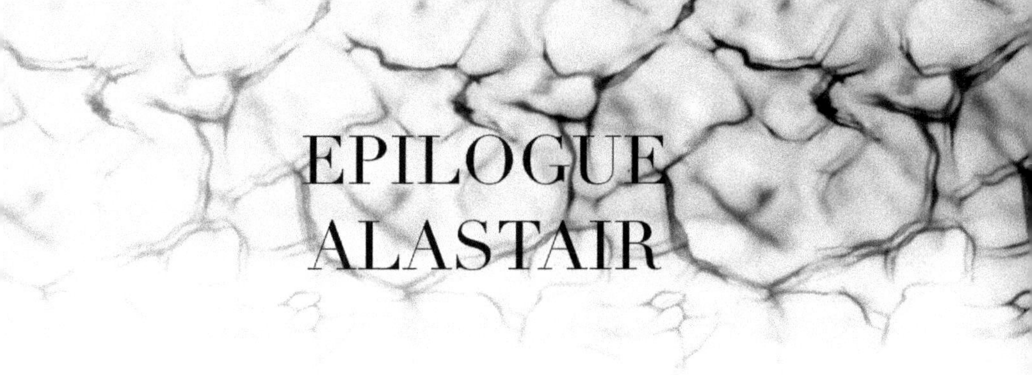

EPILOGUE
ALASTAIR

Rhesamyre is missing again when I awake, but instead of worrying over her whereabouts, I take the chance to disappear myself without fighting her on the matter. My brothers still snooze on the bed, and I survey their forms for a moment before retreating back to my chambers to dress in my leathers and arm myself with my swords and daggers. Just as I'm about finished, my magic growls within me in warning, and I whirl around with a dagger in hand to clash against another's steel.

It's Atlas this time.

My middle brother cocks his head at me, eyeing my weaponry and regalia with narrowed eyes before he inquires, "And you thought we'd let you do it *alone*?"

I snarl at him, throwing him backward before sheathing my dagger once more. "Do what?" I inquire.

"You're an easy book to read when we know your language, brother," quips Atticus from the doorway, my youngest brother leaning back against the door with crossed arms. He shakes his head at me, stalking forward as he drawls, "You know it won't work with just one of us."

"But it could work with three," provides Atlas, his pink eyes sullen even with his scowl in place.

I shake my head. "Leaving her *alone*? No."

"But it would leave her *alive*," says Atticus quietly. "If there's a chance that we can destroy the altar with just the three of us, I'm willing to risk it."

"I would never ask—"

"You're not asking," quips Atlas. "We've come to the same conclusion as you and have decided to see it through on our own accord. You don't *need* to ask, Alastair. Because while we will do it *with* you, we're not doing it *for* you. We're doing it for Rhesamyre."

I nod silently, at a loss for words. Then finally, I murmur, "Then get your shit. We better leave before she gets back."

My brothers nod, and soon enough, we're meeting back in Rhesamyre's room. I allow my gaze to roam about the space, memorizing her style and committing her scent to memory as I do so. Atlas appears to be doing the same, but then Atticus stalks over to her bedside table and pulls out the drawer. There, he pulls out a few parchments, some rings that I'm fairly certain belong to me, and a familiar tome that I never expected to lay eyes on again.

I cock my head at the sight of the Reverie. "When did she . . .?"

Atticus grins at me as he flips through the enchanted, leather-bound journal before turning his attention to the smaller pieces of parchment. *Letters*, I realize. Their replies to Rhesa when she inquired about their help behind my back.

"She and I went after it a little while ago," says Atticus. "It's how I managed to brand her. Or, well, I suppose *she* technically branded *me*." His grin widens. "Sweet spice saved me from the arachnid venom."

Atlas steps forward, ignoring the Reverie as he flicks one of the letters. "She kept them," he muses.

Atticus scoffs. "Did you expect her to get rid of them?"

Atlas flicks his gaze to our brother, pinning him with an all-knowing, pointed look. "Did you get rid of yours?"

"No," Atticus admits softly. "Did you?"

"No."

Atticus inclines his head, and Atlas seems to be thinking something over, as well. However, knowing we're pressed for time, I force myself to murmur, "We need to go."

My brothers glance up at me and then promptly put Rhesa's belongings back into her bedside table. We come together once more, clad in hellion leathers and armed to the teeth, and I open a conveyance straight from Rhesa's bedchamber to the furthest wards of the Forbidden Cities near the Falls of Man. However, upon arrival, we find ourselves surrounded by enemies.

My brothers and I stand back-to-back, shoulder-to-shoulder, at the sight of the angelic foot soldiers, and Apollo drawls from where he stands near the fall's edge, "I told you they'd come running once they figured it out. And here they are."

I narrow my eyes at the archangel, noting the being he speaks to is Taurus. The rest of the Zodiacs also stand off to the side near the falls, and my mind races as I realize we've been played for *fools*.

My brothers seem to come to the same conclusion, and Atticus snarls, "If you think you'll be safe from that tyrannical, self-proclaimed god thanks to whatever foolish bargain you appear to have made, then you're even more delusional than you appear, Apollo."

Apollo smirks, but his gaze is cold and apathetic as he drawls, "It doesn't much matter anymore. The end is near, and when it comes for me, I will welcome it with open arms. But until then, I'll see to it that I can take as many of you down with me as I possibly can. Starting with your precious *Rhesamyre* and the entirety of Hell itself."

"Don't you mean *Myra*?" inquires Atlas, seething beside me. "Your *sister*."

Apollo growls at the reminder, but I inquire with a growl, "Where's Pollux?"

The archangel smirks at me again. "Otherwise detained. As are the rest of my brothers. They won't be coming to your aid. Nor hers when the rest of my soldiers storm Hell."

"You can bloody well try," Atticus seethes.

"*Oh*, I plan to. I believe the siege is already underway now that you three are here."

"Then if *you're* here, who's commanding the rest of your armies?" I inquire.

"An old friend. But I don't believe you three will have the luxury of meeting him. Not for what we have planned for you. You see, we still need to open the passageway, and you've finally arrived to help us do it."

"Suck a bloody cock, Apollo," snarls Atlas. "We won't be pawns in your games any longer."

"No?" He pouts pathetically, dramatically. "Then how will you ever destroy the altar without first getting there?"

"We'll cross that bloody bridge when we get to it," I snarl. "And it won't be any concern of yours because you'll be *dead*. Rotting in the soil while the maggots and magics have their way with whatever is left of you after I'm through thoroughly *eviscerating* you."

"*Promise*?" he mocks, though there is an underlying desire in his tone, all the same.

He truly has lost his mind. And his will to live.

I attempt to access my power, but whatever spellwork they now have entrapping us here keeps a firm clamp on my magic as if I've been poisoned. And from the tense forms and faces of my brothers, I know they're in the same predicaments, too.

"Well, then," drawls Apollo, sighing as he stalks toward us. "Shall we get started? I would hate to keep Master Lucifer waiting."

Atticus scoffs. "*Master Lucifer?*" my brother mocks, chuckling darkly. "My, my, how the mighty have *fucking* fallen. You're a disgrace to everything your name and magic stand for, Apollo."

The archangel doesn't deny it and instead draws nearer as the Zodiacs—*Apostles*—begin to surround us. Their glittering silhouettes sway in the breeze of the falls, and they grasp each other's hands and begin chanting commands in Old Latin. Immediately, the air and magic shift around us as the ground shudders beneath our feet, and the waterfall that was once caused by *my* eruption and the Great Betrayal stops flowing. Then, the water begins to recede and flow *backward*, and the falls start to shift toward the starry sky instead of over the land's edge.

I glance at my brothers, and they nod at me. I incline my head in return, and steeling myself, I trace my trouvaille tattoo softly as I mutter, "Forgive me, my love."

Then, moving faster than any other being, aside from my brothers and maybe Rhesa, can keep up with, I unsheath the sword strapped to my back and swipe at the closest Zodiac near me. It won't do much more than *piss it off*, but the wavering of its silhouette is enough to surprise the shit out of it and force it backward, thus breaking the circle and whatever concentration they had on keeping our magic blocked.

My brothers and I erupt.

And what happens next is a mess of swords and steel and screams and snarls and shadows and stars and raw, unfiltered magic and *rage*. I cut down angelic foot soldiers and even clash with Apollo a few times, though since I am unarmed with the Zodiac Blade, I have no hope of killing him or the Zodiacs as easily as I could with the weapon. So instead, I have to rely on my magic to tear them apart, but whatever spellwork they had trapping us earlier seems to be swiftly making a comeback, and I feel my limbs and power slow to an alarming, nearly *mortal* rate.

Atlas comes in to cover my back when I am forced to a knee, my body dragged down by invisible forces toward the soil as the Apostles keep chanting and commanding forbidden magic by using the Zodiacs' bodies, minds, and powers to do so.

"C'mon, brother," grunts Atlas as he grabs me, slicing another foot soldier in the process. "We'll be no good to Rhesamyre if we die here."

I huff a laugh, driving my sword through another angel when he nears us. I've lost sight of Atticus, but I still feel him fighting nearby as Atlas and I fight back-to-back again to slaughter our angelic enemies. But then another wave of crushing magic weighs down on us, making it hard to breathe as the air around us grows stale and poisonous in nature. I can taste the miasma on my tongue, and bile rises in my throat as Atlas heaves up a mouthful of blood next to me.

"You fucking bastards!" I roar, grabbing ahold of whatever tendril of my magic I can still feel, using it to lash out at the next wave of angels coming for us.

They're all sent flying backward, their limbs twisting, armor melting to their faces, and bodies bursting and burning alive as my power slithers inside their forms to torture them from the inside out. However, it feels as though that was the last of what

I could use as the Apostles' commands have me crumbling to a knee once more. I feel blood dripping from my nose, eyes, and ears, and I spit out a dark mouthful of it, too.

The air is still thick with poison, and the starry sky above us is riddled with thunderous clouds and black lightning that crackles with strange, angry magic as the storm eye siphons the water from the reverse-falls. I attempt to rise to my feet, leaning on my sword as I grab Atlas, but when their commands and chanting grow louder, I buckle once more. Somewhere in the distance, I hear Atticus *roar*, but then I feel invisible hands grasp my ankles, and I'm hauled backward toward the waterfall.

I thrash and make another attempt to call on my magic, grasping at other bodies, trying to slow myself down, but it's no use. I hear Atlas cursing up a storm next to me, and he and I lock eyes one last time before we're dragged into the cold, poisonous waters of the falls. It shocks me to my core, rattling my bones as it steals my magic, but I believe most of it has already been stolen by the Apostles to open this fucking passageway into the Tenth Sphere.

My vision fails me and goes in and out as I am carried upward by the current, and the overwhelming noises and sounds of the wind and water and magic roaring past me and through me leave me nearly deaf. My lungs seize, unable to take in air, and I nearly drown in this strange pool of poison and power, unable to grab hold of anything solid or even feel where my body begins and ends as I am thrust into a dark, all-consuming nothingness.

And then I'm falling.

My lungs burn as I try to inhale, and the new scents of whatever place I have found myself in are foreign and strange and above all, *bloody*. The air itself nearly tastes metallic, and I hit something solid with my back first, knocking the wind out of me again. I roar and snarl and curse as I heave and attempt to clamber up onto my hands and knees, my body weak and numb and all but useless as I can barely feel my magic slumbering deep inside me. Angry and vengeful, but weakened and nearly nonexistent to a degree I have never felt before. Not since I was closer to that of a *mortal* centuries ago.

And then I finally manage to sit up on my haunches, my chest heaving as I take in my new surroundings. The land is barren of any greenery, splintered unnaturally with massive crevasses, and there are bodies *everywhere*. Some are weeks old and rotten, while others still twitch with fresher pools of blood staining the dry sand beneath them. Many are of monsters and men that look as though they should belong to the spheres back home, but then there are others haphazardly thrown into the bloody mess that I have never seen before, which means they must derive from *this* sphere.

Purgatory. The Tenth Sphere.

Rising onto my booted feet on unsteady legs, I grasp my secondary sword that is strapped to my back. My leathers are torn, but at least I still have a good amount of daggers left. However, as I continue my sweep of my surroundings, I find no signs of forests or other natural shelters for *miles*.

And there is no sign of either one of my brothers.

The sphere rumbles beneath my feet, and I jump backward as a new crevasse opens up to swallow dozens of bodies at a time; all of them fall straight into the chasm of magma lifelessly. And then behind me, I hear monsters roar and growl, surely scenting the *fresh meat* that has just arrived.

I turn to face my new abundance of enemies, my blood dripping to the ground and hissing against the already blood-soaked sand, and I size up the massive creatures of teeth and tusks and talons and too many eyes that prowl forward and stalk me from all sides. Their bodies are molded together unnaturally and haphazardly with skin and fur and limbs poking out from all sides. As if they have consumed pieces of every other monster to grow and heal their wounds, becoming stronger than they were before.

I raise my sword, snarling viciously, the sound purely a primal instinct and promising death as they pounce all at once.

ACKNOWLEDGMENTS

And with that finale, book two is complete.

Thank you so much to everyone who made it to the midway point of this series, and if all goes according to plan, I hope to publish book three by the end of this year, so stay tuned!

Of course, I couldn't have made it this far without the support and love of my friends and family.

Mom and Dad, neither of you have ever doubted me whilst along this journey. It was only earlier this year that I published Obsidian and Silver, and since then, it's been pedal to the metal, but both of you have been along for the ride without me ever having to ask for your support. You've always just given it, and for that, I will forever be grateful. I do my best to show within these stories and words what everyone and everything means to me, and whilst the Devil did not live to see this book, Cameron Burris, I still stand by what I said the first time. You are my Dad. Forever and always.

And Mom, let's be honest here . . . Rhesamyre's beauty, grace, badassery, and willingness to dispatch those that threaten what's hers, it all comes from your unconditional love.

But it was not only my parents' characteristics that bled into this series, and it was not until I re-read my work that I realized two others must also be acknowledged.

Claire Bear, I didn't know it then, but Althea is you. She has your beauty, kindness, and spirit, as well as a familiar love for giant, scaled, winged beasts.

And Uncle Taylor, every uncle has a piece of you in him. From the Horsemen to the Seven Deadly Sins, they're all loyal to a fault and dangerous when provoked, but overall, kind and full of love.

They love their niece, Rhesamyre, just as much as you love my sister and I, and I can only hope that my writing did you justice. But let's be honest here, no amount of writing will ever be able to capture how big of a goofball you are.

"In case of emergency, break glass."

It's true for Rhesa, and it's true for me.

Once again, I thank the talented Barbara Kennerly for my cover art, and Jaime Ryter for her editorial services.

Mel and Angie, I owe you my thanks, as well.

And Ethan, this one is for you.

ABOUT THE AUTHOR

Isabelle M. Guernica is a full-time equestrian with big dreams to publish as many books as possible, most of which will be written from either the barstool in the farmhouse or the couch where she snuggles with her dogs. And when she's not cuddling into the couch cushions with either her laptop or a very smutty book, she's usually outside working, riding, or acting as a treat dispenser for her horses.

Isabelle lives in a small town in North Carolina with her family of humans, horses, and dogs, and you can follow her on Facebook or Instagram for information regarding her upcoming releases!

AUTHOR.ISABELLEGUERNICA